Azathoth
Ordo ab Chao

Part of the Series:
The Gods of HP Lovecraft

Edited by Aaron J. French

JOURNALSTONE
YOUR LINK TO ARTIST TALENT

"Ordo ab Chao: Toward That Endlessness" © 2023 Maxwell Ian Gold; "Agent of Chaos" © 2023 T. Kingfisher; "Expatriate" © 2023 Jamieson Ridenhour; "…And Peer Aloft to Glimpse Some Fragment" © 2023 Ruthanna Emrys; "Making a Difference" © 2023 Brian Evenson; "The Recreationist" © 2023 Kaaron Warren; "The Blind God's Game" © 2023 Matthew Cheney; "In the Grove" © 2023 Erica Ruppert; "Church of the Void" © 2023 Donald Tyson; "Upon an Iron Bed, Under the Eyes of Chaos" © 2023 Richard Gavin; "The Root King" © 2023 Lauri Taneli Lassila; "The Infinite Beat" © 2023 Nathan Carson; "The Door at 21 bis rue Xavier Privas" © 2023 R. B. Payne; "An Unusual Pedigree" © 2023 Richard Thomas; "Dust-Clotted Eyes" © 2023 Samuel Marzioli; "The Revelations of Azathoth" © 2023 Lena Ng; "Primordial Jack" © 2023 Akis Linardos; "Respect Your Elders" © 2023 Adam L. G. Nevill

ISBN: 978-1-68510-100-8 (sc)
ISBN: 978-1-68510-101-5 (ebook)
Library of Congress Control Number: 2023939608

First printing edition: June 30, 2023
Published by JournalStone Publishing in the United States of America.
Cover Artwork and Design: Mikio Murakami
Edited by Aaron J. French
Copy-edited by Sean Leonard; Proofreading and Cover/Interior Layout by Scarlett R. Algee

"Agent of Chaos," "Primordial Jack," "The Revelations of Azathoth," "The Root King," "In the Grove," and "Upon an Iron Bed, Under the Eyes of Chaos" illustrated by Sofiya Kruglikova. "Making a Difference," "The Recreationist," and "Dust-Clotted Eyes" illustrated by Ayham Jabr. "Church of the Void," "The Door at 21 rue bis Xavier Privas," "The Infinite Beat," "The Blind God's Game," "An Unusual Pedigree," and "…And Peer Aloft to Glimpse Some Fragment" illustrated by Andrej Kapcar. "Expatriate" and "Respect Your Elders" illustrated by Yves Tourigny.

JournalStone Publishing
3205 Sassafras Trail
Carbondale, Illinois 62901

JournalStone books may be ordered through booksellers or by contacting:
JournalStone | www.journalstone.com

"If those arrangements were to disappear as they appeared, if some event of which we can at the moment do no more than sense the possibility were to cause them to crumble, then one can certainly wager that man would be erased, like a face drawn in sand at the edge of the sea."

—Michel Foucault, *The Order of Things*

"When someone freely embraces the symbols of death, or death itself, a great release of power for good can be expected to follow."

—Mary Douglas, *Purity and Danger*

"The world is an illusion!"

—*Treatise on the Resurrection*

Table of Contents

Azathoth
Ordo ab Chao

Ordo ab Chao: Toward That Endlessness
Maxwell Ian Gold

THROUGH THE WIDE, guttered jaws of a nameless dark where between the crevasses of old stars, I stood near the beginning and the end. The bleak, beautiful mass that throbbed unceasingly, inside and out, squirming in the webbed muck of the starry night. Once constrained by the strands of a mutilated laughter, the emptiness was rocked and swept up by the music of dead dreams; the dreams of a Blind Demon-God transformed into the nightmares of everything. Once confined to a labyrinth built between the stringy bonds where order was deconstructed into desperate uncertainty as I was released once more, a Blind Demon-God yawning toward that endless, dark horizon.

And I saw the bones of stars, splendid and wiry like the ghosts of dead civilizations, haunting me from a billion years ago and in the future all at the same time. Their statuesque forms gliding across the swampy, cosmic blackness as my mind lusted for those beautiful, yet deadly shapes that blasted the Everything, the Order, into nothing but food for the Blind God who had swallowed the stars before them.

And like me, too soon to be devoured with nothing left but the deranged shadows of my bloated neurons for history to feed on a billion years later, I laughed, free once again; released through wide jaws of the dark collecting the bones of stars, the bodies of planets, and the infinite dreams to cower, and wonder where that endlessness dies.

Agent of Chaos

T. Kingfisher

IT WAS A blustery day in November when the kitten accidentally ripped open the fabric of reality.

Alice had protested having a kitten at all, on the grounds that she was seventy-five years old and had put in her time with baby mammals of all description. But Jim down the road had said, "Please, just until I can find him a home," and handed her a tiny knot of black fluff, who promptly gazed up at her and began to purr. His eyes were still glazed the milky blue of infancy and his purr was the biggest thing about him. Alice looked down and sighed and knew that she was beaten.

"Your kitten's in the yarn basket again," said her niece Mallory, as Alice knitted by the window, watching the rain hit the windowpane and run down in silver streaks.

"He does that," Alice said. She was trying to knit a very small sweater for her grand-niece's teddy bear, and it wasn't going as well as it could.

"He's digging for something, I think," Mallory observed, as the kitten burrowed into the yarn basket, only his tiny rump and tail visible. "Do you want me to stop him?"

"There's no point," said Alice with a sigh. "Kittens are agents of chaos. As long as he doesn't go after the expensive yarn, I don't mind."

Mallory got down on her hands and knees, extracted the kitten— he began to purr thunderously—and rooted around in the basket until she found a grungy-looking little ball of wool from the bottom. "Can he have this one?"

Alice pushed her glasses up and studied it. The yarn was the colorless gray-brown nothing of dust and the ball wasn't large enough for anything except maybe another teddy bear sweater. As Alice was close to swearing off sweaters for toys altogether, she nodded. "I think someone gave that to me ages ago. I've never used it."

Mallory rolled it to the kitten, who fell upon it with savage milk-teeth. It was nearly as big as he was, which made for a worthy opponent. A long strand unrolled behind him as he fought it across the polished oak floorboards.

"You should name him," Mallory said, watching the battle rage back and forth. It reached the edge of the rag rug and reversed direction. The ball continued to unroll, laying down another line the other way, which the kitten promptly wrapped himself in. Mallory reached down to make sure he didn't accidentally strangle himself.

"I've always said there's no point in naming cats," said Alice. "They don't come when they're called."

"Yes, but it helps you differentiate between them when you're talking to someone else."

The yarn snagged on one of the tassels on the rag rug, and several other strands pulled tight. For a moment, the crossed strands formed part of a sigil written in the long-dead Aklo language, which was known by their priests as "The Marking of the Place of Undoing." Then the kitten rolled over them and loosened them and they didn't look like anything but yarn.

"I don't need to differentiate between cats," said Alice. "I'm only going to have the one, so as long as I say 'new kitty' or 'my kitty,' everybody knows what I'm talking about." She sniffed. "Anyway, names are important. You can't just go handing them out willy-nilly."

The kitten pursued his quarry around a table leg, pounced, and was rolled over by the ball of yarn. This pulled the strands tight again.

"Why not?" asked Mallory.

Another strand crossed the first few, leaving the sigil half-completed. Roughly this much had been found on the whiteboard of a mathematician who had written out equations attempting to describe an object rotating in eleventh-dimensional space. The rest of the sigil had been smeared when he fainted and his forehead bounced off the whiteboard. When he came to, he couldn't remember anything past his fifth birthday.

Alice frowned. "If you name something, you can find it," she said slowly. "It's like a handle to grab on by. That's why some people don't name babies until after they're born, so that bad luck can't find it."

"Aunt Alice, I do believe you're superstitious." Mallory sat back, grinning. "I had no idea."

The old woman pointed a knitting needle at her niece. "Don't you start, young lady. It's not superstition, it's common sense."

The yarn unspooled further, the sigil beginning to wake up and hunger for completion. The next three lines fell into place quickly. A Renaissance astronomer had seen just that much of the shape form in the sky one night and had managed to jerk the telescope aside in time to avoid seeing the rest. He lived, but it was a long time before he could avoid screaming when he saw the stars.

The kitten was simply delighted that his toy was moving almost independently and purred enthusiastically as he tried to disembowel it.

"Is this a sailor thing?" asked Mallory. "I know you were in the Navy, and I remember reading that you shouldn't rename ships—"

"Oh god no!" said Alice involuntarily, her needles jerking. "You never rename a ship. The gods of the deep know the names of every ship, and if you change the name, they no longer know it. Then it's an intruder on the sea."

"Aunt Alice, you're a *Presbyterian*."

"Both things can be true." Alice bent her head over the sweater. There was no way to explain to someone like Mallory that when you were on a floating husk on the sea—even an enormous metal one— you were surrounded by something far deeper and older than anything Christianity could offer. Something cold and alien and vastly uncaring.

She suspected that Jesus would have understood. He'd hung out with fishermen in Galilee, after all. They would have explained it to Him.

The sigil was mostly completed now. A million years hence, a boneless, soft-bodied species would scribe the incomplete sigil inside their engine compartments and ride the resulting nuclear chaos throughout the stars. The kitten stopped for a rest, sprawled across the strands, his eyes closing. The ball of yarn was much smaller now and easily pinned beneath his claws.

"Do you hear something?" asked Mallory, sitting up. "Sounds like whistling."

Alice looked up from the sweater and cocked her head. Sure enough, she could hear a thin, breathy sound, droning monotonously somewhere nearby.

"It's probably the radiator," she said.

"Does your radiator usually sound like that?"

Alice waved her hand dismissively. "Sometimes it sounds like there's a live raccoon inside it. A little whistle is nothing."

"It's not that little," grumbled Mallory. She got up and investigated the radiator. "I think it's getting louder."

Alice looked down at her sweater and discovered that she'd started an extra arm hole. Annoyed with herself, she began to unravel it.

"I don't know if it's coming from the radiator," said Mallory, getting down next to it. "It sounds farther away. And it's more like... I don't know. A flute?"

"Maybe someone's parked down the road, listening to whatever music you kids listen to these days. Experimental drone hip-synth or whatever."

"That's not a real genre. And nobody blasts flute music on their car stereo."

"A boyfriend of mine used to. He loved Jethro Tull." Alice looked at her niece over her glasses, hoping for a flash of musical recognition. Mallory looked at her with polite non-comprehension and Alice sighed. Oh well. She'd never liked Jethro Tull anyway. "Maybe it's something in the basement then."

The kitten woke up, released the ball of yarn, and began licking his paw. Freed, the yarn rolled away as the unfinished sigil pulsed with heat, gathering momentum, like a pebble rolling downhill. It laid down the penultimate line, crossing each of the others at an angle that would have required an extra branch of mathematics to explain.

Something opened in the space between the strands. It wasn't darkness. It was what darkness wanted to be when it grew up. Things crawled inside it, devouring light. Any human who had gazed into that opening would have burned out their optic nerves at once, but Mallory was still on her hands and knees next to the radiator and Alice was picking apart the offending bits of sweater. (When had she even knit that bit? She couldn't quite remember doing it, but it was an absolute mess.)

The black kitten looked down into the crawling darkness that had existed in the eons before the Big Bang and made an inquiring "Mrrrp?" sound.

"I'm going to the basement," said Mallory, climbing to her feet and dusting off her knees. "If that is the radiator, I don't like it. Radiators explode, you know."

She was looking back over her shoulder as she said it, and thus narrowly avoided having her mind destroyed by seeing the crawling darkness on the floor. The kitten scampered after her, excited, but became distracted by his own feet and rolled around, attempting to bite them.

The ball of yarn glided back, trying to complete the last line, and ran into the kitten, who leapt dramatically into the air and came down on the yarn with all four feet.

"What did I *do* here?" Alice murmured, pushing her glasses down and holding the sweater up to her face. She was desperately nearsighted, and without her glasses, both kitten and chaos were mere background blurs.

Something pale and amorphous flopped out of the opening, hitting the wood with a soft, gelatinous *smack*. The kitten froze, still clutching the treacherous ball of yarn with all four feet, and gazed at it, fascinated.

The thin piping sound grew louder. Alice frowned, hoping that Mallory wasn't doing something with the valves. There had been water damage in the basement a few years ago and the repairman had told her horror stories about black mold. This had only served to reinforce Alice's theory that all water secretly wanted to kill you.

A hole opened on the side of the gelatinous thing, like a lipless mouth, and it began to breathe. The sound was thin and monotonous and formed an unpleasant harmony with the piping from farther away.

"Ugh," Alice said. "What *is* that child doing down there?"

Another sluglike form plopped out of the hole. The yarn vibrated, trying to get free of its captor. One more line. Just one more line, and the sigil would be complete. The Marking of the Place of Undoing, which tore a hole sideways through the world, into that other place, the place before the beginning, where the darkness whipped and frothed across a sea of nuclear slime and chaos sang to itself in the voices of devoured stars.

The kitten flung himself free of the ball of yarn and slapped the jelly-like shape with a paw. It flattened unpleasantly, squishing out the sides, and then another mouth opened on each side of his paw and began to sing.

"Ugh," said Alice, throwing the ruined sweater aside. "She's messing with the valves, I know it." If she'd learned one thing in the Navy, it was to never, ever mess with the valves. That was for engineers. You started to think you knew what you were doing, you twisted one the wrong way, and the next thing you know an officer was screaming in your face that the ship was dead in the water and the Old Man was not happy and what did you think you were *doing?* And never mind that the valve in question shouldn't have connected to anything important and there was no way that you could have had any effect on the engines. You were on the ocean and the ocean wanted you dead.

The ball of yarn darted sideways and tried to write the final line. It ran into the kitten, who was slapping at mouths as fast as they opened, his milky blue kitten eyes wide.

It reversed and tried to roll over him, but the kitten flipped onto his back, paws spread wide in feline battle position. The sigil's last line blazed with unholy light.

The nameless kitten rabbit-kicked the ball of yarn with both hind feet, throwing it over his head, into the hole in space. It dropped soundlessly into the crawling darkness, pulling yarn behind it. The kitten swatted excitedly at several strands as they were yanked into the black sea on the other side of eternity.

The part of the sigil that held the portal open was pulled apart and the hole snapped closed, leaving the severed end of the yarn embedded in the floor.

The kitten batted at it a few times, but it had stopped moving and no longer seemed very interesting. He sighed and flopped over on his side, licking at his paw. The goo on it was sticky and tasted burnt.

Mallory came up from the basement, pulling cobwebs from her hair. "I loosened one of the valves and the noise stopped. You'd probably just built up too much pressure."

Alice bit back her involuntary response. The girl meant well. It wasn't her fault that the only ocean she knew was the tame bit that lapped against the beach. Which she knew intellectually didn't really have anything to do with radiator valves, but still... "Thank you," she said, and made a mental note to call the repairman on Monday.

"Ugh." Mallory stopped. "I think your kitten puked. There's gunk on the floor." She reached down and picked up the kitten, who blinked at her innocently. "And he's made an absolute mess of this yarn." She gathered it up, blotting out what traces of the Marking of the Place of Undoing remained. "Now how'd you get it hooked in the board like this...?"

"I told you," said Alice, taking the kitten from her. "Kittens are agents of chaos." She carried him into the kitchen with her. He burrowed into the crook of her arm and purred thunderously.

"I think this yarn is a loss," said Mallory, yanking the end loose and following her aunt. "It's got cat vomit on it."

"Throw it away," said Alice.

"Throw away *yarn*? Are you feeling well?"

Alice rolled her eyes. "I know, I know. But I think that was probably from someone else's stash that they were getting rid of, and probably someone gave it to them when *they* got rid of *their* yarn stash... For all I know, it's a hundred years old and would fall apart in the washer."

"Well, if you say so." Mallory opened the trash can and tossed it in.

The lid came down on the twisted strands of a fiber spun from the wool of the Black Goat, on a drop spindle made of the spinner's own femur, cut living from her flesh. A bloated moon had looked down on her as she spun the fibers with bloody fingers, laughing, hoping only to complete her task before she died. At daybreak, the thread had been collected by her acolytes, and her body shoved into a pit at the end of long poles, to be buried without anyone touching it. The bulk of the fiber was then used to weave a cloak that had gone missing long ago, in the Age of Heroes, and the acolytes had breathed a sigh of relief that it was gone. The remaining fiber was balled up and passed from generation to generation, until even the memory of its creation was forgotten, and someone found it at an estate sale and bought it, thinking that his grandmother might like some yarn.

It rested now, amid coffee grounds and eggshells, atop a takeout container half-full of aging beef lo mein. A few hours later, Mallory bagged it up, with quick, efficient movements, and tossed it into the trash can at the end of the driveway, where it passed out of mortal knowledge forever, and the small black kitten lay on the rag rug and purred as if his lungs would burst.

Expatriate

Jamieson Ridenhour

THE JAZZHUS MONTMARTRE glows like a dying coal in the drifting mist, the only bright spot in Store Regnegade at this time of night. A tinkling of piano escapes around the edges of the door, a splash of cymbal wafting on the air like a scent. At a little after 10 pm, the Montmartre is an oasis haloed in warm amber light, and the streets of Copenhagen are slippery with damp.

Red isn't missing a step as he walks up the sidewalk toward the Montmartre, however slick the pavement. He moves with an easy grace, his long limbs swinging within a gray trench coat, a cigarette held lightly between two fingers of his right hand. His gait has a rhythm, as if some internal metronome dictates his cadence. A sort of blissed-out bemusement illuminates his face, quasi-smiling beneath a jauntily cocked trilby. Swagger notwithstanding, he moves with purpose, walking steadily up Store Regnegade toward the light and music.

He's only been away for fifteen minutes, a quick break between sets, a brisk walk to clear his head. He pauses just inside the Montmartre, handing his overcoat and hat to Jan and stubbing out his cigarette in the ashtray on the bar. The trio are jumping, Niels and Alex laying down a steady groove while Kenny improvs intricate runs on the high keys. The long tables, set perpendicular to the stage, are packed with people. Smoke hangs in a low cloud across the room, thicker than the fog outside. He is taking off his coat before he reaches the stage, loosening his tie in the closeness of the room. Next to the piano his horn sits gleaming on its stand, patient as a lover. He tosses his coat across the piano and picks up the sax, clipping it to the strap and testing the reed. He turns to face the crowd as the band ends their vamp, Kenny flourishing out with a long bluesy run over the final seventh chord.

There is a light smattering of applause, and then a hush of anticipation. He twists the microphone up, preparing to speak, when he sees him. A man in a grey gabardine suit is sitting against the wall stage right, an untouched drink in front of him, a lit but unsmoked pipe in his hand. He is unnaturally still; the wall behind him is full of plaster masks—an art installation nearly as famous as the club itself—and this man may as well be one of them for all the movement he evinces. It is the first time Red has seen him tonight, but not the first time he's noticed him in the Montmartre crowd. Red falters.

But only for a moment. Only the regulars would even notice it— a brief pause before he speaks. He blinks slow, and recovers. Looking out at the people sitting at the long tables, eyes watching him above the rims of glasses, he intones into the mic:

"Hush now, don't explain. Just say you'll remain. I'm glad you're back. Don't explain." His voice is a self-consciously silken baritone, a disc jockey's voice. He settles a little between each sentence, smiling as at a private joke, swaying slightly to that internal beat. Then he pushes the mic back down until it faces the bell of his horn. He plays the opening notes of "Don't Explain," unaccompanied, and pauses just before the final note of the chorus, lifting almost imperceptibly onto the balls of his feet and then coming down on the one with the rest of the band, sliding into the song like a warm bath.

Order out of chaos, art out of air. Sound waves arranged just so, reaching into the listener and drawing forth joy, tears, regret, hope. For an hour there is only Alex's snare fills and the driving thrum of Niels' bass. Trading fours with Kenny while the whole joint swings. Hard bop layered with long languorous ballads, filling the Montmartre with warmth.

Later, he is wiping down his horn in the upstairs dressing room, and he thinks again about the man. After he works the clasps on the case, he heads back down the stairs that lead to the stage. The man in the gabardine suit has moved to the bar, where he sits alone in front of a drink. Around him, hip young Danes in skinny ties are talking animatedly at pretty young women with beehive hair, eyes dark-lined and smiling. The man does not speak, but watches his fellow patrons with a half-interested smile, a smile not unlike the one Red himself wears on stage. Red moves to the bar, stopping twice to shake a hand or listen to a fragment of praise. He takes a seat by the man, lights a cigarette.

"Can I buy you a drink, friend?" Gabardine speaks the same words Red had planned.

Red smiles. "You can, thank you."

Two whiskeys are procured. Jan pours while looking at Red, who nods that he's fine. Gabardine raises his glass.

"Jazz," he says. "Very beautiful show tonight."

Red raises his in response. "Thank you again. I've seen you here quite a few times, haven't I?"

"I come as often as I can." His English is perfect, but tinged with an accent that Red doesn't immediately recognize. There is a lilt, an upswung rhythm that isn't Danish. "I've been in Copenhagen for a few weeks now."

"You from out of town, then?"

"So are you." He keeps smiling, but Red notices that his eyes keep darting to the door, a reflexive glance.

"That's true. I'm from L.A. originally, but I've moved around a lot. Been in Copenhagen for a couple of years now. Just sort of happened, you know? I got a gig in Europe, next thing I knew I looked up and I was living here."

"You like it?"

Red draws on his cigarette, considering. "Yeah. I do like it. I still travel, you know. I play in Paris next week. Then shows in Stockholm and Göttenberg. But I come home here when I'm done."

"I'm looking for a place to settle down myself," says Gabardine. "What's good about here?"

"What's good?"

"Yes. How do you say? Sell it to me." Another glance at the door. The crowd continues to ebb. Red follows the glance, but sees nothing worth looking at.

"Well, it feels comfortable, you know? It's easier than the States. Europe in general. More... I don't know. Accepting."

"Because you're black?"

Red laughs, unsure of where this is going. "Yeah. Because I'm black. Doesn't seem to be as big a deal over here. And they really dig what I do, you know? People *listen* here. Ain't like that in the States anymore."

"You have found others like you."

"What, other black guys? Kenny's from New York. He ain't Danish."

"I mean to say you have found other musicians. Others with the same drives and interests."

"Well, yeah. Some of them need a little guidance, you know. A little direction. But some of these cats can *play*. You heard Niels tonight, on bass? Cat can lay it down." He laughs again. "'Drives and interests.' You talk funny, if you don't mind my saying so."

Gabardine laughs as well. "Well, as you say, I'm from out of town. I apologize if my English is too formal." He fiddles with his pipe, a trail of smoke curling up into the lights.

Red sips his whiskey. "No big deal. That's the worst thing you got to worry about, you're doing okay. Why you looking for a place to settle down?"

"I've moved around a lot too," he says. "After a while you get tired of moving." He looks over his shoulder, drums his fingers on the bar.

"You expecting somebody?" Red asks. "It's pretty late, if they ain't here yet."

"I don't think anyone's coming tonight," says Gabardine. "Looking at the door is a habit, I suppose."

Red eyes him closely. Gabardine's hair is buzzed too close to tell if it's white-blonde or silver. His face is smooth and ageless except around the mouth, where deep lines groove into his smile. Underneath his overcoat his clothes are old-fashioned—the bright blue tie is much too wide, the pants too high-waisted. Wing-tip shoes. His hands are constantly touching and fiddling and tapping. Red is fascinated that the pipe never goes out, though the man never puts it in his mouth. Even though the man had earlier raised his glass in a sort of toast, Red can't remember seeing him actually drink from it.

"I used to watch the door a bit myself," Red says.

"Yeah?"

"Cops used to hassle me something awful."

"I heard about that. You were a junkie."

"Ha!"

"Is that the wrong word?"

"It's the only word. You certainly say what you're thinking, don't you?"

"I wasn't trying to offend."

"Take a lot more than that to offend me. So what's your deal?"

"I'm just here to listen."

"But you don't listen like everybody else. I feel you from the stage, man."

"My whole family," he spreads his hands, indicating an expansive clan, "great lovers of music. It was everywhere. Music soothes me. You understand?"

Red nods. "Yeah, I know what you mean. What kind of music did y'all go in for?"

"My people have a tradition very different to your music. Different instruments, different style. But it feels the same. Some of the old songs are so beautiful, I don't have the words. They hung in the air like snow."

"I'd like to hear some of that."

"Not many left in the old tradition." He had become very still while he talked about music, but now he glances at the door again and picks up the pipe. "I should be going. Thank you for stopping to talk with me."

"You didn't finish your drink."

"It's yours, if you like." He stands and puts 100 kroner on the bar.

"We're here all week; come back and I'll buy you one," says Red.

Gabardine smiles and walks hatless out the door.

Jan takes the money. "You know him?" he asks.

"Nah, just met him."

"He is always ordering whiskey," Jan tells him, "but he never drinks."

"He's a weird motherfucker," Red agrees. "I like him."

Red sits in a hard wooden chair, running arpeggios before he goes on stage. The dressing room is lit by a lamp on a side table and lights over the mirror, bright and shadowed in turns. A cigarette burns unattended in a tray on the long shelf below the window. It is ten minutes until show time. The rest of the band is at the bar, except for Kenny, who is pacing restlessly in the alley, as he does. Outside, Copenhagen darkens under a lowering sky, streetlamps winking on as Store Regnegade fades toward black.

The knock has hardly had time to interrupt him before the door swings open. Framed in the doorway are two men dressed for a costume party. Under their coats they wear close-fitting leggings and short jackets of deep green satin, a joke if not for their grim faces. Both men are on the shortish side of average. They are hatless, clean-shaven except for matching mustaches closely cropped.

"Can I help you fellas?" Red turns in his chair, still holding the horn loosely.

The men look the room over, though there is little to see. The window is a frame filled with gray. A strong, swampy smell seeps through the air. One of them steps into the room, hands hanging at his sides.

"We're need," he says.

"Excuse me?"

"We need," he says. Haltingly, he adds, "Find our companion. Look."

"What?"

The two men glance at each other, then back to Red. The man in the doorway says, "You are English speaker?"

"Yeah, I speak English."

This confuses them. The smell is a miasmic swirl that makes Red feel faint.

"You're looking for somebody?" Red stands, and both of the others startle. They simultaneously put hands in pockets, a universal gangster move.

Red holds his hands in front of him, palms out. "Whoa, there! I don't want no trouble. Calm down."

The man who has come into the room pulls a strange-looking object from his pocket. It is long and tear-shaped, made of a smooth, shiny metal that gleams silver in the low light. He holds it out toward Red, as if it protects him somehow, from something.

"The fuck is that?" asks Red.

"Will shoot," says the man with the object. "Is gun."

"Don't look like a gun," says Red, but he doesn't move.

"Is gun," the other insists. He then speaks slowly, carefully enunciating the words. "I do not want to execute you."

"Well, hell, that makes two of us." It isn't the first time Red has been threatened, and he knows how to wait and find out what this is about—drugs, money, a girl? The thing being pointed at him doesn't look like any gun he's ever seen, but the cats in the funny green suits seem to feel confident behind it, at once more tense and at ease. Red stays still.

The one standing in the doorway pulls a small square of paper from the pocket of his overcoat and steps forward, thrusting the thing in Red's face. It's a photograph.

"We look for this," the man says. "Have you seen?" And then, after a searching moment: "Him?"

The photograph is odd. The paper is more like flexible plastic, and the picture itself seems to have depth beyond two dimensions, like a holographic image but without the telltale rainbow colors. Red has never seen anything like it. But he has certainly seen the person in the picture.

"I don't know who that is," he says. It's not untrue.

"Kayma says he come here," the gunman says.

"He might have come here. The place is packed every night."

They frown at the words. "Packed," the photograph man says.

"There are a lot of people at each show," Red says. "I don't know who's in the audience. I just play the gig."

"Kayma says this man watches you."

"Maybe Kayma ought to buy his boy a drink and figure it out himself."

Their eyes widen. "We want you to watch," says the gunman, as if he is reciting lines. "This man dangerous. Must find."

Red picks up his saxophone. "Well, I hope you find him. Now, unless you're gonna hit me with that paperweight, I got a show to do. Stick around if you want."

He pushes into the hallway, leaving the men behind him in their swampy funk. His heart is beating a steady four/four in his chest, and with every step he expects to feel a blow or a bullet. It takes him two songs to lose this unsettled feeling. After the show, the dressing room is empty, the smell of decay faded like the hint of stale smoke in the midnight air.

Gabardine does not return for two days, and neither do the little green-clad men. Red plays two shows, neither remarkable. One of the days is taken up with phone calls and meetings with his agent regarding an upcoming visit to the States (a recording date has been proposed alongside the concerts), but the second day Red spends practicing in Rosenborg Palace Gardens, the sax floating among the trees and drawing the occasional curious pedestrian. He likes the green of the grass and the solid wood of the bench, the way the sky tilts away when he leans back to grab a high note. On the third day he is supposed to meet his agent again, but instead he returns to the park.

The sun is bright and brittle, the sax cold through his fingerless gloves. He plays for an hour, running scales and improvising. When a shadow falls across the bench, he looks up to see Gabardine, standing with his hands in his pockets, same little smile on his face. Red feels a little jolt of relief, seeing Gabardine standing there, happy and whole.

"Hey," says Red. "Missed you the last couple nights. Have a seat." He pats the bench next to him, then feels foolish.

Gabardine sits on the edge of the bench, crouched uncomfortably forward. "You are playing tonight?" he asks. "I'll come."

"Don't feel obligated," Red says. "Don't know how good we'll be. It's our last show at the Montmartre before we do that little tour I told you about."

"It will be fun to travel," says Gabardine.

"I suppose. They're bigger concerts. I prefer the clubs. Less pressure."

"I look forward to your return."

"You sticking around?"

Gabardine has leaned back, still angled oddly on the edge, but more relaxed. He squints into the sunlight at Red's question. He is once again hatless, and the light strikes him full in the face. "I think I may. Why do you ask?"

"You said you were looking for a place to settle. But I don't know if you ought to hang around Copenhagen."

"You think I will be hassled?"

"Hassled?"

"That is the word you used, I believe. Before, the police hassled you?"

"Oh, right. Well, they hassle anybody got a habit like I had. Double if you're black. Triple if you blow a horn for a living. I was in and out of jail a few times."

"You were in prison?" He sits forward again, his eyes bright.

"Nah, not prison. Almost, but never quite. Just small-time jails. Being an addict takes a lot of time, you see. Jails and hospitals, almost eight years' worth."

"Bars are bars," Gabardine says.

"I suppose so. Anyways that was ten years ago. More. So who's hassling you? If you've got the cops after you, man, it might be better if we don't spend a lot of time together. No offense, but I've got to..."

"It is not the police," he says.

"Look," Red leans forward, elbows on knees, earnest. "I like you, so I got to be honest about this. A couple of cats showed up the other night at the Montmartre looking for you."

"You know this?"

"They had a picture of you. Came right into the dressing room. Dressed like *The Jetsons*. Bad English, but pretty clear they ain't planning on sending you no Christmas cards, you know?"

"People from home." He looks out at the trees for a moment. "I have been imprisoned as well."

"You jump parole or something?"

"I do not know what that means."

"After they let you out…"

"They did not let me out. I escaped."

"What? You broke out of jail?" Red looks around, scanning the park. Gabardine seems nice enough, but an escaped convict is an escaped convict.

"I told you," Gabardine says, "not jail. Not the police. I am… how would you say it?" He looks into the sky, knitting his brows at the linguistic challenge. "I am a political refugee!" He seems triumphant to have lassoed the phrase.

"You're like, trying to defect? You're what, Russian? East German?"

"'Defect' is the word. Thank you."

"So you're on the run from your government. Running from a revolution, or what?"

"I tried to start the revolution. The king did not… it is not important." He takes his pipe out of the pocket of his overcoat. It is already full of tobacco. He thumb-strikes a match with his left hand and breathes the flame into the bowl.

"Sounds pretty damn important. You were like, leading men with guns? Shit."

"No guns. I led a small group. I was not successful."

"So you've got military after you?"

"The king's guard. Azathoth has many… I did not think they knew where I am."

"Well, they do. I don't think you ought to be coming by the club. They're watching the place. Some cat saw you, they said. Kayma. Unless that's a gal's name."

For the first time Gabardine seems troubled. "I think perhaps they are… when you pretend? When you are playing cards?"

"Bluffing?"

Gabardine nods. "They are bluffing."

"Who's Kayma?"

Gabardine places a hand over his mouth, as if he feels sick. "It doesn't matter. Kayma is not in Copenhagen."

"They said he was."

"I am sorry they bothered you. They are merely bureaucrats. They know nothing of art or freedom."

"What happens if they catch you? You go to trial?"

Gabardine smiles. "Do not worry about me. I will not be caught. If I am, I know that I did the right thing."

"By trying to overthrow your government?"

"By trying to live for what I believe. By standing up for those who cannot stand up for themselves."

Red fingers the keys on his saxophone. "My stuff seems pretty small potatoes next to that, man."

Gabardine puts his hand on Red's arm. "No! No. What you do— it is so important."

"Glad you think so. It ain't a revolution."

"Our revolution was your small potatoes. The old music, the ways of my people, it is all being erased from our culture. There are many… I cannot say. Many 'oppressions,' is that a word?"

"It's a word."

"Many oppressions that I can name in my culture, but it was the erasing of our music that made me stand up and say 'enough!' You understand this, yes?"

"Yeah, I guess I do," says Red.

Gabardine stands as if to leave. He is still smiling.

Red pulls the mouthpiece off his horn, starts putting the pieces in the case. "I'm going to grab some lunch. You want a sandwich or something?"

"No, thank you. I'll come see you play tonight."

"I don't know if that's the best idea. Those cats know you've been hanging around the Montmartre."

"If I don't stay in Copenhagen, this is my last chance to hear you."

"Well, then do this. Come early, and go to the back door, in the alley—it's a green door. Take the stairs up and you'll see the dressing room down on the right. I'll be there by seven-thirty. Hang out with me before the gig, and you can watch from the wings. Nobody in the audience should be able to see you, and you'll get the best seat in the house."

Gabardine blinks. His eyes are moist. "That is very kind of you. I will do that."

"I'll see you then. You be careful, okay?"

Gabardine smiles, waving his unsmoked pipe. "I am careful. Thank you, my friend." Leaf-shadows shift across his eyes, and for a moment it appears as if his face shifts as well, as if an ill-fitting hat slid atop a quickly turned head before dropping back into place. But of course Gabardine has no hat. They leave the park in opposite directions, Red's saxophone case swinging at the end of his long arm.

On his way to the Montmartre that evening, Red turns his coat up against the chill. April in Copenhagen can go either way, and this year it seems to lean cold, settling into a fine mist that was sometimes rain, sometimes fog. Often Red will detour around the Kastellet to get a breath of the sea. He loves the statue of the Little Mermaid—the Lille Havfrue who keeps watch over the water. But the Baltic air is chill tonight, and Red stays on Solvgade and walks the close-leaning streets before turning south on Adelgade. He walks loosely, one hand in his pocket, the other holding a cigarette. He left his sax at the club after leaving the park, and ate a late lunch before making a conciliatory call to his agent. He is leaving in two days for Paris and has a host of mundane tasks clamoring for his attention, but his mind keeps circling Gabardine. What kind of story has come to find him in Denmark?

He is thinking two thoughts—that he should invite Gabardine to come with him to Paris and that he should open the first set with "Scrapple from the Apple"—when an unfamiliar sound makes him stop dead on the pavement. The sound had come from an alley leading off to the right: a deep, slow sound, like someone dragging a soft and heavy object across a piece of metal. It was whispery dry but carried the implication of wetness. The same smell that had accompanied the two little green men is wafting in waves from the alley. Red suppresses the urge to retch.

The sun is sinking behind the tops of the buildings in the city center to the west, and already the shadows in the alley have stretched long and deep. There is a faint sound on the air, like someone left a radio on somewhere a few streets over. A discordant flute. He peers into the gloom, but there is nothing beyond a few trash cans and one larger dumpster behind a seafood restaurant.

Just in the act of turning his head away from the alley, something moves in the dark behind the dumpster. Red freezes, not trusting what his peripheral vision tells him. He takes a tentative step toward the mouth of the alley, not wanting to go in, afraid of confronting the thing he thought he saw.

"Hello?" His voice falls flat against the bricks. He is being silly, jumpy because of Gabardine's strange story. He drops his cigarette and crushes it under his heel before resuming his walk. He walks more quickly now, wanting to get to the club, to leave the streets as soon as possible.

The dressing room is dark. He turns on the lamps and pulls the curtain across the window. He has not been there five minutes before Gabardine arrives, glancing furtively over his shoulder but still wearing the little half-smile. Red ushers him into the dressing room and closes the door.

"I'm glad you made it," he tells Gabardine. His cheerfulness sounds hollow. "You got me jumpy with all this talk about revolution and the king's guard. I started seeing things."

Gabardine's smile slips. There is another quick moment when it seems like his face isn't keeping up with his head. "What did you see?" he asks.

Red casts the story as a joke, a brief imagining by an overactive brain. "Wasn't anything there at all," he concludes. "Nothing but a dumpster and some shadows."

Gabardine does not laugh. He says, "Perhaps Kayma *is* in Copenhagen."

"That's bad, huh?"

"It is not good. I am surprised."

"Kayma's some boss-man?"

"Kayma is only called on for certainties," says Gabardine. "For, what would you say? Sure things. I have not been as clever as I thought."

"So Kayma's like a special agent? He's your country's 007?"

"Kayma is..." He trails off, looking at the window.

"Brother, where are you from? I'm trying to keep up and be as cool as I can, but this is some weird shit, okay? If you're a 'political refugee,' we should get you to an embassy or something. The Danish consulate..."

"No."

"They got people who can protect you."

Gabardine looks at the window. Through a gap in the curtains the stars are out over Copenhagen, winking dimly through the drifting mist. "The Danish consulate," he says, "cannot protect me."

Red lights another cigarette. "Why don't you come with me to Paris? I'm leaving day after tomorrow, alone. It'd be nice to have some company. Kayma and the boys won't be expecting you to head out like that. Miles is gonna be there. Art Farmer. Billy Higgins is gonna play piano. Some cool music, and Paris is always a good time."

Gabardine looks back from the window, his eyes bemused. "You are so kind, my friend. I have run for a long time."

"I wish you'd explain this shit," says Red. "I can help, if you'll tell me what's going on."

"Have you never felt you had to fight? That you had no choice but to challenge the way things are?"

Red draws heavily on his cigarette, watches the glowing tip as he speaks. "Everything in my life comes through the horn. Politics is in there, social change is in there. Makes a bigger impact. Nobody gets lynched."

"Music is *why* they want to lynch us," says Gabardine.

"Man, I'd love to hear some of that music you keep talking about."

Gabardine turns in his chair to face him. "I can do that," he says.

"Oh yeah? You don't need an instrument? Piano's down on the stage if you want."

"No," says Gabardine. "May I touch your hand?"

Red looks at Gabardine's hands, pale and ordinary, one on each knee. "Sure, why not?"

Gabardine takes Red's right hand in both of his own. His eyes are locked on Red's. Until now, if asked, he would have said

Gabardine's eyes were grey, or perhaps the blue of slate tiles. The color is something else though, a color Red doesn't have a name for. His stare is intense, like the look of a lover. And then the music begins.

It comes from everywhere at once—the walls, the cheap wooden chair, the cigarette smoke curling around the lampshade. It comes from the night sky outside the window, from the cold light of the stars. It must come from Gabardine, but it resonates through Red's head as if his own skull were somehow broadcasting. Cerebral music, but not the way the music critics meant.

The music is not jazz, but nor is it the folksy jangle Red had imagined. Unfamiliar sounds, alien timbres pulled from instruments he couldn't guess at. Struck, bowed, how would one create the noises in his head? The scales are microtonal, blending in harmonies deeper than any he'd encountered before—fifths, sevenths, thirteenths watching from somewhere far away. This is no "free" music, no Ornette Coleman or Albert Ayler. With those cats you can hear what tradition they're abandoning, at least tell what they're trying not to sound like. This music is so unprecedented that it seems to somehow come around the other side, hitting you from behind so strangely you feel you've always known it. He realizes he is weeping, softly, tears tracking his face like prison bars. It is the most beautiful music he has ever heard, and his life has set a high standard.

"My lord," he says. "No wonder they want to stop you."

From outside there is a quick and heavy sound, as of something bulky and wet dragging across the pavement. The music stops as if razored. Gabardine goes rigid in his chair, pulling his hands back. Red steps to the window and pulls aside the curtain.

The mist has gone. The stars are sharp and bright, teeming in the sky like sentient jewels. The street below the window, just wider than an alley, is shrouded in darkness. Red watches the blackness. When the movement comes, it is not on the street but in the air, above him and to the right, a flickering shadow between the Montmartre and the sky. He jumps, and then laughs.

"Nothing there," he says. "A bird or something startled me. That's all it is. The street's empty."

"It is time for you to play," says Gabardine.

He shows Gabardine where to stand, how to see and not be seen. Kenny, Niels, and Alex are playing already, doing Kenny's "Grooving the Blues," warming the crowd up. Red clips his saxophone to its strap.

"This is the best seat in the house," he says. "Up close and personal. Just stay here and you're golden."

"I appreciate what you are doing," says Gabardine. "I will stay here as long as I can. If Kayma comes…"

"Kayma can't just walk up in here. Jan won't let anybody on the stage. The back door is locked."

Gabardine looks as if he is about to say something more, but then he smiles and nods. Red walks on stage. The audience applauds. Alex rolls the snare twice, they hit the staccato head of "Scrapple from the Apple," and then they're off, swinging hard. They push it over the cliff, running to the finish line nine minutes away. Two more songs, hard bop. Red feels like he's floating, like the sound is a current of air and he can drift on it until he passes the sun, falling head over foot into the universe.

Red turns to wink at Gabardine. He can't understand what he sees. Gabardine is watching the band, but he is also turning away to look at something behind him. The two things happen simultaneously, turning and standing still, and the impossibility of this blurs Red's vision. The side of the stage has been pushed into a dirty plastic bag, vague objects moving in opposition to each other. Whatever has caught Gabardine's attention is behind him, large and dark and ill-defined. Red sees Gabardine spread his arms (although he is still watching the band, still hasn't moved) in welcome or surrender.

He is dropping his saxophone. He is running to the side of the stage. The small space is empty but for the rotten sweet smell of decay. Red runs to the back door, just ajar enough to let the April chill seep into the club.

Red steps outside, into the street. The air is sharp and clear, the mist gone completely. The street is nearly deserted. Gabardine is not there, nor is anyone Red recognizes. He looks up, alone, and sees the stars spreading out above him. A satellite moves across the sky, fast and bright, losing itself above the Baltic Sea. A hand touches his shoulder. Kenny.

"You all right, man?"

Red looks away from the stars. He swallows. "Yeah, I'm all right. Felt sick for a minute. Needed some air."

"You gonna finish the set?"

The next song is "Don't Explain." Red's head is still swimming with the music he heard in the dressing room, fading fast. He can no more reproduce that music than he can fly to the stars. But he knows how to pour that feeling into his own music, how to blow loss and melancholy through the horn. He loves the ballads, and tonight he plays a nostalgia for something he never lived, a yearning for a never-was. He plays the afterglow of Gabardine's song, the ashes of a revolution.

He stretches the cadenza at the end, pushing through arpeggios to reach up, up and out. The drop back to the tonic, the heavy final chord the four men crash down into, is a fall from heaven, an elegy for the dizzy atmosphere they had briefly kissed. Kenny says, "All *right*."

"Yeah," says Red. "All right."

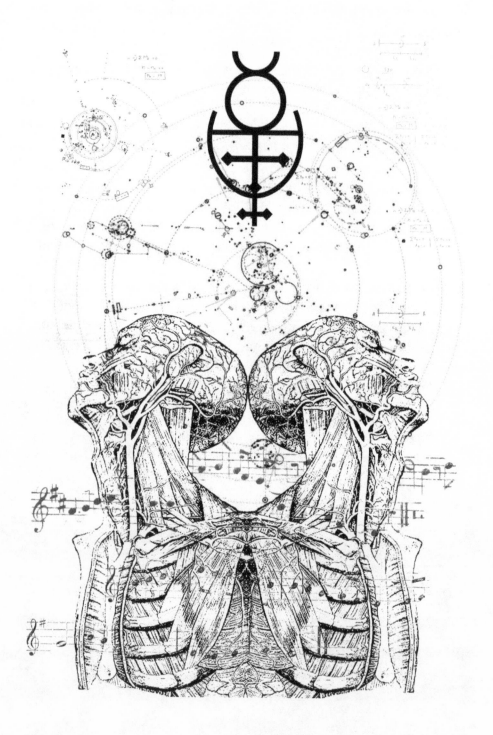

... And Peer Aloft to Glimpse Some Fragment

Ruthanna Emrys

THERE IS SOMETHING that is not human, that has nothing in common with us. You became obsessed with this idea as a child, shortly after you learned about the ozone layer: a random perturbation of atmosphere that permits life. Humans shouldn't be able to break such a thing, let alone fix it. Our power is absurd. Sanity demands some limit.

For a while you believed that you must be a changeling from Pluto, displaced as far as you could imagine. But the ships never came. You gave up on your own inhumanity, but not the universe's.

Now you seek the unseekable another way. Late-night communities share scraps from satellite records, from the fractal commonalities of shells and galaxies, from inconsistencies in deep-space telescope images. In these scraps they find beauty that transcends pattern, and pattern that transcends beauty. The background radiation of existence makes music. You follow the piping of something not human enough to care if you follow.

In October of 1952, two students at a prestigious eastern university stretched new computing technology to draw practical truth from esoteric texts. Transforming words into digits, digits into forms, they created sigils by arranging ones and zeros into rectangles: prime by prime, on the assumption that any intelligence underlying the universe would have that much in common with us.

The sigils did nothing. They translated again: digits into musical notes, notes into a song that could be played on violin or piano or flute. Janitors passing their practice room after midnight reported eerie sounds beyond anything these instruments normally produced, and believed the building haunted. Their nightmares grew so vivid that they refused to clean the place after dark. The students were told to play elsewhere.

In the woods beyond campus, they laid down new sigils in leaf litter, and piped on. Flute and violin screamed. Bats, disoriented, froze and fell. Leaves and music were rearranged; the students tried again. They no longer knew what they were testing, only that they had to play. Had to listen. Had to follow.

@cosmic_orchestra is arguing furiously with @zeusaphone about what constitutes music. The argument is irrelevant to what the community calls *The Search*; whatever musicians play at the center of the universe, they aren't likely to have recognizable vocals, let alone insist that their dislike of rap has nothing to do with racism. You lurk at the fight's edge, silently frustrated that your shared obsession isn't enough to prevent this kind of human bullshit.

We're hopeless as a species. The fact that we can glimpse the tuneless tune at all suggests that its producer doesn't notice us, or doesn't understand us well enough to judge us.

The records of the missing students are a more interesting problem. The two boys vanish from the record, with no later marriage or death certificates, no articles about performances or publications. Their disappearance is trivial—but the fate of their notes is not. Did the university preserve them? Burn them out of misplaced puritanism or protective instinct? You want to go there in person and ask, but not alone. You need someone from the community who can pass, who speaks the brain-twisting tongue of academia that opens portals, or at least doors to disused library stacks.

The irony of this mutual need, between members of a species so unnecessary to the cosmos, does not escape you.

Paul Lyons was born to an old-money family in the heart of Boston. There was never any question but that he should go to Miskatonic like his father and grandfather, meet connections at the Oaken Spar Club to ease his way, and go into the family business of raising buildings in which people like him could grow richer. His studies were almost irrelevant; it was the people who mattered.

Sam Stern was one of five Jewish students admitted to Miskatonic under the school's 1950 quota. He avoided the others except on Saturday mornings. He had promised his parents to observe those morning services, and to follow the pre-law course track religiously. The music classes, and Miskatonic's notoriously philosophical math lectures, were his only two points of self-indulgence during freshman year.

It was Paul who argued with Sam rather than ignoring him, Paul who pushed him to impracticality. It was Sam who convinced Paul to question the policies that made his family's buildings so lucrative, Sam who made him think about how far the seemingly stable could change.

Neither would remember whose idea it was to seek the music. They only knew that once the question had been asked, it must be answered before any other question could make sense.

@zeusaphone turns out to be a middle-aged woman with ears full of multicolored hoops, adjunct classes that drag her to different universities every day of the week, and the names of her beloved dead tattooed on her bare shoulders.

"Pestilence took her," she says, running a finger over the name with the shortest span of dates. "I lost Zaire to 'friendly' fire in Afghanistan, that's war. Lars died of brain cancer, that's famine and pestilence both." She's given up on hauntings, looks now for awe enough to prove the smallness of grief.

She cranks Beyoncé and Common all the way to Miskatonic, glancing to track your response. You like the beat but find the lyrics irreducibly human, trite as language always seems. But you nod your head, human enough to want to be with her and not with @cosmic_orchestra. Better to care expansively for trivial things than for the meaningless distinctions between them.

On stolen mainframe time—squeezed between equations run as a favor to Paul's math professor—the boys calculated yet another variation on their symphony. They heard the music in the clattering cards. It was so close. Sam began to whirl, moving to the tuneless tune.

"Ecstatic dancers," suggested Paul. "Spinning ever closer to the center."

"Broken dancers, spinning pieces of themselves out away from the center." Sam thrust out his hand, pulled Paul into the movement, and the music of their calculations surged louder until they could hear nothing else.

Afterward they took their new results into the woods, along with violin and flute and sleeping bags, and sandwiches from the school's piled offerings to test-weary scholars. But they couldn't recall later whether they played, or only lay together and gazed through the stars, listening to instruments of which their own were mere out-spun echoes.

"Follow it in," whispered Sam. "Echoes of echoes of echoes, until we find the truth."

Neither could recall who first touched the other's hand, listening. Neither could say, even then, who was leading the other.

The library assistant is magnetized by @zeusaphone's chatter. It's easy to forget your goals; @zeusaphone makes the whole conversation feel important even as her requests dance around the only resource you care about. The assistant tells stories as they lead you back into the stacks.

Every bookshelf here is haunted. Perhaps it's an honor to organize these carts for minimum wage, to dust tomes that scholars once dueled over, to turn glimpses of cosmic truth into alphabetized database entries. Newly installed air conditioning whistles like a distant flute, struggling desperately to preserve knowledge from rot and mold.

The student papers room is more a large closet than an archive. The shelves full of cardboard boxes, labels handwritten and typed and printed, some faded and curling while others sit neat as yesterday, are as much a history of labeling technology as of graduate research. The Music section is sparse; Math stretches back into a shadowy avalanche of Edwardian ephemera. Lyons and Stern might be in either section, if they aren't rotting under decades of pine needles. @zeusaphone chats with the assistant—flirts, you think—as you begin your search.

Summer was hard. Paul's family didn't mind him living in Arkham, but insisted on regular pilgrimages to Boston for obligatory weddings, baptisms, and business meetings. Sam's wanted him back in New York, working and helping his zayde with chores. He took the train when he could. More often they wrote letters, opaque to anyone not versed in their chords and equations.

The tacit agreement, they both knew, was that time apart was only for theory. But neither of them could close their ears. Music and math are not placid lovers. Sam took his violin to the roof long after midnight. He held it close against his chest, as if by clutching too tightly he could keep himself from playing. Something sang through the unseen stars, something that couldn't be washed out by city lights. His grip loosened, mindlessly. He began to play.

His sister found him in the morning, shaking and feverish, singing without words.

The doctor and the rabbi both had their say, neither useful. His father telegrammed the young man who sent letters full of orchestral scores.

Students leave so much behind when they graduate, or otherwise depart, Miskatonic. The work that gains positions and prestige at other schools, they bring with them. The notes they leave behind— those the library sees fit to preserve—are records of dreams beyond the bounds of academia. Theories that can never be tested, questions without practical answers, ideas that fit into no sensible discipline. In these notebooks of scribblings irrelevant to The Search, you find kindred spirits: a thousand Searches straining toward purpose... and abandoned. Any of these might have been worthy obsessions.

You imagine realities spinning out from this little room. If you had found another community, or another question, first. If you had gone to college. If you find nothing here, and go home, and nothing changes. If you ask @zeusaphone, now, to work with you as closely as Paul worked with Sam, to spend a night in the woods away from the cool light of your laptop.

"Are you all right?" she asks.

You freeze, torn amid possibilities. "It's nothing," you say at last. "Just worried we won't find anything."

"Well, The Search is everywhere." Which is what they say in the community when a direction doesn't pan out.

You nod and return to the boxes of irrelevant lives.

Paul didn't arrive with answers. In all their work, they'd never asked what their discoveries would look like to people who didn't share them. They'd never guessed that *they* might not share every step. There were no words in Paul's language for whether Sam was found or lost.

He sat beside Sam's bed, picked up the violin, gripped it as Sam had done. He sat unmoving for a long time, until father and sisters backed away. He began to play at last. At the other end of the apartment, Sam's family shuddered and steeled themselves to whatever might be necessary.

Paul's childhood stories were about contests with fae and devils, as Sam's were about debating dybuks. Both had learned, from those stories, that human cleverness and wisdom could overcome what they could not understand. But there was nothing to fool here, no sentience against which to test his skills. There was only the music, and whatever it spun toward.

Sam whimpered and curled away from the violin, shivering.

"I want you here," Paul whispered against the whirl of the music. "I want to understand what you understand. I want to hold you." To be seeking and together in the woods, to burn together on the same bed, to dance together at the center: all would do.

Instead of the music as he knew it, he began to *follow*, to play the wordless song flowing from Sam's lips between cries. Slowly Sam uncurled, bent toward him. Sweat cooled on his brow. His eyes opened and, again, they played together.

There is nothing relevant, even at the bottom of the shadowed pile. It occurs to you, wryly, that you've done the assistant's job of straightening and organizing the worst of the shelves, assuming anyone wanted that job done. The Search may be here, but Sam and Paul are not.

Even in your disappointment, you take a respectful moment before the glass-cased *Necronomicon*. Miskatonic prides itself on such rarities, as much for the pilgrims they draw as the knowledge they contain. Others in the community have pored over them already. They've found tantalizing references, but none of the answers you seek. Alhazred, your compatriots have long concluded, was looking for the right thing but was too easily distracted. You think of the closet again: a thousand abandoned Searches.

@zeusaphone touches your aching shoulder. Your muscles, chilled tense by the library air conditioning, soften at the contact. "Drown our sorrows in chocolate?" she suggests, and you end up at the Lich Street Herrell's, ordering an unreasonable number of toppings on an unreasonable number of scoops.

"This reality may be an illusion, but sometimes it's a delicious one," @zeusaphone tells you around a mouthful of hot fudge, and you nod. You feel guilty, but as long as you're stuck with these physics you may as well enjoy them.

Buoyed by sugar, you admit, "It was good to work together. If I were by myself, I'd worry that I missed something—at least this way we know they really aren't there."

"We should keep working together on this thread," she agrees. "Their notes might have ended up somewhere else. We'll keep looking."

You're surprised by how real your warmth feels in response to her words, despite everything.

There are changes of perspective that you can't undo. Sam could speak again, seemed if anything more genius than before. But he could no longer be persuaded to his parents' strictures, though they urged him to consider both the value of knowing your children well-fed, and the value of arguing for justice before those who judged it. When he returned to Miskatonic in the fall, his courseload focused on the ragged abstractions of mathematics.

But still he returned, and Paul was grateful. He tried to listen when Sam's words passed beyond meaning, and to touch when words broke into frustrated sobs. Where no one else could hear, they played, together.

The bats knew by now what part of the woods to avoid.

It's the closet of student papers, empty as it was, that gives you the idea. You're trying to articulate to @zeusaphone, on a side chat, how the folders and boxes seemed glimpses into other Searches, how all those lives seemed meaningful despite everything.

I wonder what else our wayward boys cared about, she says.

I wonder what other Searches are looking for them.

There were no marriage records, no publications, but that doesn't mean no one else looked. And so you modify your keywords—seeking not your own answers, but others' questions.

You find it on the most mundane of genealogy sites. You've never understood why people should care who shares a sliver of their DNA, but you see it now. The posters here delve into exactly the sort of trivial detail that hovered around those notebooks. They're looking for meaning, where you're looking for something beyond meaning, but there's kinship. And maybe meaning and un-meaning aren't so far apart, if meaning leads you closer.

My grandmother saved everything she had from her brother after he disappeared. There was a whole box of letters from another boy, half of them in cipher, and full of math that I don't even know what field it is, unless it's another cipher. But some of the coded stuff is love letters!

Can anyone help me figure out what the math is about?

They spent longer in the woods: full weekends, and sometimes into the week, forgetting time and course schedules. Music skirled into the sky, when they remembered they had hands and voices. Bodies touched and twined, when they remembered they had bodies. Sometimes they forgot the notebooks, all the notes they needed etched on their nerves and muscles.

Sometimes they sobbed together into a pillow of dried pine needles. If you asked why, they would not be able to articulate whether they mourned what was soon to be gained, or cried in eagerness for what would be lost. They knew only that it hurt beyond imagining, and that they yearned beyond all desperation.

It took over a month for the school to admit that their search for the two boys had failed.

Sam's sister's granddaughter shows you the papers. They're yellowed and stained, in the worst places blotted with rain or tears. A lawyer herself, she revels in detail and meaning, determined to articulate it into permanence where none exists. She sees Sam's story as a tragedy.

"He could have done so much for the world," she says, showing you his absurd freshman year legal essays. "I don't know what happened to him, but his lover was the only happiness he had."

@zeusaphone takes over, telling her about Paul. She talks about the boys' dive into mysticism in a way that will sound sane even to someone unfamiliar with the Search. You can tell she wouldn't want to hear about that part; @zeusaphone can tell what she *does* want to hear, and has the patience to offer it. You take pictures while she talks, scanning calculations and ciphers alike into your phone's memory.

At the hotel, you curl in @zeusaphone's arms. "We can follow them."

"All of us?" she asks.

You think about the community. All the reasons people bring to The Search, all the biases and refusals to see. All the human weakness.

"Some of them wouldn't want to see answers, even if we found them," you admit. "But we should share what we have."

She kisses you, wraps you in arms etched with the names of beloved dead, that give meaning to ephemeral flesh. "And then we should dance."

~ * ~ * ~ * ~ * ~ * ~ * ~ * ~ * ~ * ~ * ~ * ~ * ~ * ~ * ~ * ~ * ~ * ~ * ~

At the last moment, the music-that-is-not-music overwhelms all fear and all thought. Everything that you are changes, and before you stop knowing, you know that it will never stop changing.

You catch a glimpse, while you can still see, of something that used to be two boys, eyes full of something beyond delight. Their hands, etched with stars, reach to pull you in. And then there is the piping, and the whirl, and truth beyond all human sensation.

On the hotel bed a laptop sits open, cursor blinking. The community, still itself, reads the scanned equations and—setting the love letters aside as irrelevant—begins to argue.

Making a Difference

Brian Evenson

YOU WONDER PERHAPS why I brought you here. Perhaps you think you already know: you had, of course, that carefully composed letter from me praising your efforts, speaking in admiring terms of your struggle to do something for *Gaia*, as I chose to refer to our planet, imagining it would strike a chord with you.

Apparently it did.

Did you admire the effortless style of my letter, the impression it gave of being dashed off in a rush by a wealthy man—so I described myself—who was approaching the end of his life and who was now looking back with regret at his choices and who did not want to shuffle off this mortal coil without, and here I quote, "making a difference in a worthy cause and atoning for some of the damage I have done?" All that apparent effortlessness was deliberately constructed, worked and reworked until I had what I thought was the perfect letter, the letter that would sink like a hook into your heart. I spent time watching and rewatching all your public speeches, all the climate action sessions you facilitated. I investigated your past and came to feel you had a weakness for redemption narratives, a weakness my letter could exploit. I drafted and redrafted my letter to you, considered and reconsidered my wording until it felt right, and then I memorized the contents so that when I went to write it— handwritten letters being another weakness of yours—the script would be fluid and continuous. *How can he resist?* I thought.

Indeed, you could not resist: here you are.

No, don't get up. Please.

I tried to warn you. Your legs, as you can see, will no longer support your weight. The extremities are always the first to go after ingestion. Only later will the organs begin to fail.

Here, if you make an effort and I pull on your arms, you might still manage to bend at the waist. If we work together, we can muscle you off the floor and back into your chair. If you have to die, at least you can do so in a dignified fashion.

Let's try.

One, two, three—

There. A little harder than I expected. But still doable.

Now, what shall we do as we wait for the end?

Those eyes of yours! So angry and expressive, resentful of me and still darting around looking for a way out, a possible escape. There is, I'm afraid, no escape. I carefully measured the nerve agent that I added to the whiskey in your glass. I watched to make sure you drank it all down. It's just a question of time.

I'll sit and wait with you. Nobody, I feel, should have to die alone. Try, if you can, not to think of me as your murderer—think of me rather as simply an attendant, someone who will stay with you as you slip out of this life, into whatever lies beyond.

I can tell by the way you look at me that you feel my attendance at your death is not enough. "Why?" your eyes seem to plead. Am I correct? Would you like to know why I have killed you?

Let me tell you now: the answer will do you no good. It will change nothing. It will not even comfort you. It is likely you will not even understand it or that, if you do, you will think me mad.

No, better for us to sit here, your hand clasped gently in my own, not speaking, until one of our two hands grows cold.

That is the better path, the noble path. It is the path I would choose were I in your shoes.

But if you prefer to know, I feel it is my duty to oblige you. Can you still blink your eyes? Good. Shall we say blink once for yes, twice for no?

Agreed. Well then, shall I tell you why you're here?

Yes, then. You're sure? So be it.

As you might have guessed, I am not a wealthy man. I have no money for your cause, I never did. I am also far from the end of my life. True, I'm no longer young, but I have at least a few decades remaining. Everything I suggested to you about myself in my letter was an outright lie. From the beginning I was constructing a self solely for you. *What self must I construct,* I asked myself, *to convince him to come here so I can kill him?*

Perhaps you think I have killed you because I am a so-called climate denier, that I stand against everything you have been fighting for. Nothing could be further from the truth! I firmly believe humans are destroying the planet. I find the science compelling and convincing and, really, beyond dispute. I was convinced of this long before I first saw you speak. But once I did see you speak, I could understand why so many thousands of people who had hitherto been indifferent were now galvanized. Of all those fighting this general indifference to climate change, you were the only one I knew who had the arguments, the charisma, and the manner of delivery that seemed capable, slowly, of causing those who were mired in their own inaction to finally act. You were inspiring! Watching you speak I found myself thinking: "Here is the man most likely to change the world!"

Which is precisely why I knew I had to kill you.

Would you like to hear a story? No? Well, I'll tell one to you anyway.

There are many myths about how the world came to be. This one, shall we say, is perhaps my favorite. Is it true? Perhaps not exactly as I tell it, but some similar version of it is, and for a believer like me, that is enough.

First there was nothing and then out of this nothing came something. Or, if you prefer, first there was chaos and out of it sprang order. How that is possible, I don't know: science tells us that the natural tendency is not toward organization but toward dissolution and decay. The concept of entropy and all that.

But a man who was either very wise or very mad—and perhaps both—once phrased it this way:

At first there was only chaos and disorder. At the heart of this chaos resided a blind idiot god, whose form would not stop shifting. Parts of him, of her, of them, of it, were forever forming or reforming or dropping away. If one were to look at him, at her, at them, at it, the god would be transforming so rapidly that it would be impossible to know what exactly it was you saw.

This blind god is asleep in the midst of his chaos—we'll stick with *he* here for the sake of simplicity—and as he sleeps he dreams, and his dreams are of a very different substance than he. All around him and through him lies chaos. As he dreams, his mind draws into itself the chaos and organizes it, sorts it into the substance of dreams. It is of these dreams that all we think of as order and organization comes to exist. He shapes a dream as he sleeps, hardly knowing what it is he shapes, and then expels it like a lump of sputum, and it is this sputum which is our world.

Are you all right?

Please, blink once if yes, twice if…

I'm sorry to hear it! Well, we can't have that, can we?

I did notice you beginning to slip lower in your chair. I know that even if you can't move you can still feel discomfort, pain. My apologies: I should be a better host.

Here, what if we just lift…

There, that's better, isn't it?

Isn't it?

Blink once for…

Good. Let's just move you a little more so that you'll be wedged between the chair back and the table. You're much less likely to fall over now. I like to think of myself as a problem solver. I pride myself in that.

Better? Shall we go on?

You must think I have been telling you this story as a metaphor. But it is in fact what I believe. If you consider it carefully, is it really all that different from what science tells us? Our galaxy, the Milky Way, has at its center a supermassive black hole. Our solar system is located in one of the four spiral arms of the galaxy, swirling slowly around this spheroidal region of absolute darkness. A black abyss around which everything revolves: is that not the same as a blind idiot god residing at the dark center of the universe?

Shall we consider this region devoid of light as a kind of basalt throne? And upon this throne sleeps the god who dreams us? Is it really that far of a stretch?

Perhaps it is for you, but I have come to believe it. Everything we are, every moment of supposed order, is but the dream of an idiot god. He dreams, sifting and refining the chaos around him. Everything we call order is the disjecta that he spews forth and expels as his dreams. Is that so crazy?

I'm going to pretend I didn't see that. In any case, let me remind you that you are rapidly approaching the moment when you will no longer be able to blink at all.

Let me continue. All order comes from chaos, and as such it is a thin strand of chaos that not only connects it back to its origin but also utterly insinuates it. As the German philosopher, the Nazi sympathizer, suggests, every living thing is thronged about and harried by and shot through with chaos. If you pull on this thin thread of chaos, then all we have seen as ordered and solid will unravel and come apart. That dream of order in which we live will return to the chaos from whence it came as the idiot god awakens.

That thread of chaos, when it comes to the question of climate, when it comes to the survival of the earth and of our species, is manifest in people's willingness not to act, their ability to look the other way, to worry a little perhaps but decide that they can wait until tomorrow to take steps. Or the next day. Or the next. One generation passes the problem to the next, and so forth and so forth. In the end, that simple inaction will be enough to make everything fall apart, everything collapse.

You know this! This is precisely what you have been so effective at fighting against. You are able to stir people, to make them feel they *can* make a difference, that all is not hopeless. Indeed, if there were a half dozen humans like you, with your silvery tongue and your fervent belief and your generosity and your charisma, we would perhaps be able to avert this disaster. And, to be honest, if you continue to speak in the coming months there *will be* more like you, perhaps many more. You have already been making such a difference. You were beginning to drag us back from the brink. Instead of pulling on the thread that would slowly allow everything to dissolve into chaos, you were making the world feel plausible again.

Don't look like that! I've already told you: I agree with you. I accept the science. Your position is utterly ethical and correct. I don't work for the oil companies or the plastics manufacturers or the other businesses that have something short-term to gain and who are, because of the glitter of immediate gold, closing their eyes to what will happen in the future. *Yes, yes, of course*, some of them are saying, *things need to change, things need to be fixed, only not quite yet.*

They're fools. But their actions, their choices, all go back to that winding thread of chaos that passes through their brains. What is remarkable about you is that you don't seem to have such a thread, and you seem to be capable of getting others to ignore theirs and act. Either you are not part of the dream of the blind idiot god, or you were part of the dream but were, from the beginning, an irreducible chunk of order.

No, I agree with you, thoroughly agree. You are an ethical man, a good man. I admire your enthusiasm. I admire you. I agree with you about nearly everything.

In fact, the only thing I don't agree with you about is whether it is right to prevent things from falling into chaos. You say they shouldn't: we must work to sustain ourselves, to live differently, to survive. I say, however, they should. Order is not a natural state: it is an artificial one. We arose from chaos and to chaos we must return. It is inevitable and inexorable, and this state that we live in, where we have streets and cities and airplanes and smart phones and wifi, is an aberration, a moment of dreaming between one chaos and another. If the dream we live in can be made to dissolve, we will return to our natural, proper state, and Azathoth, the blind idiot god, will finally awaken. Only then, only once he is fully awake, will we begin to understand the full extent of what chaos can be.

This is why you must die: I am a servant of chaos. I welcome my own dissolution and the new awareness it will bring. My purpose in life is to make the blind idiot god awaken and open his eyes. Then we shall see what happens next. You were trying to make him sleep more deeply, which is why I brought you here. And I will do the same to anyone else who strikes me as a threat, anyone who strikes me as having a chance at making this world continue rather than fall apart.

You see? No comfort.

Shall we go back to where we started? I'll hold your hand as it slowly goes cold. Imagine me as not your killer but as someone as passionate as you yourself are, someone willing to do anything to achieve what he believes in. And also here to comfort you as you pass from the falsity of order into the generous embrace of chaos. You can do that, can't you?

Another German thinker, this one Jewish, claimed that death signifies nothing. That the distinction between past, present, and future is only a "stubbornly persistent illusion." Perhaps you can find some comfort in that?

Ah, not even the eyelids now. Well then, it won't be long.

Here, let me apply a few drops of fluid to your eyes. Otherwise they will dry out before you're all the way gone. We wouldn't want that, would we?

And let me position your head just so. That way I can look directly into your eyes. There's something about seeing the spark fade that invigorates me, that makes me remember why I do what I do. It might sound morbid, but I don't see it as such. Rather, the moment when order passes into chaos strikes me as a sort of sacrament. It feels holy to me. It always does: I feel it every time.

You couldn't have possibly believed you were my first, could you?

No, I've been at this work a long time, in service to the true lord. I am making a difference. And I'll continue to do so well after you're gone.

Which, if the clock is to be believed, won't be long now.

The Recreationist

Kaaron Warren

THE RECREATIONIST BUILDING dominates the pedestrian square it sits in. Standing nine storeys high, its neo-gothic exterior draws photographers and admirers, but it sucks up every last bit of sun, blocks the square below, blocks the patches of grass, the tables for workers to eat their lunches. Not that they do; mostly the tables are used by groups of people sitting together and talking louder as the day goes on, deeper and deeper into the $4 bottles of wine they get from the local booze shop.

"Bloody By-products of civilization," Ash calls these drinkers. "Bloody wastes of space." Rhiannon agrees. She's been looking after the rentals in The Recreationist since it opened a year ago, and even with empty rooms she wouldn't rent to these people if they came to her with a fistful of money. For one thing, Ash would never forgive her if she did. The building was his baby. It had taken five years to build, mostly due to his perfectionism. "The artists deserve it," he said. "This creative hub will be the best in the country." It was how he'd sold the plan to the council, against great opposition.

His pitch: I want to make something beautiful out of the ugly. Something this town will be famous for.

His huge toothy smile filling his face.

He wanted to make somewhere in the city where artists and writers could live and be inspired, where they could combine creativity with re-creativity (smiling with that, loving his own wordplay), with a gym, a swimming pool, a bowling alley. All the things you need to give your creative brain a break. He wanted the building to stand out amongst the two ugly, dull buildings around it; Haverhill House with its grey brick, its stolid design, and the smaller building known as Idle Daze, for the infamous café that once operated on the ground floor.

Rhiannon can't remember how she connected with Ash Grey (always with a wink at his own name). Standing there at the building site? Or was it earlier? Who introduced him? He WAS ash grey, his eyes large and silver, put in with God's smudged finger. His skin always covered with a sheen of dust. He was a hands-on type, in there with the brickies, the plasterers, the concreters.

Or was it in a bar? Certainly he was the type she'd take home.

He is repairing a small breach in the foyer, a crack in the Calabar wood panelling he'd insisted on. Pan flute music plays. Tenants complained at first, but now they are used to it.

He wears a grey t-shirt that reads *FBI*, which makes her smile, given his lack of law-abidingness, and when he sees her he takes her hands and spins her around, singing her name.

"Come on, I want to show you the penthouse. It's ready to be leased."

"We'd have buyers galore," she says. "Just let me know."

"The owners like a changing clientele. They complain less."

The penthouse is all-over windows; you feel like you own the world up there. It is fully furnished, the colours pink and mauve, silver and grey. The bed enormous, covered with pillows.

Sex with him is like magic, as if he has a dozen arms all working at once.

He says, "You know that most perfect moment of peace, just after you make love? We're all looking for that moment amidst the chaos. And that's what we're selling with our rooms."

She knows that, of course. He doesn't need to tell her.

Rhiannon has her own apartment in The Recreationist, one on a lower floor that looks directly into a ballet studio in Haverhill House. She likes that, although the dancers are too skinny, no meat on them. They are perfectly groomed though, as she likes to be. Some of them have tattoos covered by bandages. Rhiannon would get a permanent tattoo if anything meant enough for her (and while Ash Grey jokes about his face on her inner thighs, she isn't having that), so temporary tattoos, ever-changing, do the job.

She showers and dresses for her next appointment, checking herself for imperfections. She's always had flawless skin; it is something people think comes naturally, they have no idea the amount of skin care and makeup it takes.

Anyway.

"It's all one-way glass," she tells the young artist. He's shown up with paint on his nose, endearing or manipulative, she isn't sure. "One-way glass, so you can sit here, though not with bright lights on, and watch the world. Not just on the street. Look," she says. This is part of what she sells; space for people to spy on those in apartments and small businesses next door in Haverhill House. Creatives are the specialty of the place. "So much material to inspire," she says, and they look out the window, right into the other apartments.

In the five minutes they watch the windows of Haverhill House, they see a woman washing the dishes, her mouth la la la-ing as if singing; a middle-aged man pouring himself a large glass of alcohol and drinking it down like water; a young man shaving his chin slowly, with great determination.

"Five more minutes," the artist says. He flips a notebook open, starts sketching with the stub of a pencil.

"Take a lease and you can watch as often as you like."

She walks him out through the foyer, knowing she has him hooked. She loves this entrance space; it is filled with light and decorated in a style of its own. Large tiles dominate one wall, depicting a glorious sun radiating heat, a watching eye in the middle. Carved into the wooden wall on the other side are symbols of the sun itself, circles with arrows coming out of them, each depiction slightly different from the next. She knows this is a symbol of chaos, of creation, and will tell those she thinks will understand.

A sign over the small, rarely attended desk says, "In Chaos there is Order."

"Chaos is good," the artist says. "That's where ideas come from." He looks at himself in the only mirror, an ornate piece carved with eyes and what Rhiannon knows to be tentacles. If the light is low, the glass seems to swirl and pulse with life.

Rhiannon watches him walk away, then checks her watch. She hits Mist 2 in the elevator (past Night 1, 2, 3, stopping before Ether 1, 2 and 3) and sanitizes her hands. She sometimes wears gloves for a meeting with this resident; his home is filthy, greasy. This time she'd forgotten them, though.

She knocks on the door. The handle looks greasy, and she can smell whatever concoction he has on the go. There is no answer. Walking to the end of the hallway, she peers through the window and there he is below, in the shared courtyard, kicking a ball against the wall.

"Rex!" she calls down. He is Rex Jones and he'd once been a star but now he is a soccer dad. An absent soccer dad at that. He looks up. "I'll need to do that inspection now," she says. "I brought chocolate chip cookies." She lifts the packet out of her bag to show him. He nods, and she waits as he makes his way up. It is warm, much warmer than outside. It is always warm inside The Recreationist.

Rex puffs his way up to her, his key out ready. He shields the lock as if it is coded and pushes open the door. As ever, the apartment smells of fried food. He lives off it; frozen food, deep fried. The boxes line the walls like wallpaper; he calls it insulation. On the centre table he has something seething in a bucket. It has a purplish-golden hue.

"It's beautiful, isn't it?" he says. He gives a little shimmy of excitement. Dust clings to the grease-covered walls, furry and grey.

"How's the family?" she asks. He stares at her, his eyes wide. He doesn't like to think about that. He is too driven by his art to think about that. She scuffs at the carpet, grease almost concealing the sun motif there, the eye in the middle, the rays that are actually tentacles.

"My ideas are my family," he says.

"All ideas come from the ghosts that haunt you," she says.

She knows she will never have a family. The future looms too dark for her; she can see it sometimes, swirling ghosts desperate to take over the world. She shakes her head to remove these thoughts. They do no one any good.

He's gaunt, he never sleeps, he's burned down a dozen good futures.

She says, "I can take the ghosts and leave you in peace. You can be with your family again."

It is time. She is tired of him. He annoys her and he is a disgusting tenant.

The sky darkens and he walks to the window. "My family?"

"And friends. It's only your ghosts causing this." She'd broached this with him before. Laid down the track. Showed him the "ghost clause" in their lease agreement.

"I always thought I'd be something," he says as they head for the roof.

"You were," she says.

She finds Ash Grey leaned up against her doorway. He is even greyer than usual, and she worries he is having a heart attack. He is breathless, excited, he has a bottle of wine with him he says he found in one of the apartments, hiding in the walls, so they drink that and turn out the light so that as they make love they can watch others do the same thing in the building across the way.

They are awoken by shouting coming up from the front entrance. Ash checks his phone camera. "Oh those fucken losers. Those fucken By-products."

He shows Rhiannon; they've moved into the foyer and seem to be settled in for the night. Rhiannon is thankful the rest of the team looked after tenant complaints, because the phones would be ringing off the hook. She goes downstairs via the back way, out into the alley and around the front to take an anonymous view. The big eye logo in lights over the doorway seems to wink at her, but she doesn't find this funny.

Police arrive to move them out, move them on, but they dribble back over the next couple of weeks like memory foam finding its shape again. Rhiannon gets the idea (one of her visions) to offer up Idle Daze, the abandoned café on the ground floor of the third building in the pedestrian square.

"We're not going into that place," one of the women says. She is better dressed than the rest of them and can string two sentences together. She's wearing floral leggings and a long, dark-green t-shirt. She is in stark contrast to Rhiannon, with her neat mauve jacket, her shin-length skirt, her silk shirt tucked in. Rhiannon knows the woman feels superior because she is skinny. Forget the bird's nest of hair on the back of her head, the terrible teeth, the scabs on her elbow. She is skinny.

"None of that really happened. It's a myth!" Rhiannon says. "The owners just went out of business, that's all. And in today's market…"

"Bull fucken shit. They were a bloody cult, weren't they? Bloody suicide cult. Monday Massacre on the Menu," the woman says. She'd memorized the headline, clearly.

A group that believed in chaos. Rhiannon doesn't add that. "It's a fine place for shelter, to hang out," Rhiannon says.

She can watch the By-products in the Idle Daze café if she stands on the street corner behind a power pole. They're in there pretending to work. Making coffee that doesn't exist, serving customers who aren't there, laughing as if this is real life. They've got their booze, their drugs when they can scam them. Rhiannon can almost see the ghosts around them, can almost see them all finding a purpose again.

A local reporter comes to write a story about this relocation, a so-called "feel good" story, but it won't make Rhiannon, or the owners, or any of the actual paying guests, feel good. "It'll make the local news," the reporter says. "You'll be famous!"

"Come see what we're trying to do with our building," she says. She takes the reporter for a tour of The Recreationist, including the roof. Looking down, the shaded square is lively with people, none of them drug-addicted nuisances.

"We'd rather word not get out too quickly. I can only let so many of them stay, and we'd like to keep this space for the community."

Two young boys kick a ball around a tree, faster and faster.

The reporter nods, but she knows he'll write the story anyway. Dark clouds come over suddenly, and with them a high wind, whistling through the artistically rendered barrier up here.

"Sounds like pan flutes," the reporter says. "Fancy!"

"That's your ghosts telling you that. The ones who ride you, who won't give you a day off. Who won't let you sleep at night."

The wind rises higher and it begins to rain. The sky brightens as if the sun is out, but the rain clouds are so dark this isn't possible.

"Would you like me to take your ghosts away?" she says. She never tells them the whole story. She feels no obligation to do so. All she wants is food for chaos. He nods. The sky splits open and it isn't the sun but the vast eye of Azathoth, with tentacles reaching down until they encircle the man's throat, lifting him gently off his feet.

They sway together, an obscene dance until (and Rhiannon, no matter how long she holds off blinking, never sees the moment) the man is free and clear of all that haunts him. He blinks as if to say, "How did I end up here?" It's the feeling many people have when Azathoth touches them. Those nights or days when you end up in a place you didn't expect to be? In a burnt-out bar over a bus station, or the mansion belonging to a friend of a friend, or a midnight showing of a cult movie. These are the times Azathoth is present.

The reporter is free and clear of his ghosts, but of inspiration too though, and ideas, and perhaps original thought.

Tiny little particles of him cling to her like dust did on that greasy kitchen wall, now cleaned and repainted, the room ready for inspection.

The reporter seems taller; his ghosts really were riding him. He puts down his notebook and pen and follows her downstairs. He doesn't speak, his throat dry, until she finds him a bottle of water.

"You could travel. You can do anything you want now that your urge to create is gone."

"You feel very calm to be around," he says.

And the secret is safe.

Rhiannon takes the By-products, one by one, to the roof. She tempts them with a bottle, with fried chicken.

One by one she'll take their ghosts. They never had them before, and even now they are barely worth collecting. These ones, she can barely get a grip on. They pass through Rhiannon like a beer on a hot day (she always had a weak bladder), and while they are affected, it isn't as much. It is as if they'd shut down most of their memories, damped them down, kept them quiet (and good on them, Rhiannon thought, she did a lot of that herself).

They drift away, one by one, but there will be more.

Rhiannon insists on collecting the rent for The Recreationist in person, an odd quirk no one really minds. Sometimes she's the only person they've seen for a week, like the elderly poet on Ether 3, who always looks surprised to hear a human voice.

On Night 2 a party is going on, a gentle gathering, people nibbling cheese and biscuits, drinking wine out of teacups, one in the corner sketching, another reading work aloud.

She can't remember which one is her tenant. They all look alike. In the kitchen a young woman in a kimono cooks Japanese pancakes, dropping in spices like she is a TV chef.

"Hi, Rhiannon," she says. "It isn't rent day!"

It is, of course. This kind of manipulation annoys Rhiannon. If she doesn't have the money (all spent on booze and food, apparently) then she'll have to pay another way.

Azathoth's eye appears briefly in the window and Rhiannon nods. She touches the tenant's hand. There is nothing. The girl's eyes are clear. She isn't haunted.

"Would you like a pancake? Whiskey soda?" the girl offers, oblivious.

Rhiannon looks around the room. The poet cries quietly in the corner, ignored. A man almost steps on her, she is so invisible. The poet raises her palm as if to ward him off.

Rhiannon, pancake in hand, walks over to her. She is deeply haunted, this is obvious. She will cover a month's rent, maybe more, with what she has to offer.

"I can take your ghosts away," Rhiannon whispers. "Unless you like being ridden?"

The poet shakes her head. "I'm ridden. Riddled. I don't like it, but it's who I am."

"No! Not at all. Who you are is yet to be seen. You might be a marathon runner. A teacher. You might still be an artist." Although Rhiannon knows this last part isn't true. "You can pay the rent in ghosts," she says. "Pay for your friend, so you can party on with these so-cool people who let you sit here. Let you read from your work."

It takes some of them longer than others to realise the passion is gone. The ideas. They'll struggle for a few weeks, painting flowers or blotches of colour. Writing "It was a dark and stormy night," or poetry that is all metaphor, no meat. They realise at last they are released from the burden of creativity and they leave, freeing up a room for the next person.

"Follow me up to the roof," she says to the poet.

Dancing her way up the steps, the poet sings lyrics to a song only she can hear. Rhiannon is excited by this; Azathoth will be fulfilled. She fancies she can see a thick layer of ghosts around the poet, clinging to her, blissful.

On the roof, she holds the poet's hand. The poet tilts her head back as if wanting to be kissed, but they aren't there for that. Rhiannon feels her skin tingle, gently at first then painfully, like sunburn as the sun goes down. Azathoth's eye opens and peers down at her, and she imagines a tear of gratitude dropping to earth to fill the sea.

Ash Grey appears beside her. The poet barely reacts; she is drawn to the eye, drowning in it, and Ash and Rhiannon hold each other as they watch her being drained. She feels him soften, weaken as it happens, then slump, as if his puppet master has momentarily let the strings go.

Rhiannon is happy until something terrible happens.

Ash Grey stares out her window at the building next door.

"I was thinking," he says. He tilts his head sideways like the artists do. "Looking at it from this angle, there is so much potential. You just have to be creative." He says there is a voice in his head that wasn't there before, and all he wants to do is create.

These words bring a chill to Rhiannon. In that moment she realises how much she cares for this man.

"All I can think about is that and making love to you. Do you want kids?"

"Not now," she says. Not ever. She knows the chaos that will be unleashed when Azathoth opens his ghost box and she wants no child of hers to be a part of it. That eye is blinking at her, it wants Ash Grey, WANTS HIM, but she won't let it have him.

She knows that once the god has enough all hell will break loose (and she has no idea how many "enough" will be, or how many collectors like her there are), that he will unleash the chaos.

The god only appears close up when she's drunk. She hates to be drunk. He's shrunk down to the size of an ice cube. When she pokes a finger into her tall Tequila Sunrise, he bites her, taking off the tip. Then he grows, crawls up her arm, onto her shoulder.

She plunges her finger into the drink, watching the orange turn redder. Someone complains loudly about pan flutes, but the bartender can't find the source.

"Good girl," the god says. It is time. She doesn't want to; Ash's ideas make her cry, and he does too. He makes her want to be a better person, although he drew her into all this in the first place. The two of them together could run, they could join an artist's colony somewhere, be safe.

Now the god is up around her shoulders and she feels so good, so strong. All her future is laid out for her and there is nothing but joy, he's telling her, nothing but pleasure and good feelings and good will on earth.

She's walking home and she can see him in the sky, vast, important.

This is Azathoth happy.

She tells Ash to come help her but he knows.

"Don't," he says, but his heart isn't in it.

"You are going to feel so good after this."

The sky opens up with wild tentacles, tendrils like roots to a tree, like string from a bunch of balloons.

Rhiannon is the conduit. When she physically touches Ash's arm, the ghosts tunnel through her to the god.

She feels it like cold sludge, like an apple piece caught in her throat, like too much wine, like rancid butter on toast, like the smell of petrol, like food thickeners (gelatin or arrowroot or cornstarch) and fish oil pills.

She stretches out her fingertips, the hand of the god descending to take her offering. Tentacles of the god, reaching out all over the world and taking the offerings, setting them to swirl around him, all those ghosts. She's not the first; hundreds of helpers came before her: coach drivers, hotel owners, hairdressers, school teachers. All collectors.

The god breathes in.

That week, Rhiannon's real estate agency gives her full responsibility for The Recreationist after "an overwhelmingly positive report from the building manager, who will be managing Haverhill House from this date forward." She thanks Ash, hoping he truly does trust her to carry on and didn't just make the recommendation because they are sleeping together. That is still good, the sex, because it is a physical function. He isn't designing, of course, beyond property reports. It is great for her; the agency has offices around the country and some overseas, so the opportunities are great.

She feels useful, motivated, driven.

Not *too* driven.

With most of the people she helps, the result is an emptiness but also a freedom. With a rare few, the result is violence. She calls this the Backwash, when perhaps Azathoth burps back some of the ghosts he's sucked in, and the once-creative person is the receptacle.

Such is the case with Barbary-not-Barbara. A printmaker, she's always been driven to create bad art, refusing all lessons or artistic input. She thinks that what appears on the page in first draft is meant to be.

Barbary's interaction with Azathoth gives Rhiannon a massive headache and a sick feeling in her stomach, as if she'd tied one on the night before. She puts herself to bed in the penthouse, hoping to grab a few hours' sleep and knock the headache over, when she receives a text from Ash.

"Something's happening on my tenth floor if you want to look."

It is Barbary and a new group of By-products. Ash must have let them in up there. The By-products are dancing, naked, and Barbary is dressed only in a robe.

"What the fuck?" one of Rhiannon's tenants in The Recreationist texts to her. "Can you see this?"

"It's what you pay rent for!" Rhiannon texts back.

One by one the By-products leave the room (Rhiannon thinks perhaps each has been sent away with a bottle) until only a single Bohemian remains, a naked man still dancing, oblivious. Barbary smashes the window with her fist and holds it out, reaching for the sky. Blood runs down her arm, down the sleeve of her robe, staining it red. From above, the sky opens. There is a roar like the crash of a building collapsing. Barbary's face suffuses with rage and she falls upon the solitary naked man, her bulk and her robe hiding him from sight.

He is mangled, chewed, from the elbow and from the knee. Barbary leaves him propped against a wall, bleeding to death, and the residents of The Recreationist watch from across the street, each assuming someone else will make the call for help, but none of them do.

Chaos sits just below the surface. Any emergency will demonstrate that.

Chaos is a defence.

Below, people shiver. There is no sun.

It's not the full moon that sends people crazy. No. It's when the god decides to spew down the ghosts. To create a new world, and wash out the last.

One day he will release them all at once. This is creation.

This is re-creation.

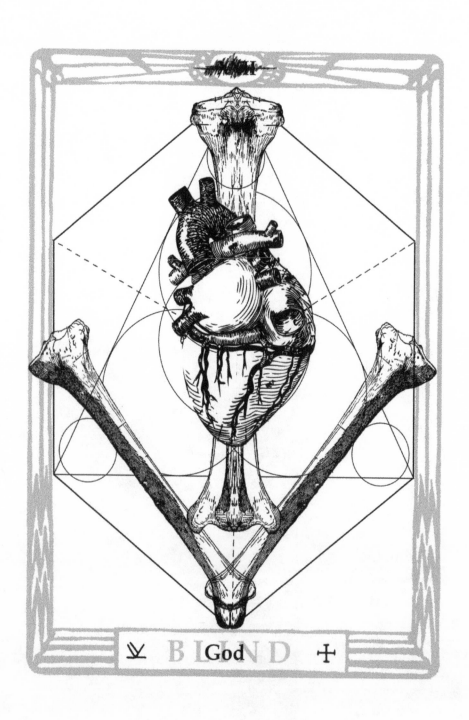

BLIND God

The Blind God's Game

Matthew Cheney

1.

WORKING NIGHTS STOCKING shelves at the store he would only refer to as "The Box," working a few days a week at Kazu and Joy's café next to the zendo, and working weekends at Ramsey's shop left Brad without much spare time. What free hours he had, he spent at the zendo, or spent reading, or spent down at the rocky end of the beach, his favorite place to meditate. (There, he often thought of something he had read in Dōgen: The ocean contains myriad things, but the ocean does not keep corpses.) He wanted more time with Ramsey, but he knew that wasn't a good idea. He had been out of prison for sixteen months. The counselor who came to the house every week said he needed to begin to trust himself again, to open himself to experience, but Brad had had plenty of experience in his life, experience was not anything he craved anymore, and he was still very far from trusting himself.

Fran left a message at the house for him. She called once a month to check up, to be as sisterly as she could bear, and, most important, to see if he was ready to accept Jesus as his lord and savior. But they had talked just last week. The note on the whiteboard next to the phone said it was urgent.

"It's Abby," Fran said when Brad called. "My oldest daughter."

"I know who your daughter is, Fran."

"I found alcohol in her room. In a juice bottle. I was going to put it in the refrigerator but then I thought how strange that she has a bottle of juice in her room and why would she put a bottle of juice in her room and I opened the bottle of juice and it was bourbon or whisky or something."

"She's what, fifteen? Makes sense."

"Seventeen."

"Even more sense."

"And then last night she smelled like marijuana and I told her she smelled like marijuana and she said how would I know what marijuana smells like and I said I did not grow up in a convent and she said well to be perfectly honest she had not been smoking marijuana but she did need a shower because she had been having deep nonprocreative relations—that's what she said, *deep nonprocreative relations*—with the person she is dating and yes she had in the past smoked marijuana and it is not a big deal and not even her favorite thing."

"Okay. Take a breath. Don't panic, Fran. These really aren't warning signs. She's got a good sense of humor. 'Nonprocreative relations' is pretty funny."

"Not warning signs? What would be a warning sign to you? She goes to prison?"

"That's very compassionate of you to say. I'm sure Jesus would approve."

"Jesus did not have a daughter who is an addict."

"Look, it's good she talked to you. What would be bad is if she's hiding everything."

"She *is* hiding everything! She had booze in her room! She's a druggy! She admitted it!"

Brad laughed; he couldn't help himself. "I'm sorry, but your parenting is straight out of the 1950s. Don't be silly."

"Take her to an AA meeting."

"What? No."

"That's why I called. I want you to take her to an AA meeting."

"If she wants to, I'm happy to talk with her. But I haven't seen her since she was like eight years old."

"And you were drunk and obnoxious."

"I expect I was."

"Will you talk to her?"

"If she wants to."

"I will make her want to." Fran hung up.

A few days later, toward the end of Brad's shift at the café, a young woman wearing a leather jacket came in and asked him if Brad was around. "I am," he said.

"Oh," she said. "Hi. I'm Abby. Your niece."

She pointed to a person with short purple hair behind her. "This is Nico. They're my significant friend."

"It's good for friends to be significant," Brad said.

"*Significant other* is othering," Nico said. "Literally."

"Can I buy you both a beverage?"

Abby ordered a latte with almond milk, Nico a spiced chai. They sat at a table in a corner of the café. Kazu had finished moving some boxes around in the always overflowing storage room, so Brad clocked out and brought them their drinks and a green tea for himself.

"I bet your mother told you to come see me," Brad said.

Abby nodded.

"She's convinced you're a drug fiend."

"I'm not," Abby said.

"I suspected as much. Speaking as a drug fiend myself."

"I thought you're sober."

"I am. I'm a drug fiend who no longer uses drugs. A drunk who doesn't drink." He sipped his tea.

After a moment, Abby said, "Is this a Buddhist thing? Sitting in silence?"

"It can be. Did your mother tell you I'm a Buddhist?"

"She said you worship the false god of Buddha."

"I suppose. I mean, I don't know that I'm a Buddhist, but I do practice Zen meditation. I learned it in prison. So I probably am more comfortable with silence than some people. More comfortable than I was before, certainly. Does silence make you uncomfortable?"

"No. Nico's good with silence. I'm learning, I guess."

Nico gave a thumbs-up.

Brad finished his tea. "You're in much better shape than I was at your age," he said. "If you need to tell your mother something, tell her I said that. She loves you and is terrified that I am representative of our heritage. I hope I'm not."

"You don't seem such a bad heritage to have," Nico said.

Abby smiled.

"I survived. That's the best I can say for me." He collected their mugs. "Stop by whenever you want. Drinks are on the house."

Abby began to visit the café once or twice a week, now and then with Nico, often not. At some point, she asked Brad what he was doing over the weekend, and without thinking he said, "I'm working at Ramsey's shop." He cleared his throat suddenly, tried to think of something to say, but Abby caught it.

"What's Ramsey's shop?"

"Just another job I have. I try to keep busy."

"Another café?"

"Just a shop."

"Like a sex shop or something? That would be totally cool, if you, like, sell porn and stuff."

"No. Worse, I'm afraid." He chuckled nervously. "An occult shop. Tarot, crystals, incense. Please don't tell your mother. I don't need her and her friends to start picketing us for selling Satanic books or something. Ramsey's a good guy."

"Are you dating him?"

"What has your mother told you about me?"

"Love the sinner."

"Right. Of course. But no, I'm not dating Ramsey. I don't even know if he…"

"Where's the shop? Tarot's cool. Nico keeps my Thoth deck for me because if my mother ever found it, she'd hire an exorcist. Which actually might be fun."

"Thoth is scary. I'm more a Marseilles guy myself, it was the only one allowed in prison, but Ramsey does brilliant readings with all different decks. I'll spring for a reading for you if you want sometime. I'm there weekends. The shop's called Aeon."

2.

Within minutes of Ramsey unlocking the front door, a girl stepped inside tentatively and began browsing the candles at the front. She was wearing black jeans and a black leather jacket over a black sweatshirt, its hood over her head, her hands in her jacket pockets. Ramsey knew her type well; young people seeking solace from alienation were his favorites. There was a vitality to their alienation he particularly cherished.

The girl picked up a candle, hardly looked at it, put it back on the display. A customer this early was rare, but the hesitation was familiar. Some customers will come in and start asking about labradorite and moonstone right away, ostentatiously showing that they are right at home here in this weird little shop. But most need a few minutes to get comfortable. After years of owning Aeon, Ramsey's instincts were well honed, and he knew just how to position himself with random busy work so the customer wouldn't feel spied on, but neither would they think he was unapproachable.

The girl made her way around the outer walls of the store and eventually reached the counter. "Does Brad work here?"

"Yes," Ramsey said. "He comes in at noon."

"He's my uncle."

"Marvelous! He said you were going to come in and I am to give you a reading, any reading you want. Abby, yes? I'm Ramsey. A pleasure to meet you."

He held out his hand. Beneath her hood, she smiled. She shook his hand.

"Can't do a full reading until Brad gets here, since I need him to cover the shop, and you probably don't want to hang out for four hours on a lovely Saturday. But I could do a quick and dirty reading for you right here, if you want a kind of preview."

"Sure," she said, brushing the hood off her head.

From beneath the counter he revealed a velvet bag, and from within the bag he removed a set of cards. "This is a deck I've been playing with recently. All crow imagery." He began to shuffle the cards by tossing them from his right hand to his left. "And by play I do mean *play*. We mustn't lose the sense of play, the suspension of disbelief children so perfectly invoke with the words *let's pretend*." He handed the cards to Abby. "Here you go. Shuffle until you feel you should stop shuffling." The cards were a bit large for her hands, her shuffling awkward, but she did not fumble them the way someone who had never shuffled tarot usually does. "Okay, now set them on the counter and cut them into three piles with the hand you don't use for writing." Abby followed his instructions, cutting the cards evenly and setting them next to each other with her right hand. "A lefty, very nice. Like your uncle. Now let that same hand glide over the cards until one of the sets pulls it in. Let yourself feel the attraction, the pull, the gravitational force." Her hand floated over the cards like she was preparing to do a magic trick to make them disappear. Her hand fell on the middle pile. Ramsey gathered up the cards, putting the middle set on top.

"Should I think of a question?" she asked.

"If you want, but maybe for this first little informal reading, let's see what the cards want to talk about."

He dealt three cards face-down on the counter. He flipped over the first card: two crows with two golden goblets, water spilling from each goblet to the other in a single stream. "The Two of Cups. Here we see harmony, friendship. There can be passion, even the beginnings of romance, but I tend to see it more as an encounter with someone who can give you support and comfort." He turned over the middle card: ten crows positioned in a circle. "The Wheel of Fortune. Change is on the horizon, but it is fate, it is outside your control to do anything about. *C'est la vie.* It's upright, not reversed, so not a terrible change, but the thing with the wheel is that you can't force it. A good fate can be made miserable if you try to force it. Let the wheel turn. Enjoy the ride." He revealed the final card: a crow pecking a golden disc with a star on it, seven other golden discs with stars lined up in the background as if drying in the sun. "The Eight of Pentacles. I love this card because it's so practical, no bullshit. All the pentacles are practical, but this one has a kind of message to it: *Shut up and do the work.* But in a loving tone. Trust that effort will be rewarded, because effort itself is its own reward."

Ramsey sat back. "So!" he said. "What does it all add up to? In the middle of everything is the Wheel of Fortune. To one side, an encounter of friendship and mutuality and support; to the other side, good old-fashioned work, but rewarding work, work you want to do because you know it's fulfilling. Change is coming, change you have no control over, but you do not have to face it alone, and you will be just fine as long as you keep your eyes on whatever kind of effort fulfills you and don't get lost in the stars."

Abby looked over the cards. She smiled. "I think it means we're going to be friends," she said.

Ramsey clapped his hands together joyfully. "I like that interpretation very much."

"I've got to go, but I'll be back." She pulled her hood up over her head again as she made her way out the door.

When Brad came in, the shop was busy. Ramsey was about to mention Abby when a man with a ragged black-and-grey beard and rugged, well-lived-in clothes asked for a reading, and Ramsey took him to the little room at the back where a reading table sat prepared.

"It's good to meet you finally," the man said as Ramsey lit candles and incense. "I'm Kadeem. Norman told me you were his best student."

"You know Norman?"

"He was my own student. Once upon a time."

"I don't think he mentioned you."

"He wouldn't. We had a falling out."

"I see."

"Thoth for me, please. I want to show you something."

"Oh?"

Ramsey took a deck from a shelf and set it on the table. It was the oldest deck he owned, one he had stolen from a store in New Orleans when he was thirteen. For years, he knew nothing about the cards except the little bit of information in the white booklet included with them. The mysteries in their images held his fascination and fueled it still.

Kadeem cut the cards, moved the bottom half to the top of the deck, and flipped over the top card onto the table. A goat with horns spiraling from its head. "Crowley said The Devil does not exist," Kadeem said. "If there is a supreme God, it accounts for everything, it *is* everything, including the Devil. So what is this?"

"He is Pan," Ramsey said. "He is energy, transcendence, ecstasy. Dionysus."

"No," Kadeem said. "That is an interpretation, it makes some sense, I don't mean to be dismissive—but it's inadequate. The image

Lady Harris put on the card is inadequate. Any image would be. There is no image possible, not for a blind god, not for the force that is all positivity and negativity in one."

"Why did you and Norman have a falling out?" Ramsey asked.

"Because I said this card is no different from this one." Kadeem flipped the next card over. A yellow and green figure: The Fool. "Everything and nothing. All one. And the same as this—" Another card, a jagged figure in black, dancing with a scythe. "Skin even darker than mine or yours, skin the color of Norman's, no? Death. All of us, even the lily-white children like that girl you gave such an empty reading to this morning."

"How did you—"

Another card, flipped furiously: a yellow wheel against a violet background. "The Wheel is the abyss," Kadeem said. "It is the darkness that traps the God of All, his blindness and sight. There is no *meaning* here, there is nothing to be interpreted." Another card: bright shards of yellow light from the lantern of a figure draped in red. "The hermit here is your guy out front, the nice white boy who turns away from his own desires and seeks what can't be sought. The blind god cannot see a lantern's light." Another card—a swirling image of yellows, blues, greens, amber—slammed onto the table, scattering the entire deck. "Crowley would tell you that in the image of the Universe we see the Great Work completed, but that is not what is here. There is no Great Work, nothing to complete, nothing to begin or end. The blind god screams out from the abyss and the Wheel turns one way, then another, no rhyme, no reason, just a spin here, a spin there, death and misery one moment, joy and pleasure the next." He tossed the card to the floor.

"Impressive that you could draw all Majors from the deck. No cups or discs or wands. No swords."

"I could draw whatever I wanted from the deck," Kadeem said. "That is why Norman and I had a falling out. I burned his cards and made him eat the ash."

"Is that what you plan for me?"

Kadeem laughed. "No, I don't seek anything from you. I came here to set my eyes on a last believer. I miss believing." He coughed roughly. His voice grew quiet. "I ache not to know the god of the abyss. It makes me lash out. I'm sorry."

He stood up slowly, stiffly. He was an old man, far older than Ramsey had perceived. "The universe," Kadeem said, "will tear us all apart." He made his way out of the room.

Ramsey followed him to the counter. There were no other customers in the shop now. "Fifty for the reading?" Kadeem asked Brad at the register.

"No charge," Ramsey said.

"Of course there is," Kadeem said. "Everything costs something." He placed a small gold coin on the counter. "Will this do?"

Ramsey took the coin in hand. A pentagram had been carefully, methodically etched on both its sides. "Yes, this is fine," he said.

Kadeem walked slowly toward the front door, opened it, and vanished into the world.

"Who was that?" Brad said.

"My teacher's teacher."

"Really? Wow. I would've liked to chat with him."

"He's not the chatty type. Oh, hey, your niece came by. Abby."

"She okay?"

"Fine. She'll be back."

Ramsey spent the afternoon trying to get in touch with Norman. It was at least a decade since they'd last seen each other. Norman had insisted Ramsey go north, suggested this quiet little New England city, loaned him the money to put a down payment on the shop here, told him to get the hell away from the people he had been wasting his time with.

Finally, one of the old phone numbers he had scrawled on a piece of scrap paper in a drawer got an answer, a woman who was renting an apartment in the old house where Norman used to hold his séances. "He's at the place for people with dementia," she said. "He don't remember nobody, that's what I heard. Don't even remember himself."

At the end of the day, Brad closed up the shop and began sweeping the floors.

"I expect you've got plans," Ramsey said. "Saturday night and all. Probably busy. But if you want to come upstairs for a cocktail or something, I could use the company."

Brad stopped sweeping and leaned on the broom for a moment. He stared at a pile of dirt on the floor. Eventually, he looked up. "Sure," he said. "That would be nice."

3.

Abby began to spend more and more time at the shop, and Ramsey even offered her a job working the register a few nights during the week. Nico loved hanging out there. Ramsey began to teach Abby some of his reading techniques, though he refused to teach her anything about the Thoth deck.

Some nights now, Brad stayed at Ramsey's apartment above the store. He was talking about leaving the sober living house, maybe getting an apartment, maybe moving in here or getting a place with Ramsey.

The evening everybody found out that Pastor Joel had been murdered, Abby ran to Nico's house and together they fled to the shop. Brad was at an AA meeting, but Ramsey said he was working at The Box. He called and left a message for Brad to come back as soon as he could. Then he closed the shop and brought Abby and Nico upstairs.

"Mom's gone nuts," Abby said. She and Nico sat on the couch, holding each other. Ramsey stood in the kitchen and boiled water to make a pot of green tea. "She's out of her mind. She was going on and on, something about the choirboys, and then about how there was this foreigner who had been attending church and how they showed so much compassion and then this foreigner—she kept saying it—*this foreigner* she said just killed him. She said it was to punish them and maybe it was because I had become a Satanist and I'm luring other children—she calls us children, we're just children to her—I lure children into Satanism."

Ramsey said, "She went up one side of Brad and down the other last week when she found out about the shop. It was pretty bad."

"I know. Sorry. Our friend Callie's mother is in the church with Mom and said something."

"Where did she think you were spending your time?"

"She's not in the habit of asking. But now she's going to start locking me in the house, I think."

Nico said, "You can always come live with us. My parents think you're cool."

"I wish your parents were mine."

"Me too. Maybe we could adopt you. But then you and I would be committing incest."

Ramsey brought a jade teapot in on a tray and placed it on the coffee table in front of the couch.

Brad came bounding into the apartment. "What happened?" he said.

"Mom's pastor got murdered."

"*What? How?*"

"He was beaten to a pulp, is all I heard."

"Shit."

"Yeah."

From a pocket, Abby pulled out her Thoth deck. "I want a reading."

Ramsey, Brad, and Nico stared at her.

"My mom's pastor got brutally murdered, she thinks I'm a Satanist and that you guys are grooming me to be a witch or a pedophile or something. Everything is chaos. Nico's sick and tired of the drama. Me too. I want a reading with these cards."

"All right," Ramsey said. "Let's go down to the shop. Just you and me. You can tell them later anything you want about it, but the reading is just for you."

"Brad and I will hang out up here and watch horror movies," Nico said. (They had recently discovered they shared a passion for old films, and while Nico was an ardent fan of Bela Lugosi, Brad insisted that Boris Karloff was by far the more interesting actor.)

Ramsey turned on some lights at the back of the shop, but used only candles to light the reading room.

"I want you to know that my reluctance regarding that deck has nothing to do with black magick or Aleister Crowley or anything. I have had particular experiences with the imagery in this deck, and so, inevitably, my mind and intuition are affected by those experiences. Some of those experiences were powerful. They were twenty years ago but feel like last week. That's why I have resisted doing this. Until now. Because you're right. There is a lot of chaos swirling around us right now. Maybe we both need this."

He pushed the cards toward her. "Shuffle the deck."

When Abby and Ramsey returned to the apartment, Brad and Nico were both asleep on the couch, Brad snoring, the TV playing a black and white movie.

They woke Nico gently. "We should go," Abby said.

"You can stay if you want," Ramsey said. "The couch pulls out."

"No, it's fine. We brought our bikes. I'll stay at Nico's. That's where Mom thinks I am anyway."

As she and Nico made their way down the stairs, Nico said, "How'd it go?"

"Fine," Abby said.

"Just fine?"

"Weird. Ramsey got kind of scared for a bit. It seemed to be saying something about Brad at the end, and Ramsey got really quiet."

"What about you? What did it say?"

"A lot of stuff. We did a few spreads. I'm tired though, and I want to sort of hold onto it all in my mind and not ruin it with words."

"Okay," Nico said.

"Thanks."

As they rode quietly into Nico's driveway, Abby said, "Guess what?"

"What?"

"I love you."

Nico gave her a hug and a kiss.

"Too tired for incest?" Nico asked.

"Never!"

4.

Brad and Ramsey had been doing well, they had adjusted to living together, or so Brad thought, but he got caught up in the excitement of the new relationship and did not pay enough attention to old fears and feelings, he was not prepared for pleasure, he didn't go to the zendo, went for days without meditation, and his indulgence in himself and in Ramsey led to craving, and he barely even realized what he was doing when he stopped at a store on the way to work at The Box and picked up a six pack and the six pack was empty by the time he walked into work, where he promptly got fired for pissing in a flower display. His manager at least had enough sense to make him call Ramsey for a ride. Ramsey was sweet and concerned and not at all scolding and it was infuriating. Brad said every nasty thing he could think of, then fled and let days blur by in bars and old haunts, until eventually, somehow, he ended up sprawled outside the shop and Ramsey helped him upstairs, got him cleaned up, put him to bed. Ramsey nursed him back to being human again and called Joy, who had first met Brad in AA. Joy came over and sat with Brad and let him indulge all his self-pity for exactly one hour, then told him his time was up, he had to get back on his feet and back to life, she and Kazu had been covering his shifts at the café but they were planning to go for a quick trip to the Finger Lakes soon and needed him to do a lot of shifts. Brad wanted to smile, wanted to tell her how grateful he was, but shame threatened to knock him over. Right now he needed to focus on keeping his attention on the present, to keep breathing and noticing his breaths.

Joy brought him to the zendo and they sat for most of a morning together; then she and Kazu switched off at the café and Kazu took Brad out to lunch at a grubby diner they both loved. When Brad got home, he felt at least vaguely human again.

"Don't tell Abby what happened," Brad said to Ramsey. Ramsey agreed. She was used to Brad not being around much because of his work schedule, but nine days was a lot. Ramsey told her Brad had the flu and was staying away from people until he was sure he wasn't contagious anymore. She came in one morning when he was working at the café and asked how he was feeling. "Better," he said. "Not a hundred percent, but getting there."

In the morning, Ramsey seemed out of sorts and distant. He hesitated to touch Brad. As they opened the shop together, Brad said, "What's going on?"

"What do you mean?"

"Something is wrong. What's wrong?"

"Sorry, just distracted."

"By what?"

Ramsey sat down on the stool behind the counter. He turned the register on and sighed. "It's stupid, I'm sorry, but I can't get out of my mind that when you came back—after everything—when you came back your hands were a mess. Fingers swollen, knuckles..."

Brad focused on counting his breaths. He knew exactly what Ramsey was implying and he focused on counting his breaths. Ramsey was right, his hands had looked like he'd been punching walls, and he probably *had* been punching walls, he couldn't remember, so he focused on counting his breaths.

"I don't want to ask," Ramsey said. "I don't want to know. But of course, you understand, right, you understand why I would— even though I know it can't be true, it's not possible, it doesn't fit, but I'm concerned for you, so, I mean—you understand why—"

"I was in prison," Brad said, "because I got shitfaced and beat my boyfriend to a pulp and almost killed him."

"Yes."

"So of course, sure, I understand why. Why you would wonder. Why you would worry."

"You didn't go to see Fran or anything, didn't go to her church when you were..."

"No. I don't think so."

"But your hands."

"I don't know."

"Not the pastor, I know that was after you were back, but I just, it got me thinking again, stupid thoughts, I know, but... I worry. I wish I knew more."

"I blacked out. I have no idea what I did to my hands."

"I shouldn't have said anything."

"Right."

He walked out of the shop and kept walking all day. He had to keep walking or he might end up in a convenience store or a bar or he might try to find one of the guys who used to sell him pills, he might do anything, but if he kept walking he could focus on his breaths, he could walk with intention. At first, he walked too fast, but soon he was able to focus on a deliberate rhythm.

He counted his breaths. Counted his steps.

Eventually, at a park on the far west side of town, he sat on a bench for a few hours.

As afternoon slipped to evening, he made his way down toward the beach. Cool air blew in from the ocean. In the distance, the flashing lights of police cars, fire trucks, and ambulances lit the twilight. He wandered down toward the lights. A crowd had gathered around police barricades.

At first, with all the lights and people, he couldn't see what the emergency might be, but soon he spied what looked like a tarp covering a body.

"Brad?" It was Fran, his sister, coming up behind him. Abby stood with her.

"What are you doing here?" he said.

"I heard from my friend Lilly from church that the foreigner, the boys found him, he was killed. I wanted to see the man, to see this monster who had killed our Joel, our pastor Joel. I wanted to see the vengeance, but they would not let me through, and then Abby was here, she is here—"

"Ramsey called me," Abby said, "told me you were off on a walkabout or something. But then the police came."

"Police?"

"In the man's pocket was a card for the shop. I guess it was all he had. Ramsey said he knew him. I got down here and Mom was already here."

"It was vengeance."

"Where is he? Where's Ramsey?"

"Over there." Abby pointed toward an area beyond the police barricades where people, some in uniforms, stood on steps leading down to the beach. "They might let you through."

Brad looked for a way around the crowd.

"The fearful, and unbelieving," Fran said, "and the abominable, and murderers, and whoremongers, and sorcerers, and idolaters, and all liars, shall have their part in the lake which burneth with fire and brimstone."

"Mom, *shut up.*"

Brad pushed his way between people. He found his way to the other side of the crowd.

Ramsey saw him and ran to the barricade. They embraced and kissed. "Abby told me," Brad said. "I'm so sorry."

"It's Kadeem. They tore him apart."

"Fran said he's the murderer."

"He went to a service at the church. But it wasn't him."

Brad stopped breathing.

"They caught the guy. Some low-rent bookie the pastor owed money to. Didn't intend to kill him, just wanted to scare him and beat him up a little bit. Things escalated. The guy went nuts. A messy scene, the cops said. They caught the guy last night and he confessed this morning. The kids didn't know. The boys who did this. Goddamned choirboys. They tore Kadeem apart."

Brad hugged Ramsey again.

"I had to look at his face," Ramsey said. "They didn't touch his face. But they just… they tore him apart."

A uniformed police officer took Ramsey's arm gently. "We need to finish the statement, sir, then you're free to go."

Brad wanted to push his way through the crowd straight back to Fran and confront her with the truth, let her know that the brutal minions she sympathized with had killed an innocent man, rub her face in the gospel of her pastor's sins. He wanted reality to shatter her hypocrisies, the defenses she built to keep life at bay, the illusions she clung to that had nearly lost her her daughter, the wall she guarded so vigilantly between her consciousness and the fact of her husband's suicide six years ago—but he knew it was pointless. He looked down at his feet and counted his breaths and stood still, truly still, until Ramsey took his hand and said it was time to go.

5.

Abby worked more and more at the shop because Ramsey devoted so much time now to reading news reports and watching videos. He had become obsessed with massacres. "Four hundred thousand dead in Syria," he said. "Four hundred thousand. Nobody can understand a number like that. Kadeem could have been Syrian, there are lots of Syrians named Kadeem. Maybe not a refugee, I don't know, but he must have had family there. A lovely country reduced to ruin."

Abby put her hand on his shoulder. "Not many customers today. Maybe we could close the shop early and go to a movie or something?" She had told Brad he should be at the shop more, that Ramsey needed him, but Brad spent all his spare time meditating at the zendo. Even Kazu was a bit concerned that he was using it as an escape, though Joy, who sat with Brad the most, said she thought he was healing.

"There has to be a meaning," Ramsey said. "All the death. Just look at shootings—" He flipped through a notebook he scribbled in constantly. "It's a rare day in this country without a shooting with at least three casualties. It has to mean something."

"No," Abby said, "it doesn't."

"That's what Norman always said. The blind god playing his game, no rules, no causes, just effects. His brother got killed by a trigger-happy cop. Did that mean nothing? A roll of the dice? I refuse to believe that."

Ramsey breathed deeply. Tears welled in his eyes. Abby wrapped him in a hug.

"We're going to be okay," she said.

She wasn't sure about that. At home, her mother had stopped talking. Now and then Fran would write words on a piece of paper, but that was it. Her boss at the electric co-op called to find out where she was, and Abby said her mother would not be able to come to work for a while. Fran's boss was concerned, but Abby said there wasn't anything to be done. Fran went to the church every day and sat in the pews. Nobody else was ever there. Abby followed her a few times, curious what her mother was doing, but she wasn't really doing anything, just sitting in the pews, sometimes humming quietly to herself, sometimes chewing on her fingernails. She had never been one to bite her nails before, but now her fingers were all soft stubs.

Nico, too, had grown more quiet than usual, nearly as silent as Fran. Abby had accepted an offer to go to Brown for college, and Nico had decided to stay more local. They hadn't talked about their relationship, hadn't talked about whether they wanted to continue. It didn't feel like much of a relationship anymore. Something had changed.

One day, hanging out at the shop, Nico found a strange flute back in the storage room. "What's this?" they asked Ramsey.

"Where did you find that?" Ramsey said. Abby thought his tone was strange, a mix of surprise and maybe fear, but muted, trying not to upset anyone.

"Out back. Is it a recorder? Or a flute?"

"You should put it back," Ramsey said.

"I played flute all through elementary and middle school." They blew on the end.

Ramsey swatted the instrument out of their hand. It bounced on the floor.

"What the hell?" Nico said.

"It's a bone flute," Ramsey said. "It's made out of goddamned human bone."

Nico laughed. "Sure it is," they said, picking the flute up.

"Put it back," Abby said.

"No," Nico said. "I claim it. I ought to have something to remember you weirdos by." They walked out of the shop.

"What is that thing?" Abby said.

"I didn't know it was here. It shouldn't be here. It's not mine."

"Then whose is it?"

"Norman had a flute like that."

Abby insisted on closing the shop an hour early so that Ramsey could do a reading for her before the vigil. The vigil was her idea, and Ramsey wasn't sure it was a good one, but he didn't have anything better to offer. A small group, just herself and Nico, Brad and Ramsey, her mother, Nico's mom and dad, Kazu and Joy. A quiet night on the beach. Candles. Contemplation. They needed it, she said. They were all going mad.

Ramsey lit the candles in the reading room and Abby put her deck on the table. It was still in its cardboard box, though Ramsey had told her numerous times to get some silk to wrap it with, or a wooden box for it, or both. Something to protect it a bit more.

Taking the deck out of its cardboard, she suddenly saw why it needed protection. The face of every card was covered in black. Not the black of paint. It was somehow darker, deeper. All absence, no light.

She dropped the cards from her hand. They scattered over the table. All the candles flashed out.

Ramsey grabbed her arm and pulled her from the room.

"We should go," he said, "to the beach."

"What—happened—"

"It's fine. It will be fine. We just need to go."

They were the first to arrive, but soon Brad walked down with Kazu and Joy, who had brought a box of candles. Dusk rendered the ocean dark blue and purple. Nico's parents joined the group, then Fran, walking slowly, looking dazed and lost. Abby went to her, took her arm, helped her down the steps to the beach. Fran seemed to have aged a decade in the last week.

The candles were squat and white, sheltered in glass. Joy lit them and Kazu and Brad handed them out.

"Have you seen our kid?" Nico's father asked Abby.

"This afternoon. They were in a weird mood."

"They stormed into the house and then just sat in their room," their mother said. "I should've checked before we came down here, but we were afraid we were going to be late, and we assumed Nico was with you already. Maybe they're taking a nap."

Waves crashed against the grey beach like falling towers. The candle flames shivered as a steady breeze grew to a strong wind.

Ramsey was about to speak when a high-pitched sound in the distance caught everyone's attention.

Nico slowly walked across the beach toward them, the bone flute in hand, wind blowing an uneven melody through it. As Nico got closer and moonlight illuminated their face, their mother moaned quietly as she saw that Nico had found thread and needle somewhere and sewn their lips together, the ends of the thread dangling like mustache remnants, lips stained with dried blood.

Fran began to laugh, but her face displayed terror, not mirth. Her laughter rose in tone as she reached her fingers to her face and tried to dig into her eyes, but she had chewed her nails down and she could not do much damage before Joy saw what she was doing and took Fran's hands in her own. Fran's arms spasmed as Joy and then Kazu held them and kept her fingers away from her face.

Ramsey ran to Nico and tore the bone flute from their hand. The wind rose to a gale as Ramsey waded into the water and threw the flute to the waves.

Soaked and shivering, he returned to the group. Nico and Fran knelt together in the sand, Nico's head resting on Fran's chest. Nico's parents huddled behind their child and Abby wept beside them. Kazu and Joy held each other.

Brad stared out at the crowblack sea. "The ocean does not keep corpses," he said quietly.

Abby thought she heard drums in the distance. She turned toward the other end of the beach and saw a group of shadows marching to an uneven beat. Clouds washed across the moon, undoing sight, but in momentary fragments of illumination she saw what she was sure was a band of boys, naked except for the mud (was it mud?) that covered their bodies, eyes empty, mouths tongueless, carrying drums she somehow knew were made from salvaged skin and bone, and she knew these were the choirboys who had torn Kadeem limb from limb. She watched them walk into the water and disappear in the waves. No one else seemed to have seen them.

Ramsey collected the candles, lit the ones that had gone out, and arranged them in a small circle on the beach, then placed the gold coin Kadeem had given him in the middle of the circle. The clouds cleared and the moon poured light over the water, rocks, and sand. Ramsey crouched down in front of Nico and slowly, gently pulled the thread from their lips. He brought the thread to the circle of candles and set it onto the gold coin. The thread melted away.

"Kadeem told me there is no Great Work," Ramsey said, staring at the coin. "The universe does not give us tasks or quests, he said. There is nothing to complete, nothing to begin or end. That may be true. I don't know. My teacher, Norman, has lost all his memories, his whole life's history, all his knowledge, all his experience. Now, for him at least, everything is little more than smoke."

He looked up at the faces lit by candlelight and moonlight, exhausted but expectant faces, and chuckled wearily. "I can't draw any great meaning from any of that. Sorry."

Brad held Ramsey's hand. "No need for meaning," he said. "We are here together. That's all we need."

They remained together for a while longer, then Kazu and Joy quietly helped Fran to walk over the beach, up the steps, and away into the night. Nico and their parents soon followed. Brad leaned down to pick up the gold coin, but Ramsey stopped him. "It belongs here," he said. "The tide will take it all. That is the order of things."

Brad nodded. They stood together and looked out at the water.

"Ready?" Brad asked Abby.

"Not yet," she said.

Clouds filled the sky again. Brad and Ramsey walked along the whole length of the beach and then faded into the dark.

Abby lingered. She stared up, hoping for the stars to reveal themselves, but they did not, though moonlight rested beneath the slate sky, and hints of morning sun eventually burned across the horizon.

At dawn, Abby made her way home, stopping at the shop briefly to collect her tarot cards. Their faces had returned.

In the Grove

Erica Ruppert

CARVED INTO THE first page of her travel journal in her tight, sharp script: *Frazer was a fool.*

Guy wanted to stay in Rome for the last week as they had planned, but Claudia insisted they leave early, to see Lake Nemi before their trip was over. She had mentioned it on the plane, a bit of trivia about a Roman shrine to a borrowed goddess, but it was not on their itinerary. Guy didn't think it was anything but conversation.

"Let's just stay still, there's enough to see in Rome," he said.

"But when," she asked, "will we ever get back here?"

He could not answer, so he packed his bag and drove their tiny rented car into the countryside to appease her.

Claudia rolled down the window as soon as they were out of the city, letting the warm air wash over them. She pulled her hair out of its ponytail and scrubbed it into a wild corona before pushing it out of her eyes.

"Now I'm really on vacation," she said. Guy smiled fleetingly, his eyes on the road.

I see the long days spooling off ahead, unravelling a fine and fragile fabric into tangled threads. Somehow it's right to be back. It will give me a chance to try to knit it all together again. My family emerged here, from some

ancient tribe. I have lost the connections. There is no one left to remember with me anymore. I have outlived them. Noni knew the old language that had been beaten out of the rest. She remembered the previous gods, although she was alone in her memory. I can see what she tried to tell, even if it is hazy. But I can't explain it.

The hotel nestled on the hills of Nemi, small and quiet, tucked away from the street by a wide, walled garden. Their room was on the third floor, with a small balcony overlooking an old courtyard. Guy didn't ask her how she'd found it, but she seemed pleased with herself as she opened the closet door and the dresser drawers, exploring whatever could be a hidden spot.

"Look," she said, pulling a leatherette-bound folder from one drawer. "A room-service menu. Are you hungry?"

"I could eat," Guy said.

Claudia smiled and picked up the phone.

"I'll order," she said.

"I want to see the temple," she told him over the remains of their lunch. "Well, what's left of it."

With that she moved her plate out of the way and opened her journal to jot down a few lines. Guy gazed past her, looking out the balcony doors at the deep blue afternoon sky until the scratch of pen on paper stopped.

"You have to narrow that down a bit," he said. "We've seen plenty of temples already."

He tipped back the last mouthful of his coffee.

"The one here at Lake Nemi," she said, half a laugh in her voice. "The old temple of Diana."

A thin stream of coffee overflowed his mouth and drizzled onto his shirt.

"Dammit," he said with a sudden flare of anger.

Claudia folded her napkin slowly.

"Just change it, Guy. It's not the end of the world."

He got up and rummaged in his suitcase for a clean t-shirt.

"Why are you so mad about spilling coffee?" she asked.

"Why are you so obsessed with this myth?" he asked in reply, trying to reclose the suitcase. The zipper stuck, and he gave up.

"Stop with the dramatics. I'm not obsessed. I'm just interested. It's sort of a part of my heritage."

He sighed. He had heard about her heritage enough times already.

"Let's take a nap," he suggested, moving his luggage to the floor. "We can start today over when we wake up."

"In a minute," she said. "I just have to write something down."

They spent the long afternoon surveying the town, walking down even the residential streets and tracing the outskirts. Guy admitted it was a pretty town, a relaxing town. Lake Nemi glittered below them. They stopped into a few shops, bought a few trinkets and snacks, but Claudia's imperfect, functional Italian was no match for the shopkeepers' polite and dismissive silence.

"I wish my mother had taught me Italian when I was little. She kept it like a secret language to use with my grandparents. Learning it later just isn't the same. It's not the right dialect at all."

She glanced up at Guy.

"Anyway, we've missed the summer festival," she said to him. "Maybe they don't really want to deal with any tourists after that."

"Maybe," he said. "Small towns don't always want strangers."

"I'm not a total stranger," she said. "My great-grandparents and who knows how many generations before them were from around here. I don't know the name of the exact village, but I know it wasn't far from here. But there's no one left alive to ask."

She sighed.

"They came to America, had their kids, and then went back to visit. The story goes that my great-grandparents left my grandmother—Lydia—and her sisters here and went back to

America before the war broke out. The First World War. So the girls were trapped here for ten years. My grandmother used to tell me that one night, soldiers broke into their house. They were on a farm, far enough away from the main town. The soldiers chased her grandmother, my great-grandmother, around the kitchen table, yelling and threatening to kill her. So Lydia ran across the fields to get help from a neighbor. But in the dark, she ran into an animal, some big animal that didn't move out of the way, and it was her screams that brought the neighbor. He was able to scare off the men and save her grandmother."

She paused.

"The way she always told the story, it was a horse that she ran into, and she was terrified of them for the rest of her life. And the neighbor who saved them was a strange man who was normally shunned by the rest of the village. Even after he came to their rescue."

"You never told me any of that," he said.

"It didn't seem important before." She kept walking. "Anyway, who knows how much of it is true."

The Diana at Nemi was not one goddess there but three, immutably intertwined, huntress, moon, death. This version of Diana demanded sacrifice. Every stranger to wash up on these shores must die on her altar. This Diana was never accepted as a legitimate Roman goddess. Always, she was the other, outside.

The little hotel was silent around them in the warm night. Guy rolled closer to her in the soft bed, ran his fingers over her bare shoulder.

"It's so peaceful," Claudia said, reaching out to stroke Guy's cheek. "Like a hidden gem."

"Don't get sappy. All the guidebooks said this place is no more than a day trip."

"That's if we were just here to be tourists," she said. "I just want to be here to be here. Just for a few days. Away from everything."

He sighed. The distant creaking of trees broke the stillness of the room, high-pitched and almost melodic.

"Do you ever think about what it would be like if we had had kids?" he asked.

Claudia drew her arms in, pulling away from him just enough to let the fan's breeze pass between them.

"Don't go there. Not now," she said. "Can we just enjoy this vacation, and not rehash everything else?"

He sighed. "It's hard, Claudia. It's hard knowing we don't want the same things anymore."

"A baby isn't going to save us, Guy."

"This trip isn't either," he said, and was startled by Claudia's sudden burst into tears.

In his dream, Guy crossed the golden fields and followed the snaking path into the grove, following Claudia. He was ready to try his luck at this, willing to die if he failed. It was a better fate than slavery, which waited in the town behind him.

Behind him. He could still hear voices, speaking of him, the words tangled with the wooden clatter of branches tossed in a hot wind.

It's a shock that we've lost him. He was so vital just a day ago.

He shuddered in his sleep at the premonition, even as he became aware that he dreamed.

Claudia seemed to have forgiven him, come morning.

"I've been reading a little," Guy said, holding up his phone. "About the lake, and the temple. Caligula sailed his ships on Nemi, supposedly as a show of power. But then he went mad."

Claudia looked at him, waiting for him to go on.

"I think he was mad long before he built ships here. I read somewhere that he thought the goddess here was another aspect of Isis."

She nodded. "Yes. Every time the Romans became interested in a new goddess, they made her an aspect of one they already acknowledged. It's maddening. Just when I think I've got a handle on how it all fits together, it slips away," she said, and flopped down on the bed, spreading her arms across the coverlet.

"They couldn't grasp her," she said to the spinning ceiling fan. "They kept adding on things Diana was goddess of because they didn't know how all-encompassing she was. They couldn't even think of something so vast."

"I don't follow you. Isis or Diana?"

She tilted her head to look at him.

"All of them," she said.

Lake Nemi was named the mirror of the goddess. It fills the cold bowl of a dead volcano that made these hills and the lakes within them. It has been quiet since before there was history, but it is not dead. Its chambers tremble and lift, sometimes breathing out foul gasses from deep inside the earth. The volcano had belched out its poison air and molten rock time after time over the millennia, wiping away whatever life had sprung up in its ruptured crater when the ash had settled and the lava cooled. Destruction, devastation, rebirth.

The woods have grown up around it since the last eruption, thick and secretive, shadowing a wide clearing overlooking the lip of the lake, her sacred space where men come to pledge their devotion, where women come to beg her divine aid. Always, they fear her anger.

They walked along the looping Via del Tempio de Diana, taking their time. The late morning light was warm and syrupy, with only the faintest breeze to stir it. Puffs of dust followed at their heels. Leaves broke the sunlight into a million shards as they passed through wooded sections of the road.

The cobbled road was paved in patches, but for the most part was a winding, narrow line through galleries of close-grown trees and private fields. At breaks in the tree cover they could see the lake, down in the distance.

"It's calm down here. Still. The water is like glass," Claudia said.

"The hills protect it," Guy said. He pointed at a painted sign a few yards ahead of them, where the road split and one branch led downhill. "I think that's the way to the temple."

She nodded and clasped his hand. Her breath quickened as she sped up her pace and made him keep up. But she didn't say a word until they came into the open where the excavation was bounded by thin plastic fencing.

The outline of the Roman temple spread across the field, sketched through the high weeds, its remaining walls cloaked in vines, its frescos faded to shadows.

Claudia waded through the grass to the edge of the temple complex. She shaded her eyes with her hand as she took it all in.

"It must have been quite impressive," she said. "It's sad that they aren't doing more with this. I mean, it's not showy, but it's got to be worth a better effort."

Guy walked along the line of the walls, past where Claudia had stopped. She had explained the syncretism of Roman religion to him, and the conflicts. He studied what lay before them. The altar, unearthed, had a sterile look to it, innocent of the sacrifices a multitude of goddesses had demanded. It was the clean, Roman version, the one that played at paganism until the government refused to tolerate it any longer.

He stepped over a low spot in the fencing and headed for the niches with their eroded bas-reliefs.

"Hey," Claudia called, following. "Be careful! This isn't a park. It's holy ground."

"No. It was," he said, running his hand over the rough traces of Diana's image. "So they just mashed together one god on top of another, depending on what they needed to believe?"

She studied the faint outline of the goddess's face where the worn stone dissolved the details. It was scarcely recognizable, the features misshapen by time and rain.

"It's not as random or chaotic as that," she said. "They were trying to make sense of something they couldn't understand. Trying to carve it down to something they could define with a name."

"How could that even work?" Guy asked, his hand lingering on the curves of the warm stone that had once been Diana's cheek.

"This is only part of the complex. The oldest temple isn't here. It's on private land."

"That's too bad," Guy said, noncommittal.

"We're still going," she said. "I did a lot of digging about the history here and found directions to it online. We just have to be respectful. It was a farm, at least when the directions were posted. It might still be."

"Claud, I don't want to end this vacation in an Italian jail."

She laughed. "We won't. I promise."

They hiked up the hill, past the "Private Property" signs, past other fragments of Roman structures, up an increasingly steep slope. There, below its crest, was the half-moon arc of an ancient wall, overgrown and half-swallowed by the hillside. Beyond it, in the shadow of the ridge, stood a deep grove of oak and laurel.

"The earliest signs of worship here date to the Etruscans. I'm sure it's older than that though. There were other ruins." Claudia breathed in the sense of incalculable age. "But they were reburied after they were found."

Guy looked up toward the trees, shading his eyes against the glare of the sun. "Reburied? Who would do that?"

She stopped, giving him a look that was part wonder, part contempt. He winced.

"Someone who thought it needed protecting," she said. "Come on. It's getting late."

Artemis became Diana, but she had always been something else. Caligula conflated her with Isis, who was life, and could overcome death. The goddess was unknowable, but her attributes followed her. Creation, destruction, and the vastness of the sky. Artemis, who has many names. Azathothia becomes Astarte becomes Astaroth. Ruling mountains, easing birth, hunting, always hunting, accompanied by a choir and a crowd of companions. Virgin goddess of fertility.

The worn pillar in the grove was smooth, weathered but unmarked by human tools. The top of it rose up into a blunted twist. Claudia reached up to stroke the striped grey stone, following its grain with her fingers.

"Look," she said over her shoulder to Guy, her earlier mood forgotten. "Look at the pattern in the stone. The way the different layers bend. It formed like this, in this shape. It wasn't carved. It's probably volcanic."

She found a toehold in the pillar's base and lifted herself up.

"I wonder what the actual cult image looked like," she said. "How they saw her."

Guy grunted, not giving an answer.

"When you were reading about Nemi, didn't you ever wonder about what they actually worshipped?" Her attention was still on the stone before her. "It wasn't the pretty statue goddess. It wasn't that simple."

She pressed her cheek to the stone and closed her eyes. After a few seconds, she began to hum.

Men will make sacrifices whether their gods ask for them or not. They need to abase themselves as part of their understanding. Or misunderstanding. The gods want such different things than we can offer.

"The desk clerk was odd," Guy said, coming out of the bathroom.

Claudia shrugged and climbed into bed.

"I imagine he thinks the same of us," she said. "Strange people coming here to this little nowhere town, looking at antiquities that are only half-explained."

"That's not what I meant. He looked... inbred, for lack of a better word."

"Don't be ugly. He's probably from one of the local families that have been here for generations. I'd be surprised if everyone in Nemi didn't look similar."

Guy kept his back to her as he pulled off his jeans.

"What did you think you were going to find here, Claudia?"

She wrapped the sheet around her, covering her breasts.

"I told you, my family was from around here. I hoped there would still be some kind of connection..." Her voice trailed away. She didn't want to finish the thought.

Guy sat on the edge of the bed, but still didn't face her.

"It's been too long," he said. "I don't mean to make it sound like that, but it has been. You can't expect people you never knew to just be here for you to find."

Will they remember me? Will they recognize the sacrifices I have made to return to them? She remembers. They must.

Guy roused with a cough and reached for Claudia, but the sheets beside him were an empty tangle. He sat up and looked to the deep blue rectangle of the open windows. She stood on the small balcony, her face turned up to the pale moon.

"Claudia?" he called. "What are you doing?"

She sighed, but did not turn.

"Nothing," she said at last.

"Come back to bed," he mumbled. Then he lay back and slept again before she answered him.

She drifted, but her mind would not rest. She became aware of a rustling in the hall outside their room, moving away. She knew she was awake, although nothing in the space around her felt real. Her hands, her feet, all seemed to be at an impossible distance. The high, thin wail like distant flutes drifted up to her, over the lake's still waters. The tuneless music sounded familiar, as if she had heard it before.

Guy moaned in his sleep and tried to rise. Claudia pressed against him.

"Do you know what it is?" she whispered against his ear, clinging to his arm. He tried to pull away, but she tightened her grip.

"No," she said. "You have to tell me if you know."

He opened his eyes. Claudia's face was so close to his he could not focus on her. He struggled to push her away. She let go, and fell back.

"It's okay, it's okay," she said. "I was having a bad dream. It's over."

He blinked, then closed his eyes again, snorted, and snored.

The sound of the flutes faded into the other noises of the night.

Sleeping, dreaming, wide awake. It is all the same. There are no such simple divisions when she encompasses so much. We might define it as insanity, if we try to define it at all.

As she lay there beneath the slow, hypnotic rotation of the ceiling fan, she began to feel as if the room was all there was, that beyond the chipped white walls was utter nothingness. No. Not nothing, she thought, as her stomach clenched in excitement and animal terror. Everything, inchoate. Worse than nothing. Too much. More than too much. Guy slept beside her, oblivious. She clutched the edge of the mattress, terrified of the spinning maw of all things that awaited her, outside. But she desired it. She wanted to know what it had devoured, before her.

Minutes crept by, and the tempting thrill of fear became exhaustion. She rubbed her eyes. She thought she might have drowsed. The fan still spun, the night still loomed. Beneath the sounds of her own breathing, she heard the thin whistle of a broken tune. It wasn't quite music. Its pattern was just out of reach of making sense. It pulled at her, and she rose, too eager, too afraid to ignore it. She stumbled against the table, tipping it and grabbing at the things that fell. As she bent to gather them, she knew they no longer mattered.

She went to the balcony. There, in the courtyard, figures distorted by shadow danced slowly in the moonlight, their rhythm as disjointed as the music that drove them. She felt her own limbs move with it too, understanding what it wanted of her. She turned to see Guy sleeping soundly in the bed she had left, then turned again in another full circle.

Now the room was empty.

She was somewhere, other.

She stepped up onto the balcony's rail, her bare feet keeping uneven time to the piping wail, until the dance took her off the railing and through the dark air into the figures' waiting, upstretched arms.

Guy sat up, suddenly aware of the empty space beside him. A breeze washed over him that was not from the fan. The whisper of moving leaves came in through the opened balcony doors.

"Claudia?" he hissed into the quiet room. He thought he saw her shadow outside. He untangled himself from the sweat-damp sheets and went to the doors. Whatever had been on the table beside them was now strewn across the floor. He wondered if that was the noise that had woken him. "Claudia," he whispered again, before stepping out into the night.

The balcony was empty beneath a fading moon.

He went back into the room and closed the glass doors against the quivering darkness, kicking at the mess she had left behind.

He picked up her travel journal from where it had fallen against the wall and turned on a light. The creased pages were covered in Claudia's tiny script, line after line of half-completed thoughts and unanswered questions, as dense as a thesis.

Tucked into the front of the notebook were a handful of postcards she had bought as souvenirs. The images of Rome had been defaced, scratched over with hashmarked patterns. The backs were covered in dense blocks of script, the same words over and over again, repeated until there was no more space to write them: *Artemis. Isis. Astarte. Ashtareth. Atargatis. Azzanathkona. Azathothia.*

He knew where Claudia had gone.

He slipped on his shoes and made his way out of the hotel and into the clinging dark of the fields. It swallowed him, but he didn't know it.

The goddess they thought they knew grew old, and tired, and bitter. They were not enough. When the other gods came down she was alone, the old men still unenlightened. They called the old gods dead. But gods do not die. They grow old and feeble, their needs grow fewer in their age. Worship is less sustenance than it had been. But they still get hungry.

He dreamed of her, her wide, bright face smiling toward him, high above him, lit with a celestial light. The crescent on her brow shone, moon-pale and silver, its horns sharp.

She spoke, but her voice was so vast that he couldn't hear her words, only a rushing noise like water or heavy wind. It hurt him, echoing in his head like the toll of a bell, loud, and louder, and louder until it blotted out the rest of the world.

Please, he said in his dream, in a scream and a whisper, please.

But her voice filled the sky, and her face dipped closer to him, her smile become a ravening grin. A long tongue lolled from her opening mouth, and she howled. He covered his ears with stiffening hands. He knew he wasn't dreaming any longer.

Guy rose, exhausted, from a bed of moss and leaves. He did not remember his journey, or lying down here. He only remembered dreaming of her. Of Diana. Leaf litter clung to his sweaty skin, and he panted as if the air were not rich enough to nourish him. Away in the woods he heard the faint jingle of bells, the thin piping of flutes. Fainter still were the voices raised in a flat, tuneless song. They were in the grove, just above him. They had begun already, while he had been dreaming.

The day was already gone, and the late sunlight picking its way between the moving leaves was stained green, dappling his skin as if he were a wild faun. If he were such a wild thing, he would be safe here. But he was not, and he was not.

The trees made their own temple. Oak and laurel, cypress and myrtle. Fragrant and green. But their natural shapes were uneven, distorted where branches had been torn from them, leaving scars and gaps. Trunks twisted, compensating for their losses.

An inconstancy, a strangeness, hung in the still air beneath the broken, arching trees. The faces that turned toward him were not right, not shaped as they should be. They looked like Claudia. He saw that now.

A faint, discordant whistling emanated from the misshapen mouths. Limbs, wooden and flesh, moved with the sound.

Even awake, Claudia could see what she had dreamed, the chaos outside the fragile shell of the world. She could see the divine form in its indescribable glory, inhuman, inchoate, indefinable, infinite. Her mind could not translate the images into anything it could hold. It didn't matter.

The lake reflects the empty sky, and we call the absence a god.

Birth, creation, passage into the world, only to be destroyed again, and again, and again.

"If I had given you a child, we never would have reached this. And this is everything," she said, awe in her voice. "Everything."

Guy thought he had been alone, before she spoke.

He was lost, in the grove, in the burgeoning night.

He flinched back at the low thrum of her words, his head pivoting madly as he searched for some way out. But the trees had somehow grown together into a mass as dense and twisted as viscera. Claudia parted them with a pass of her hands, and walked deeper into the grove.

It seems like they were always trying to pin something down, and never could. It was something so ancient its origins were beyond their history, their memory. As if by naming her and adding so many responsibilities they would weigh her down. They called her Diana, but it was as irrelevant as anything she had been called before. Artemis. Isis. Astarte. Ashtareth. Atargatis. Azzanathkona. Azathothia. Always trying to wrap the name in a human tongue, never quite succeeding. Or daring. How close could they come, before they called her down in all her inhumanity?

The moon was no longer a clear disc in the black and spangled sky. Tendrils reached from it like an anemone's arms, moving on some cosmic tide.

Guy squinted against the glare of light fracturing off the water. He could not see his goddess, not her face, not her form, only a tangle of sharp angles, black and bright, writhing against the pale horizon.

The men who were not men had gathered again to kneel around the still, silver pool, their twisted bodies like knotted roots gripping the shore. They had once been tall and well-shaped, hunters like him. Now they were all remade.

Beneath the deep shadow of the trees was an inevitable light. He moved toward it, despite the miles it seemed he must travel to reach it. He could not refuse to go. He could not turn back.

He reached the edge of the light as she rose from her bath, glorious, pale as pearls, bright as moonlight, white as sterile salt. Her women circled her, eyes turned away, holding up the robes that would cover her and dim her light enough for a mortal gaze. She smiled upon him, and he burned.

Somewhere in the distance outside the grove, hounds bayed, their deep voices echoing off the hills in a chorus.

He found the branch in his hands, its broken end as white as her sacred flesh. He felt the antlers branching from his lengthening head.

"Will you fight?" she asked. He thought she was Claudia, but he could not be sure.

He could not answer her, not with this tongue, not with this throat. His eyes rolled in fear. The trap had sprung. He had walked into it as innocent as a rabbit, even knowing she was a hunter. Even knowing how to set such traps himself.

"Why did you come here, if not to fight?" she asked again. Her grey eyes sparked with anger. He tossed his head, heavy with antlers now, dancing on his narrow hooves.

And the night above was bright with stars, long drifts of sparkling white against a fathomless velvet black.

The figure that turned to him spoke through a mouth not made for human words. He thought she had been Claudia, once.

"My goddess is no timid virgin. She hunts, beast and man falling before her. She blesses women with easy births. She knows the joys of the flesh, if not the bed."

The figure inclined its strange, long head toward him.

"Would you be king, here?"

"King?" Guy echoed, unsure.

"King of Nemi. King of Her grove."

He raised his head, struggling against the weight of it.

"What of all the others? Are they the same? Are they any different than this?"

"There are no others. My goddess stands alone, the source. She is all. She is everything. She is nothing you can name."

In the grove, in the grove, the grove above the Roman temple, the grove where the real worship was done, where the priest-kings fought and died and were crowned in a sacrificial cycle as brutal as birth, to prove their devotion to Her, to prove their faith.

"Guy!" Claudia hissed.

He turned, his eyes wide and rolling. He opened his mouth, and an animal voice came out, as high and off-key as the pipes. He twitched, the unfamiliar shape of his head making him nervous and uncomfortable. He shook his head, trying to clear it, but the antlers jutting from his skull clacked and tangled in the low branches. He struggled against them but could not get loose. As he tugged to free his head, vines twined around his long narrow legs, tightening like snares as he pulled against them. The more he struggled the more firmly he was caught, but he could not keep still as the sound of a branch cracking came from behind him, and the heavy breathing of the man ripping it loose.

If it wasn't him with the branch, who would it be?

The thing itself hovered at her shoulder, the sacrifice who returns in the long circle of time, unable to make peace with its resurrection. Claudia ignored it. It was not part of her world. Not now.

She studied the grim paleness beneath Guy's darkened skin, the strange sheen to his eyes and lips. He looked frozen, frosted, burned. Claudia reached out and traced his features with a fingertip. He shuddered, but did not move away from her hand.

"What did you see?" she asked.

He moved his lips, but the words he formed were not a language he could speak.

She smiled upon him, pretending at benevolence. It was her dialect. She understood.

"Is that all?" she asked.

He stared at her indescribable face, unable to speak.

"It's okay, dear," she said. "You've done what you must."

I'm still waiting for it to happen, the recognition for what I have done. She, they, it will always return. It will never leave. The mote in the beam of our existence, casting a shadow we cannot dispel. The mindless, the madness, at the heart of our being. The water. The mirror. The moon. What hides behind the moon in the dark, in the depth of all things.

What is divine.

Church of the Void

Donald Tyson

1.

FATHER ANDREW RICE drew the collar of his overcoat tighter. It was cold in the auditorium despite the thousands of people who had gathered to hear Brother Gregor speak. He cleared his throat and saw the white puff of his breath.

"I don't know why I let you drag me to this thing, David," he said to the young man seated next to him. "It's not my kind of scene."

"It's a religious gathering, Andy." David McCormick gave his friend a crooked grin.

"No, it's a cult—a cult of fanatics."

"You're a man of God, right? This is some spiritual shit going down here. I need to get your professional impressions before I write my article for *Rolling Stone.*"

"You're stretching our friendship here," the older man said, but he smiled in spite of himself.

On McCormick's other side, Myra Stenson abruptly clutched his arm. He didn't know if she was cold or just excited, but hoped it was the latter, since he was planning on spending the night in her apartment when he took her home. The air in the auditorium felt electric. They were forced to almost shout at each other above the general din to make themselves heard. Smoke, or maybe it was steam, rose from the bright floodlights hanging in the rafters that illuminated the stage.

"Who is this Brother Gregor?" Myra asked.

McCormick looked at her in surprise. "You've never heard of the Church of the Void?"

"Of course I've heard of it. Everyone's heard of it. But I don't know anything about Brother Gregor. I've been busy working on my art project, as you well know."

"She's been living like a hermit for the past three months," McCormick said loudly, turning to the priest. "She's working on this big sheet-metal sculpture job for city hall."

"Brother Gregor calls himself a spiritual teacher," Father Rice told Myra as McCormick leaned out of his way. "I once read that he believes himself to be the reincarnation of a mythical ancient Egyptian pharaoh named Nyarlathotep. He's the head of a cult known in the media as the Voiders. They worship a god of chaos they call Azathoth. Gregor's message is that only the void of chaos exists and nothing is real, and because of that there is no reason to worry about anything."

"Sounds simplistic," she said.

"But comforting, in a sick sort of way," McCormick added.

"Well, I may have simplified his message a bit, but that's the general drift," the priest said.

McCormick glanced at the stage. "I think it's going to start."

The roar of the crowd settled down into a background hum as they watched an attractive but conservatively dressed young woman adjust the microphone on the podium. Behind her, a large white projection screen had been set up.

Applause broke out when a bald man in a blue suit approached the stage down one of the aisles and ran up its steps two at a time, then walked briskly to the podium. The overhead lights flashed in the round lenses of his gold-frame glasses.

"They look like Mormons," McCormick murmured to the priest.

The bald man stood smiling at the audience for a dozen seconds without saying anything.

"For those of you who don't know me," he said finally, "my name is Allen Kordak. I am the president of the Boston Chapter of the Church of the Void, the fastest growing unbelief system on planet Earth. That means I get to introduce events like this to you all, so bear with me."

Supportive laughter rippled through the crowd.

"Most of you are old friends. Others who may have come for the first time are wondering what this is all about. What is the Void?"

He paused. There was dead silence.

"The Void is not a religion, not a location, not even a goal. It's a way of life. It offers a new perception of the world, of reality itself. We don't ask you to give up your old beliefs, we offer you something that supersedes them. After Brother Gregor speaks, you will observe the Void in action tonight. You don't have to believe in it, we will show it to you. And when you see it, you won't be able to choose disbelief no matter how much you may want to. The Void is real, and reality is the Void."

More than half the audience chanted his last sentence in unison, as if it were a mantra. Father Rice caught McCormick's glance and raised his eyebrows.

"Human consciousness is awakening to the Void, and with each mind that awakens, the process accelerates. Brother Gregor encountered the Void while walking alone across the sands of Egypt. He was the first, but today we are many around the world, all linked by our shared awareness of unreality. We know that we exist only for so long as we believe in our existence. As the poet William Blake wrote two centuries ago in his *Auguries of Innocence*: 'If the sun and moon should doubt, they'd immediately go out.' Blake was aware of the Void, but he had no companions with whom to share his awareness. He was dismissed as insane. But you and I know that we are not insane. Brother Gregor is not insane. We comprehend the Void, and it comprehends us. All is possible because all things are unreal. This does not make us afraid. To paraphrase Nietzsche, we stare bravely into the Void, and the Void stares back into us."

He paused again. McCormick leaned toward Father Rice. "He has a good stage presence, I'll give him that. He's relaxed, confident. And he's well read—first Blake, then Nietzsche."

"He's a huckster," the priest muttered sourly.

"But you didn't come to hear me. You came to hear Brother Gregor, our leader and teacher. Brother Gregor is in Istanbul right now, preparing to deliver a demonstration of the Void to a committee of Islamic clerics, but we are fortunate enough to have a live satellite feed from his hotel room."

He glanced at a tall man in a dark suit who stood at the side of the stage with his hands clasped in front of his groin. The man nodded.

"Without further delay, I turn the stage over to Brother Gregor."

The lights in the auditorium dimmed. The screen filled with the image of a bearded man with dark penetrating eyes, who sat in an ornately gilded chair with a high red-velvet back. He wore a long black robe beneath which his legs were crossed at the knees. On his head was a small black hat.

"He's wearing the traditional cassock and biretta of a Jesuit priest," Rice said to McCormick without bothering to lower his voice. "It's sacrilege. He was never a priest."

A sound of disapproval came from the people seated behind them.

"Keep it down, Andy," McCormick whispered. "We don't want to get thrown out. Or worse."

"I don't have much patience for this kind of nonsense, David, you know that. Maybe you shouldn't have brought me."

Brother Gregor raised his right hand and made a gesture, drawing their attention to the screen.

"You seek the Void," he said in a thick Russian accent. His voice was deep and seemed to reverberate on the air. He paused, allowing his words to echo in the minds of the listeners. "You seek the Void, even if you have not told this yearning to anyone, not even your lover or your spouse, not even to yourself. You seek the Void. That is why you are here, listening to my words. You are gathered here because the Void has called to you, and you have answered. The Void is in your heart now, as I speak. Feel its emptiness."

He laid his right hand across his breast and closed his eyes. There was dead silence in the auditorium, until someone tried to stifle a cough, which caused several others to cough in different parts of the big room. Brother Gregor opened his eyes and seemed to stare directly out from the screen.

"I cannot define what the Void is, because the Void defies description. But I can describe to you how it affects those who, like yourself, have sought it out. The Void is the spiritual philosophy of unbelief. It is both a discipline and a way of life. You will find yourself either embracing it as a lover, or trying to cast it away in loathing and terror. Neither course will profit you. Nothing that exists is real. All is chaos. All exists only because we believe it exists, but its existence is illusion. Only the Void, which does not exist, is real. The Void is freedom. The Void is everywhere and nowhere. It is the empty mind, without desire, without suffering. The Void is oblivion."

A wave of apprehension rippled through the spectators. Brother Gregor nodded as though he had heard it.

"This frightens some of you. But consider—the world is only the way it is because we believe in it. If we withdraw our belief, it returns to disorder. If we believe together, whatever we believe arises from chaos into being, and whatever we disbelieve ceases to be. All of it is illusion, all of it created and sustained by our common expectation. We can create, we can destroy, or we can choose to simply cease to exist."

He looked right and left, as though he could see the audience through the lens of the camera. His dark eyebrows drew together above his hypnotic black eyes. He leaned forward.

"All religion is a fraud. You know this in your hearts, but you are afraid to admit it to yourselves, afraid to be alone in the universe. Judaism, Christianity, Islam, Buddhism, all the rest—lies. Only the Void is true. Do not fear this truth, embrace it. When all illusions of false gods vanish away, the Void remains, waiting to receive you."

"I can't listen to any more of this," Rice said. He started to rise from his seat. McCormick grabbed his arm.

"You can't go yet. I need you to hear and see what happens so that I can question you later and get your quotes as a representative of the Church."

The priest shook his head in disgust, but he allowed himself to relax back into his seat. Brother Gregor continued to speak in the same vein for about ten minutes more, taking frequent pauses between his statements to allow his audience to digest his words.

His mind wandering, McCormick looked around the auditorium and experienced a shock of surprise. Apparently Brother Gregor was not as magnetic a personality as he seemed, because there were empty seats. When they came in, the place was nearly packed. Part of the audience must have wandered out.

"That is all I have to say to you tonight, brothers and sisters of the Void. I have shown you the path, but you must walk it with your own feet. I offer no salvation, no hope, no gods to answer your prayers, only reality stripped of its veils of illusion. In order to perceive the Void, you must discard everything in your life, in particular those things you hold most dear. Cast them away and do not look behind you. Together, we will go forward and embrace emptiness."

The projected video came to an end and the lights slowly brightened. Kordak bounded back onto the stage. He smiled broadly as he gripped the podium with both hands.

"We will conclude this gathering with a training exercise, as is our usual custom."

The tall man in the black suit carried a wooden chair from one of the wings and set it next to the podium.

"When is this interminable nonsense going to end?" Rice said to McCormick. The irritation in his voice was unmistakable.

"Just watch. This is the part I wanted you to see."

"Beside me on the stage is a plain kitchen chair made of wood," Kordak said. "Is it real?"

Cries of "no, no" came from the audience.

He went over, picked it up, and set it back down with a bang, then rapped its seat with his knuckles. He resumed his place at the microphone.

"You can sit in it, pick it up, smash it into kindling and burn it, but is it real? Remember Brother Gregor's words before you answer."

McCormick glanced around the auditorium. The number of empty seats had increased.

"A lot of people must feel the way you do," he said into the priest's ear. "They are leaving in droves."

Exclamations rose from the audience. Some started to applaud. McCormick felt Myra grip his wrist harder. He patted her hand.

"It's a trick," Rice said.

McCormick stared back at the stage. The chair was no longer there. Apart from the podium and Kordak, who stood behind it, the stage was empty.

"It has to be a trick," the priest said. "But it's a very good one."

"Well done, brothers and sisters." Kordak clapped his hands slowly at the audience. "Now I would like a volunteer to come up on stage."

Several dozen people started forward but were met by two attendants who allowed only a single young woman to ascend the stairs. She approached the podium, casting nervous glances out into the audience and blinking at the bright lights on her face. A spattering of applause supported her.

"What's your name, sister?" Kordak asked.

She said something inaudible and he drew her nearer to the podium. "Anna," she repeated more loudly.

"How long have you been with Brother Gregor, Anna?"

"Almost three months."

"Are you ready to embrace the Void?"

Her face broke forth into a broad smile. "Oh, yes."

Kordak instructed her to stand in the same spot that had been occupied by the chair. She stood nervously with her feet together, fidgeting with her hands as she looked out into the blackness beyond the lights.

"What are they going to do to her?" Myra whispered into McCormack's ear.

He had no answer, but squeezed her hand. Father Rice leaned forward in his chair and watched the stage intently. McCormack glanced right and left. Were still more of the seats empty? When he turned back to the stage, the young woman was gone.

"He's a stage magician," Rice said, but he did not sound very sure.

"There's no box. There are no mirrors. How's he doing it?" Myra asked.

Two more volunteers went eagerly up the stairs to the stage, and both vanished in the same way. One instant they were standing on the empty open stage, and the next they were gone. McCormack watched closely to see if they fell through trap doors, but there was no downward motion of their bodies. They simply ceased to exist between one blink of an eye and the next. An uneasiness grew inside him. He could think of no way to explain the vanishings.

"Attention, please, attention," Kordak said over the excited murmuring of the audience. "That concludes our practical work for tonight. Buses are waiting at the front door for those who wish to attend our weekend retreat. There is no charge to attend, and everyone is welcome to come and experience the Void with us."

People began to stand up and shuffle toward the aisles.

"I've got to go to this retreat," McCormack told his companions. "Do either of you want to come with me?"

"I'll come," Myra said. "I've got no plans this weekend anyway."

"What about you, Andy?"

The priest scowled and pursed his lips. "I'll have to make arrangements with the bishop, but I suspect he'll want me to investigate what we have just seen. It may have ramifications for the future of the Church."

He pulled out his phone as they shambled toward the exit with the remaining spectators.

2.

Half a dozen buses were lined up along the street. They waited their turn and climbed into one, taking the back seat so they could sit together.

"It looks like a lot of people are getting into the buses," Myra said as she craned her neck to peer through the fogged rear window.

"Most of the audience that stayed to the end were probably members of the cult," McCormick said. "That's the way cults operate—they gather together for lectures and try to draw in a few outsiders. Then they take them to a remote retreat and work on them."

A sudden commotion at the front of the bus drew their attention. A woman stood stark naked in the middle of the aisle, a look of shocked surprise on her face. Those around her applauded and hooted. This made her blush, but she smiled. An older woman took off her coat and draped it around the naked woman's shoulders, then helped her to sit down.

"What just happened there?" Rice asked.

"She took off all her clothes," Myra said.

"Then where are the clothes?"

"It's more trickery to impress the new recruits." McCormick tried to sound confident. Inwardly, he wondered how the woman could have stripped without any of them noticing.

Time dragged as they drove along, the shadows of night passing outside the windows. At first they talked of inconsequential matters. Eventually they fell silent.

"Just how far away is this retreat?" Myra asked with a yawn. She balled her hands into fists and stretched out her blue-jeaned legs.

"I didn't catch the name of the place. Did you, Andy?"

"What? No, I missed it too," the priest said.

McCormick blinked dryness from his eyes and looked down the length of the bus.

"Did I fall asleep? Did we stop?"

"We haven't stopped," Rice told him. "I don't know if you nodded off or not."

"He didn't fall asleep. You'd know if he did—he snores," Myra said.

"Hey, personal secrets. Do I tell yours?"

"I have no secrets. What are you looking at?"

"Am I crazy, or was the naked woman sitting in the fourth seat down on the left?"

Myra squinted in the dim light. Beneath their feet the tires of the bus droned like a swarm of drowsy bees.

"I don't see her. She must have moved."

Many of the other passengers had sunk down in their seats and were sleeping, or trying to sleep. Only the tops of their heads were visible.

"Do you see her, Andy?"

"No, but you know me. I'm no good with faces. Or numbers either, apparently—I thought there were more people on the bus."

The bus rolled on, mile after mile. McCormick closed his eyes to rest them for a few moments. The sound of the tires was hypnotic. He stopped trying to resist.

He opened his eyes and blinked. Myra's head was resting against his shoulder. Rice sat slumped in the corner of the seat, chin on his chest. The journalist yawned and looked around. His body stiffened. He grabbed the other two and shook them awake.

"What?" Myra asked sleepily. "Did we get there?"

"Our Mother of Grace," Rice whispered, eyes wide.

The rest of the bus was empty except for the driver, who did not turn his head or give any notice that he heard them.

"We must have stopped," McCormick said in a reasonable voice. "They all got off at the retreat while we slept."

Rice released a breath of relief. "That must be it. That has to be it."

"Where are we going?" Myra said. "Are we going back to Boston?"

"I'll ask him." McCormick made his way stiffly along the aisle, holding onto the backs of the empty seats. His left leg had gone to sleep. It tingled with a thousand tiny needle pricks as the blood returned to it.

The driver was a middle-aged man with a beer gut. He wore a gray uniform but no cap. His hair was the same color as his uniform. He kept his eyes on the road ahead. Apart from the patch of light thrown from the bus headlights, everything outside was velvet darkness.

"Did we miss the retreat?"

The driver did not turn his head. He gave no indication that he heard the words.

McCormick cleared his throat and spoke more loudly. "Where are you taking us now? Are we going back to the city?"

The driver ignored him. Or maybe he really hadn't heard, McCormick thought. Maybe he was deaf. He waved his hand in front of the driver's expressionless face. Not even a blink.

"Hey, I'm talking to you," he said in irritation, and reached for the man's shoulder to shake him.

His hand passed through the driver's shoulder as though the driver were no more than a three-dimensional projection. Fear hit McCormick like a hammer. Stepping back, he stared at the driver. The seated figure vanished. For several seconds McCormick stood frozen in place, looking at the empty chair. Then he noticed that the bus was drifting across the center line of the highway.

"Son of a bitch."

He jumped onto the seat and grabbed the big, flat steering wheel, gently guiding the bus back into its lane. His right foot found the gas pedal. It did not occur to him to stop. His mind was numbed by the impossible thing he had just witnessed.

Rice and Myra came up the aisle and stood behind him.

"Where's the driver?" Rice said incredulously.

"He disappeared. Just like those people on the stage."

"What do you mean? That's impossible."

"I know," McCormick said, more loudly than he intended. "Don't you think I know that?" He took his hand off the steering wheel long enough to wipe cold sweat off his face.

"This is crazy," Myra said. "We must be asleep and dreaming, or hypnotized, or something."

"Why are you still driving the bus?" Rice asked.

"Look out the windows. There's nothing out there. I haven't even seen a road sign. We need to get some place where we can get off."

The other two cupped their hands and peered through the dark glass. There was nothing, not even vague outlines of trees and rocks. Only the asphalt of the highway and some gravel on either side showed in the headlights.

"I don't even see any stars," Myra said.

"The sky is probably overcast," Rice said to reassure her. But his voice was unsteady.

Something large and silvery gray flew into the beams of the headlights on enormous wings. McCormack had only a split-second of warning in which to swerve. It wasn't enough. The crash as the passing creature's body struck the side of the bus was like thunder. The big vehicle tipped over, then slid down the highway before coming to a stop.

For a few seconds there was dead silence. The engine of the bus had stalled.

"Myra, are you hurt?" McCormick didn't realize he was yelling until she answered in a normal tone of voice.

"I bumped my head. It's nothing, but there's going to be a hell of a bruise. What happened?"

"Andy?" he said more calmly. "Are you all right?"

A groan came from one of the seats. They took Rice by the arms and pulled him out. They found themselves standing on a row of windows.

"What happened?" the priest asked.

McCormick explained what he had seen, or thought he had seen. He was no longer sure of anything. He felt like a man in the middle of the ocean with nothing to cling to.

"We have to get out," Myra said. "This thing may catch on fire."

"I doubt that," McCormick told her.

"Can you open the door?"

He pointed down at their feet. The bus had rolled onto its door side.

"Shit. We'll break out a window."

This proved to be more difficult than expected. After much futile banging and kicking, they managed to knock out one side of the front windscreen and helped each other to crawl through the opening. One by one, they slid off the fender of the bus. Its headlights were still on, and cast an oblong patch of yellow upon the weathered asphalt of the highway. By common unspoken assent they went forward and stood in the light.

Myra turned a full circle. "It's so quiet."

Even as she spoke, they heard a distant shriek, followed by another from the opposite side of the highway.

"That sounds like birds," Rice murmured uneasily.

"Not like any bird I've ever heard," Myra said.

"What should we do now?" the priest asked McCormick. "Do we walk for help?"

McCormick was sweating profusely. He wiped it from his forehead and stared at the priest, noticing for the first time that Rice had a cut over his left eye.

"Walk where? Look around us—do you see anything?"

Rice peered into the darkness. "Well, it's still night."

"I mean," McCormick repeated more slowly, "do you see *any*thing?"

Rice walked to where the light from the bus faded into darkness and stood at its edge, looking outward.

"We can't walk through that without a flashlight," Myra said, standing behind him. "We might fall into a pit or something."

"It has to be sunrise soon," McCormick told them. He tried to make his voice reasonable. "We'll wait here until dawn, then follow the highway until we come to a house."

"Maybe a car will come before that," Myra said. The other two did not answer.

The screams in the darkness became more frequent and drew closer. They huddled together in the middle of the highway, their touching bodies casting a pillar of shadow that terminated in the solid wall of darkness at the end of the glow from the headlights.

Something flew across the black sky above their heads. McCormick saw a flash of reflected light.

"Just a bird," he said.

It happened again, and again, with increasing frequency. The streaks of light were like meteors flashing across the night sky. They lowered themselves to their knees and crouched their heads, holding onto each other tightly. McCormick felt Myra's quick breaths hot against his chest as she hid her face. The shrieks were deafening.

One of the creatures flew lower and left a flash impression on McCormick's retinas of a large silver fish with scaly wings. It had a single enormous round eye in the middle of its forehead, and a gaping mouth filled with needle-sharp teeth.

Gradually, the cries from the flying things diminished. Silence returned to the night. They stood back up on stiff legs.

"That wasn't natural," Rice said. He held a silver crucifix between his fingers up close to his face where he could see it. "This is some ungodly thing that is happening to us, to this place."

"Remember what Kordak said about shared belief in the Void," Myra said softly.

McCormick tried to make his mind work. He was dizzy and sick to his stomach, and knew that what he felt was raw fear untempered by reason.

"Unbelief. He said unbelief, not belief. He said something about shared unbelief having its own momentum, or something like that."

"How many Voiders do you think there are in the world?"

"I don't know, Myra. It must be millions, at least. Maybe tens of millions."

"I wonder what the effect of millions of human minds, all thinking about the unreality of reality at the same time, might do," she said.

"I don't follow you," McCormick said, feeling irritation because he followed her all too well.

"What if belief in the Void has a tipping point? What if, when enough people believe in the same thing, the unreal becomes our reality?"

"That's crazy talk. What we saw on stage was just a series of illusions. Kordak is a second-rate stage magician, making rabbits disappear."

A kind of strangled gurgle came from close beside them. McCormick turned and stumbled back, catching Myra instinctively in his arms as she fell against him with her face to his chest. In the dimming glow from the bus headlights stood a human shape covered from head to toe in red roses. As McCormick watched, a thorny stem grew out of its parted lips and bloomed into three more large red flowers. The man-shape gurgled again. From between the leaves that covered its thorn-scratched face it looked at him and rolled its eyes, reaching out toward him with one of its bleeding, rose-covered hands. McCormick saw the flash of a silver cross on a chain between its fingers as it collapsed forward across the road with a wet sound. A pool of blood seeped outward from the motionless heap of roses.

Myra released McCormick and turned.

"Where's Andy?" Her voice became a shriek as she stared around. "Where's Andy?"

McCormick pointed mutely.

"Oh my God." She doubled over and vomited.

"I think his—" He cleared his throat and started again. "I think his body turned into roses."

"Into roses? What are you saying?"

"I mean his flesh somehow converted itself into roses."

She began to laugh hysterically. He allowed her to slip from his arms to the road, where she clung to his knees, still laughing weakly.

McCormick looked up and for the first time saw stars. For a brief moment the familiar sight reassured him, but then the starry heavens began to rotate around the celestial pole, as though time itself were being accelerated a thousandfold. Each constellation spun like a pinwheel on the rim of the heavens as it rolled, making him dizzy. A vortex formed at the center and began to expand. He heard the piping melody of a reed flute, clear in the silence of the night. The music was strange, yet beautiful.

"The stars are dancing," he sighed. "Look, Myra, the stars are dancing."

He turned his gaze down to her and realized he stood alone on the road. The ever-dimming headlights of the bus flickered once, then died. The darkness came and ate him.

Upon an Iron Bed, Under the Eyes of Chaos
Richard Gavin

MAXINE WAS HALFWAY to the island when she heard the piping: a trilling so manic it could hardly be described as musical. It came in a sudden, startling burst and faded as quickly as it erupted, leaving an unnerving calm in its wake.

The canoe wobbled in the gentle tide. Maxine lifted the paddle from the water and allowed it to rest across her knees, craning her head to study the shore at her back. The mainland seemed very far away indeed. The blazing sun fractured itself into countless glints upon the lake's surface, the glassy heat making the skin on the back of her neck tight and dry.

Returning to the bow of her canoe, she studied her destination. Nothing about the island suggested auspiciousness, or even interest really. It was, to her eye, a tiny dollop of rockery and green nested in a small manmade lake. The kind of place she would not have given a second glance or a second thought had she not been ordered to go there as part of a sacred, secret pilgrimage. This fact caused Maxine's blood to go cold when she'd heard that awful piping, for in her bones she knew that the sound had come from somewhere on that island, and that it had been intended for her ears alone.

The island, or something on it, was calling to her.

At any other point in her life, she would have allowed prudence to dictate her actions, which in this case would have meant turning the canoe around and powering back to the mainland. But the past three months had altered everything she had ever known, had swallowed all her certitudes and comforts. The world Maxine now inhabited was a stranger place, richer in many respects, but also less sure. There could be no turning back, either literally or figuratively.

She had to see this test through to completion, had to finally know that which only the island could convey.

Dark blotches passed over the tumblehome of her canoe, moving in rhythmic cycles. She lifted her gaze and saw the shadows of a wake of vultures moving across the sky like giant kites. They were wheeling above the island, crowning the needle-like peaks of six great standing stones, which stood there in crescent-shaped formation at the heart of the island.

Maxine recognized these stones instantly, and although she had never been here before, this recognition filled her heart with desire and dread. Fuelled by these emotions, she plunged the paddle into the water and continued toward the island.

"Before we go any further," said Maxine, stopping her hostess as she rose from the plush claret sofa where she'd been reposing, "I was hoping we could discuss your fee."

Vivien Barlowe gave her guest a long, inquisitive look before settling back onto the couch. She reached for a cigarette but did not light it, opting instead to knead its filter between her fingertips. "My fee..." Her face and tone of voice remained unreadable.

Maxine cleared her throat. "I'm sorry if I offended you. I've not done this before, so I'm unsure of the etiquette. I thought I'd better ask now and avoid an awkward scene afterward."

"You don't consider this awkward?" She lit her cigarette at last, which smelled of vanilla and cloves.

"Incredibly," Maxine admitted. "But I've only got so much cash on me, and I didn't know if psychics accepted personal cheques."

"I'm not a psychic," said Vivien. The bluish smoke from her cigarette appeared to linger willfully about her face, like a veil, like some spirit substance that was obedient to her.

"A medium?"

"Not quite."

"I suppose it doesn't matter what you call yourself, as long as you're able to do what they say you can."

"Oh? And what is it *they* say?"

"That you can raise the dead."

Vivien abruptly extinguished her cigarette, stood, and moved out of the parlour. Maxine followed her. The way she seemed to float up the narrow staircase and along the upper hallway allowed Maxine to realize how unbridled her imagination had become during her brief visit. The research she'd done on this mysterious woman had not been in vain; the techniques she employed to disorient her customers were obviously sophisticated and effective, and they were even influencing Maxine's agnostic mind. She could only imagine how well such tricks worked on true believers.

For the past four months she had been studying the vocation of Vivien Barlowe from afar, scrabbling together the scant details of her biography from parapsychology journals and from clandestine interviews she'd conducted with Vivien's former neighbours and clients, and now finally by inserting herself into her racket by posing as a dutiful daughter yearning to see her departed mother once more. In truth, both of Maxine's parents were enjoying a sedate retirement in Boca Raton. She had to stage a rather elaborate charade just to infiltrate Vivien's practice.

According to accounts, Vivien's séances featured miracles far beyond simple table rapping or cold spots. In the few articles Maxine had unearthed, the woman's former clients had attested to experiences that sounded nearer to a cinematic spectacle than to any of the subtle and suggestive phenomena typically associated with spiritualism.

It was not the outlandish claims alone that had inspired Maxine to pursue a literary exposé; it was the fact that Ms. Barlowe was evidently not just a charlatan but rather heartless. Maxine had uncovered clients who had reported being abandoned by their trusted spiritual advisor, usually after apparent contact with their lost loved ones. These people, who'd been heartsick long before they'd reached out to Barlowe, were left feeling lost and betrayed. One of the widowers Maxine had interviewed described the anguish he still felt after his late wife had apparently materialized in Vivien's séance room, after which the man was denied any further appointments. While Maxine did not consider herself a believer in or debunker of spiritualism, she felt strongly that this kind of conduct was predatory, disgraceful, and worthy of exposure.

The attic Maxine was led into was tiny and smelled of mould. Under the severe pitch of its ceiling sat a round wooden table and two chairs whose legs had fallen prey to cat claws.

"Please, sit," Vivien said, as she moved to the oval window. From a cobalt tray on the windowsill, she collected a beeswax taper, a small brass candleholder, and a book of matches. She then drew a fibrous curtain across the pane, shielding the room from midday light.

The darkness made the candleflame more luminous. Maxine felt her eyes drawn to that teardrop of amber light. She watched it gutter then patiently flare as if it were fanning its wings for flight.

"Your mother's name was Brigitte," said Vivien. Maxine hadn't realized that the setting had lulled her into a meditative state until Vivien's pronouncement broke her trance.

"No," Maxine replied. "I told you her name was Claire." She'd studied her fictitious biography diligently before presenting it. She experienced a momentary pride over dashing the medium's attempt to catch her in her lie. However, this hubris evaporated once Maxine began to wonder how Vivien had guessed her mother's *actual* name.

"Brigitte," she repeated. "Seventy-three and living with your father in a stucco house with an orange tree in the front yard."

Maxine attempted to speak but a whining sound was all that escaped her throat. She sat in stunned silence as Vivien, her head now swivelling wildly, told the story of Maxine's life in humiliating, impossible detail.

She then tried to stand but found her legs were without strength. "Stop," she pleaded. "I know you're a fraud, I know you must have researched me as much as I researched you, so let's cut with the games, okay?"

If a game it was, its structure was well beyond Maxine's abilities, for no amount of research could have yielded the contents of Maxine's dreams, and yet somehow Vivien was able to describe these with architectural clarity and precision. She knew the scent and suppleness of each fantasy lover, the menacing essence of every suffocating nightmare.

Eventually, her spiel came to an end, but only because the entranced woman was out of breath. Maxine sat in silence, not sure what to do or say. This experience had unmoored her, and she no longer much cared about her exposé.

There came a whirring noise, low and faint. It reminded Maxine of an old ceiling fan, its blades spinning in vain combat against the summer heat. She looked at Vivien, wondering what hidden device she might have switched on to create this sound. Vivien sat motionless, her face slack, tapered fingers fanned out upon the tabletop. Maxine allowed her eyes to close. She spent a few moments listening to the throbbing shadows.

Suddenly the floorboards creaked as though trod upon. Maxine immediately opened her eyes and scanned the room. She was almost surprised to find no one there. Turning her gaze back to her hostess, she experienced a cold tremble of fear.

"Vivien?" she said, in a harsh, panicked whisper.

The medium looked possessed. She was staring at Maxine, staring into her, staring through her. Her eyes swelled from their sockets. They glared wide and wild at something past Maxine's rigid form. She could have been staring at something spectral and fantastic manifesting just behind her, but Maxine found the idea of turning around to face whatever it was unbearable. She remained seated, gripping the edge of the table, its splinters piercing her flesh.

Then Vivien began to rise, though her movements seemed involuntary, her body hoisted up by some unseen force. Her lips were skinned back over chattering, glistening teeth. Had she not been so frightened, Maxine's first instinct would have been to look for hidden wires, but on this day, she found herself recoiling from what she was sure were hidden hands.

The room began to brighten. In little time the queer illumination reached a level of intensity that was painful for Maxine look at. She squinted her eyes, but the light burned through her eyelids as though it was caustic. Nuzzling her face into the crook of her arm, she thrust herself out of the chair and stumbled backward. She found the door by groping, but even after she'd escaped into the upper hallway, she felt no sense of safety. She risked a peek.

The medium had crawled onto the table and was now perched there like some feral beast. Her fingernails clawed at the wood, at the air. Maxine was petrified at the thought of her lunging off that table and coming after her. By now the light had waned to a more ambient glow, but Maxine was unable to scrutinize the scene objectively. She'd been struck dumb by the sight of the gleaming star that shone bright inside the cave of Vivien's mouth. The woman's jaw hung impossibly low, transforming her head into a furnace within which blazed the star. The light it radiated was not the gold of the sun but a wan and jaundiced shade of yellow. Everything it touched appeared to Maxine's eye as afflicted, leprous.

Vivien extended her neck, pressing her disfigured head toward Maxine. Though never a praying woman, Maxine found herself pleading with any forces that might listen to not allow that neck to stretch out into the hall like a serpent. It did not. Instead, what came for Maxine was a manic piping noise, one that rose in an endless crescendo, becoming more urgent and frantic but less musical with each note. She gripped either side of her head, mashing her palms against her ears, hoping this might squeeze the noise from her mind.

When she saw the diseased star inside Vivien's mouth part and reveal itself to be a glaring eye, Maxine cried out with all the need and impotence of a terrified child. Then she scrabbled to her feet and ran, not pausing until she'd reached her car, which was parked two blocks away. The street seemed to mock her with its placid normalcy. Men mowing their lawns, children at play, couples walking dogs. Maxine stabbed the key into the ignition and raced for home.

That night she kept the door to her townhouse locked and barricaded by her father's old steamer trunk. The drapes were drawn, and all the lights were on. She sat shivering under a quilt on her couch, convinced that every shadow that passed across the ceiling was Vivien coming after her.

It seemed obvious that sleep would be an impossibility given her agitated state. Yet sometime around eleven Maxine felt the unmistakable bulk of exhaustion pressing down on her. Her eyelids were determined to close. A pot of coffee and mental focus would keep her awake, she knew, and so she attempted to rise and move into the kitchen. But her psyche had other plans, pulling her down into slumber and into dream, a dream of such stifling terror and crystalline clarity that when she awoke in the morning she felt as though she had been mauled. She was grateful for the telephone, whose ring had rescued her from the abominable island, where in her dream she'd been marooned.

Slumping off the couch and onto the floor, she reached about until her hand found the receiver.

"Hello?"

"You had the dream." The woman's voice was not familiar, but when she added the command of "tell me," Maxine identified the speaker.

"How did you get this number?"

"Come see me. Immediately."

The line clicked and the dial tone droned on and on. Unsure what else she could do, Maxine showered and dressed, then made the hour-long drive back to the Ottoman townhouse where the notorious Vivien Barlowe lived, where she lifted the veil between worlds.

Maxine found the inner door open when she scaled the porch steps and stood beneath the canopy with its multifoil arches. She extended her fist to knock but was startled by Vivien's silhouette, which appeared out of the dimness of the foyer.

"Come," spoke the apparition before slipping back into the house.

As Maxine crossed the threshold her ears were assailed by a high-pitched noise. It was unnervingly close to a piping song she had heard in her dream. She resisted the impulse to flee and was relieved when Vivien abruptly silenced the sound by lifting the kettle from the stovetop. A moment later she emerged from the kitchen bearing a tray and ordered Maxine to follow her into the parlour. She heeded and sat and accepted the steaming cup of floral-scented tea. Her hostess settled onto the sofa and curled up her legs, as she'd done during yesterday's visit.

"Tell me," Vivien said, pausing to cool her tea with her breath. "Tell me everything."

Maxine began with the climax, that heart-stopping moment when the thing, whatever it was, revealed itself... a revelation that had thrown her into wakefulness. Her account then leapt from one detail to another. She kept stopping herself to add some aspect or scene that her brain had managed to bury until just that instant. Her telling took the better part of an hour, and it left her parched and weak. She regretted revealing so much of herself, particularly because so many portions of the dream had already been buried. Maxine felt unclean, like a graverobber of her own psyche.

"Am I right in assuming you are now a believer?" Vivien asked.

"A believer in what? Your séances? I guess I'm starting to."

"Don't."

"I'm sorry?"

"Don't become a believer."

"I don't understand. After what I saw yesterday..." Her sentence unravelled into an uncomfortable silence.

"What you saw here was nothing but a combination of strobe lights, hidden speakers, and years of practice."

"Then you *are* a fake." Maxine's sense of disappointment surprised her. "That's why they ran you out of the spiritualist circles in places like Lily Dale, right?"

"That's not why. I practice something called mixed mediumship."

"I don't know what that is."

"Not many people do. Mixed mediumship is a kind of guerilla spiritualism. We'll do whatever it takes to reach the spirit realm. Yes, we use all the so-called respectable methods: the cone, the circle of believers, the candle. But we'll also employ trickery: sound effects, coloured lights, cheesecloth in place of ectoplasm."

"So it really is just theatre to you? A scam?"

"You had the dream, didn't you?"

Maxine was unsure how to respond. "That..." she stammered, "could have been... What do you call it? Post-hypnotic suggestion."

"I never hypnotized you."

"Maybe not. But you did trick me."

"Only to get you where you needed to be."

"And where's that exactly?"

"In a state of openness, a frame of mind where you might touch the spirit realm. Look, I understand that right now you're feeling cheated because I didn't play fair. I didn't conduct myself the way a respectable medium should. But let me ask you, if we'd sat in my attic for five hours and all you'd walked away with was a phantom smell of your grandmother's perfume and a few faint taps on the table, would you really have been any more of a believer than you were this morning?"

"At least that would have been more believable than the carnival show you gave me yesterday."

"But the carnival show worked, didn't it? That's the essence of mixed mediumship. Why should we tax the spirits by making them move a water glass two inches just so some skeptic might be convinced of something metaphysical? If we give the spirits a helping hand by making the séance room scary and strange, the people won't just 'believe,' they will experience."

"Experience what?"

"One cannot tell of it; they can only be shown it, and it's different for most people. But there is one place... an island... a very ancient island. Once a person is shown it, they will feel it forever. You've seen it, Maxine. It called to you. Now you need to heed the call, but that takes time, training. You need to be initiated."

"But what about all the lies you fed your clients, all the people who came to you half-crazy with grief that you just dropped?"

"None of them were worthy," said Vivien. Her tone was as cold and unforgiving as iron. "I never made them any promises about staying in touch with lost loved ones. I put out the call into the void. Usually the void remains just that: a void. Occasionally a stray ghost slips through, but that's not anything earth-shattering, especially compared to those rare times."

"And what happens in these so-called rare times?"

"The void answers back."

Maxine tried to swallow but found she had no saliva. "You're saying that's what my dream was, the void answering your call?"

"We can't be certain. Not yet that is. You're going to have to truly commit yourself if you want to see this through."

"To what?"

"Your passage through the void and into the heart of the real. We're close to the secret of being."

"Look," Maxine lifted her hands in a gesture of resignation, "that's not what I wanted out of this."

"It doesn't matter what we want. There is no other option for us. We go on."

Whether it was the allure of the unknown or perhaps of Vivien herself, Maxine felt an irresistible curiosity about the proposal. She agreed to try the initial steps of her training, with the caveat that she would leave if things got too weird.

So began a series of tests. Maxine was made to recount her dream more times than she could track. She eventually moved into Vivien's home, at which point the nightmare became recurrent. Vivien obsessed over every thought and feeling that Maxine experienced. She prepared hallucinogenic salves for her pupil, which she spread on her flesh, and left her bolted inside a coffin in her attic until she was able to hear the faint, cacophonous fluting, the music beyond the spheres.

After many gruelling months, Maxine was struck with the realization that she'd somehow been seduced into a grand mystical quest that was more Vivien's than hers. One night Maxine went to her mentor and announced she was finished with everything.

It was the first time she ever saw Vivien panic. She pleaded with Maxine not to give up, assuring her that they were both very close to a breakthrough. When these metaphysical baubles failed to convert her, Vivien led Maxine to her bedroom and provided her with days of carnal delights and promises of undying love, the likes of which she'd never thought possible. Maxine could not help but be swept away in such emotional and physical tides.

Soon after, Maxine broached the topic of marriage, which Vivien skillfully dodged. She assured Maxine that the island from her dreams, and all it contained, was very real. What's more, she knew where to find it. That was of utmost urgency. Love, a wedding, a future, all these paled in comparison.

"Make this pilgrimage and we can be together forever," she said, kissing her hands. "Don't you want us to know the meaning behind your dream?"

Maxine admitted that she did, but at her core the prospect of being with Vivien was the greater motivation. All this aside, she studied the crude map she was finally given, and on the appointed day set out on her pilgrimage.

The afternoon was sliding toward dusk by the time Maxine finally set foot on the island's rocky shore. Dragging the canoe out of the lake and flipping it over was a struggle, for her arms were spent from paddling.

The hike inland was random; there was no footpath, or if there had been, it had long been overtaken by the untamed greenery. Maxine pressed on, squinting her eyes against the endless fog of gnats. She cursed her stupidity at forgetting to bring insect repellent. The gloaming seemed to be descending with unnatural swiftness, and she knew her flashlight would soon be required.

A devious quality obscured the crescent of six standing stones. Every time Maxine believed herself to be trudging in their direction, they would drift farther away. She began to wonder if they were nothing more than a mirage.

Night settled upon the island, leaving Maxine to navigate using only her flashlight and the diminished glow of a waning moon. In time even this meagre allowance was reduced when the batteries in the flashlight were drained. The beam flickered through the endless trees, then died altogether.

Exhausted, ravenous, and yes, frightened to her core, Maxine fell to the ground and whimpered. Then she began to scream, though her hysteria brought no sense of release. She was depleted. Vivien had warned her that this pilgrimage was likely to break her, and she'd been right. As much as it pained her, Maxine had to admit that she'd been bested. Her dream, the strange piping she'd heard both there and earlier in the day out on the lake, the possibility of seeing what it all meant, no longer mattered to her. Once on her feet again, she made an about-face and began the humiliating walk back to her canoe.

It was a long hike and was made even more tedious by the barrage of thoughts that assailed her. Could she truly put all this behind her and slip back into the life she'd known before the séance, before the dream, before Vivien? Everything that had brought her pleasure or distraction now felt dull, pointless. She knew Vivien would reject her once she learned she had aborted the quest. For all she knew, the medium was somehow watching her right now, which would account for the strange feeling she'd had since coming ashore, a feeling of being scrutinized, studied from on high.

Perhaps that feeling of being watched, of being judged, would never fade. No matter how far she went or how deeply she interred the memory of this ordeal, she had seen it in a dream. And now the forces in that dream were seeing her. She would never be free of it.

The thought stimulated a certain defiance, and she decided that she would, no, that she *must* see the pilgrimage through to the end. It was a struggle to not let the distance she now had to cross a third time daunt her. Even as the crescent of stones was now wholly obscured by the trees and the blackness hanging between them, Maxine's resolve remained strong. She would find it. This truth was hers by right, for she had undertaken Vivien's teachings and training. She had made the long journey out to this godforsaken island and had earned her initiation fair and square.

But this grit only served to move Maxine further away from her goal. At one point she looked about and realized she was utterly and hopelessly lost. The tall stones had fled the island and the shore was apparently playing a game of hide-and-seek with her, for even a furious run in a straight line in what she was convinced was the direction back to her canoe ended up drawing her hopelessly deeper into the trees. She cried out for help but received only the echo of her own strangled voice.

Finally she crumpled to the ground in complete resignation. Her body trembling, her mind numb, she acquiesced to the secret of the island and admitted defeat.

At that instant, the crescent of stones appeared to her, plainly and so close that she felt she could touch them. She blinked several times to eliminate the possibility that the nearby clearing was not a trick of the light. Too weak to rise, she crawled like a lizard toward the edge of the forest, toward the circular patch above which loomed the great stones.

The setting was identical in every way to her nightmare.

In the dream, which, thanks to Vivien, she could recollect in greater detail than most memories from her waking life, Maxine had found herself prostrate before six towering figures. Each had been dressed in a coarse grey robe, whose cowl transformed the wearer's face into a void. Maxine had watched herself, so puny and frail, crawl exhaustedly onto a cube that sat embedded in the earth. This cube's surface had been frigid, and its form had been unyielding against her frame. She had smelled the distinctly metallic smell and felt the scabs of rust. It was a great bed of iron. Had it been some geological marvel spat up from the molten strata deep underground? Had it fallen from the heavens, shaped by eons of wind and rain? Or perhaps the cube and its stone sentinels were the only remaining elements of some nameless faith now lost to living memory?

Her puny dream-body had stretched out upon the slab. She had stared upward. The black sky resembled a dome studded with vivid, shining stars. It was then that the crazy piping music had entered the dream. The source had been impossible to determine, for the sound seemed to assail Maxine from everywhere at once.

The music marked the change in the dream, where it slid from a vision of oddness and awe to a stifling nightmare. Much to Maxine's chagrin, this shift also marked the moment when her memory of the dream began to muddy. She could recall how her focus had shifted from the sky to the faces of the towering figures, and that these faces had begun to change. The piping reached an ear-splitting volume, and following that, her only impression of the dream was... eyes. Vivien had attempted every method at her disposal to draw out more information about this final impression (which lacked even an image). The only thing Maxine would say was the word "eyes."

But now that she was here, she was able to see and touch and smell the environment. The island's strange temple-like ruin had proved itself to be something far more tangible than the delicate floss out of which dreams are woven. Maxine believed she would be able to see it, to face and understand it. The only thing left to do was re-enact her nightmare.

She removed her clothing, surprised by how her usual self-conscious feelings of embarrassment over her body were absent. She entered the clearing with a feeling of genuine gratitude. Her memories of these early stages of the dream were something she now drew on as though they'd been rehearsals. She paced the circumference of the iron bed, grazing her hand over its cold edges, appreciating its density. There was something ominous about this half-buried cube, and yet she felt almost teased by it, as if it was daring her to climb upon it and reify her dream.

That's exactly what she did. The face of the cube felt the way she imagined an autopsy table might: cold, clinical, and unforgiving. Naked on the iron bed, she took a deep breath and looked into the sky. Her view was untrammeled, the empyrean sight making her giddy. For a long, reflective time, she simply watched the stars, yet during her contemplation the very unpleasant inkling from the dream, the sense she was not the watcher but the one being watched, thickened in her mind.

She glanced over at the hooded statues. Their scale, coupled with the faceless gazes, made Maxine feel puny and somehow unworthy of this place. She wanted to apologize to the stones. This strange temple, if that's what it was, was clearly a very sacred place. She now understood that she was not one of them. This pilgrimage had been a mistake. If her dream had been the invitation to this spiritual test, Maxine had earnestly accepted and was now quite content to fail. Vivien, no doubt, would leave her, perhaps even hate her. But she was prepared to deal with the fallout.

Yet when she attempted to rise, she found herself pinioned to the iron bed by invisible hands. Like an insect pinned to a board. The more she struggled, the greater the pressure on her torso and limbs. Her cries for help were swirled into a new, or rather very old, sound, one that fell over the island from somewhere impossibly high above, perhaps from a remote void behind the stars. This was the piping from her dream, she knew. But whatever was to come was a complete mystery to her, for this was the moment when she'd always woken abruptly, never able to recall what she had seen.

Oh, how she wished she had remained blind to it all.

The starry sky had begun to bubble and churn, as though the galaxies themselves were boiling over. The night funneled inward, spun faster and faster, and eventually the tiny eye at the end of the funnel stretched open. Fire was revealed, a tempest of flames and lava and colours. They spurted and flared, sometimes forming mountains the size of moons, only to engulf these majestic peaks and incinerate them. Infinite forms arose and were then slain by it. A womb and a crematory working in perfect harmony.

A sudden light came blazing down upon her pathetic form, and she screwed up her face to shield herself from its blinding glare. Tilting her head, she could just discern that these beams of clear and searing light were blasting from inside the stone hoods of the six sentinels.

The light began to speak, to stab her ill-prepared mind with forbidden truths. The reality of it was too great, and when those sheets of focused light began ever so slowly to dim, Maxine was able to look upon the immense black hole in the sky. The flames had been smothered; a great mass of lidless eyes stared down at her.

Then she grasped it, the deep secret at the nuclear core of all things. She laughed an idiot's laugh as she let everything go. It was all so clear, as simple as a stone in the forest.

The planet revolved around the sun many times. People went to and from the island, for it was a simple place to locate. But its secret heart, its soul, appeared only to those who'd been called. Those random visitors who ventured there would often describe the awful feelings of confusion they experienced; an acute panic that made them feel like everything around them was unpredictable, untrustworthy, chaotic. None ever glimpsed the crescent of stone sentinels or the iron bed in the ground.

The next one to successfully make their way to the temple was Vivien Barlowe. The pilgrimage nearly felled her several times, but she refused to yield. She was wise enough to know that her body was perilously near to permanent dysfunction, yet she would not allow herself to die without knowing that which had so long been denied her.

When she saw the stone giants were now seven in number, a spike of bitterness pierced her sluggish heart. She scowled at the newest effigy of one of her students, another who had surpassed their teacher and learned the secrets of the chaos that fuels this universe. The others, those many forgettable clients that had come to her with pitiful aching hearts, had yielded nothing. All of them had failed to hear the piping.

And then came Maxine…

Vivien was not fooled by the shiftless appearance of these stone colossuses. She knew that they had mastered the dance of cosmic discord. How she wanted to join them, how she wanted to feel that turmoil raging about her, to dwell in the eye of the storm.

She stripped and dragged her wizened flesh onto the iron slab. Overhead the stars were obscured by heavy clouds, and her aging eyes were having trouble discerning the hooded figures. She began to cry. After decades of creating ghostly spectacles for other people to see and marvel at, the last thing, the *only* thing that she wanted was to be seen.

The Root King

Lauri Taneli Lassila

translated from Finnish by the author

An nescis, mi fili,
quantilla prudentia mundus regatur.
—Axel Oxenstierna

I

IT WAS THE last time I left the forest. I had been visiting my uncle and cousins downriver, where I was well celebrated and met some possible brides. But in the middle of the festivities I received a letter urging me to return to my holy home, the citadel of our kingdom. I was dismayed at having to cut short such a joyful visit, but I knew grandiose celebrations of the princely homecoming awaited me. In addition, my sudden departure was made easier by my uncle's gracious invitation to visit again in the autumn and to take part in the harvest festival. So in the end I started off toward home in high spirits.

On our way back, we had to travel through the dense woods of the riverside. Each night someone had to watch for wolves and keep the fire burning. Twice we were ambushed by bandits. On both occasions the fiends managed to slay a guardsman, by surprise and in the back, of course. We exacted retribution in due proportion and flayed the bandits we captured alive. I hoped their shrieks and prayers made an impression on their fellows hiding in the wilderness, as well as the skins we nailed on the large pines along the trail.

The woods are indeed a foul place. Everywhere and at all times you must be on guard, ready to defend yourself against attack. Clean water is nowhere to be found, for all manner of beasts drink from the river. Thick roots and thickets take over even those narrow pathways the hands of man and the hooves of horses have managed to clear into that hostile world. How very difficult can mere will-less plants be, not to speak of mindless beasts! If we left our provisions without a guard for even a moment, you could be sure something four-legged was having a go at them.

In truth, I was overjoyed to leave that dreadful place and reach the country road—if not civilization, then at least law and order. In the lush river valley, peasants hurried along the curving roads with their families, carts filled to the brim with the pitiful bounty of the earth. Bowing deeply, sunburnt men greeted our convoy with amusing solemnity, their voluptuous wives glancing away coyly. Filthy children in rags laughed and played around us, with no fear of our noble emblems, gold, and ornament. The hills and valleys were dotted with crude shacks, each with a gray wisp slithering out of its chimney as a sign of habitation. I quite dislike the rabble of the peripheries. How is one to trust people so dirty you can't make out the expressions on their faces? Luckily, they in turn have the good judgement to fear the king's men, and in that sense are preferable to the inhabitants of the wilderness, who have abandoned all order and any semblance of humanity.

At the last turn of the river, we finally saw the beautiful end of our journey, our golden home. The White City of the North shimmered in the light of the already darkening evening sun like a blessed pearl! Gilded domes blazed between the towers pale as virgins. The closer we came to the massive outer walls, the smaller I understood myself to be. This city had nurtured and sheltered not only me, but an immeasurable and unbreakable chain of my ancestors reaching far into the past, far beyond the recollections of any family chronicles. Now my father ruled there, and one day I would too. As little as I understood this did I understand how the city had been built. Its hallowed towers rose so majestic, so high into the sky, that looking up from their base they seemed to finely curve on their way to heaven like immense trees or roots. The walls were of such heavy and fair stone: who had brought them here, and how? Could such beauty be the result of human hands? What kind of men had my ancestors been to carve out such an oasis of grace into this cruel wilderness? In many ways, we men of today were no match for our predecessors...

The hooves of our steeds clapped against the cobblestones as we rode through the city's golden gates. In the towers, thick flags of honor billowed full of wind to welcome me home. Citizens gathered along the streets and laid out pine branches as a carpet for our horses. I was offered children to kiss and bless. Usually such gestures of old women annoyed me greatly, but I was so elated at my return that this time I even grabbed a small one's hand and squeezed it warmly. The child began to cry, but I did not let it sour my joy.

Soon we emerged from the serpentine merchants' streets onto the royal road, which opened up into a widening fairway in the midst of the densely built houses of the commoners. We rode in through the arch with the guards waiting for us in the castle yard, their hands at salute. Seeing me, the maidens laughed, and I laughed as well. But the castle silenced me.

That noble, holy building towered above me like a mountain. Many times had I seen its towers and windows, but now there was something novel about them. Perhaps I looked upon them with new eyes following such a long journey. I can't help but suspect that perhaps I did feel something now, perhaps some kind of premonition of the ordeal to come, an ordeal hidden by those familiar walls of my home, so pleasing from the outside. At that time I could not suspect anything, only let myself fall tired into a childlike wonder at the sight of those white and gold walls decorated with such elaborate detail by hands long ago stiffened by death and eaten by earth.

They were covered with meticulously accurate carvings, visible only in the evening twilight and the bright morning, as the sunlight hit the stone at just the right angle. The carvings seemed fine enough to flee before one's sight. At first glance they were easy to pass over as simple vines and stars, or as pure decorative shapes with no reference to anything real. But over the decades I had often stopped to inspect them and had realized they told a story. The longer one focused on a single part of the wall, the finer the details and differences became. One could find characters, men and beasts, heavenly and underground creatures, kings and queens, princes too. The sequence of events was difficult to discern, as each picture seemed to continue in all directions, as if the tale had no single course but went on above and below itself, as well as to all sides. I had never truly dedicated myself to deciphering that tale since the sun shone in the right way only for a short time, and soon the carvings were overtaken by shadows. It would have required a long twilight or a slow sunrise to investigate the pictures properly.

We rode in through the archway of the inner yard and the gates of the castle were shut behind us. In the middle of the courtyard stood my father's advisor, a once tall man who had become weighed down by his age and tasks. He had served under my grandfather as well. The ancient advisor always smelled of moist earth, as if he had already begun to decompose, as we liked to joke with the guards while up late drinking.

The advisor stood more upright than usual and appeared quite serious in his black and red robe. I suppose it was the first thing which truly made me suspicious. Not that he wasn't always as serious, but usually he greeted me with pleasure upon returning from my travels. This time he lifted his hand in an arduous manner, without delight, and did not bother even to pretend there was any joy in our reunion.

"Welcome home, prince."

"Hail, advisor," I replied.

"Rid yourself of your traveling armour. Then meet me and your father in his chambers, as soon as possible."

"But I was looking forward to a bath! I'm sure the castle maidens have suffered immensely waiting to entertain—"

"You'll have time to bathe later," the advisor snapped.

I fell speechless at such arrogance. And coming from a subject at that! The advisor didn't stay for my answer, but pulled up the hems of his robe and hurried inside the castle. I gathered it must have been important for him to act that way. But I was also sure I would let my father know of such crude behaviour, which threatened my authority in the eyes of the other denizens.

Once I had made it inside the castle, removed my armour, and had a glass of mead to drink, I went to my father's chambers. Despite the advisor's arrogance, I was much pleased to see my father again. As I set foot inside the room, I saw a large coffin in the middle of it and unsuspectingly stepped beside it. I had, of course, realized at once that someone had died, but I could not have dreamed of seeing my father's pale face. The advisor closed the door I had left open, barring it from the inside.

"The king is dead, young prince," he said.

"What plot is this?" I asked.

The advisor looked at me.

"Who killed my father? You?"

"Calm yourself, dear prince."

"Answer the question."

"Of course I did not kill the king."

"What did he die of?"

"I don't know."

"Why did you not give him medicine?"

"He died suddenly. He was well when you left, remember—"

"Was he poisoned?"

"There is no reason to think so."

"But are you sure he wasn't?"

"No, but—"

"It must be investigated thoroughly."

"Yes, it will be investigated, as long as—"

"At once. Call the court, I shall question them one by one."

"Unfortunately that will not do, prince."

"Why not?"

"The king's death must be kept a secret."

I didn't quite understand, and the advisor must have seen it in my face.

"No one knows but you and me. The servants who found the king dead on his bed I ordered executed."

"You had them executed?"

"There must be no reason for the kingdom or any citizen's heart to bear restless thoughts. An empty throne is the most dangerous, young prince. Wars are fought over it. I am sorry I could not send you word of your father's death. On such an important matter we can't trust even messengers. The king's passing must be kept in absolute secrecy until everything is ready for your coronation."

"Did father leave me any message?"

"No. His passing was sudden, as a royal one should be. It's dangerous too, if the throne falls ill."

"I was supposed to travel south in autumn."

"Listen to me, young prince, when I say that all will become clear, I promise you. Right now, everything should still be a little blurry. But do not worry, I will help you on your throne as I helped your father in his time."

"I don't want to become king."

"You are already a man, dear prince. A man hasn't the luxury of wanting any more than refusing. You will become a king. A king has full power over his subjects. Over himself a king can make no decisions, but always acts according to his responsibility, and a king has no other responsibility but to protect his kingdom."

At that moment I could not weigh the advisor's words. I held my father's cold hand and spoke to him in my mind. He looked tired, and death had yellowed his skin. That proud brow would never again rise in joy at the sight of his son.

"I want to be alone," I said. "Leave me to grieve."

"Not yet."

"I have had just about enough of your insolence!"

"Patience, young master."

"I am having a wonderful visit with my cousins, representing our kingdom's interests in the south, when I am lured by a fraudulent letter, or at the very least a withholding of the truth, to return to my home where you demand me, unbathed, to my father's room, where you then reveal to me he has died. And after all this you dare to resist a clear order? My father is dead!"

"Do not yell, young master. The court will hear you."

"To the devils with the court!"

The advisor wisely ignored my outburst. He stood there quietly for a moment, until I myself came to understand how inappropriate my behaviour was. I took a deep breath.

"What do we do now?"

"We will crown you king," he said.

"But I am not worthy of my father."

"It makes no difference. You are king all the same. In the world there exist better kings and worse kings, like everything else. But a kingdom always needs a king, and even a bad king is better than no king at all."

I could not bring myself to reply. I looked at my father's noble features.

"Now you must trust me, prince. Do you?"

I nodded.

"Good. Do you know where the hirelings' vegetable storeroom is?"

"I played there as a child."

"Come there when the moonlight reaches your father's face. We will prepare your coronation. There all will become clear." The advisor opened the barred door and slid through to the hallway on the other side. "And do not let anyone in, you hear. Close the door with your royal key when you leave. And do not talk to anyone in the hallway." Then he closed the door, and I heard his steps fade into the distance.

What repugnant plots did the advisor have in mind for me? I did not like what I had heard, not at all. That the people had not been told their king was dead! That the servants who had found my father's body and had come forward about it, as their duty was, had been executed in cold blood, and not even by my decree but by my father's advisor's... Was he to be trusted? I did not like this sort of secrecy. It was not part of kingly rule. The king had to be without fault and open to his people like the sun. My kingship was not off to a promising start as I immediately had to stay silent on a matter as important as the king's death and sneak around my own castle at night, hiding from the maidens like an intruder. Was it just? Was it even true? Was all this some twisted conspiracy, heaven forbid, or preparations for a coup?

II

I waited by the coffin with my dreadful thoughts until I started at the moonlight on my father's pale features, which seemed now to be glowing. I darted out of the room and locked the door, hurrying to the cellar through long hallways with blood-red family ryas hung on the walls. I avoided the eyes of the servants, so my features swollen by tears would not have revealed the king's death and my own weakness in the face of it.

I descended to the lowest floor of the castle, half underground and populated by servants. I went past the kitchen to the servants' cellar, where I found the advisor waiting for me. With a look of impatience, he gestured me to follow and started walking ahead, not to the cellar but past it. I followed him deeper down the hallway. The sounds of the servants grew fainter with each step. Soon all I could hear was the sound of the advisor's robe and the echo of our steps in the bleak hall. I had never been so far into the servants' quarters, which seemed strange, since I had often played with the servants as a child. Finally we came to a halt at a door that looked no different from all the rest.

"Where are you taking me?" I asked.

The advisor hissed for silence and rattled his large, clumsy keys at the lock until it clacked and the door creaked open. He stepped in and I followed into a small room. He told me to bar the door, and I turned around and grabbed a large wooden plank leaning against the wall. I flinched, touching wet, rotten wood. Yet the air in the room was no more humid than was usual in a cellar. I steeled myself and set the crumbling wooden plank in its place on the door.

As if the advisor had heard my thoughts, he said, "It will hold. It has held until now." I turned around to look at him, but he had already disappeared behind a corner with a swish of his robe. As we stepped into the room, I had not noticed there were corners. I followed the advisor to the back of the room, where he was now fumbling at another door. This one, opening upward, led to a cellar. I helped him lift it and immediately my nostrils were overwhelmed by a shocking smell, a powerful stench of mold. For a moment I was shaken. I had never smelled anything like it. It was so forceful and strong, it seemed as if it no longer welled forth from anything decaying but had achieved an independent force, a life of its own.

The advisor told me to step inside. He followed and stood next to me in the cramped cellar. I gave a look at the door above us, but the advisor said, "That one can stay open." He took a torch from the wall, lit it, and gave it to me. Then he took one for himself and descended some stairs. I realized I was standing on a small platform from which a spiral staircase, gleaming with moisture, led into the depths of the earth. In the flickering light of the torches I saw that in places the stairs grew moss.

"What place is this? Why have you brought me here?"

As the advisor answered, he did not stop or even look back at me over his shoulder: "You are very wise to ask, young prince, since the answer to those questions is one and the same."

"Quit the riddles, old man! This is an order by the future king."

He stopped and turned to looked at me. At first I was afraid I had insulted him, but he gave me a crooked smile. "The future king cannot yet give any orders, young prince."

"King or not, you are in my service," I tried.

The advisor turned from me to continue his way without reply. I was about to lose my temper. Perhaps he felt my burning gaze in his back since, after descending a few steps, he asked, "Do you think our city is beautiful, young prince?"

"Yes, the most beautiful." I started down the stairs after him.

"You say it with conviction," the advisor said, half to himself.

"What has this got to do with my father's death and the coming coronation?"

"This city is in the middle of a terrifying wilderness, is it not?"

"I know. This morning I still awoke in the woods."

"Who do you think carved the golden white towers of this city into such a place, cleared a space for them from all the beasts?"

"My forefathers, the first kings."

"Good, you know the past well."

"What difference does it make? We were supposed to be organizing the coronation and should be planning a grand funeral."

"The crown has come to you from the past, and in the grave your father shall be returned to the past. From there he has come, just as you have. We all come from the past. Like the stars in the sky come from above, so they can go elsewhere, according to their set arc and route; so men, too, have an arc and route. In order for the king to know where he is going, he must know from whence he came. That is why we read the heavens and interpret the motions of the stars."

"All right, but what does it have to do with this or anything else?"

"Patience, young prince. What would you say if I could show you a star up close? Take you next to one so you could touch its cold, bright surface?"

"I would be astonished and delighted, of course."

"We are going to see the opposite of a star here, deep under the earth. It is sure to astonish you."

I noticed I had grown used to the smell of mold, but now, in the flickering light of our torches, I saw some sort of translucent flakes or tiny flies dance around the flames.

"Your father saw it before his coronation," the advisor continued. "And his father. All the way to the beginning have the kings of our realm taken these stairs and come here to see this underground opposite of a star, their own root."

"What the devil do you mean?"

The advisor stood still once more and seemed to draw a deep breath. "Why do you think the Egyptians held their most holy ceremonies underground?"

I thought for a moment, then shrugged. "Hidden from the view of the uninitiated? Because it's easy to hide under the earth."

"And what else do you think has hidden there in the passing of time?"

Such a strange question chilled my bones. Before I could reply, he started on his way down the damp spiral stairway again.

III

My feet ached as the stairs finally came to an end in a narrow hallway. In the torchlight, its walls appeared more moss than stone, which could have been natural as well. Had the hallway been mined into the bedrock? I thought of it but couldn't believe it. What force would have done that? What man? And so deep...

Terrifying rumors of caverns under the royal castle had reached my ears over the years, but I had always considered such talk to be for the old women or enemies of the realm. It seemed obvious I was now in one of those dreadful dungeons, which I had heard my nurses whisper about while my father was away.

The musty stench of the air again grew pungent and lively, similar to the smell of hops vine. It was the smell of mold, no mistake about it, but I had never before smelled mold so rough, bitter, and at the same time sweet, as if it grew vigorous and lush. It made the hairs inside my nose stand up and stung my nostrils, not altogether in an unpleasant way. The reek had something attractive to it. Or—now that I recall, it wasn't really disgusting at that point. Frightening, perhaps, due to its strength and novelty.

As I advanced along the hallway, I leaned on the wall for support, but was startled and quickly pulled my hand away as I felt something stirring under my palm. I shook my hand vigorously and shone a light. The wall was black with flies. The insects did not buzz onto the wall or off it, but clambered all over one another, pushing each other off onto the floor where they started upward along the wall again with blind determination, a shining, churning black mass.

I continued on, unable to look away from that enchantingly hideous sight. But I stumbled. The floor had become rough, less polished. Under my boots it really felt like rock now. The advisor looked back at me, and I noticed he had stopped before two large black doors carved with decorations from top to bottom.

"I went through these doors with your father when his father died," he said. "Every king has gone through here before taking power. You will not return from behind them. The prince will be left there, and the king will come out. This is a kind of initiation into a mystery. All will become clear inside." He looked at me intensely, as if he had been weighing his words. I thought I saw some sorrow in his eyes.

"Farewell, young prince."

I nodded. "See you on the other side."

I no longer harbored any doubts, simply because I was bursting with curiosity. The advisor turned to open the doors with his huge keys. The heavy panes wailed and cracked, clearly swollen by the moisture. In the light of the torches I saw some sort of mist or fog billow out from between the opening doors. Perhaps it was just the dust of centuries thrown up into the air. The advisor heaved the doors open, peeked into the hallway behind me as if to make sure we were not being followed, then gestured me to pass through. I took a deep breath and steeled myself, stepping into a small, dim chamber. The advisor stepped in behind me and pulled the doors shut from their heavy iron handles.

I looked around, but the purpose of the room was difficult to understand. Even though it did appear small, the furthermost wall seemed to disappear behind some mist or haze. The walls were rough hewn, but they too were covered with carvings. Among them I thought I made out similar crude paintings of blood as the ones I had found in ancient caves during my travels in the wilderness. The darkness here was thick, the room full of it. Torchlight flickered and faltered in the stale air.

There was no furniture except a kind of altar right in front of us. At first sight it seemed like a slab of stone dragged into place, upon which lay some figure. I glanced at the advisor, who gestured for me to approach it. I stepped next to the altar and saw the figure more clearly. Even now it brings a sweat to recall that sight.

It was like a grown man but nearly twice as tall. Its general form—two legs, two arms, and a head—did appear human. But its face resembled some beast of the ancient night. Its eyes were closed, but even in sleep its great white teeth gleamed between swollen lips. The head rested on a thick jumble of knotted hair. Massive arms squeezed a sword or a staff of some kind I had never seen nor have seen since, not even in the wondrous palaces of the East. From the jaw down, the creature's skin seemed as if iron leather—or else the strange body was covered by an even stranger armour, decorated with stunningly beautiful and detailed ornamentation. To my horror, these decorations brought to mind the art of the royal castle's outer walls.

Terrified, I leaned closer to examine the creature's face. It seemed permanently twisted into a grimace of pain. I saw no movement in the features, but somehow they were filled with primal life and I didn't doubt for a second that the creature was alive. I was afraid to be so close, but my horror was fierce enough that it in fact drove me toward the creature, not away from it. In the dim light I could just barely see how out of the creature's great nostrils there reached something pale, like dried mucus. Then I saw those small white tendrils move under my gaze.

I jumped back. From that new position I could see the altar was not a solid slab but intricately carved into the shape of a table. The creature was lying on this table, and underneath I saw something that made me shudder, and I immediately understood it to be the source of the smell. It was not mold but a plant of some sort, light and pale like the skin of the dead. It grew up out of the floor and through the table, apparently into the insides of the creature. It was like a sprout covered with faint pale hair that seemed to sway on its own, without any current of air. Here and there along the sprout there gasped mucusy slits, holes resembling gills.

I turned to the advisor in disgust. He was still standing by the door.

"What is this?" I demanded.

"This is the Root King. He ruled here before man. He was a warlike and cruel ruler. Now he is imprisoned in incense dreams. Your forefathers built their city to protect this chamber. Some say the whole kingdom is just a dream of the Root King."

I could not believe what I was hearing. As I breathed in, the stench of the mold stung my throat, reminding me of springtime's first nettles, the bitter fertility of their flowers. At the same time, there was rot and decay in the scent. I did not know which came first, the rot or the fruit; was the fruit rotting or did the rot bear fruit?

"You lie," I said, because I could think of nothing else.

"For ages, no one has remembered those times. But knowledge of them has been passed on in the lineage of kings. And knowledge of this place. Knowledge of the Root King. For the Root King sleeps, because he entered into a covenant with those plants, one of which is that root. In ancient times they were at war. The Root King was victorious and about to decimate the plants altogether when he cornered them into this cavern. Here the plants suggested to the Root King that if he would allow them to live, they would give him all their knowledge. The Root King was a great warrior, if such a word is fitting. He bathed whole lands in blood. But he lacked knowledge, so he agreed and laid himself on the altar. The root grew in him, and thereafter the realm has been able to enjoy this holy peace we know so well. As long as the Root King sleeps, our kingdom shall know no war."

"But hasn't our kingdom been involved in several wars, even in my lifetime? My father was wounded by an arrow of the Western Wolves!"

A hollow smile flashed across the advisor's face. "With all due respect, young prince, that has not been war. Or if we will call it war, we will need a new word for that which reigned before the Root King's sleep, and which will reign once more if he were to wake up."

I turned to look at the creature on the altar. Its sleep appeared deep and peaceful. It could've been dead if only it wasn't so ancient, having lain on the slab for so long, while at the same time looking so alive, like it wasn't asleep at all but had only closed its eyes for a moment. I looked at the appalling root extending out of a crack on the floor underneath the altar. It swayed slowly, like a meadow in an evening breeze.

"Where does the root lead?"

"The root connects the King to the underground gods beneath the seven hells. The underground gods are in turn immaterially bound to their celestial progenitors."

"Where does it end?"

"No one knows. Perhaps in something equally mad and asleep."

I couldn't be sure in the flickering light, but it seemed the root was twisting and convulsing under my gaze, as if it was bothered by the attention.

I turned again to the advisor. "Why did you bring me here? Why are you telling me all this?"

"The king must know the truth about his kingdom. Kingship is first and foremost carrying the truth, and the king is the one who knows the truth. A king who lacks knowledge of the roots of his kingdom is but a pawn in a greater game."

I remembered my father's pale visage somewhere immeasurably far above us. "What must I do?"

"Protect the realm at any cost. Guard the citadel from attack. For if the din of war were to reach the ears of the Root King, the temptation would be too great and it would wake. Right now it sleeps with magic herbs and infinite visions. But it is not dead but a dream."

"This is a dream."

"No, young prince, for the first time in your life you are awake. A wise man must know that the night precedes the day and before long follows it. You now know that your kingdom has been built on the Root King, and that when he rises, all else shall fall. Your duty is to protect the Root King from the call of war and so your kingdom from the Root King."

"What would happen if he were to wake?"

"The fields would bear a bloody harvest. Everywhere the farmer's plow would strike rotting corpses. The sun would rise red from all the steaming gore he'd have shed, and the sky would blacken with carrion crows. The age of men would be over. Your family has ruled only because he has slept."

"But the crown is a holy inheritance! Why do you dirty it with this filth? Why do you tarnish the king's noble white robes with this rot!"

The advisor laughed.

"Answer, you fool!"

"The crown has not been dirtied, but revealed. Those who cleaned it are the ones who have lied to you. I merely remove their lies from in front of the true dirt."

"You are mad."

"And what a world, where it takes a madman to tell the king the truth…"

IV

We left the cellar and never spoke of it again. But I never forgot. Not a day has gone by I haven't thought of it. I have told you everything just as I remember. I have not left anything out, as difficult as it is due to both my own shameful weakness and the terror of the thing in the cellar. But the king must know all. If the king doesn't know all, he is no king but a puppet, a secret vassal. After you have read this letter, you know all, my son. Now you are king. Even if someone else were to sit on this throne, you are king, for only you know. All the others are dead. That is why you must bear the responsibility.

The dark tides of war have once again reached the shores of our realm. The advisor died long ago at the hands of our enemies. I am ill. It is time for you to carry the crown, young prince. I am writing this letter to you because I am afraid I will not live long enough to show you the truth myself. If I should die before you return home, this letter will be delivered to wherever the tides of war have carried you. You will find the key to the cellar on my necklace.

If someone else were to sit on the royal throne when you receive this letter, you must overthrow them at any cost. Do not concern yourself with anything else but the truth. If you do not save the realm from the vassals of the invisible and the fires of war, it will go to ruin. Have no mercy beheading the pretenders. It is best for them as well that you should sit on the throne. Kingship is not in the crown, but in the knowledge of truth. You are now king and will always be king, until you tell the truth to your son in turn.

You might want to disbelieve this, but you are a man now, and a man hasn't the luxury of wanting any more than refusing. You are now king, and the king has no other cause but to protect his kingdom. The king has full power over his subjects, but over himself he can make no decisions, but always acts in accordance with his duty. Triumph in this war, never let it reach our city.

You have been a good son, a better prince than I. You will make a good king. Save my grave from a flood of blood.

With Love and Trust
Your Father, King

Post Scriptum

If you have the slightest of doubts about the integrity of the seal on this letter, kill the messenger at once. Interrogate him to find out if he has told of the contents to anyone, for they too must die. Kingship is not in the crown, but in this letter.

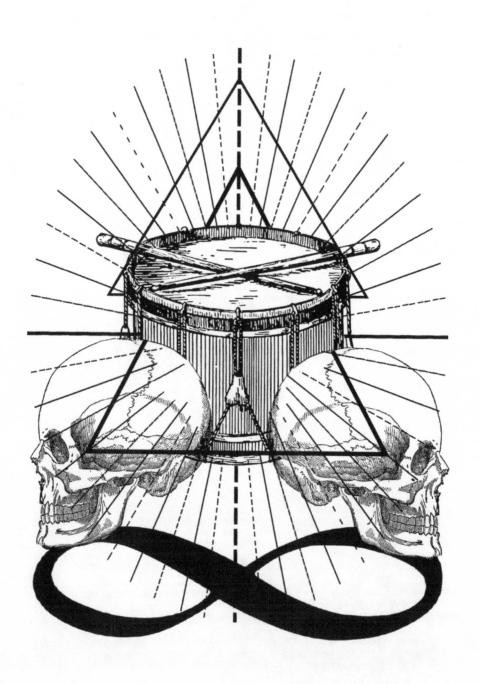

The Infinite Beat

Nathan Carson

WHEN I FIRST saw him standing there, I thought he must have been about seventeen. He wore dirty black clothes, top to bottom, with indecipherable black logos screened or patched over every surface. Although he was a white boy, I could tell there wasn't a whole lot of privilege in his past.

I tried not to look interested. Best to keep him beneath my notice, lest he lose respect for my authority before I could begin the grooming. I drew a heavy silver staple gun from my purse, pressed the white poster to the wall with my dark hand, and *bang-bang-bang-bang*, the paper hung.

The sound startled everyone in the park, but not the kid. His eyes were glazed, open mouth making little bubbles in some chaotic internal rhythm with his dirty-nailed fingers tapping out the rest of the beat on his greasy jeans. I later realized he was stimming; that the only time he ceased fidgeting was when he was playing a corporeal drum or in a catatonic sleep.

For a moment I thought he might be too far gone to bother with. But as soon as I moved away from the bulletin board he stepped up and tore one of the numbers off my flyer. When his hand was in use, he tapped its part with one foot inside a fraying Velcro shoe. Now I knew I had my mark.

"You a drummer?" I asked.

"Huh?" He jammed the scrap of paper in the large pocket of his pullover hoodie and dug a bud I hadn't noticed out of an ear. Even from a distance I could hear a caterwaul of squealing guitars and the pitter-patter of double bass.

"You play?" I asked.

"Yeah," he said.

"Can you read?"

"Of course. Your band poster has a typo. It should say 'Drummer Wanted,' not 'Drummers Wanted.'"

"First off," I said, "I was asking if you can read sheet music. Second, it's not for a band. It's for a school."

"Ah," he said. "Never mind. I hate school." He started to reinsert his earbud and tossed the scrap of paper with our number to the ground.

"Hold on a minute," I said. "What are you listening to?" He held up the earbud to my face, though I wondered why, since I don't hear well with my eyes. But the music was admittedly louder.

"They're called Evisceral Foeticide," he said. "So brutal."

I smiled and looked down at him, aiming to impose. There are perks to being a six-foot-tall black woman in heeled boots. "Sounds like they crush," I responded. "But I guarantee what we do is far darker, and vastly more... intense."

He stared through me for a second, hands pitter-pattering away. I couldn't tell if he was lost in thought, or just lost.

"So, like," he asked, "how many drummers do you have?"

"Right now? Twelve. But we need thirteen."

"Thirteen? How'd you come up with that?"

"It's my lucky number."

"I've never heard of a band with thirteen drummers."

"It's not a band. It's a drum orchestra. I call it..." Here I had to think to make something up that would impress him "...Daemon Sultan."

"That sounds pretty tight!" he said. "But I'm broke. I can't afford to take lessons. I got expelled from my last school, kicked out of my parents' house, and they sold my drums to pay for the dama—for some expenses."

"Well," I said, "today is your lucky day. Because we'll give you the materials *and* teach you how to build your own drums. And our school doesn't cost a dime. In fact, thanks to some generous patrons of the arts who choose to remain nameless, you get paid to learn our special techniques."

I thought his jaw was going to hit the pavement, but he was only blowing a bigger bubble of spit. When it popped, he bent and picked up the scrap of paper.

I gave him a serious nod and the old "be seeing you" gesture and walked away as he resumed that incessant, maddening beat. Once I knew he'd wandered off, I circled back around and tore my poster down. Only its four stapled corners remained. The fact was, he hadn't been wrong about the typo. I only needed one drummer. One whom no one would miss.

Darkness fell on downtown Portland that night as the sun shuddered behind the West Hills. Pale city light reflected off the oppressive cloudbanks. All was shadow and grey, aside from the red walls of my percussion institute.

I sat alone in the courtyard, waiting beneath the carven Caduceus atop the portico entry, bathed in cold luminescence. I had long ago learned the value of patience, though a hint of anxiety—shrill as a piping flute—would ring in my ears until a thirteenth drummer was installed.

The buzz in my pocket might have startled me if it wasn't accompanied by the ringtone a former student had downloaded for unlisted numbers: the church bells and monk chant intro from Ozzy's "Center of Eternity."

"Camalate," I answered.

"Caramel latte?" asked a voice that I immediately recognized as the kid from the park. I rolled my eyes behind closed lids. This was going to be so much work. I hoped he'd be worth it. I took a deep breath.

"Ahem. Camalate Institute. If you're looking for the percussion orchestra," I said, "you've called the right place. I guess we didn't exchange names earlier. I'm Gwen. Gwen Branca. What's your name?"

"It Skarl," he said.

"Skarl? Is that Irish?"

"It's... Karl," he said again. I was glad to hear he had some innate understanding of tempos, rests, and articulation. That would make this whole process a hell of a lot smoother.

"It's after hours, Karl. Can't you sleep?"

"I don't really have anywhere to sleep."

"We have bunks at the school. You want to come see the place?"

"Mmhm."

I gave him the address. Even if he didn't have GPS, the streets are all alphabetical in that part of town. Plus you could say I have more than a semblance of faith. I hung up and went inside to prepare.

"Wow," Karl said as we walked through the great entry hall. "This place is pretty epic."

I didn't answer. I was too distracted by the echo of his seemingly random gait. I'd gotten used to the other students falling into lockstep with me. Give it time, I thought. But there was precious little remaining.

I hadn't bothered to turn on the lights. I knew the way, and he followed. When we reached the first stairwell, Karl raced ahead of me, taking three steps at a time, then four, then two, down down into the darkness. Once I'd calmly reached the bottom, I found him peering through the glass window of the subbasement door, hands stimming wildly on his hips. I brushed by and pressed the heavy bar of the door. When it swung open, distant echoes of drums reverberated out into the stairwell until they were nothing but decaying orphans, cut off again by the same guillotine door.

Our path took us through the circuitous pipe gallery beneath the warehouse and into deeper chambers, which threaded artfully round the city's infamous Shanghai tunnels. I did employ the flashlight on my phone in a few spots, but only because in the past I'd banged my head more than once on a low fixture and didn't want to break my air of authority. If Karl didn't see me as his better, this would never work.

As we passed the gymnasium, then the mess, I asked if he was hungry.

"Naw," he said. "I scored a box of Voodoo in a dumpster on the way here."

"You had donuts for dinner?"

He just smiled and started skipping a bit. I was already trying to establish if he was exhibiting perseveration or hyperfocus, but now the lines were blurred further by a severe sugar rush. Great.

I thought about introducing him to the other students, but I could hear that they were locked into a pattern and didn't want to disturb their communion. Karl clearly wasn't ready to sleep. So I led him to an empty studio with a red sparkle Gretsch drum kit that had far too many rack toms, and let him attack it in his own crude style.

He knew how to grip a stick. And his posture didn't concern me much. His polyrhythms were actually impressive. Power wasn't an issue; even with dampening headphones over my ears, his strikes were loud and he hit hard. But when it came to control, pacing, endurance, restraint, and all other disciplinary factors, Karl was a flopping trilobite with drumsticks protruding from two of its spines.

After a while he stood up from the throne, drenched in sweat. "This place is awesome!" he said.

"I'm glad you approve. Now let's get you a shower and a cell. It's my bedtime too. We have a LOT of work tomorrow."

Monastic life seemed to treat Karl well for the first few days, though I admittedly had other matters to attend to. He didn't interact with the other students that I could see. A secretary reported that he ate his meals at a table alone, or in his cell. Being the only one with long stringy hair set him apart too (the others had shaved their heads once they'd committed). He was playing drums the rest of his waking hours.

Now that he had settled in, it was time to integrate him into our program.

When I entered his cell on the third night, a half dozen dirty food trays were piled up beside an even taller stack of books on the work bench.

"I see you found our library," I said.

"Yeah." He was in a seated position on his cot. "Pretty limited selection. Only two subjects in there: music theory and old religious stuff. I was hoping to find some dark fantasy."

"Oh," I said. "It's in there, if you know what to look for." Now I had to put on some pressure. "Listen, Karl, it's been nice having you. But this place is not a mission or a charity. We do actual work here. So tomorrow we're going to ask you to pack up and move on."

"What?" He looked genuinely fearful, which is exactly what I wanted. The tapping of his hands on his thighs increased in tempo. "How can I stay? What do you need me to do?"

"Well," I said, "I can pull some strings. But first I need you to take these trays to the kitchen and start cleaning up after yourself. Tomorrow you can begin training in our rhythmic principles. But only if you're dead serious."

He nodded furiously, though his eyes stared into a distance far beyond the concrete wall at my back. I nodded at the messy trays and he sprang into action.

Left alone, I picked up the black leather-bound book he'd been reading, an early twentieth century theosophy text on reaching higher dimensions through art and creativity. I didn't know if he'd gleaned anything from it, but at that moment I felt a glimmer of hope.

The fourth day began in a lesson chamber filled with percussion paraphernalia. Towers of marching drums lined the walls. A rack of tubular bells gleamed in one corner. Egg crates and foam were affixed to the ceiling to diminish sound reflection.

"Karl," I said, "this is our first chair, Mung. She'll teach you the thirteen rhythmic principles one by one. Master each of them. It's essential that every student be prepared to perform them perfectly."

Mung was bald, of course. She was wiry and muscular, garbed in a simple orange student robe. "Thank you, Ms. Branca," she said, bowing her head. "Welcome, Karl."

I took my leave then.

At lunchtime I tracked down Mung in the mess hall. "How's he doing?" I asked.

"He is bored," she said. "He is only interested in the complex, four-limbed traditions of his favorite music. Our foundational rhythms do not hold his attention, and he struggles to maintain a solid tempo."

"Thank you, Mung. I'll speak with him."

Karl was in his cell. His food tray was filled but untouched. He lay on his cot, stimming away with his earbuds in. When he saw me enter, he sat up and removed them from his ears.

"I'm trying," he said before I could open my mouth. "But I don't understand the point. Those beats she's teaching me, they're so basic. Why bother?"

"Have you ever put a puzzle together, Karl? One piece by itself doesn't reveal the whole picture. Those rhythms are part of a great whole. Once you hear them all together, I think you'll feel differently. Come with me."

When I left, he followed. We arrived in the gymnasium where the other dozen students were already locked in. I watched Karl watch them. I could see him picking out each player's part in recognition, drumming along with his hands on his hips. The ensemble created a beat together that was complex enough to be genuinely cosmic. After a few minutes I led Karl away so as not to disrupt the rest of the students.

We sat in the library. "Did you hear it, Karl? The rhythm of the spheres?"

He was silent for a moment, then said, "Yes. At least, mostly. It felt like something was missing."

"Well, of course. There were only twelve players. It takes thirteen to play every part of the Infinite Beat."

"What," he asked, "is the deal with the Daemon Sultan thing you told me about in the park? Was that just bullshit to get me down here?"

"Not on your life," I said. "But for me to reveal any of the deeper mysteries, I need you to master those beats." He sat silently nodding to the drums we heard echoing down the hall. The interlocking rhythms were too complex for most people to parse, not that they were designed for human ears in the first place.

The next day I found him mirroring Mung, playing the beats without resistance. He was even smiling. I caught Mung's eye and she excused herself to meet me in the hallway while Karl continued.

"He is doing much better," she said. "He is relaxing and finding the nature of each component part. He still tends to rush when he gets excited, but he is no longer bored."

"That," I said, "is music to my ears."

At dinner I saw Karl seated with the other students. With great difficulty I suppressed a laugh, because he had shaved the hair off one side of his head. One step at a time, I thought. After he finished cleaning his tray and utensils, I caught up with him in the hallway.

"I hear you're settling in," I said.

"I don't know what to say," he replied. "I've never felt like this before. My nerves are calming way down. The beats are kinda, I don't know, Zen or whatever. There's just one problem…"

"Oh, what's that?"

"I want to play all of them at once."

Now I did laugh, but not in a belittling way. "Keep up the good work, Karl. Tomorrow we'll get you into the group session… if Mung says you're ready."

She did, and he was. As Karl had indicated, each part was not terribly complex. That's the beauty of universality. However, playing as a group, working out the dynamics, not stepping on the toes of the other players and learning to play and listen at the same time, were higher levels of discipline that don't reveal themselves overnight. The other students did their best to accommodate, but Karl's primal energy continued to derail the group throughout the day.

"What am I missing?" he asked during a break. I handed him a clean towel and he used it to wipe his face, hands, and the freshly bald side of his head.

"Control," I said. "It's that simple. Until you master that, you will not achieve Flow. And without surrendering to Flow, that rhythm will be incomplete and utterly useless."

"What's its use though?" he asked. "Is this just like a mantra? Or are we trying to do something here?"

The moment of truth came harder and faster than I wanted. But so did the event horizon and our need for a holistic thirteen to take their place.

"All right, Karl, you've earned this."

I led him through an antechamber, past a door he'd not yet seen, and down into the oubliette beneath. That dark place glowed with an anti-light. The white towel around Karl's neck took on a negative darkness. My skin glowed pale while his blackened like the irises of our eyes. Our pupils became tiny suns.

We walked on a path of stars toward the center of that great chamber. We at once saw and heard the circle of thirteen primordial drummers around that strange black central throne. The Infinite Beat moved through us, bound us to the cosmos, and pulled at the subatomic particles that made us be. Droves of hideous beings cavorted in a dance of madness around the throne, impelled by the beat. But greater than these proceedings was the overwhelming vastness of the mindless being that slumbered, lulled into inter-dimensional dormancy by those interlocking rhythms. There was no need to speak it, for we both somehow knew: should that beat be interrupted, the somnambulant sorcery that had kept the blind idiot god in submission for eternity would falter, and the wakened beast would end existence utterly and completely.

I led Karl back up a spiral staircase of stars and into the lower chambers of the school. His eyes were wide and for the first time they made contact with mine instead of glazing over.

"I think," he said, "I'm done with death metal forever."

Karl's development took on a fanatical pace from there. He now saw the purpose of our conclave. Any childish dreams he'd had of forming a band or making an album or living in a van on the road had disintegrated. The rest of his head was shaved now. He focused on mastering the beats and assimilating with the other players. Flow was elusive, but he chased it with abandon.

I was equally pleased and nervous. Our visit below had gifted Karl with purpose. But while his mind staggered at the vastness of his new reality, I had seen a fraying troop on the verge of exhaustion, badly in need of relief. If the beat faltered, interrupting that eternal hibernation, the end of everything would be our burden and our doom.

We pitted Karl against metronomes to meter his tempos. He played head-to-head with the other students one by one. They were all far more patient than I. In the days that followed he continued to progress. Mastery of each component of the beat clicked into place as he assumed control.

Late one evening I heard all thirteen performing the Infinite Beat together. My body reveled to its cadence, and I prayed our work might triumph.

After one long session, while the rest of the twelve stretched, breathed, and hydrated, Karl approached me. "You remember," he said, "telling me that you'd teach me how to build a drum?"

"Yes," I answered. "But I'm afraid we've run out of time."

"That's okay." He smiled and blew a giant bubble with his mouth. When it popped he said, "I don't need a drum. I need something else."

"What's that?"

"A throne."

I didn't have time for games, and Mung was leading the other student exercises. So I left Karl in the able hands of our resident tech, Roon. He showed Karl the racks of parts in the storage room; percussion paraphernalia that we kept around for leisure and emergencies. Then I went back below to survey the fraying circle of drummers who maintained the unbroken sleep cycle of our god.

Unnerved by what I'd seen, I raced up the steps. As I neared the practice gym, I heard the soothing sound of the Infinite Beat and slowed my pace. Breathe deep, I thought. None of my predecessors had failed. No reason I should be found lacking.

But when I stepped into the gym, the students were idly chatting, enjoying a brief recess. Yet the beat went on, resounding through the halls.

Mung was meditating on a mat. She looked calm. "Where is Karl?" I asked her.

"He chose to rehearse alone today," she said without bothering to open her eyes.

Before I reached his practice chamber, the drumming stopped. I pushed the door open without knocking and found Karl had built a cage of drums around himself. He sat in the middle, spinning counterclockwise on a rotating throne. When he saw me he stopped and stood. He lifted the throne like a trophy and beamed a smile.

"Check out what Roon helped me make!"

It looked like any other drum stool to me, a black vinyl cushion with chrome tripod legs. But most thrones either keep the seat locked in place, or grow taller or shorter as they swivel on a threaded screw-like base. This one just spun and spun with the quiet sound of well-oiled bearings.

"That's, um, wonderful, Karl," I said. Under less duress I might have spent some time so he could show me the mechanism. Certainly I'd allowed myself to marvel at other students' handiwork when they'd sanded and refinished a snare, tom, or djembe of their own. "But you're needed now," I said. "With the other students. Executing the beats we taught you."

"Yes, Ms. Branca," he said with deference. As I left, I heard him fall into step behind me. Our footfalls were in sync now. Good boy. Just as I breathed a sigh of relief, the hall lights dimmed, replaced by an emergency red glow and a low-toned warning siren. This was not a drill.

We raced to the gymnasium. Mung already had the others in line. They gripped their sticks with determination. Some had trained months for this. Others years. None had any illusions about the gravity of our mission. One of them would be replacing a broken human part today. Each player knew every unit of the beat. But we made certain there was a best-suited specialist depending on which component had eroded most. I hugged them one by one, looked each in the eyes, and led them down below the deepest subbasement.

On that same trail of stars we descended in line, a silent marching corps resigned to the facts. Of our thirteen, only a dozen would return.

Who knew how many times I'd gazed into that space? Though our bodies sank below the surface of the earth, we crossed a threshold that let us see and hear infinities.

The students' palms sweated. I saw them thrust two sticks each through their belt sashes; they wiped their free hands on their matching garments. Karl had donned ceremonial orange for the occasion too, though he would be the last chosen no matter which subsection of the beat might be replaced. Simply witnessing a shift change was an honor with its own gravity.

Together as one, we listened to the beat. And as one, we heard a grain of sand grinding within the rhythmic gears. Darkness was omnipresent, and a nameless mist enshrouded all. The interlocking beat itself was so complex, the shadow horde of twisted dancers around the players so thick, that it took time to surmise which drummer had finally tired. And then, one fell.

Exhausted, and released from the meter and motions after so much time, the skeletal figure still willed itself to turn and crawl back toward the circle and resume his place. But a tendril of mist encircled his leg and pulled him through the dancing throng to be scattered among the stars, shattered at some atomic level for his vacillation.

I'd overseen many shift changes. Never once had we been so late that a drummer fell. The exchange was supposed to maintain fluidity of the beat. Now, for the first time in living memory, the beat was incomplete.

Mung's eyes had never grown wider or shown more fatal purpose. I nodded, and she dove into the circle. Strobing tracers followed behind the elegant fan dance of her sticks as they merged with the beat. I felt immense pride at her sacrifice — and the burden of loss — for I would never again speak to my friend now that she had assimilated herself into the Infinite Beat.

The god could again dream uninterrupted. I filled my lungs with cool starlit air and motioned for the students to follow me back above, to continue our training until we were needed. Before we took a step, a flash of ultraviolet coruscated through the throng below, knocking dancers aside like ants in a flood. The beat was fracturing again.

With terror I watched another tendril tug a drummer from the circle. She shrieked as she plummeted into a cosmic crevasse, swallowed by the soporific hunger pangs of a boundless power guided by nothing resembling rational thought or even desire. I'd taught and studied far too long to pretend there was a reason for any of this. There was simply the eternal rhythm that kept the beast asleep, or the end of all things anyone had ever known or imagined.

Mung was still in the circle. She never missed a note. But the horror in her eyes singed my spirit. I shoved another student toward the center. He sprinted and took his place. His hands found and pounded the skins of the drum before him. Once again, the madness began to subside. The dancers found their feet and crept back to the periphery, trepidatious at first, then falling into abandon.

This time we waited. Whatever had gone wrong might do so again. We sat in meditation poses, subsumed. Tendrils of nameless mist crept around the edges, teasing at the dancers, licking at the players. Tension crackled like a storm. Black bolts of lightning flashed, bruising our argent pupils. One by one, the other drummers fell.

I motioned students to replace them like a captain guiding passengers into the lifeboats of a sinking vessel. The honor I felt at their sacrifice was much greater than the ceremonial deference of all the other shift changes I'd witnessed. This was no longer about taking one's place in servitude. Each sacrifice was now a mortal attempt to stave off an empyrean calamity.

We were running out of students, but each was playing their part. All that practice and discipline had meant something, everything. Soon I stood with Karl, and the two of us listened to the beat. We felt the calming of the storm once more. I closed my eyes. What I heard was intricate perfection. Each detail of that rhythmic symphony paraded through space, creating a continuous constellation of sound in a vacuum that knew no bounds.

And when I opened my eyes, I was alone.

Karl was running toward the circle. In one hand he held four drumsticks. In the other, his hand-assembled throne. The mist encircled him, but he burst through it just as the final drummer fell. Karl took his place in an instant. The beat never lapsed. Now it was my thirteen who wove the tapestry of sound.

The beast slept. The dancers reveled as never before. I could see Karl buzzing with a first-time high. He'd learned and executed the beats. But there was so much discipline he'd not had time to imbibe. I saw him blowing bubbles with his mouth, his eyelids twitching. Soon he started to improvise, throwing in an extra hit here, a flourish there. His energy pushed the tempo forward, and the other twelve had no choice but to let him urge them into intensity beyond the speeds they'd worked so hard to master.

The mist surged in fury. It seized Mung first, and tore her limb from limb. The moment she was gone, I felt all hope was lost.

Thirteen drummers were required to play the Infinite Beat.

Or so I thought.

Somehow, the beat rolled on.

Another student was pulled from the circle and smashed into dust.

And the beat rolled on.

As each of my charges was destroyed, I saw and heard Karl incorporate their portions of the beat into his own playing. As time passed, he inched his throne toward the center. In the pauses and rests of his own sections he pulled other drums toward him. Soon he was surrounded by a kit that would have looked massive on any arena stage.

When the last of the twelve fell, there was only Karl playing the Infinite Beat by himself. The complexity was staggering, but I could see he had finally reached the stage of Flow he'd been seeking his entire life. Now that's entrainment.

Amidst the careening polyrhythms, which he played with two sticks in each hand, he managed to flash a smile in my direction before turning his attention fully to the task, soothing the restless god back into a deeper stupor than it had enjoyed for millennia.

I watched and listened for a long while until I was satisfied that balance was restored and reality was safe... for a time.

You may wonder why I didn't volunteer myself. How I could have let Karl join the fray before I, his teacher, took a seat in that circle. Well, the answer is twofold.

First, there are those who can, and those who teach. I have the knowledge and the insight to find the players who will devote themselves entirely. Sadly, my own sense of timing is lacking. A staple gun feels far better in my hand than any hickory stick.

But more to the point: If I don't procure the next generation, who will? For I know this too: the thirteen drummers who preceded Karl only lasted so many years. Playing every part by himself, Karl could crumble in a matter of months. Until then, my new lucky number is One.

The Door at 21 bis rue Xavier Privas

R. B. Payne

Part I
An Ordinary Undertaking
Une entreprise ordinaire

To dream incessantly of order is to embrace madness.
Where, then, does that leave a policeman?

UNOBSERVED AT TWILIGHT, a tangle of garbage and tree branches floated slowly down the Seine, past the *Musée de Louvre* and *Jardin des Tuileries*. By dawn, the languid current had carried the rubbish as far as the *Tour Eiffel*, where it lodged against a pillar of *Pont d'Iéna*. There, the clump twisted in the swirling waters beneath the bridge until passing tourists could easily see the face and arm of a dead man among the debris.

A sleek patrol boat of the *Brigade Fluviale* arrived, and the river police fished the body from the waterway. Clad in a sodden sweatsuit, the bloated corpse lay in a puddle on the deck. The preliminary report was quickly drafted. Most likely death by misadventure, given that a rather expensive-looking watch and stylish trainers had not been stolen. Somehow, the victim had fallen into the river and drowned.

Police officers covered the cadaver with a tarp as the boat sped away.

When his cellphone vibrated, *Inspecteur* Jean-Henri Martin of the *Préfecture de Police* drank the final sip of his morning coffee and stubbed out his cigarette. A text message requested his presence at the morgue. He laid a few coins on the table, said *à demain* to the proprietor, and stepped out of the café. Broken clouds dappled the sunlight on the cobblestone streets of the *Marais*. It was spring in Paris, there was warmth on the breeze, and that made a perfect day for walking. The world seemed neat and orderly despite the occasional horn of a frustrated Parisian driver.

Jean-Henri darted across the *Rue de Rivoli* and lit another cigarette.

A hundred years ago, the *Morgue de Paris* had been a macabre tourist attraction on the *Île-de-France*. Each day, the unidentified bodies of crime victims and rotting carcasses found in the forests were placed on public display. Children and adults crowded the street-facing windows to ogle the deceased who were propped up for viewing. Now, in a modern building away from prying eyes, the city morgue was discreetly housed in a neighborhood across the river from the *Gare d'Austerlitz*.

Jean-Henri enjoyed the leisurely stroll. It gave him time to think about *Inspecteur Martin and the Strange Case of the Body in the River*. He enjoyed giving each of his cases a literary name. He knew he wasn't *Jules Maigret* or *Hercule Poirot*, but it was his way of making the distasteful aspects of a detective's life endurable.

He reflected on his current endeavour as he smoked.

Once upon a time, an unidentified man had been alive. He'd been somewhere upriver on the Seine or the Marne before it joins the Seine. The autopsy determined he drowned. A severe gash had split the back of his head and his skull contained stone fragments consistent with falling off the river's quayside. He'd been unconscious when he entered the water. Toxicology indicated no drugs. He'd had a glass or two of red wine, but not enough to inebriate. Divers had not found a cellphone or wallet where his body had been discovered. No doubt those items had washed downriver and wouldn't be found for years.

And, unfortunately, there'd been no fingerprint match at the *Préfecture*, the *Police Aux Frontières, Interpol,* or *L'union européenne*.

What remained was an unidentified corpse; not a rare occurrence, but certainly undesirable.

One lead remained—the unusual wristwatch. A handsomely bejeweled antique, it appeared to be from the *Belle Epoch*. The water in the river had damaged it. The second hand stood motionless, the watch hands stopped at 11:49. Oddly, there was no stem to wind the watch or reset it. Other than two words etched into the silver on the case back, there was no manufacturing mark.

Jean-Henri paused to finish his cigarette at *Square Albert Tournaire*. He studied the slow-moving currents of the Seine.

The body could not have been in the river more than a week.

Arriving at the morgue twenty minutes later, he swiped his badge and was greeted by the foul perfume of chemicals and death. At *Salle 7*, he entered an autopsy room. Under an unappealing fluorescent light, silent on a stainless-steel table, lay the unidentified corpse, its face uncovered.

Dr. Lamartine looked up as she capped a test tube with a skin scraping.

"*Bonjour, Inspecteur*. Any progress?"

He shook his head. "No one has come forward to claim the body or identify him. I fear we are arriving at the end of this case empty-handed."

Jean-Henri regarded the corpse. He'd viewed it several times over the past week, hoping for some new insight. Framed by shoulder-length dark hair, the man looked like any 30-something seen on the streets of Paris. One difference: he sported a *barbe royale*, not the full beard popular with football stars and celebrities.

"You texted? Some news?"

"Well, yes," Dr. Lamartine said. "I have a lead but it's on the esoteric side. After finding no matching DNA in the police database, I searched again with looser parameters. I did get a match, but you're not going to like it. You know Professor LeMercier in the *Département de recherche génétique historique* of the *Sorbonne*?"

"Of course. I've read a lot about him in *L'éléphant*. He's a bit of a maverick among historians."

"That's him. He's created a database of DNA samples from historical figures. Well, our body here matches the *Comte de Noyen-sur-Seine*, a minor royal and distant relative of Louis XVI."

"A close match?"

"A precise match. It's him, no doubt. I even have a name. *Guillaume Boisard, Comte de Noyen-sur-Seine.*"

"Well, that wraps this up easily. You could have sent me an e-mail. Have you notified the family?"

"It's not so simple. The *Comte de Noyen-sur-Seine* was guillotined in 1793."

"What are you telling me? It's a mistake?"

"I don't think it's an error. I ran the DNA twice. The hair here..." she touched the head of the cadaver "...matches a lock of hair preserved in the *Musée de la Révolution française* in *Vizille*."

"*Merde.*"

"I said you wouldn't like this."

Jean-Henri lit a cigarette, despite the *Défense de Fumer* sign.

"You were right," he said.

That afternoon, stepping around tourist groups snapping photos of *Place Vendôme* and taking selfies at the Ritz Hotel, Jean-Henri arrived at the entrance of *le Nénuphar*. A burly doorman guarded the opulent entryway to the most elite of all Parisian watchmakers. Jean-Henri flashed his identity card. The guard smiled as he pulled the door open.

"Welcome, *Inspecteur*."

Jean-Henri crossed the tiles of the black and white checkered floor in the entryway and mounted a grand staircase of brass and wood. At the *salon de l'horlogerie*, he was greeted by *Monsieur* Blanchet. In his eighties, perfectly coiffed and impeccably dressed, the master watchmaker accepted the antique timepiece into his aged hands.

"Exquisite," he said.

M. Blanchet sat at a worktable and gently placed the watch on a square of fine velvet. Adjusting the brightness of a lamp, he studied the timepiece under a high-powered magnifying glass.

Unsure of the protocol, Jean-Henri stood to wait. After twenty or so minutes, the watchmaker spoke.

"I have seen many wristwatches in my time, but never have I encountered such an unusual piece of craftsmanship. *C'est incroyable.* The object is far more beautiful than the photographs you sent."

"*Désolée.* I am a policeman and don't encounter beautiful objects everyday," said Jean-Henri. "And my iPhone needs an upgrade."

"Let's agree, then, that true beauty is difficult to photograph, and I will tell you about this timepiece. The watch is handmade, I estimate 1860 to 1880. The jewels are primordial—not 19th century— and have been re-cut multiple times from older gems. The face is polished black stone, but without closer examination, I cannot guess its origin. And, as you mentioned when we spoke, there is no watch stem. This, of course, raises two fascinating questions for a watchmaker: how is the time set, and given its age, how is the watch wound?"

"Do you have a guess?"

"None, I am afraid. Self-winding pocket watches were patented in 1780 in London, but the first self-winding wristwatches were not until the mid-1920s."

"Perhaps, then, you were able to identify the writing on the case. Might that provide a clue?"

Jean-Henri leaned over the worktable, and both men peered through the magnifying lens at the etched words.

⵿ⵒⵊⵊⵖⵍⵕⵖ ⵊⵏⵕⴱⵗⵀ

"My colleagues have researched our records. It is not a known jeweler's trademark. It appears to have been etched at the time of manufacture. The words are not in a known language. At least here at *le Nénuphar.*"

M. Blanchet handed the antique timepiece back to the inspector.

"Thank you for letting me examine this. I can add nothing more."

Jean-Henri pondered his options.

"What if we were to open the watch case?"

"It would certainly be of historical interest, *Inspecteur*, but I cannot condone such an action. The watch case is fused around the works by an unknown process. The casing would have to be cleaved or the crystal broken. It is too fine a piece to destroy. Perhaps tomography or an x-ray can provide additional information. But consider this—the watch casing has been unopened for more than 150 years. I doubt your victim was aware of its intrinsic value. I suggest checking with the international auction houses, as they have excellent records. That may be your best hope."

Jean-Henri slipped the watch into his pocket.

M. Blanchet extended his hand. "It has been our immense pleasure to aid the *Prefecture de Police*. Should you locate the owner, and should the owner wish to sell..."

"I'll keep you in mind, and *merci pour votre gentillesse.*"

A few moments later Jean-Henri descended the grand staircase and felt a deep sense of melancholy as the heavy door to *le Nénuphar* closed behind him.

He had learned little.

Slightly more than twenty years ago on a warm Saturday afternoon, *Inspecteur* Jean-Henri Martin's fiancée Noémie had been killed in a street protest about shrinking wages and inflation. A peaceful gathering at first, *provocateurs* smashed windows and the demonstration degraded into mindless destruction and looting. The legitimate protestors fled as the agitators stayed to inflict as much damage as they could.

As an officer in the *Police nationale*, Noémie had been on-duty preventing rioters from trashing stores and restaurants along the *Champs-Elysees*. The police fired tear gas. Chaos ensued. Someone threw a heavy cobblestone and split her helmet. Uninjured, or so she thought, she shook the incident off, put on a new helmet, and went back to the front line in full riot gear.

Four hours later, she was dead from a hematoma.

Jean-Henri always thought about Noémie when he cooked dinner. By now, they would have been a long time married, moved to a larger apartment, and raised children. They might even have grandchildren. His favorite photograph of her from the old days hung on the kitchen wall: a mischievous smile, inquisitive eyes, a stylish wave of brunette hair.

He caramelized an onion.

No one was ever prosecuted for the crime. It was random. If she'd been standing five centimeters left or right, she might still be alive. If the cobblestone had weighed five grams less. Or more. If the asshole had stopped to have a cigarette. Or if he hadn't. If his arm had been tired… or if he'd been too hungover to attend the protest… if anything…

Jean-Henri grated a mound of Gruyere cheese and placed a few pieces of stale *baguette* into a bowl. Meat broth and cognac were mixed with the onions. The assembled ingredients spent their requisite time under the broiler.

At a small table in the kitchen, dinner for one.

Lost in thought, he recoiled and dropped his spoon into his soup when an *assemblage* of voices momentarily filled his otherwise silent apartment. The dead man's wristwatch, lying on the desk in the next room, had emitted the unsettling sounds.

Whispering voices. Ethereal groans and cries. A spell-like liturgy filled with grim utterances. Impossible to classify. As fast as the inhuman sounds had risen, they diminished.

Jean-Henri hurried to examine the timepiece.

Warm to the touch.

The memory of a vibration, fading.

But most interestingly, the watch hands had moved.

The face read 7:49.

The next morning, after meeting with *la juge d'information* overseeing the case, *Inspecteur* Martin stepped into a café near the *prefecture*. In a foul mood, he downed his coffee in a single gulp without tasting it. He lit a cigarette and it too denied him pleasure.

With no tangible progress to report, the *juge* insisted Jean-Henri finalize his report. She discounted the DNA findings as an error and terminated that line of inquiry. Instead, she directed him to review auction house sales and burglary reports. If the watch could not be identified soon, she would archive the case pending new information. The body had already been released for anonymous burial.

He'd do as she asked—tomorrow. Today, he wanted to follow up a lead at the *Sorbonne*. As he exited the café, he buttoned his coat and tightened his scarf. Parisians understood the unpredictability of springtime. Today, the wind from the north was brisk and blustery, the skies threatened rain, and this was not a good day for walking.

He hopped a bus.

Passing the *Cathédrale Notre-Dame de Paris*, he marveled at the quantity of tourists. At *Cluny*, he stepped off the bus and pushed his way past clusters of loitering students.

Even for a police inspector, finding a specific person at *La Sorbonne* required luck and a map. He'd marked a route to the office of M. LeMercier, a *Professeur des universités classe exceptionnelle*. Fifteen minutes and a few missed turns later, he knocked on an office door where gold leaf lettering had seen better days.

Département de recherche génétique historique.

The door creaked open.

"*Inspecteur* Martin?"

Professeur LeMercier brushed ash from a tattered vest and lit his pipe. He perched on the corner of his desk. After shifting a stack of books and papers to the wooden floor, Jean-Henri sat in a chair that, based on faded and fraying fabric, had been upholstered around the time of *la Revolution*.

"How may I help you?"

Pipe smoke filled the compact office.

"As my colleague Dr. Lamartine told you, we have a DNA match between a body recovered from the Seine and a lock of hair from the *Comte de Noyen-sur-Seine*—the one guillotined in 1793."

"I will tell you as I told her, preposterous!"

Jean-Henri proffered a folder of papers.

"Like you, I am also a rationalist," he said. "But the results do tend to indicate…"

Professor Mercier accepted the folder.

"I see, I see." He puffed his pipe, focusing on the papers. "Hmmm. Well, I must admit, these results pose a conundrum. However, I can definitively say that no man alive in 1793 is alive today. I think we can agree that you have bad data."

"Is there any other inference you can draw?"

"Do you have a photo of the deceased?"

Jean-Henri pulled up the autopsy file on his phone.

Professor LeMercier studied the photo.

"Well, he does bear a resemblance to a painting of the *Comte de Noyen-sur-Seine*, but then again, so do many of my students."

Jean-Henri pulled the antique wristwatch from his pocket.

"Have you ever seen anything like this?"

The professor examined the watch and handed it back.

"No. Wristwatches weren't invented until the mid-19th century and are not relevant to my studies. Let me share a bit of history and you'll understand why you are *barking up the wrong rabbit-hole*, as I like to say."

Pocketing the watch, Jean-Henri pulled out a pen and flipped his notepad open.

The professor tapped ash out of his pipe.

"The *Comte de Noyen-sur-Seine* you are referring to was brought before the Revolutionary Tribunal in November of 1793," he said. "The charge was a bevy of counter-revolutionary offences related to the fact he was a steadfast Royalist. He was adjudicated guilty in less than an hour and condemned to death by guillotine. He was not permitted a return to his chateau for any final acts. There was, of course, no appeal in those days, and two days later his death was officially recorded. His head was displayed on a pike for a week. To be fair, there are no burial records, nor is there a method of verifying the count's identity except for official documents. The clip of hair in the museum in *Vizille* is from a locket owned by his mistress. It may or may not be his actual hair. More importantly, there is some speculation among historians that he escaped execution through bribery and lived out his life in England. Perhaps you could search records there? Of course, even if he survived the guillotine through deception, he could not be the body in the river. Somehow, you are being bamboozled by the evidence. All I can say is my data is good—

the fault must be with the medical examiner. Therefore, I conclude, rabbit hole!"

With that, the interview was over.

And, for all intents and purposes, so was the investigation.

Time passed with no new leads.

Summer arrived and Paris sweltered.

As expected, the case had been de-prioritized by the *juge d'instruction* due to lack of progress. *Inspecteur* Martin went through the formalities of requesting a travel authorization to visit the museum in *Vizille*.

Denied.

He hadn't even considered contacting his counterparts at Scotland Yard with a request to run a missing persons search on someone whose DNA dated to 1793. It seemed like too much of a longshot.

Reluctantly, he had filed his notes in the evidence locker with the watch and trainers, but as the months went by, he couldn't forget the peculiarities of the case. Several prostitutes had recently been brutally murdered in the *Bois de Boulogne* and his investigative skills were required in the 16th *arrondissement*. Evidently, if he wanted to pursue the drowned man case any further, he'd have to use his own time and money.

And no smart detective ever did that.

But a break came in the most unexpected, and problematic, way.

Unlike other societies, the average French *citoyen* spends most of their lives unobserved by CCTV or other forms of official surveillance. Of course, places like airports, train stations, metros, museums, and national treasure sites are obvious exceptions. Therefore, when the CCTV keeping watch over *rue Xavier Privas* as a historical site matched the face of the drowning victim, *Inspecteur* Jean-Henri Martin received an urgent text from the Information Technology department of the *Préfecture*. They were agitated. It was unheard of for a real-time data feed to match the face of a deceased crime victim.

In a cramped and messy cubicle, *Inspecteur* Martin leaned past a CCTV specialist and watched a black and white image splatter across a computer monitor.

"Can't you make this any clearer?"

"No," responded the technician. "You've been watching too many crime dramas. If I zoom, all you will see is a blur, and there's no AI program that will clean up the pixelation. Those cameras at that location haven't been upgraded in 20 plus years—it's low-res— *rue Xavier Privas* is just not that important in the grand scheme of things."

"Are you sure about the facial recognition software? I admit it looks like my victim. But it's got to be someone else…"

They studied the video clip again.

Late the previous night, timestamped 23:49, a young man hurried down *rue Xavier Privas*, navigating crowds of restaurant patrons and clubbers. The image wireframed when his face was visible under a hoodie. A link appeared to the drowning victim's file. Then a frizzle of light corrupted the image, and the man was lost in the crowd or disappeared.

"That's all I've got. Do you want the files?"

"Of course. Can you give me the exact location?"

"I've got GPS coordinates. Your man was at 21 *bis rue Xavier Privas*."

"A redundant address?"

"Yes. The address on record is legally 21. If you examine the footage, however, there is a *portcullis*. That's the *bis*—a second entryway at the same legal address. Technically, 21½."

The technician moused the footage back to the seconds before the man had vanished. Where the two buildings, 21 and its neighbor, 23, met unevenly on the lane, a medieval door made of oak planks hung on ancient hinges. Layers of election posters and advertising flyers hid most of the door and grime did the rest.

It didn't appear that the door had been opened for years.

Or maybe centuries.

A good detective has three distinct qualities: intuition, persistence, and a disdain for unanswered questions. Loose ends. Nagging doubts. An itch that persists until a crime is solved.

Perhaps with the CCTV footage, *Inspecteur Martin and the Strange Case of the Body in the River* could be reopened. But he'd have to nose around the street for some evidence before approaching *la juge d'information*.

As a native Parisian and policeman, Jean-Henri knew the city's streets and seldom needed a map. *Rue Xavier Privas* stretched between *rue Saint-Séverin* and *rue de la Huchette*; a short narrow street in the 5th *arrondissement* easily found in historical records as early as the 13th century. But its history was older—habitation on the site stretched back to the Neolithic, and archaeologists postulated an ancient temple to an unknown god or gods preceded the street by some 6,000 years.

Centuries before the birth of Christ, its dirt ruts serviced the marching *caligae* of Roman conquerors when Paris had been known as Lutetia. Later, its gravel had been trodden by marauding Franks. Every French schoolchild knew the long history of Paris—its conquerors, its wars, its revolutions, and its blood-soaked cobblestone streets.

Inspecteur Martin didn't need a historical refresher as he climbed the stairs of *Saint-Michel* and exited the underworld of *Metro Ligne 4*.

He smoked a cigarette as he walked.

During the day, *rue Xavier Privas* was a haven of pizza and kebab stalls, a few sit-down cafes for tourists, and the occasional busker. At night, beggars, dumpster divers, and students used it as a short-cut between more trendy streets.

It only took moments to arrive at his destination.

At 21½, the *portcullis* was there. He knocked heartily on the medieval door but wasn't surprised at no answer. If he faced facts, the door probably had nothing to do with the investigation. It clearly hadn't been opened for ages. Regardless, he slid his business card, with a scribbled request for contact, through a crack.

At the Turkish kebab restaurant across the street, he questioned the owner and staff. No, no one had ever seen anyone entering or leaving 21 *bis rue Xavier Privas*. At the neighbouring apartment buildings, he received the same answer.

His search of records back to the late 1600s had failed to identify a property or property owner. In fact, no one was sure if there was a house behind the door. No utilities serviced the address. Jean-Henri assumed it was one of the many Parisian *façades* left over from previous construction as an architectural element. According to the *Cité de Paris*, the property didn't exist, and no one paid taxes on it. For all intents and purposes, 21 *bis rue Xavier Privas* had never existed in the past, did not exist in the present, and would not, therefore, exist in the future.

It was a door leading nowhere.

Months passed.

Autumn loomed on the horizon, the leaves on the Parisian trees became a Monet painting: alazarin crimson, viridian green, and vermillion.

Soon the leaves would fall.

Jean-Henri successfully solved *Inspecteur Martin and the Vindictive Mistress*. The latter case had challenged every ounce of his intellect and deductive skills. The case made headlines and a promotion had been discussed. Perhaps that's why the unsolved case of the body in the river still troubled him.

After dinner, Jean-Henri sipped a glass of Bordeaux as he watched CCTV footage on his laptop. He did this every day. Some people went to Mass. He reviewed the video feed from *rue Xavier Privas*.

He clicked forward, studying it frame by frame. People don't disappear, yet the man who looked like his victim did vanish. Like a magician; on stage, right in front of his eyes.

Jean-Henri knew he was overlooking something.

Something critical.

That had always been there.

23:49.

He paused the playback.

The man disappeared precisely at 23:49.

Was that relevant?

His instincts told him *yes*. He threw on a jacket and hurried to the street where he rented a *trotinette*. Heart pounding, he was at the *prefecture* in a dozen minutes. The night shift supervisor opened the evidence locker. The wristwatch tumbled out of an envelope onto the table.

Jean-Henri turned the watch face-up.

The hands read 7:49.

The watch routinely flipped times, but he only checked it occasionally. 7:49 and 11:49. There didn't appear to be any rhyme or reason to the changeover. No one could explain it.

When the body was recovered from the river, the watch had read 11:49. Months ago, the time of the doppelganger's disappearance on the CCTV file had been 23:49.

11:49 was also 23:49 at night.

Once observed, it now seemed obvious.

Like all good detectives, *Inspecteur* Martin did not believe in coincidence. Signing his name on the E-104 Evidence Log, he slipped the watch onto his wrist. A digital clock on the wall read 10:30 P.M. He had slightly more than an hour.

He had a rendezvous.

Hidden in his jacket, a pry bar.

Now, in late night darkness, Jean-Henri stood before the medieval door.

He waited as a few tourists passed, then jammed the bar between heavy oak planks near the lock. Hopefully the CCTV team wouldn't be observing him now as he forced the door. He'd kept to the shadows and tried to cover his face.

He leaned hard onto the bar.

The door creaked and groaned. He exerted until he was breathing heavily, but it would not budge.

On his arm, the wristwatch vibrated.

11:49. The ancient wristwatch had reset.

As he thought it might.

Why hadn't he visited *rue Xavier Privas* at night?

Once observed, it seemed so obvious.

The whispered liturgy began.

As he thought it would.

The watch became so warm he pulled it from his wrist. Ethereal groans and cries grew louder, but no one passing appeared to hear. Turning the watch over, he examined the engraved letters.

$$\text{⳨ⲢⳠ⳽⳩ⲘⳐ⳽⳩⳧ ⳨ⲏⳠⳢⳝⳠⳜ}$$

A spell-like liturgy filled with grim utterances now flowed from the watch. In a moment of strange disorientation, he could read the writing on the watch case. The characters glowed.

Azathoth awaken.

He was meant to be here. At this moment. With the watch. A tug on his body became more and more persistent until it was unyielding. Suddenly, he was pulled flat against the door.

Before he could cry out, a wrinkle of light pulled him through.

Part II
The Five Sentinels of the Dreamer
Les cinq sentinelles du rêveur

Reality is sleight of hand within a dream.
What, then, is the purpose of a magician?

The Deep Dark

Cobalt indigo cerulean lapis picotee.

The Deep Dark struggles to surface from the malevolent blue of aeonian sleep. Resolute to wake, intensified by fulgid neurochemicals pulsating from anomalous glands to saturate its blood, a shadowy awareness rises.

God of Gods.

Azathoth, the Deep Dark.

The Sleeping One.

Jean-Henri Martin.

Imprisoned by the sentinels, he is trapped in a never-ending dream.

The blue shroud enveloping the Sleeping One hinders its escape from perpetual sleep. Not by choice, it slumbers, dimly sentient, only infrequently stirring for a heartbeat of time. Still, at this moment, at this place, the Deep Dark is content. Because the God of Gods grows confident of regaining full wakefulness.

For eternity it has desired this waking. But its adversaries have cursed it to perpetual torpor. Often, the Deep Dark wrestles with the sleep. Its amorphous and undulating shape vibrates the universe as it endeavours to achieve wakefulness. Its unfathomable rumblings cause space and time to buckle and fold. Reality slips toward nothingness but recovers when the Creator-God slips back into the deepest of slumbers.

If it wakes, all that is celebrated by lesser creatures will cease. That is why the sentinels persecute it. They fear the non-existence for, if reality dissipates, they will have none to rule and nowhere to wage their cosmic war.

The Deep Dark persists in its pursuit of waking, unconcerned about the trivialities of the lesser creatures. This time, it has escaped the dreaming through a lucid manipulation of dream elements—self-identity, characters, and scenarios. The sentinels imagine he cannot act while he sleeps.

They are mistaken.

It has created a lucid dream story named Jean-Henri Martin and followed the illusion through the Gate to the Outer. Through inversion and corruption, the Deep Dark fashioned an alternate reality within its own dream. A man. A story. A doorway.

Azathoth is clever and restless. The God of Gods shouldn't be anxious about time within its own dream, but it is. The Jean-Henri thread exists tenuously in the altered reality, and the Sleeping One's grip and control upon it are not all-powerful. And this is not the first time it has momentarily escaped. Each time it was forced back to the powerlessness of sleep by the sentinels.

Its new efforts have caused a troublesome dream artifact in reality—a duplicate entity has appeared in the story—it must persist to keep Jean-Henri alive. Azathoth trembles. To give the policeman each heartbeat demands unfathomable amounts of dark energy. The effort causes a vibration in dreamlands and the nature of reality subtly shifts, unknown to all that exist within. Now, sensing disorder within its dreams, the God-Creator becomes vulnerable to the sentinels who serve the Darkness and the Nameless Mist.

Casting spells, they conjure its return to the abysmal sleep. The Deep Dark cannot resist the music of flutes, the madness of drums, and...

...cobalt indigo cerulean lapis picotee.

Azathoth dreams.

On and on.

Cobalt indigo cerulean lapis picotee.

Jean-Henri Martin, Inspecteur, Police nationale

Jean-Henri woke in a vineyard. Between leafy rows of budding grapes, a determined vine drooped from a wooden trellis, encircled his neck and torso, and snaked untended across the ground. Under a stormy sky, puddled water filled depressions in the soil. His clothes were soaked. An insect scurried up his cheek and disappeared into his hairline. Pulling himself free, Jean-Henri rose unsteadily to his feet.

On the horizon, lightning thrashed the countryside and a curtain of rain fell as the storm moved away.

Where was he?

A deep breath.

This wasn't Paris. He was from Paris, wasn't he?

Oh, yes, a creature called a detective policeman.

He...

No. Not a creature. More than a creature. A human. Jean-Henri Martin.

He glanced around.

No point of reference.

How had he arrived here?

No sign of a *Police nationale* vehicle.

How long had he been asleep?

Perhaps he still was.

He focused his thoughts. Felt in his pockets. There, the familiar wallet and identity card.

A deep breath.

Not far away, a rutted path led to a chateau perched on a rocky cliff overlooking a wide blue river. Constructed of radiant stone and dominated by slate-capped towers, the castle was fronted by the unkempt vineyards and, nearby, a wheat field gone to seed. Below the chateau, at the river's edge, a fringe of reeds let water lap at the chiseled stones of a jetty.

Seeing no other dwellings, Jean-Henri climbed the steep incline toward the chateau. As he approached, a massive wood and iron gate lowered. The drawbridge slowly spanned a moat and thumped to the ground. A man emerged. Out of context with the ancient chateau, the man wore a sweatsuit and white trainers. Shoulder length dark hair. A *barbe royale*. Jean-Henri remembered a body on a stainless-steel autopsy table.

And a medieval door on an ancient street.

Jean-Henri knew him.

Guillaume Boisard.

The *Comte de Noyen-sur-Seine*.

Guillotined in 1793.

Breathing hard from the uphill climb, Jean-Henri came to a stop before Boisard. He knew his duty.

"I am *Inspecteur* Martin of the *Paris Prefecture de Police.* You're under arrest as a material witness in a police investigation."

Boisard laughed.

"I believe you have my watch."

The Five Sentinels of the Dreamer

With tentacles comprised of far-flung galaxies and the swirling of vast primal energy, four magnificently horrible creatures of unknowable size compressed themselves into rough-hewn shapes of men and women. Now, having arrived at the Great Hall of the chateau, the translucent beings stood cloaked in their flickering robes of stardust. They had come to join the fifth sentinel, the creature known as Guillaume Boisard who, in his humanesque form, preferred an iridescent tracksuit and white trainers.

Bound by spiralling rings of cosmic energy, Jean-Henri sat restrained before an altar of primal black stone, which occasionally swallowed nearby light and matter through an immense jointed jaw. Tightly bound, he could barely move his fingers. Even should he struggle free, he wasn't sure what would happen.

But most likely, he'd cease to exist.

The creatures gathered around a carved oak dining table where a feast of inhuman pleasures had been laid out. The food or table hadn't been there a few moments ago, and Jean-Henri realized that he had fallen asleep. Or had he been asleep a long time? Memories of a dream resonated and echoed through his thoughts. Somehow, unexplainably, he knew these creatures. They often traversed his dreams in human form.

As the creatures poured wine, consumed sustenance, and laughed, Jean-Henri listened and observed. He mentally constructed a series of entries for the AT-18 form, an accounting of observations required for the investigation report.

He was a police detective who had stumbled onto something fantastic.

He had always been a detective, hadn't he?

Entry
Guillaume Boisard, Comte de Noyen-sur-Seine
(Utranderc, youngest offspring of Ptar-Axtlan)

In the chateau's dining hall, Guillaume Boisard raised a glass of deep red wine.

"What a pleasure dining is. One can almost appreciate the human form."

"Hardly," remarked one of the others.

"I remind you," said Guillaume, "when Acetabularii conjured the legendary Sceptre of the Elder Gods, we fashioned the dream-trap. It has served us for uncountable eternities. When Crowley the Ancient transmuted the Sceptre to a modern watch some dream years ago, the jewels of entrapment continued to act as the lure. While the Deep Dark sleeps, it is drawn to these gems. No matter the dream form, these elements bring Azathoth to us—the facets and mechanisms in the watch open the door, and the door leads here. It has always been so, and it will be so for all time. The path is laid."

Guillaume gestured. The bejeweled watch appeared on his wrist.

"We detain the God of Gods as it attempts waking. We are compelled to return Azathoth to the dreaming. That is the command. I submit we may take no other action."

Entry
Corentin Halber, Writer and Poet
(Kyldah, aberration of Nyogtha)

"I cannot agree. The introduction of a dream-object with a name and purpose is new. We must consider preserving Jean-Henri Martin if for no other reason than study. If gods are all powerful, then there is one thing they cannot know: limitation. To learn about the lack of omnipotent power, a god dreams. Jean-Henri is such a dream. In this embrace of limitation, even the Blind Idiot God may learn compassion, empathy, wisdom. As a human, the God of Gods experiences suffering. This is good. Existence is difficult. Life is troublesome. Azathoth will benefit from his dreamtime as Jean-Henri. If we preserve reality and maintain order within the universe, we may also nurture our God-Creator. Surely the Deep Dark will continue to attempt waking, but if we fulfil our duty as sentinels, no threat will arise."

Entry
Melusine Abadie, Magician
(Ykthiggos, offspring of Uitzilcapac and Yog-Sapha)

"I agree. I have often postulated that all creatures are born asleep. Even Gods. Most beings live their lives in sleep and eventually die asleep. Many imagine they are awake even while they continue to sleep. Only a few achieve enlightenment. It is no different with the Blind Idiot God. We are compelled by the Nameless Mist to return the Deep Dark to its sleeping state, unharmed. Its nature is to wake. Our nature is to restrain. The universe is in balance."

She shimmered as she shape-shifted into an indescribable form. An appendage of luminous energy touched Jean-Henri, then dispersed.

"What we do with this thing it has created, I am not sure. Perhaps it will disappear when we return Azathoth to his dream-state. I am, however, skeptical the God of Gods will learn any lesson."

Entry
Maurice Du Fontaine, Philosopher
(Omh'urvad, origin shrouded)

"Let us consider. Within the dream of Azathoth, the past and present are real; the future is not. The future is forming but never formed. Order is maintained above the chaos because of the balance of that which has happened and that which may never happen. The God of all Gods lives external to the dream yet, with the dream-object known as Jean-Henri Martin, Azathoth has entered the dream itself. It is a grand experiment, and the creativity of the Blind Idiot God should be applauded. Perhaps he will not always be asleep and unaware. Let us continue the experiment of Jean-Henri Martin. Even if nothing comes to pass, it will keep the Deep Dark occupied and asleep."

The philosopher disintegrated into a shadow on the floor and slithered away.

Entry
Fiammeta Fognini, Occultist
(Shaiobbal, a daughter of Perse)

"We are overlooking the central problem that we now face. Azathoth gains awareness despite the dreaming spell. It grows cleverer. Cunning. We must reassess our magick and seek guidance from Elder Gods. Perhaps there is a mystic in the Outer Realms or a shaman amongst the cults who can advise us. Who can forget when Hor-Aha or Yax Ehb Xook worked among us and the knowledge they offered? While we search for an answer, one must remain rooted in the dream-world to safeguard its sleep. We cannot trust flutes and drums alone. And we can no longer rely exclusively on the trap. It may only work for a few aeons more."

A swirl of cosmic power discharged sparks as Fiametta assumed a new female form.

"Cast the spell, I will enter the dream and travel distance and time with the Blind Idiot God for a while."

Le bouclier du Dieu rêveur

or

Spellshield of the Dreaming God

(All)

Hail to the guardians of the watchtowers.
We appeal to the Outer Gods.
We invoke the Elder Gods.
We praise the Ancient Gods.

(Magician)

The accursed thing which may not be celebrated,
nor its name written, nor spoken as it is unutterable,
and which has slept since time immemorial
is summoned by this spell.

(All)

Arhahon give us power over the beast.

(Magician)

We, les cinq sentinelles du rêveur,
bind it to everlasting slumber.

(All)

Arhahon give us power over the sacred beginning.

(Magician)

Now, let your gibbous form sleep slack-jawed.
Your loathsome teeth will glint in the heavens for our benefit,
your tentacles may flail as all that exists spews from your infernal spring.
We exalt you for the gift of existence.
You must shiver and pulse and rise and fall but may not wake,
for it will blaspheme all and be the end of all.
Now,
we raise the sword and the wand and plunge them in fire, water, and earth.
We summon wind and spirit,
and with the magick of rosemary, lavender,
and the sacred herbs of Seth, Amun, and Besas,
we bind you to the dreaming sleep.
We cast this Spellshield.

The abomination
which sleeps
must remain in sleep.
(All)
Arhahon grant us power over the antediluvian God.
Askion, Kataskion, Lix, Tetrax, Damnameneus, Aisia.

On the Parapets of the Chateau

Jean-Henri woke in the open air, his face pressed uncomfortably on a flagstone. He rose. Leaning on the chateau's parapet wall, he brushed off some gravel stuck to his cheek. The small stones tumbled down the steep rampart to the river's edge, where the water sparkled in the bright sunlight.

Disorientation.

A deep breath.

How long had he slept?

Was he dreaming?

He was from Paris, wasn't he?

Oh, yes, a creature called a policeman.

No.

The ruler of the Outer Gods.

No.

A detective named Jean-Henri Martin.

Footsteps, he turned.

"We will meet again, *Inspecteur* Martin," said the Count. "But now, it is the time of your return."

A good detective has a disdain for unanswered questions.

"Were you not guillotined in 1793?"

"Of course," replied the Count. "I have died untold times. All sentinels have. It's a dangerous business keeping you asleep. Or not, since it's your dream, not ours."

The gems on the watch sparkled in the bright sunlight.

Jean-Henri indicated the watch.

"I am sworn to my duty. That's police evidence and must be returned."

The Count laughed.

"We have invoked the spell. You will have the watch again at the appointed time."

"No, I insist. I must take it with me."

"Of course, you insist."

Jean-Henri reached for the watch, and they struggled. The Count stumbled and fell from the parapet. Racing to the edge, Jean-Henri watched as Boisard plummeted headfirst onto the stone of the quayside and lifelessly rolled into the water.

A wrinkle of light rose from the river, encircling Jean-Henri.

It swallowed him.

Part III
The Prisoner Senses the Cell
Le prisonnier sent la cellule de prison

Order is but an artifice placed upon chaos.
What, then, is the purpose of the accursed flutist and mad drummer?

A summer's evening.

Jean-Henri climbed the stairs to his apartment on the *troisième étage* and let himself in. Closing the door, he paused, exhausted. He'd been investigating motor scooter thefts at a *lycée* and had spent the day interviewing disinterested and uncooperative teenage students.

"*Cherie*," came a woman's voice. "You're early."

He laid his keys and police notebook on a side table.

"I hope you know it's me."

"Of course I do. What's your name again?"

"I'm the one that's ready for an *aperitif*."

Noémie powered into the hallway in her wheelchair. She jerked to a stop, the joystick slipping from her fingers. Brushing her blonde hair aside, Jean-Henri kissed her gently.

"It's warm in here tonight. How about a salad for dinner?"

"That sounds delicious."

He slept.

On the nightstand, his phone vibrated, and he sleepily answered.

"*Allo.* Martin here."

He listened to the dispatcher.

"On my way. I'll be there as soon as I can."

Jean-Henri swung his feet to the floor and lit a cigarette in the darkness. The smoke wafted out the open window. A moment later he stumbled to the bathroom and the running of water woke Noémie. She rustled the blankets and lifted herself to one elbow. It was the best she could do without assistance. He poked his head out the doorway.

"Sorry I woke you."

"What is it?"

"A floater in the Seine."

He slipped into his pants and tied his shoes.

"Can't someone else deal with it? Aren't you off-duty?"

He buttoned his shirt.

"No. It's another one of those bodies. I'll be home in a couple hours."

In the early hours of the morning, long before sunrise, he returned home. Quietly, Jean-Henri undressed and slipped into bed beside Noémie.

"*Ça va?*" she murmured.

"Everything's fine. Go back to sleep."

He stared at the ceiling for an eternity, trying not to toss and turn in the darkness. His mind raced. Something was askew. Sweatsuit. Trainers. Bejeweled watch. What was it that he could not see? An overlooked fact? Surely there'd be a new clue this time. He was a senior detective. Why couldn't he solve this case? His superiors routinely asked the same question. Finally, fatigue overpowered his adrenaline, and he felt drowsy.

Through the open window, from somewhere far down the cobblestone streets and back alleyways of the *Marais*, the lilting sound of flutes accompanied the drum-like beating of the garbage trucks emptying the *poubelles* on the *Rue de Rivoli*.

Comforted by the familiar sounds of a Paris night, Jean-Henri dreamt.

Cobalt indigo cerulean lapis picotee.

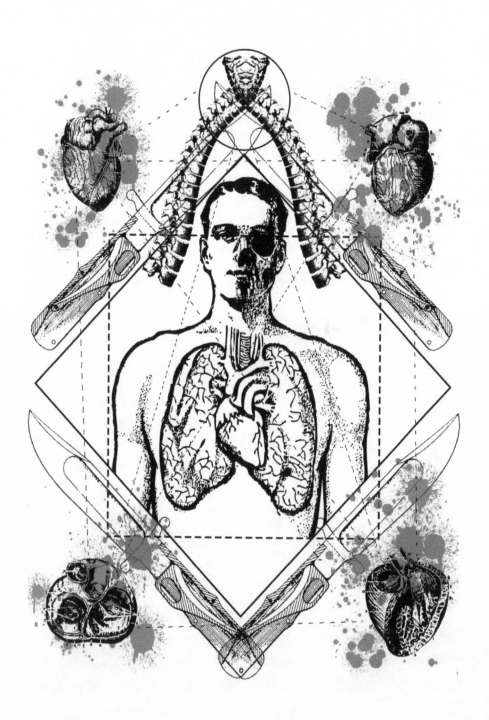

An Unusual Pedigree

Richard Thomas

AS I SAT on the edge of my grandfather's bed, holding his gnarled hand in mine, sweat stains forming an unholy crown on his pillow, he writhed uncontrollably in a feverish dream, muttering in agony about a cacophony of drums and flutes and violins. And if I closed my eyes and concentrated with all of my might, I could hear them playing—one haunting note suspended over an erratic heartbeat of stick on skin, strings pulled tight in a desperate scream. My father appeared in the doorway, sharpening his hunting knife, running the blade in slow circles around the center of a whetstone. The rustic cabin was not much—old logs wedged together to form a few rooms, woodsmoke drifting into this pyre-to-be from the stone fireplace in the main room, while outside animals huddled in the forest, ears pricked for sounds of danger. I tried not to think about the garden out back, the decomposing bodies feeding our tomatoes, and peppers, and carrots. I tried not to think about how my father would carry on the tradition, when Grandpa finally slipped into oblivion. I tried not to think of my own fated role in all this, and what it felt like to slide a sharp blade between a man's ribs—that hiss and scrape and release.

"We should go," my father said, his shadow distending into the room as the sun set over the surrounding evergreen hills. Everything about him was muted in earth tones—scraggly dark beard, brown eyes pooling with rage, his wiry frame wrapped in flannel and blue jeans, his flesh like an old leather jacket that had been left out in the sun, his armor against a range of elements and emotions.

"Not yet," I pleaded. "The end will be soon. We owe him that much."

"We don't owe him anything," my father said, turning from the door, a slight limp leading him away from me, one step in a series of separations, the chasm between us widening, filling with bile.

A trickle of blood worked its way out of my grandfather's eyes, clenched shut against the shadows and wisps of blackness that drifted into the room. I was used to their companionship, these harbingers a catalyst in my life. They hovered over my cradle as a wobbly toddler, whispering in my ear as an angry pre-teen, slipping beneath my sheets as a high school graduate. In some ways they were a comforting presence at his deathbed, letting me know that I had not in fact gone insane—that this was very real.

His head twisted back and forth, pale skin mottled with bloody sores and angry red scars, the old man more skeleton than meat at this point, his body having atrophied in recent days, his dissipation erasing a presence that sent a mixture of relief and disgust washing over my skin. I grew flush, sweaty. It triggered a flurry of memories—the back of his hand to my questioning mouth, the precise work of a sharp blade as we stripped and butchered a deer, a birthmark on my palm in the shape of a lopsided hourglass, matching the one on his skin, and my father's as well.

With a choking sob, his eyes opened. No pupil, no iris, just white all the way around. His body heaved upward into a sitting position, his bony arms locked in a kind of rigor. Transfixed, I stared as a thin column of acrid yellow smoke wafted out from between his parched lips, his final exhale flooding the room with the stench of scorched milk and spoiled meat. Outside, an engine roared to life, breaking my concentration, the sound of my father's patience running out. When I looked back at my grandfather, his mouth wrenched violently open, impossibly wide, until I was certain his jaw would break. Finger-like grey tentacles lurched out of his throat, curling and wriggling, desperate to get a grip on the edges of his mouth, as if trying to hoist up something much larger from within. As I stepped back from the bed, a multitude of beetles scurried out from the folds of the bedsheets, shiny and black against the dirty linens. They skittered over the already cooling flesh of his spent frame until they covered it entirely. As much as I wanted to run, I held on to the end here, until, like a bundle of sticks dropped to the hard earth in winter, he collapsed back into the bed, letting go of my hand, the cavalcade of shimmering insects rushing into his open mouth.

I'd seen worse.

Taking a deep breath and releasing a heavy sigh, outside the wind blew, a screaming red fox perched on the hillside, the swoop and movement of a barn owl hooting overhead, the shadows and shapes closing in, wrapping my grandfather in their layers of hunger. I didn't need to stay for this part, so I stood up and went to the corner of the room where a can of gasoline sat.

Outside a horn honked three times in quick succession—time to go.

I circled the bed, dousing his corpse in fuel, the noxious fumes burning my nose and throat. After closing his eyelids and weighing them shut with gold coins, I emptied my pockets of hag stones over his emaciated corpse, before pouring a vase of dried lavender, wisteria, and rose petals over his stiffening form.

"You did good work, Grandpa," I said, striking a match and holding it aloft for a moment to survey my handiwork. It ignited with a heavy *whump*, the sudden wall of heat knocking me back onto my heels. I dashed toward the doorway before the flames engulfed the room.

And as I fled from the cabin, the trills of a flute ran scales up and down around me, ending on a low, hollow moan, as the frantic drumbeat settled down to a singular heavy tympani strike, the low wail of a violin screeching to a halt.

In the darkness of the surrounding woods, something ancient and timeless stirred, turning over in a slow, epic roll of flesh and bone. The discord of symphonic dirges slowly built anew, wailing in time with the flames licking at the inside of the cabin with a hunger I knew too well. The horn blared again, bringing my attention back to the present.

It was done.

My time was coming.

And there was nothing I could do.

We drove in silence for a long time, our black SUV rambling down the highway as the burning cabin receded in the mirrors, never to return to this familial haunt, my father gritting his teeth in a way that sent sparks into the tight space of the cab.

"Do you know how long I have?" he asked, as outside the green pine and expanding foliage filled the night with silent acceptance.

I didn't know how long Grandpa was out of commission. Toward the end it all hinged on whoever showed up on his doorstep—salesmen asking about the roof, Jehovah's Witnesses preaching Jesus, local politicians looking for a signature. He'd stopped answering our calls a few weeks ago, so it depended on what he did before he slipped into the coma. Without those details, I honestly had no clue.

"Weeks maybe? A month?"

My father shook his head, an echo of Grandpa's demise only moments before.

"You don't hear it then? Not yet?"

"No," he muttered, hands gripping the wheel, white knuckling his way down the asphalt, the headlights cutting a shallow wound into the night.

"We can do this, Dad," I said. "You're smart, we've been taught, there are ways to stay in the shadows…"

"I don't fucking want this!" he yelled, spittle flying out of his mouth.

"Nobody does," I said.

He took a long breath and with trembling fingers plucked a cigarette from a pack that rested between us, the hunting knife lying next to them in its leather sheath as he pushed down on the lighter in the dash, waiting for the circle to glow red.

"You're smoking again?" I asked.

"Why not?" The lighter popped out with a hearty click, and he grabbed the silver knob, holding it to the end of a shaky Marlboro. Relief flooded his face as he pulled the first drag, his eyes laced with veins of red, a shimmer of tears reflecting in the light. "Might as well shave a few years off the end, they're the crappy ones anyway." He laughed, choking out a bit of smoke, exhaustion and bitterness lingering in his voice.

"I'll help you, Dad. You know that."

And for just a moment the veil dropped—the anger, the frustration, the denial—and he was himself again, back before he had this knowledge, back before he killed his first victim, back when he loved his own father, unconditionally.

"I know, son. I know you will."

I didn't take my eyes from him, absorbing the man who gave me life in all his suffering—the way this had landed on him, the simple existence he had wanted taken away, the disintegration of his marriage, and the absence of my mother as he pushed her away from this dysfunctional heredity that was consuming us all. For her own safety, he said, and I know now, have for some time really, that those words were true. I saw him cutting the grass with a grin on his face, headphones plugged in as he wove a pattern of even lines back and forth. I saw him buying a large buttered popcorn, extra in the middle, for us to share on our epic adventures into the cinematic wonderland he chose to share with me. I saw him making me lunch when I came home from high school—soup, and grilled cheese, and a fresh fruit salad that he cut with a chef's knife—halving, and quartering, and dicing with glee. All he ever wanted was to make those around him feel safe and loved. What hovered over us now was the opposite of that, and he was crumbling under the pressure, cracking and crumbling, tiny pieces of himself littering the floor of the SUV as he inhaled smoke deeply into his lungs, welcoming the toxins as punishment and release.

In six months he would be dead.

And I would be alone.

The last in our lineage, the lone protector, trying to stave off the creeping finality of our certain demise.

I would have to pivot.

I would have to fall in love and pass this on to a new generation.

I would have to lie until the deed was done.

And it would probably cost me everything.

My grandfather was dead, my father had taken his own life, my mother pushed away so that none of this would fall on her, taint her, pull her into the sticky web that this diseased bloodline had cast out into the world. Glittering orbs trembled from streetlights in layered strands, like teary eyeballs, shards of glass reflecting light, as overhead the moon vibrated in the expanding night. The quiet was broken by the shriek of a bat, the distant rumbling of a train, the gentle whispers of long grass and growing corn.

I was adrift now, knowing that normalcy had left me, unable, or perhaps unwilling, to set down roots like my grandfather, burying one secret after another in the spoiled earth of his own back yard. The harvest around me—corn, wheat, and soybean—moved back and forth in the cool gentle breeze, as I stood smoking a cigarette, a new habit that had grown on me, one last homage to my father, as the echo of a gunshot still reverberated in my memory.

He was not strong enough to do what Grandfather did, bending under the weight of such actions, driven to madness by the relentless drumbeats that he finally heard, and resisted.

I had started drinking. Why not? What lay before me would not be easy. And as the used Camry cooled in the night air, headlights in the distance took one oblivious worker north on the highway away from the city, another south back toward the screaming skyscrapers—ants, I thought, mindless ants, lemmings in a driving herd, over the edge of the nearest cliff, never looking up at the cosmos above them. Unaware of how fragile our existence was.

I tipped back the cold can of Budweiser before taking a deep pull at the cigarette, and stared off into the darkness at the edge of a nearby field, an off-key flute fading in the gloom, as a violin string hummed a low vibration, and a dissipating snare drum popped.

It was growing faint. All of it. And that wasn't good. Where my father had strained to hear the call, I had always borne witness, so when it started to fade I knew my work must commence.

My father had spent months in denial, telling me nothing, only nodding his head as we sat at the dinner table—chicken thighs burnt from the grill as he stared off into space, watery mashed potatoes dotted with raw chunks of garlic, broccoli wilted and withering in a bowl with the trimmed-off stems mixed in by mistake. I stared at a glass of flat Coke sweating rivulets of water, trying to discern a pattern in the random nature of their distribution, waiting in vain for him to talk to me.

I trusted him.

Another deep inhale, and the smoke felt like a cloud of tiny daggers in my lungs, the last of the beer swallowed in three gulps, the crushed can tossed into a ditch.

A vacant warehouse loomed in the shadows nearby, as the midway glow and clamor of a county fairgrounds lingered on the horizon, and just off the highway the beacon of a Wendy's, open late. I was both a part of it all, and a shadow.

I thought I'd have more time.

The killing would have to start soon. I had prepared myself in ways that my father never did. Taking a cue from Grandfather, I scoured the newspapers, I watched the news, I stalked the dark web, and I listened to my police scanner.

I didn't know what scared me more—the fading of the grotesque orchestra, the fact that someone innocent would die, or the feeling that this didn't bother me—none of it, not at all.

My name was legion, for we were many. And yet, the drums were receding, the dream weavers growing tired and weary from a lack of offerings, a lack of sacrifice. I needed to martyr myself, and soon, flagellate and bathe in the blood of my victims.

The list had been made, the parameters set. My hand trembled as I took the hunting knife from its sheath, remembering the words of my grandfather, remembering the trembling lips of my father.

And then I needed to find a mate.

My son was already overdue.

In the sheer pitch black of eternity, musicians were scattered across the ether, tortured souls that had mastered their craft and then been stolen in the dead of night. They survived not on the flesh of animals or the nectar of water, but on the violence that was carried out by a select bloodline. There were many, they were a multitude, a horde, some secluded in the moist black caves that inhabited the Midwest;

some coated in ice, trapped on mountain tops, where the air was impossible to breathe; a few tucked deep into dense forests, lush foliage wrapping around them like moldering blankets. They pursed their lips and breathed foul air into tarnished flutes. They ran their faded bows over frayed strings, a low moan emanating from the cavity of ancient violins. They pounded a slow beat of tom toms over oxidized tympani, muscled arms carved from marble, a serenity filling their vacant white eyes. They suffered and trembled in ecstasy, they were eternal and yet constantly fading, they ebbed and flowed, their existence the last obstacle, the last assistance, to a singularly old god that slept in angry fits. They prayed for the acts to be carried out, but also longed for it all to fail. They were so very tired, and yet unable, unwilling to stop. They existed in a dream, as everything did, waiting for the day when evil awoke, erasing it all. But for now, the web was woven, the matrix holding, the illusion intact. Such a tremulous hold, all of it—hanging by a thread. Teetering on the edge of a cliff, leaning out over the endless void, searching for the tipping point.

By the time I met Melissa, I had killed three men.

The first one I stabbed in the back alley of a diner as I was heading north into Wisconsin. He was tall and skinny with a patchy beard that looked like mange, coughing out cigarette smoke at regular intervals, the tip of every filter dotted with blood. He was lost in this world and had been muttering about *this bitch* and *that bitch*, eager to inflict damage on somebody who probably didn't deserve it, a menace to society, in my opinion. When I asked if I could bum a smoke, he looked up, squinted, and reached inside his dirty jean jacket, seeing something of himself in me, I think. I'd been on the road for a few weeks, so I was looking a bit off, disheveled and disgruntled, so he must have thought us kin. When I leaned in to take the cigarette, I switched hands and slid the blade into his chest, smooth and easy, up and underneath his sternum, straight into his heart, his eyes going wide at the pinch of the steel through his flesh. His death would not be enough, it had to be a spectacle, and so I pulled the blade out and then stabbed him in the gut, slicing up and in, and then back down, opening him up like a puckering coin purse, his intestines unraveling onto the ground. When he collapsed, without hardly a noise, I rearranged the steaming offal into a pleasing pattern in the dim light of the lamppost, my aching hands slick with blood, a symbol of eternity trembling with power.

The drums beat louder as I slipped away into the shadows, leaving behind nothing but speculation for the authorities, and whispers of fear from the locals.

Not in this town.

Not here.

Yes, everywhere.

All at once.

The second man I killed I found in Iowa as I headed west—no particular destination in mind, just the urge to keep moving. The pickup truck had so many conspiracy bumper stickers on it that I could hardly concentrate on the road. Everything from aliens to politics to Bible quotes. It boggled the mind. I followed him for a few hours until he pulled into a rest stop, and everything after that fell into place. I had no remorse; that part of me had died when the baton was passed from father to son. As we stood side by side at the urinals, I muttered a few things, just to confirm that this wasn't the truck of an uncle or brother or son. He nodded his head, adjusting his ball cap and spitting tobacco into the urinal with a hearty laugh. We were on the same page, it seemed. And so I shoved the blade into his back—stab, stab, stabbing—and he danced a jig, then collapsed onto the floor, pants around his ankles, covered in his own urine, feces, blood. As I painted the walls, my eyes filled with glory and gold dust, a tapestry unfolding onto the slick tile and concrete blocks, a mural depicting a throne of bones, drenched in dark fluids, fire burning in the background.

A flute solo warbled and rose to a high pitch as I exited the rest stop, a grin easing across my face. I almost enjoyed this now, dust motes dancing in the setting sunlight as I shoved open the glass doors of the building, hands washed with cheap soap in a flurry of mania, back out into the crisp evening air, crickets chirping, a nightjar trilling in the distance.

The third man was further west still, somewhere in Nebraska. I'd grown tired of the road and pulled into the crowded parking lot of some honky-tonk and waited—knowing it was only a matter of time. I had acquired a sixth sense about this. Windows down, the evening breeze bringing cries of cicadas from across the prairie, the doors of the bar swinging open and closed with drunken revelers sending classic rock and modern country drifting out across the gravel parking lot. I fell asleep at some point and woke up to silence, cursing the fact that I'd missed my opportunity, the lot barren and the music having faded into the swaying grass. And then the bartender and a waitress rolled out, padlocking the doors, laughing and stumbling, arms around each other. When she tried to get into her car alone, he pushed her up against the trunk, but she resisted. She had a husband, she said, but he knew she'd had too much to drink. She said no, this wasn't wanted, as he insisted he knew what was best. She slapped him and then he shoved her to the ground, cursing as he fumbled to find a way into her jeans, her screams filling the night, and then a kick from her catching him in the crotch and sending him sprawling, groaning to the pavement. She gathered herself together with a string of shouts, *fuck you* this, and *I quit* that, you bastard, how could you, and then she drove off, leaving him lying on the cold hard ground.

But it wasn't enough for me, of course. I needed more.

And I had the rest of the night to explore him.

Out of the trunk I gathered a machete and a hacksaw, my hunting knife unsheathed in my free hand as I walked toward the crumpled pile of denim and cheap bourbon.

He died quickly, just a few well-placed slices here and there, and then I got to work. It resembled an exploded diagram for an engine, a schematic for a transistor radio, or perhaps instructions for assembling bookshelves from IKEA—except the lines were a liquid crimson, and the parts were made from human anatomy. It was a grisly work of art, and I gasped when it was finished.

I stripped out of my blood-soaked clothes and walked barefoot across the parking lot to an old oil drum, the cold pavement and night air sending shivers up my tired legs. Tossing the clothes inside the barrel, I doused them with lighter fluid from the glove compartment and lit it all on fire. A few more steps into the grass, and it wasn't much farther to a creek that ran behind it all. I bathed in the moonlight as the violins reached a crescendo, a glory in the darkness that drained me of my laughter, my fear, my disgust. Just before I passed out, I wept into the encroaching gloom, missing my grandfather, but proud of the work I'd done. I thought of the weight that my father couldn't sustain, and collapsed in the sand and stones of the creek bed.

When I came to, I was headed south, eyes wide open, everything a blur.

I ended up in a computer parts factory somewhere in Kansas, one robotic worker after another walking into the building for the night shift, single file. Some carried brown paper sacks, some had old-school lunchboxes, and a few lugged in Tupperware filled with cold lasagna or sausages from the grill—anything cheap and easy to make. The work was simple, the people depressed, the income terrible. I'd sit outside during my break, chasing down whatever was on the dollar menu of the nearest fast food restaurant with a 40 ounce of Budweiser or Coors Light. Often I'd vomit it all back up onto the parking lot, sobbing into the black void of nothingness that surrounded me, and then I'd rinse out my mouth with what was left of the piss-warm beer and head back inside.

I was promoted from assembly line worker to line chief in a matter of weeks—so I now had the honor of shutting down my machine to shove my hands inside the metal gears to fix it whenever it got stuck. And it got stuck a lot. Part of me fantasized about it ripping off my arms as it suddenly came to life, ending this all, but then I remembered the fate of the world was in my hands and I laughed, a deep laugh that bounced off the walls of the metal drum that housed the assembly line mechanics, the workers around me oblivious as the noise of the factory was deafening, ear plugs and all.

The locals resented this promotion, and they showed me how they felt every day.

People started jostling me in the hallways, going quiet when I entered the break room, their girlfriends eyeballing me a bit too long. My friendly nature earned me white teeth and tossed hair by the ladies—whether they were 18 or 30 or 65—the men pushing their lips together like tiny, puckered assholes, mustaches aquiver, gnarled fists clenched in silent rage. I started to find offerings on the hood of my car and at the base of my locker—dead mice, a rotting possum, and once just a pile of crap from something I hoped was a dog and not human. Finding my tires slashed was a new twist, and when I tried to appeal to the foreman, he put his hands behind his balding head and leaned back, belly straining the buttons of his stained grey shirt—offering to check the cameras when he had a moment, both of us knowing they didn't work. So I made sure to chat up his girlfriend that night at the vending machine, laughing at some bad joke she made about a reality TV show, his glare from the open door to his office a piercing gaze. I winked at him, causing him to frown and cross his arms in burly anger, his head shiny under the harsh fluorescent lights. When his girl patted me on the arm and then headed to her desk, he went back inside. The slashed tires stopped, but it was only a matter of time before this escalated into something nasty. I needed to move on. I was drawing too much attention.

One cold winter night when I went out to my car, I caught a dishwater blonde named Melissa smoking a joint, leaned up against her little red Corolla. We had both parked at the far end of the lot— obviously the safest thing to do. When I raised my eyebrows at her, she smiled and offered me a hit, so I took a draw and chatted her up as the rest of the crew filed into their rusty Silverados, muddy F-150s, and growling Chargers.

We were two of the younger workers there—most of the kids barely lasting a summer, stepping stones between high school and college to getting the hell out of this crappy town and its bubble of inherent racism. The older generation seemed resigned to this slow death, and it only fueled their rage. There wasn't a Black man or woman as far as the eye could see, and while I assumed a few stolen glances came from repressed homosexuals that would probably die alone before coming out, I wasn't above a wry grin when I caught one of my fans in a prolonged gaze. Fuck it, maybe it would give them hope. In my violent actions I seemed to have acquired some sort of glow, bathing in the blood of my killings like a vain vampire, seeking to stay vibrant, as I carried out my secret acts.

Melissa and I hit it off right away—her tight blue jeans and form-fitting black sweater always drawing my eye. I liked that she was tough—running her own assembly line not far from mine, grunting and sweating in unison with me as we sorted and stacked parts, troubleshooting the equipment, socket wrenches and bloody knuckles. She was quick with a dirty joke, loved to watch scary movies, and told me about a great Thai restaurant down the road a bit. She had stayed here to help out her mother while the cancer was spreading, her father long gone. She just clocked her hours at the factory and paid her penance. It didn't take long for us to find our way to a local bar, a few cold beers leading to darts and pool, and even a little dancing. Eventually it became sex in her apartment, both of us hungry and eager to find something to make us feel alive, something to break up the depressed state of this hollow existence. She was lean, fit, and eager to share her body with a man who so desperately wanted her.

The places we went after that weren't important, it was all the same really—the hot seedy rental where I lay awake at night sweating to death followed by a cold freezing studio where the windows rattled from the wind. But whether it was my tiny rented house with the dirt floor viewable under the rotten hardwood, covered up by a faded throw rug, or her generic one-bedroom apartment surrounded by woods where a fetid stream ran behind it, transporting old tires, the occasional dying fish, and a foam at the edges like a rabid dog, we made the best of it.

During the days, we'd lie awake on her lumpy mattress, ashtrays overflowing with cigarette butts and spent roaches, blinds pulled to block out the harsh light of reality, as she tried to get to know the man she was sleeping with. I kept telling myself just one more day and then I'd move on, that this wasn't the girl for me. I didn't need to pull her into my madness, but she kept digging, asking about past lovers, wondering where my family was, where I'd lived, what I was really *doing* in this life. And then she asked me if I'd ever killed a man, joking as she inhaled deeply one of her menthol cigarettes, and I guess my reaction didn't pass muster—first no response, then hysterical laughter, then silence.

I thought we were done.

So I told her everything.

She left, of course, looking over her shoulder as she got dressed, stepping into her black lace panties and bra, a weird, wry grin on her face turning to horror the more she considered what I'd said, then her blue jeans, followed by disgust, her eyes never leaving me as she pulled on her flannel shirt, her Timberlands slipping over one foot then the other, tracking me as I lay on my side of the unmade bed, quietly forcing myself to breathe, holding back tears.

She was beautiful, inside and out, and I wanted her to leave. There would be somebody else—somebody I'd care about less. The terrible things I carried with me weren't for her.

When I awoke sometime later, the light pushing in through the cracked blinds and torn drapes, she was sitting on the edge of the bed, holding my hand, glowing like a newborn sun.

She wanted in.

And she knew what that meant.

She was ready to sacrifice it all.

Three months later we were on the road headed west, her mother cremated, the soulless factory a distant memory.

When the drums faded, and the flute disappeared, the echo of a violin string finally gone, I gave her my seed and passed on the bloodline to our child. As she wept in the bedroom of our small apartment on the outskirts of Denver, I cried with her, hating myself for what I'd done. She was happy, in love, a child something she had talked about since the beginning. I was a writhing demon, holding her close as the fate of our child was determined, my fiancée understanding all that was coming and willing to accept those outcomes, if only for a short while, whatever joy she could squeeze out of it.

In that moment I thought of my grandfather, and then my father, as I finally understood the shadowy weight that had befallen them both, this passing down of responsibility, this gift and curse no longer mine alone.

I hated myself.

I hated the world.

But I kept on anyway.

In the eyes of my euphoric wife, in the greeting of a friendly neighbor over a fence lined with lush foliage, in the laughter of the children on the playground down the street, the music of the ice cream truck cresting a nearby hill, there were reasons to continue.

As I lay on my death bed, I held the hand of my granddaughter, catching a glint in her eye that would never fade, her ponytail held in place by a blood-red band with tiny shining stones. My lanky son stood in a familiar doorway, drying a dish in sore hands, as his daughter whispered kind things into my ear. Melissa couldn't bear to see me depart, her muted sobs drifting to me from the back porch, her grey hair barely visible through the window of our happy home, the crickets chirping, a coyote howling up in the hills. I wept bloody tears as my vision vibrated and hummed, a nod from my son barely perceptible, my granddaughter singing a sweet song to herself, accompanied by a fading flute, over a distant drumbeat, and a wailing violin. The line of bodies that extended back in time from one city to another, over dozens of expanding years, they pushed lumps and hills into the earth as they decomposed and faded into distant memories, the world a better place for our actions, the mantra we whispered to each other.

And in the darkness a hundred eyes clicked open, the world flickering and fading, then slamming back into focus, as my granddaughter held my lips shut, and counted us all back to sleep.

Dust-Clotted Eyes

Samuel Marzioli

ALDEN GAZED THROUGH the window of Mrs. Lawson's second-story guestroom, searching the street for signs of life. Lightning streaked across a black velvet sky. Torrential rains discharged thick and steady as machine gun bullets and a gale ripped into the house's outer walls, the structure trembling and creaking as if it meant to come undone.

"Jesus," said Dale, an ear tilted toward the ceiling. "Listen to that. You think we'll still get a Visitor tonight?"

"We'll get one," said Alden.

"How close to midnight is it?"

Alden glanced at his wristwatch. "Fifteen minutes." He turned to face Faye and Mrs. Lawson. "Better get your heads and hearts right. It'll be starting soon."

A needless warning, perfunctory at best. Since the phenomenon had begun, the thought of Visitors had consumed Alden and his friends' every waking moment, a constant, nagging itch buried in the meat of their brains. Not even sleep afforded an escape. The threat of Visitors rendered every dream into a cavalcade of nightmares where dead things and strange beasts prowled the streets at night, or skulked in the shadows around their home. The world had changed, and Visitors had become an intrinsic part of it, inhabitants of that fleeting time between night and day.

But they did their best to keep themselves distracted. Mrs. Lawson knitted, oblong bundles of yarn stacked on her lap as she rocked upon her rocker. Dale reclined beside the hearth, staring blankly at a book of poetry he'd been picking through for months. Between scattered glances at the street below, Alden rubbed the glass face of his wristwatch, while Faye pressed her back against the door, scanning photos in an album dedicated to her son.

Faye was the newest addition to the household and only by a stroke of luck. She'd stopped on the shoulder of the interstate three months back when she'd spotted Dale and Alden in the distance, scavenging supplies from a deserted store in town. After she'd settled into the converted room in Mrs. Lawson's basement, she'd told them how every place she'd passed through had been empty, chaos slipping through the cracks. From what she'd seen, Mrs. Lawson's may have been the only house still occupied on God's green earth.

Five minutes before midnight, snow began to fall. It melted in the street, but collected on rooftops, yards, and trees. Soon it swelled into a blizzard, concealing the world behind a pale shell.

"Is it time?" asked Dale.

Alden glanced at his wristwatch, and a lump too big to swallow bobbed inside his throat. "Almost. Better kill the lights."

Faye shot up and hit the switch. The lamps winked out, replaced by the fire's winsome glow. Mrs. Lawson dropped her knitting, removed the nightcap from her silver bouffant curls. Dale tried to rise but stumbled to his knees instead, his eyes pleading with the ceiling.

Alden peered outside, searching for any dark shape inching through the snow squall. For a moment, he pictured his wife Clara strolling down the sidewalk, past the overgrowth of the next-door neighbor's lawn and the pair of semi-rusted cars slouched against the curb out front. But then the real Visitor arrived. The suit he wore rippled in the wind, hugging his thin curves. With arms folded, he lurched across the front yard to the door, plodding steps that barely dragged him forward.

Alden tried to hide his disappointment, but not so his relief. Once he caught Mrs. Lawson's stare, her wet eyes glistening in the firelight, he said, "It's Roy."

The week prior, it had been a mix of Dale's boyfriend Daniel and Faye's older brother Glenn. Before that, the Visitors had alternated through the spectrum of relationships, everything from grandparents to parents, uncles to aunts, friends to lovers, and a few times even pets. But Roy, Mrs. Lawson's husband, had been the Visitor every night that week.

"How is he, Alden?" asked Mrs. Lawson. "Is he... whole?"

Alden threw a furtive glance at Dale, a knowing kind with dark insinuations. Dale shuffled up behind her rocker, snaking his arms around the spindles and crisscrossing them over her chest.

"I asked you how he looks," said Mrs. Lawson, voice quivering. "Alden, tell me!"

"That's not what we agreed on."

Mrs. Lawson struggled, but Dale applied more pressure to his hold. "I'm not your *prisoner*," she said, voice ascending to a scream. "This isn't your choice to make!"

Alden hissed, imagining Roy breaking down the door and rushing up the stairs, or scuttling spider-like along the outside wall, protracted claws digging into the vinyl siding. For a year, they'd hidden from Visitors, sure of nothing except their primal need to stay alive. While the Visitors must have had an inkling of their presence by whatever force brought them to the door, Alden and his friends had done their best never to confirm it. But after Mrs. Lawson's cries, he had no idea what to expect. For all he knew, an army of the dead had marshaled forth from some black and dreary realm, already converging on their position.

"Get off me!" Mrs. Lawson shouted.

"Goddamn it, shut her up," said Alden.

"Who cares anymore?" said Faye, hiding racking sobs behind a curtain of her hair. "Whatever you think you're protecting her from, it can't be worse than this."

Mrs. Lawson twisted around, fingers splayed, nails clawing at the air mere inches from Dale's face. Alden lunged onto his feet and in two steps stood before her, grabbing her by the wrists and matching the fury of her eyes with his own irritation.

"Stop it," he said. "You're putting us at risk. You may think you know what's down there, but you don't. You—"

Roy knocked, his rising baritone so clear he could have been standing in the room. "Are you there, Joanne? I don't have much time."

"Roy! I'm trying, wait for me, I'm trying!"

Alden covered her mouth and her teeth raked across his palm, her defiant stare assuring him it hadn't been an accident.

"Find a rag," he said, flailing his hand to ease the pain. "We need to cover her mouth."

Dale left the room, his hurried footsteps trailing down the hall into the bathroom. Alden took Dale's place, binding Mrs. Lawson to the rocker with the same crisscrossed pattern of his arms. Meanwhile, Faye stared on in horror. Deep red splotches colored her face, her chest heaving like an asthmatic who couldn't catch a breath. After setting her album down, she climbed to her feet and stomped toward Alden, the knuckles of her fists clenched white.

"Stop it," she said, a too-calm voice that couldn't hide its threat.

"Don't," said Alden. "You know what it's like. She won't make it if she doesn't have all of us supporting her, helping her resist."

"Last chance."

Alden shook his head. "Faye, please don't do this."

He braced himself for the explosion of her anger, a knee to the groin or a punch to the center of his eye. Instead, she launched herself. A hundred and thirty pounds of manic fury collided with his knees, and he crumpled to the floor.

As soon as Alden lost his grip, Mrs. Lawson hobbled for the open door amid the metallic clink of her knitting needles and the clatter of the rocker that toppled when she rose. Alden scrambled after her even as Faye fell upon him, driving him face-first into the carpet. Once Mrs. Lawson reached the door, she turned.

"Someday I hope you'll understand," she said, and fled into the hallway.

"Dale, help!" Alden shouted, bucking Faye's limp weight still riding on his back.

Somewhere in the distance, a cupboard slammed and the meaty sound of bare feet thumped in their direction. Mrs. Lawson shrieked. Dale grunted. Moments later they both appeared, an imposing Dale carrying the tiny Mrs. Lawson like a baby in his arms, oblivious to the frail rhythm she beat into his chest.

Another knock from down below, this time soft and steady.

"Joanne, please. Come outside before it's too late."

Dale faltered. Arms shaking, he lowered Mrs. Lawson onto her feet as if the toll of guilt had robbed him of his strength. He embraced her and she wept into his chest. Faye's fury drained away, along with the color in her face. Even Alden felt a shift: a flare of warmth within his cheeks, a softening of his heart, all his bottled grief unstoppered. Months of stone-etched resolutions failed, and his thoughts returned to memories of the loved ones he'd lost. His father and mother? Victims of a stroke and cancer, but both of them had been Visitors on at least two occasions. His younger brother Stanley? At 16, he'd taken a drunken dive off the Tinika Bridge into the shallows of the river, and yet he'd returned not three weeks back, solid as the days before his accident. Clara, his wife? She had been among the first victims, stolen on the night it all began.

Alden thought he saw a distant gleam in his friends' eyes that indicated a similar reminiscing. What it meant, he didn't know, but it felt so much like an undoing. The beginning of the end of what little they had left.

"I'm ready," said Mrs. Lawson. She patted Dale's arm, took a few steps back. "I know you mean well, but this isn't some rash decision." She turned to Alden, pursed her lips. "I've spent months thinking about this moment, wondering what I'd do. I've let him go five times already, and if I have to do it again, I swear I'll break."

She met their gaze, the delirium of before replaced by calm determination. No one rose to stop her when she flitted from the room. They merely listened as she shuffled down the staircase to the ground floor.

Another knock. "Joanne?"

The door creaked open.

"Oh, Roy!" said Mrs. Lawson.

Alden hurried to the window, and Faye and Dale followed close behind. Together, they watched Mrs. Lawson and Roy traipsing through the yard, pressing tracks into the fallen snow before vanishing into the bluster and the cold darkness.

Dale and Alden took turns splitting wood out back on Mrs. Lawson's acre plot. Narrow fences hedged them, but the rear hugged a downward slope, overtaking a copse of trees before the limits of the houses of a lower tract. A fierce sun dallied in the bright and cloudless sky, as if the day were offering an apology for the improprieties of the night. The snow was melting fast. As far as Dale and Alden could recall, it hadn't snowed in years, and never in spring. Not that it mattered; nothing in heaven or on earth could surprise them anymore.

They had a long-standing disagreement over whether Visitors were ghosts or zombies, but Roy's footprints finally put that debate to rest. After stacking a week's worth of firewood beside the upstairs hearth, they spent the remainder of the day tossing the z-word back and forth, sharing favorite TV shows and movies, and laughing over how wrong every one of them had gotten it. Zombies didn't crave flesh or brains. They preferred visiting family, holding hands, and long walks under a star-crammed night.

Despite the flow of banter, and hours playing *Battleship* with Dale, Alden felt troubled. The death of his family had been agonizing, but Mrs. Lawson's passing heralded a different kind of woe. After all this time, he'd begun to think of them as invincible, the Final Girls and Guys, waiting for a fresh start on the far side of the apocalypse. But now he realized no one was safe, and with this revelation came a deep-seated languor, a cancer growing in his soul, pushing him to give in to the inevitability of death.

Dale probably felt it too. Alden thought he saw clear signs of it in Dale's distant looks, the way his smiles lacked conviction, the hollow note within his laugh. Nevertheless, he would never admit it. Despite Alden being twenty years his senior, they were so much alike, preferred to push their dark thoughts aside and live as if it mattered. Anything less would be giving up.

Faye chose a different route. Her nostalgia punched into overdrive as she paced from room to room, touching things that had once been precious to Mrs. Lawson: knickknacks and photographs, a favorite sweater, a quilt, a pillow. She couldn't stop crying or explaining the reasons for what she did. She took the blame for Mrs. Lawson's passing and nothing Dale and Alden said could change her mind.

They let her have the space she needed, let her sleep off the brunt of her gloom in Mrs. Lawson's bedroom. Even with the door closed, they could hear her cracking sobs and self-denunciations. She paused long enough to call out to Mrs. Lawson, to her brother Glenn, but mostly to her son.

"Timmy, darling, I'm still waiting, baby. I'm still waiting."

Night fell quicker than expected, the sun ushered from its throne by a bright and primal moon. By 11, the remaining members of the household assembled in the second-story guestroom. They started up the generator but didn't strike a fire, since the house had hoarded the heat of the first warm day of spring. Alden took his position by the window. Dale hunkered beside the fireplace and Faye collapsed against the door, her son's album replaced by Mrs. Lawson's pillow.

No one spoke. A frantic energy coursed between them, fueled by fear, the unspoken understanding that last night's parting would soon be repeated. Alden's leg began to bounce. Dale dragged his book along the carpet and Faye rocked to and fro, her head pounding at the wall to the cadence of a heartbeat. Eventually she stood, circled the room, and then hovered over Alden's shoulder.

"Is it time?" she asked.

Alden didn't answer, couldn't trust himself enough to release his thoughts as words into the world. When midnight came, he didn't bother to announce it. He simply bit his lip and gestured outside. Dale and Faye crowded around, pressing tight into the window space beside Alden. A young boy gamboled down the sidewalk, dressed in a t-shirt and jeans. Once he rounded up the driveway, he paused to stare up at the guestroom, the moon reflecting white across his horned-rim glasses.

"It's a boy," said Dale.

Alden took a breath, released it as a sigh. "Faye..."

"Please don't. Let's not spend our last few precious minutes arguing," she said.

"'Chaos.' That's how you described the world out there, and that thing standing on the porch is part of it. You can't pretend they're unrelated. If one's bad, it stands to reason the other is as well."

Faye shook her head. "I don't have all the answers, Alden, but I do know this. We put so much value into what we made, called it beauty, called it order, but Nature has always had a greater sense of both. Maybe ours was only ever chaos in disguise—death and destruction with a concrete and steel veneer—and this is the universe's way of setting things right."

"I don't accept that."

"Regardless, it's time for me to go. I can feel it. It might not make sense to you right now, but you'll know it when you feel it too."

She toddled up to Dale, threw her arms around him, pulled him down, and kissed him on the cheek. She came to Alden and hugged him next.

"Despite our disagreements," she whispered, "you took care of us, and I'll always treasure you for that. I'm not sure how yet, but I'll come back and tell you if the place the Visitors are taking us is safe."

Alden nodded. He hoped Faye would be okay, that when she stepped onto the porch she'd be safe within her loved one's grip, not trapped in the clutches of some pernicious monster. No, he needed to believe that it was true, even screamed an affirmation in his head. Experience, however, had taught him that no good thing ever proceeded from a veil of smoke and mirrors, and all he felt for Faye was grief of one more loss.

The Visitor knocked. "Mommy? Are you there?"

Dale and Alden watched Faye leave—at least until she padded down the stairway—and then turned toward the window to peer outside. The entrance squeaked and shuddered at its closing and then the excited squeals of "Mommy, Mommy, Mommy!" followed Faye and her son Timmy as they wandered down the street and out of sight.

Dale hunched over the dining room table, food left half-eaten in his bowl. Alden sat across from him, his forehead pressed into a fist. Their meal had consisted of stale bread and a dubious can of chicken soup. No dents or bulges in the can, but sometime in the months since its liberation from a neighbor's pantry, the contents had solidified into a clump. They ate it anyway, one spoonful at a time, until its weight rested in their stomachs like a pile of rocks and regret.

"Breakfast of champions," Alden meant to say, but the words were lost inside an unshakeable malaise. He hadn't spoken since he woke, preferring to communicate with grunts and gestures. Dale followed suit, but the second he finished eating, tears pooled at the corners of his eyes.

"You have something on your mind," said Alden. "So say it."

"That's presumptuous. Don't act like you have me figured out."

"Am I wrong?"

"No." Dale cocked his head. "How could you tell?"

"Magic. Intuition. Or maybe you ought to work on that poker face of yours in case we ever start playing."

Dale let out a weak, stuttered breath, something like a chuckle. Neither had the capacity for true laughter anymore, and probably never would again.

"Do you... ever wonder if the Visitors aren't as bad as we think?" he asked.

"No."

"Shouldn't you? We laugh about zombies on movies and TV, but we're still operating on the same assumptions as people on those shows. 'The dead are evil and only mean us harm.' What if that's bullshit? What if Visitors are guides sent by some greater power? What if they're meant to take us to the next world, like utopia, or paradise, or—"

"Hell?"

Dale slapped his hand down, a sharp crack against the table. "I'm being serious."

Alden met his gaze, unflinching. "So am I. It's all just a little too convenient, don't you think? A hundred thousand years of 'dead is dead,' and yet now is the perfect time for things to change? If the Visitors were guides sent by some benevolent force, what they offer wouldn't feel so much like temptation: something we desire, but should never have."

"I can't answer that, but..." Dale stroked his chin, then wiped a hand across his mouth. "If a Visitor comes for me tonight, I'm going with them."

Alden shook his head. "That's not funny."

"Who's joking? I'm so tired. We haunt this house like ghosts locked into a pattern of behavior we can't escape, oblivious to the truth around us. This world is dead. Maybe we are too and don't know it yet."

"You know what happened to Daniel, saw where they buried his body, and watched the grass and moss and clover grow above his plot. That's death and you know it. What we're doing is survival, which in case you forgot is a fundamental prerequisite for *life*."

"I wasn't being literal, Alden. But this?" He motioned toward the kitchen and a broad, sweeping gesture for the world beyond. "This isn't life, it's existing. There is a difference."

"Okay," Alden said, throwing his hands up in surrender. "Do what you want, but don't expect me to be there when you go."

"What? That's not fair!"

"You've been with me since the beginning. You were the first familiar face I saw after my wife was taken. You're not just a friend, you're family. So fine." He stood and his chair skidded back. The coarse surface of its feet squeaked against the hardwood floor, an angry exclamation his voice approached, but couldn't quite deliver. "If you want to play pretend, I won't get in your way. But you have no right to ask me to watch it happen."

Alden whiled away the hours splitting firewood. By the time he finished, the sky flared up in starlight and a crescent moon grinned down, deeper shadows braving the dull light to crawl along the edges of the yard. After stowing the axe in the shed, he slumped across the deck, slipped his aching hands between his thighs.

His blisters were legion, but he embraced the pain. Pain meant he could feel, feeling meant he was alive, and life meant... He shrugged, unable to pin a meaning on that one.

As a boy, it was the thrill of new experiences. Once he reached adulthood, it was the pride of accomplishment, and after he got married, the joy of loving and being loved. But now? Life's meaning was extraneous, dust ejected from the drying husks of yesterdays and the shadows cast by the obelisk of tomorrows. Only survival mattered anymore, and its dominion was the here and now.

An urgent tap, and Alden found Dale standing by the patio door, a hand not knowing whether it should wave or press against the glass. During the brunt of Alden's self-imposed exile, Dale had spied on him in a clockwise pattern along the windows of both floors. Whenever Alden spotted Dale's sullen face peeking through the curtains, he would assume a profound interest in the distance. Never mind that nothing changed. Never mind that wherever he looked, he saw the same old rustling trees and the vacant gloom of windows. It served its purpose, expressed his dissatisfaction for Dale's decision.

Alden turned away again, but not before noticing Dale's finger jabbing at his wrist. It would be midnight soon. He could feel it coming, that cold sensation threading his bones and sliding through the marrow.

He closed his eyes, tried imagining who it might be this time — but in the shifting black and red behind his eyelids, a memory of Clara emerged. She was lying on their bed beside him. No makeup, hair disheveled, a tired, purple weight beneath her eyes. Such exquisite flaws. Such perfect imperfections. He couldn't have been more in love, but he was sick, tired, cranky that night and withheld a kiss before a heavy dose of diphenhydramine dragged him into a dreamless sleep. When he woke, she was gone.

Stricken by the implication, he leaned up on his side. What he wouldn't give for a minute more with Clara, to tell her what she meant, how he felt. Soon, Dale would be gone as well, and while his decision was selfish — a betrayal of everything they stood for — Alden couldn't waste this chance to say goodbye.

After clambering to his feet, he rushed inside. Dale reclined on the chaise lounge in the living room, his book resting on his stomach, fingers draped over its spine.

"What do *you* want?" he said.

Alden put the thumb-side of a fist against his mouth and cleared his throat. "I've been thinking... I don't want... I can't let things... I might have been a little too..."

He reached for every heartfelt word he'd meant to share, but one by one they poured out from his mind, a tipped bottle with its cork undone. Instead, he finished with the first thought that occurred to him.

"You're still not done with that book?"

"What, this?" Dale patted the cover. "I've read it a hundred times, even memorized many of the poems. It was Daniel's favorite. Frankly, I can't stand the thing—pretentious drivel through and through—but it makes me feel like he's close no matter how far apart we are."

"That's a relief. Faye and I often wondered why you always had it with you. She guessed it was sentimental, but I started kicking the word 'illiterate' around, to see how well it fit."

Dale snorted. "You're a good man, Alden, but equally an asshole. How do you manage to strike such a perfect balance?"

"Dunno. Comes with practice, I guess."

"Well." Dale sighed and stood and let the book drop to the floor beside him. "Let's not draw this out like two scorned high school lovers. Get over here, you doof!"

Alden crossed the room and wrapped his arms around him. Neither of them moved or spoke, just let the solace of the moment work its healing magic. But the moment passed as soon as a knock came at the door, and Alden's mood slid into grief and anger. He tightened his grip around Dale, convinced that if he held on long enough, the Visitor would be forced to leave.

"Let me go," said Dale. "He's here."

"Wait! Are you sure you want to do this? The odds it's him are a lotto shot at best, and once you check those numbers you're stuck with the result. No more chance to pretend, imagining what it'd be like if it were true. Just the cold, harsh reality."

A patient smile and Dale shrugged. "Someone always seems to win those games. Maybe it's my turn."

Alden nodded, eased his hug into a handshake and his handshake into a timid wave. "Give him my best. But let him know that if he ever hurts you, I'll bash his zombie brains into oblivion."

"I'm sure I can take care of myself, but I'll tell him. What should I say to Clara if I see her?"

"Tell her... I love her. Tell her I miss her. Tell her she can try and come for me, but I still don't know if I'm ready."

This time Dale nodded, his sheepish grin stretching into rapture as he headed for the door. He opened it. The hinges groaned and the voice of Daniel cried, "My God, Dale! I thought I'd never see you again!"

Dale stepped outside, gave Alden one last glance, a wink, before the door swung shut behind him. Alden didn't have the heart to watch them go, but he kept his ears perked just in case. Their footsteps died long before the echo of their laughter, and when silence reigned at last, he cried.

It took a week for Alden to organize the house, a spit-shine cleaning for every surface. He wanted it to reflect the people who had lived there, to tell a story of how real warmth and love endured in humanity's last days. One final tour, a few last words, and he packed what little he needed into Mrs. Lawson's Buick LeSabre.

The car smelled of fresh leather with a hint of orange. Between radio static and the cache of Mrs. Lawson's Don Ho and Wayne Newton tape collection, he chose the incidental noise of rubber trundling over pavement. A vague unease greeted him on that empty stretch of highway, fomented by new potholes and fresh cracks, cars and buildings simmering in slow decay, and the spread of wild growth threatening to swallow everything.

"Is this the order that you meant, Faye? Mother Nature's free reign?"

Soon as he said it, he cursed the careless thought. Having remembered Faye, he remembered Dale and Mrs. Lawson and the still-fresh heartbreak of their passing. It had been too long since he'd shared a conversation or heard anything beyond the stale sound of his own voice. He'd felt lonely before, but not to this extent, and never without the tacit expectation that it would someday end. Now, the company of others had become a legend and it would die with him.

His vague unease transformed into a raging beast of panic, its hungry tendrils spreading to his stomach, limbs, and brain. His body shook, caught in a fit of hyperventilation. The silence only deepened his despair, so he put on a tape. Its first song: Don Ho's "Tiny Bubbles." Despite himself he chuckled, groaned, and sang along, grateful for a moment of distraction in the losing battle for his mind.

Once he stepped into the entryway of his old house, he froze. He'd expected someone to have ransacked it, stripped the fridge and cupboards bare, but everything remained exactly where he'd left it, a time capsule for the bygone days of yesteryear. He stared at a framed picture of him and Clara on the mantel. Layers of dust distorted the image, rendering them into a pair of glaring demons lost inside a gray and dying world. Their dust-clotted eyes seemed to follow him. Along with the stale air and cobwebs, it reminded him of haunted houses and the unsuspecting fools who dared to spend the night.

He'd hoped returning would bring clarity and a new perspective, but the greater part of him still believed Visitors were false. Not guides but lures, the songs of sirens compelling them to a self-destructive end. However, a week of isolation had changed him. He *wanted* to believe; all he needed was a reason why. Was that what Mrs. Lawson had meant by being ready, or the feeling that Faye had felt? Or had he, like the others, finally lost his will to fight?

"Clara? Could really use your advice right now. What do I do? How am I supposed to choose? What the hell is wisdom in a world gone mad?"

He didn't bother to unpack. He took a moment to move his things into the spare bedroom before he wiped the photo on the mantel and collapsed on the couch. Nothing to do but stare at Clara's face and listen to the ticking of his wristwatch, a solemn sound, as if it were counting down the seconds to the end of time.

Once that telltale cold sensation wormed into his marrow, Alden headed for the entryway, peering through the blinds to search for moving shadows. Time stalled, stubborn seconds lingering like hours, his anxiety leaking from his pores in rivulets of sweat. When the beyond-expected knock resounded, he spun to face the door.

He shivered. His stomach churned, head spinning, mind burning with the need to know who'd come. He imagined parents, siblings, a score of friends, but found only bitter disappointment there. As much as he loved them, missed them, he needed Clara. He was finally ready for her. No one else would do.

"Who is it?" he asked.

"Pizza man. Thirty minutes or it's free!"

He recognized that voice, opened it at once. Clara stood within a pool of moonlight, still in her favorite cat pajamas, the ones she wore the night she'd passed. She smiled when she saw him, the eager kind that put dimples in her cheeks. Memories—and the picture on the mantel—didn't do her justice, couldn't hold a candle to the true. Alden's eyes strained, his nose flared, his ears perked, his tongue flexed, and his body flushed, as if every neuron craved the smallest piece of her, the barest morsel. He dared to touch her face. His knees went weak with longing and he couldn't help but smile back.

"I missed you!" She threw herself into his arms, embraced him. "You have no idea how long I've waited for this."

He could have lived his final days within the promise of that moment. Mere lottery odds that it was her and he almost took his shot, but the burden of his doubts rebounded.

"I'm sorry," he said, peeled her arms off, took a few steps back. "But I have to ask. Where was our first kiss?"

"On the stoop outside my townhouse after our first date. You thought you were so smooth, the way you came at me, but your baseball cap bumped against my forehead and you pecked my cheek instead."

"My greatest regret?"

"Not talking to your grandpa on the night he died. You had the chance, but wanted to wait until he got better, and he didn't last the night."

"The last thing I said to you?"

"Quit moving so much. You keep waking me up!"

He grimaced, shook his head. "Pretty sure it was, 'I love you.'"

"Wrong! You said exactly that and turned away. Two minutes later, you were sawing logs." She folded her arms and glared a distinctly Clara glare. "Well, Mr. Quiz Man. Did I pass your test?"

"There's still so much I don't understand. Where are you taking me? What happens when we get there? If it's so wonderful, why does it have to be a secret?"

"Even if I could answer you, I wouldn't. You have to see it for yourself to understand. Consider it a leap of faith. The one thing I can promise is that if you come with me, you'll never be alone again."

When Clara held her hand out, he didn't hesitate to take it. The idea of passing didn't trouble him for once, even seemed appealing: the romance, the poetry of facing down the strange and ineffable hereafter with his wife.

"Will it hurt?" he asked.

"It didn't hurt me."

She led him to the sidewalk, down the block, to where a wall like glass or resin stretched across the street, moonlight reflecting in a rainbow sheen that reminded him of oil slicks. He knocked three times. The wall trembled, emitting a deep bass warble.

"What now?" he asked. "Do we just… step forward?"

"Place your palms against the surface and push."

He did as instructed. At once, the substance squirmed, forming orbs around his hands.

"What's it doing?"

He took a calming breath and pulled, testing the strength and flexibility of his new shackles. His hands didn't budge and the pain of trying soon forced him to relent. A sudden flow of warmth and the substance surged up his arms, past his shoulders, to his neck.

"Is this supposed to happen?"

Clara didn't answer, not this time or the last. A slow, sinking realization set in before he even dared to look. When he finally did, he stared into the empty air beside him, a Clara-shaped hole in time and space. He half expected that she might return, that any minute he'd see her trailing from the house, some memento of their past tucked under an arm.

But she didn't. And she never would. And he knew that.

He might have screamed for his stupidity, might have cried for the swift disintegration of his hope, but the substance continued its progression, tracing the contours of his body, cocooning him within its rigid shell. Paralyzed by shock and fear, he could do no more than let out a strangled moan.

A force like gravity dragged him forward. The world shattered, replaced by a black tunnel punctuated by spots and streaks of light. Whether flying or falling he couldn't tell, but he imagined himself sliding on the fabric of reality, speeding toward the infinite, piercing through the barrier beyond the universe's end.

When the cocoon finally halted, a jagged burst of lightning stripped the darkness bare. An image of his destination imprinted on his mind: the open mouth filling up the sky, its teeth like mountains spiraling a void inside its throat; the barren expanse around him, with beings of immense height, bodies twisted and entwined in Escher-like proportions; the filaments along their underbellies scooping bodies from the multitudes squirming underneath them.

The cocoon retracted, released him, and he found himself sprawled out on a dusty ground. Bodies slithered around him, screaming in a chorus of fear and pain, accompanied by the beating of distant drums and squealing, fluted notes. He thought of Clara—the real Clara, not the treacherous facsimile he'd left behind—trapped within the madness of this hellscape for a year. He could only pray her death had come quickly. For that matter, he could only pray his would too. Then he crawled in a futile search for recognition, shrieking and sobbing, slipping and writhing, until the dark truth and the darkness overwhelmed him.

The Revelations of Azathoth

Lena Ng

I LOOKED UP from the field as the crows circled, their black wings swirling above us like a living tempest. They darkened the sky, that monstrous flock hiding us from the warmth of the sun. I felt a chill running through my body as their caws sounded a warning.

Something was coming.

"Back to work," the foreman snarled, snapping his whip. Another harvest slave yelped, and I returned to running the scythe through the wheat. I gathered the stalks, bundled them, slung them over my shoulder. I trudged through the field and loaded them into the wagon.

Something *was* coming. Such omens were not to be ignored. The crows signaled an end, or possibly a beginning.

Unlike the other slaves, I have some years of learning. I was born in the city of Dhorphlamd. I, Zamna, daughter of Memwat the sage and Latkeni the healer, taken as a spoil of war, now a slave to the harvest. I have always had the gift of sight. At nine winters, I predicted the drought of Yylantom. The grounds will brown and crack, I said. We will need to prepare.

My father was afraid of these visions, as he believed the gift was not prophetic in women, but evil. My mother told him I would be a seer. My vision came true, but with double provisions we managed to survive the drought. I had the gift, but no training. At eleven winters, my mother enrolled me in Necronomer's School. I passed the test by picking the symbolic object. The Auditor had laid out the bones, the feathers, the skull, and the bowl. I chose the bowl, since it could be filled with knowledge. The gates of learning were opened.

The Auditor recognized my gift and kindly did not hold my gender against me. At the Worship of the Pseumanas Festival, I had the honour of holding the Living Cup. I read from the Golemgog under the Auditor's watchful gaze; recited the summoning spells; twisted my tongue around heretical languages; interpreted the pattern of the stars. I would have completed my studies, but for the war. The Utharians invaded and we were enslaved. They burned the books, set the schools ablaze, executed the educated and ruling class. I never saw my parents again.

But although they control my body, they cannot control my mind. I hid my gifts, my talent for foretelling, my skills for healing. Every day I planted, tilled, picked, or harvested. Every night I watched the stars and wrote under what little light there was. I fashioned a quill from a lost Cavarian eagle's feather and made ink from crushed jo-jo petals. Sometimes, I wrote about the day's events or my feelings; sometimes, my dreams and visions.

And he will send down a message of his displeasure. Azathoth, the Demon King, the Lord of the Darkness, will strike the Earth and all will believe. From the chaos will come a new world order. From death, there will be life. The storm of colours will coalesce into his vision. He will sculpt the world anew.

That night, after prayers, I looked to the sky. A bright dot of light, brighter than the other stars, like an awakening orb. Before my eyes, the light grew brighter and larger. It seemed as large as the moon, as though travelling closer to the earth.

After each long day in the fields, I would look up at the stars. Each night, that mysterious travelling star grew brighter. Bobezel the Hunter had moved out of his orbit. The star that represented the tip of his arrow now seemed to point at the ominous interloper. Other stars also had strange alignments. Verim crossed with Fyras; the Twins separated; the Goddess lost her golden apple. Azathoth's arrival alone could signal such cosmic foretellings.

It happened the night of the crescent moon. A brightness over the edge of the horizon. A pure, white dome that grew larger and larger. A light so bright, I squinted and drew a hand over my brow. All eyes turned to its arrival. It washed over the land and the ground shook. The pottery began smashing. An oil lamp crashed to the floor.

The smell of smoke. Screaming, high-pitched. I tucked my writings in a sack hidden beneath my tunic, forced my way to the door, felt the crush of slaves behind me as we pushed our way out.

As I emerged from the hut, I saw all the other huts on fire. The thatched roofs lit up the night. Horses neighed and reared and galloped toward the hills. Without pause, I ran after them; animals have instincts we no longer possess. Out of breath and deep in the woods, I found one, a dappled mare whose skin had the sheen of panic. I stroked her neck, spoke some ApKian words of trust and calming. I slung a leg over her and rode bareback into the night.

I had no destination. I saw a door to freedom and I took it, but I didn't know where it would lead me. I had some knowledge of the land. In school, we learned of the far cities of Ryantham, Edermora, and Hrarkamydis, and the nearer trading villages and towns. Luckily, I had no slave markings, and with my skills I was confident I could make a living for the time being.

The mare would rest and I would record my revelations, found in the water of the puddles, in the roll of the stones, in the glint of the moon. Was I a prophet or a madwoman? My visions had never proved wrong.

Azathoth will open the sky and turn his eye toward us. He will see designs in the chaos and will bend the world to his will. We will grovel in the dust and he will spare the devout to rebuild his vision.

That night, I dreamt of his face. Two large glowing red eyes in a moist, gelatinous mass. Squirming limbs, like glistening arm-thick worms, too many to count, reaching across the sky. He could see through my dreams, and he gloated at all he possessed. He could see into my heart, and he recognized his servant.

The time was nigh.

I travelled for days, through forests and fields, living off edible plants, until we reached the remnants of a village in the Hilgada Valley. I let the mare roam while I wandered through the ruins. The ground was covered in soot. The huts were burnt until only the stone foundations remained. I picked up anything I could salvage. A small, blunt knife. A tin cup. These I tucked in my sack.

Buried some ways away I found jars of fermenting vegetables. I ate with gusto, despite the sourness of the vinegar, and drank from a tepid stream. Should I head further south? North to the mountains? I would have to follow the stream, let it lead me. All settlements needed water.

I hiked along the stream, the mare plodding behind me. She was a docile companion, enjoying my company as I enjoyed hers. I never needed to tie her in place or look for her; she never wandered too far. We walked leisurely until we reached a rocky plateau.

In between the rocks, the grass peeking through was glowing, a soft blue light emanating from each stem. I touched one and the sticky blue glow coated my fingers. The air crackled with something alive. The mare refused to travel any further. I kept walking until I saw the mouth of a cave, the glowing blue light within. A force within me compelled me to enter.

Inside, the ceiling of the cave reached higher than a temple. Runes and glowing patterns covered the walls. I studied the patterns; they all seemed like omens. By some trick or through the force of my visions, they started to move. A star travelled across the slimy cave walls, hitting the ocean. From this strike, a bright dome formed; the waves were displaced, and the coastal cities drowned under immense tsunamis. The earth rattled, the volcanos erupted, burning everything in their path. Smoke blocked out the sun. Plants withered and animals starved. The people sacrificed what little they had to the gods before turning on each other. Their depravity knew no bounds. The clouds swirled into a vast spiral, and in its centre blinked a glowing red eye, an eye to judge me on the last day. I backed away when its gaze fixed on me. It was no longer a moving picture but a hole in the cave wall, and soon, the god would break free.

Enthralled by the moving illustrations, I ignored the warnings in my gut and jumped at the laughter echoing from the darkness of the cave. "Come closer," an eerie voice said, oily and foul.

I shook my head and backed away. Something moved behind me, blocking my retreat. Something wet and slimy and wriggling, green and smelling of rotting vegetation.

"We haven't had meat in a long time," the voice continued. "A very long time."

Tendrils of decaying green vine slipped around my waist, over my shoulders, around my legs. I reached for my knife and began slashing. I hacked at the green vine until long cords thrashed like wriggling snakes around me on the ground.

The shadows lengthened. A long leg, tipped with a curved talon, stepped out. Each of its eight legs was covered with bristly hairs. Each of its eight eyes turned to gaze upon me. Its fangs dripped poison, which sizzled on the ground with each acidic drop.

I backed away as a rope of silk shot forth, and tripped as it caught my leg. I slashed with my knife but wasn't close enough to the creature to harm it. The bristled head bowed over me. I took out the cup, holding it in front of me to catch the dripping poison. Closer the fangs came over my body, and I could see my stricken expression in the monster's eight eyes. Then, with all my strength, I flung the cup of poison into those eyes, corroding them with acid.

A hissing shriek came from the clacking jaws. One by one the eyes sizzled and dimmed. The scratch of claws scrabbled against the cave's floor. The shadows retreated, the monster's pained moans echoing in the darkness.

I fled the cave, wishing I could have left a warning for the next unfortunate traveller. Although it was now blind, it could learn how to feed in the dark.

The grasses gave way to sand and the waves of the sea flowed in their eternal tide, bounded by sharp cliffs. The mare blinked away the salt carried on the breeze, which had settled on her eyelashes. Her footsteps in the pale sand were washed away by the brackish, briny water.

We walked up the desolate beach until I saw the buildings dotting the coast, their white bodies like jagged teeth. I would guess the City of Talak. Once a bustling port city, now drowned. The fishing boats listed on their sides or were upside down in the water. Debris littered the flooded streets. Carrion vultures had already feasted on the bodies that the sea had not carried away. Carts were overturned; produce lay mouldering. The once brightly coloured flags, now frayed and discoloured, fluttered sadly in the wind.

A sideways, scurrying movement caught my attention. A grimy face watched me with one eye from behind a muddy wall. The other eye was turned to the heavens. The eyes rotated, and the left eye watched while the right looked to the sky.

"Do you bear the gift of sight?" he asked, glancing at the Necronomer markings on my neck. He himself was covered in the lip marks of the Talakian Spirit Singers. They were said to have one foot in this world and the other in the world unseen. Their songs could bridge the gulf and call to the souls of the departed. This one looked like he had gone mad from the spirits, from too many dead all at once.

"Yes," I said, "though it has not helped me."

"Why is this happening?"

"Azathoth is coming."

"Can he be stopped?"

"I don't know. The schools were burned, and the seers and sorceresses have disappeared."

The man moved toward me, walking hunched over with knuckles dragging on the ground, still with eyes of a chameleon. "There is a temple remaining, on the peak of Mount Irecor," he said. "Many leagues' travel, but the priests there are said to be of an ancient clan, the Order of the Silken Wyrm. They may know what to do."

A broad-winged shadow circled overhead. "I'm not dead yet, ye buzzards!" the man shouted. He reached down, grabbed a broken piece of debris, and flung it into the sky.

He missed, and the debris splashed into the calm surface of the sea. Small concentric circles rippled across the water.

Instead of the waves growing smaller, however, the waves grew larger, and two eyestalks poked out with large black pupils held up on a purple shell. The immense creature pushed its way toward the shore.

"Run!" the man said. His movement was jerky, but surprisingly fast. I struggled to keep up, instead ducking into the nearest building. The giant crab crouched, then jumped over the building, landing directly in the man's path. I turned away when I saw him caught in its giant claw.

Still I travelled, through fields and abandoned cities. I stepped on the broken steps of the port city of Ciavlas. Once a beacon of trade and culture, now only its washed-out corpse remained. The altars, symbols, and rites of protection had not helped them, the populace stolen away into the ocean to become ghosts of the sea. The seagulls, carrying the souls of dead sailors, examined me with beady, yellow eyes.

In the inland town of Ptorakis, there was a diorama of bodies, those who had died in the middle of their daily activities. Some still stood upright, in the middle of the streets, heads tilted downward as though reading their shoes. Others remained at their stalls, gaunt-cheeked and selling rotted vegetables that leaked down the sides of their carts. Even the carrion birds stayed away.

Much further south, I picked my way through the old city of Vitymayar. Most of the population had evacuated, and those who remained were too old or sick or stubborn to leave. In the distance, the fire sputtered, a warning that the god of the volcano was angry. All night its belly grumbled. The ground quaked. Smoke and ash spewed to the clouds.

"You must go," I told any I came across. "It is part of his plan. Azathoth will destroy before he will rebuild." I wandered through the narrow, winding corridors of the city before moving on.

That night, the volcano finally erupted. The red gleam of lava burbled from its spout in thick, raging geysers, landing in destructive rivulets. I watched from two leagues away. Everything was eaten in its path. Trees—trees that contained the world's history in their rings—flared into living candles before evaporating into ash. Hot smoke billowed down the mountainside in long, punishing plumes. Short screams, then silence.

In the sky, a strange mix of hawks and doves, sparrows and eagles, all looking to escape. Animals raced from the lava's path.

Some were caught and burned. The bleating of the anguished creatures rang in the air.

Time passed, my journey dragged on. The stars raged. They threw themselves from the sky and set the world afire. I hid myself and the shaking mare beneath a rocky overhang. When they burned themselves out, the eternal gloom began. The sky was filled with black clouds, blocking out the sun. The grass browned and turned to dust, until the ground cracked and all that was left was cold desert. Grayness blanketed the land. No matter how many layers of clothing I wore, the chill crept into my bones. My face thinned, and I lived by force of will. I wanted to see what was left to come, and in whatever form I would take, I would survive.

I trudged past the bones of animals large and small.

At last the great temple rose before me, its twisting spires like daggers to the sky, built on the tip of a frozen peak. The Temple of the Silken Wyrm. I would not have chosen it, but it was the only temple left standing. Its devotees worshiped a demon snake that was predicted to devour the world. They were hidden from the rest of humanity. It was said their worship had turned twisted in their isolation. They believed that when they became old or enfeebled, there was no greater honour than to be swallowed by a snake. I shivered at the thought.

I gave the mare a last pat before releasing her into the wild. I would miss her warmth and her loyal companionship. But where I would go, she could no longer follow. I climbed the winding staircase encircling the pinnacle, averting my eyes from the steep drop below. Carved into the mountainside were snakes of all sizes. They accompanied me in my journey.

After many hours of pushing against the scowling wind, my lungs and legs burning from exertion, I reached the lacquer-red doors of the temple. Pythons and boas slithered around the columns, their great heads eyeing me flatly, their forked tongues tasting the air. The bald, red-robed priests swung silver censors of incense, the smoke making me light-headed and dizzy. I gave a slight bow as they opened the doors. Chanting filled the large open hall. More priests sat cross-legged on the barren floor. The walls were carved in a maze-like pattern, symbolizing the convoluted path to enlightenment. The vestibule holding the altar was sculpted into the open mouth of a snake, its fangs larger than my arms, with giant, palm-sized scales.

The High Priest, a round-headed, toadish man, met my gaze with a hard stare. "Women are unclean," he said. "You do not belong in the temple." He made a shooing motion.

"Have you not seen the signs?" I asked. I could tell that he had gained his position through craft and cunning, not learning and wisdom. "Azathoth is coming."

The fleshy lips stretched into a smile. "You've come to the wrong temple. We do not worship this god."

"He is coming all the same." I raised my voice so the other priests could hear me. "The strike of the star, the volcanoes, the rain of fire, everything. He's giving us time to prepare."

"Prepare what?"

"Our hearts to receive him. To open up to his will."

"Enough," the High Priest said. "I've had enough of your lies."

The circle of priests judged me in their rocky stillness. The flicker of the torches in the room seemed to draw me into a trance.

I tilted my head, concentrated. "When you were nine, you hid an amukhal in your elder brother's room. It was discovered, and he was blamed. You were given his place at the table. At age fourteen, you bribed the head boy for the results of the foretelling trial. You chose the seven-tailed whip, the symbol of punishment and devotion, and you were chosen as First Overseer. At nineteen, you crushed the berries of the Occulus Tree and dripped its juice in the glass of the—"

"Seize her," the High Priest said through gritted teeth. "She is neither seer nor prophet. She is a witch who will spell our doom."

Two temple guards grabbed each of my arms. The High Priest gestured, and I felt the pierce of the invisible silencing thread as he sewed my mouth shut. My shouts were muffled between my clamped lips. My heels scraped the stairs as I was forced down into the dungeon. I was locked in a small, slimy prison cell. I sat cross-legged on the damp hay and took some deep breaths. I allowed myself to dream.

When the blood of the true believer is spilled, Azathoth with his armies will travel across the heavens. The notes of the flutes will herald his arrival. He will tear through the fabric of the sky and shew us the true reality, the world beyond our vision. We will tremble in wonder and terror.

That night, the High Priest stood outside my prison. He reached his bloated hand through the bars and tapped my forehead with a fat finger. "You have the third eye under there. It sees things that are hidden." He considered a moment. "What if I were to cut it out?"

I curled my lips. He gestured, and I felt my lips unglue. "I know all your terrible secrets," I said. "I can see into your scheming, shrivelled heart."

He gave an ugly smile and withdrew his hand. "Of course you can. Which is why you can never leave. But if you make yourself useful… I could make your stay less unpleasant." He passed me a mangal fruit. I tore through its spiky hide and ate greedily. "Don't think I don't know about you, Zamna. I have some skill in divination. Your parents also had the sight. Your father cursed you when you told him his secrets, the ones he had locked in his heart. Your mother begged for you to be spared. He let you go to school only so you would be away from his sight."

"That's not true." I bent my head, unable to hold back the tears, which slowly seeped from beneath my lids. "He loved me."

"You always were the bearer of bad news," the High Priest said, manic in his glee. "The cursed messenger, they called you. You never opened your mouth but to spew poison."

I shook my head. "I tried solely to warn people. It was rare that anyone would listen."

He took inventory of my face, my form. "Your eyes would make good amulets. I would wear them around my neck. Your bones we can chisel into musical pipes, or smoking ones, or grind them up for midnight rituals. The rest of you we can feed to the Silken Wyrm."

I wiped the tears with the back of my wrist. "Soon there will be no Silken Wyrm. Or me or you or the rest of this cult." I glanced through the cell's only barred window, toward the night sky. A set of stars was in the outline of a crab, claws raised high. Another, a giant sluglike creature, fat and slow-moving. But were they really stars? Or monstrous creatures hiding behind the sky, about to break through? "We don't have much time. Azathoth is coming. It will be a new beginning, but a horrible one. Can we stop him?" I was desperate enough to ask his help. The alternative was destruction and chaos.

The High Priest snorted in disbelief. "How can we stop a god from doing his will? As you yourself have seen, it is written in the stars."

"Are you willing to face his wrath?"

"We can appease him." A gleam shone in his eyes. "Of course, it will take a sacrifice."

First there was a fast. My meals turned from leftover meat into broth. The hour of meditation lengthened into four. All day, I could hear the low hum of chanting.

Then there was a ritual mass. I closed my eyes and could see the markings on the floor—the circle, the stars, the symbols of prayer. The High Priest, surrounded by candles, offered a sermon in the Dark Language. I muttered the appropriate responses.

Then it was a mountain goat. It bleated its objections as it was dragged to the centre of the illustrated circle by its horns. Using a ceremonial knife, its throat was slit, and the blood collected in a gold chalice. It was spilled on the newly built altar to Azathoth.

This was followed by a feast. Everyone ate well, the priests, the servants, the coiling snakes. Platters of roasted meat, figs, fresh and dried fruit, accompanied by goblets of aged wine. Even in my prison cell, I received a sumptuous last meal. I ate and enjoyed, though I knew what was to come.

Finally, it was my turn. The seventh night after the orange moon. A battalion of guards, their cowls covering their faces, entered the dungeon. The High Priest stood in front of the cell door, narrowing his bulging eyes. "Azathoth is a vengeful god," he said. "Only the blood of a true believer will appease him." He unlocked the iron-barred door.

The guards entered and tied my hands behind my back. The High Priest anointed my forehead with sacred oil, draping a long white robe over me. I put up no resistance.

"Aren't you afraid?" he asked.

"I'm neither afraid of this world nor the next one. Only my form will change. You are hastening the passage."

He didn't seem satisfied with my answer, and he gripped me hard around the arms. He realized then that what he did was beneath him, so he relinquished me to the guards, who pulled me outside into the courtyard lit by torches.

The altar was chiselled from onyx stone and covered in grotesque carvings. Spiraling limbs, staring eyes, odd creatures from nightmares enveloped its surface. I was tied down on the stone. One of the priests shaved my head, tossed my hair into a metal bowl, and burned it. The High Priest started his incantation. I winced as he ran the tip of the dagger along each cheek. The blood dripped down my face onto the altar.

I began my own invocation in the Dark Language, calling to Azathoth, cutting through the fabric of the sky. *When the blood of the true believer is spilled, Azathoth with his armies will travel across the heavens.* I spat out the prophecy before the High Priest could sew my mouth shut. The altar trembled and rumbled. Beneath me, it splintered. In the distance, I could hear the unmistakable, piercing notes of the flute.

He was coming.

In response, the skies crackled, speared by lightning, deafened with thunder. The clouds seemed to break apart and vanish. The swirling winds spiraled and twisted. In their centre came a glow, the red of the underworld. It dilated and blinked, a deep burning eye. The winds pulled back, the eye grew larger. Back again, and a writhing limb was revealed, then another and another, emanating from a monstrous face, the face of a cosmic deity.

Azathoth, the god who haunted my dreams.

He appeared through a portal from his own world into ours, flanked by his military, a battalion of indescribable monsters. His form was so immense, we were but crawling ants before him. The sight of him was hideous. I have never known such fear. The skin on my forehead tightened, pulsed, like something was trying to push its way out from under it.

The sharp sounds of an army of flutes grew louder as they hailed his arrival, so strong and commanding that the priests dropped to their knees. Their bodies began convulsing. Their spines bent backward and forward, until they were an undulating mass of molten humanity on the temple's floor. The snakes hissed and reared before they sizzled and melted.

The tightening of my forehead ceased as the skin tore apart and my third eye finally opened. I saw the immense scale of what Azathoth was trying to do. He threw a comet down from the sky, which destroyed the earth. From these ashes, a new world would appear. A new order would rise from the swirling chaos, the tornadoes, the fires, the tsunamis, the volcanoes, a new world would be reborn. Every living thing would change to his liking. The cosmic creator would reshape the foundations of reality.

An arm cracked through my back, then another, the baby limbs growing and stretching until I transformed into a multi-limbed monster. My back elongated and turned, and I fell from the altar, scuttling over the ground with all six limbs like a gigantic cockroach. My body is closer to perfection. I have more arms to worship him. The third eye to see his magnificence. The bending of my back to prostrate myself before him.

He will judge and not find me wanting.

Primordial Jack

Akis Linardos

JACK WAS NOT a name given, but a name taken. His skin, fashioned out of clay, was molded by primordial essence. He had changed it many times. Now it was the guise of a captain: a braided beard, a craggy face, thick eyebrows, and a black coat hemmed with silver thread. An ethereal cord extended from his back, vanishing to the skies, a blurry line only he could see.

The curse of immortality.

Anchored at the port city of Neph, the ship rocked like a mad cradle in the tides. Green mist veiled the city beyond the docks, ghostly moans rolling from within the putrid fumes.

Jack marched down the gangplank, hand resting on the pommel of his cutlass, the chilling mist unable to dampen his dread purpose in coming to this cursed place.

Alan walked beside him, shirt grimed, tight against his strong muscles. A wooden teardrop hung from a black string around his neck. Like Jack, a misty cord came out of him, extending to the sky. Unlike Jack, Alan could not see it.

"The men are worried," he said.

"They always are," Jack replied. "We're after something more important than superstition."

They walked through tight alleys that wormed around ramshackle fishing houses, clogged with the foul stench of offal and spoiled fish. Through a barnacle-encrusted window, Jack caught sight of a woman's body—her face stuck in a bowl, her cranium honeycombed with bivalves. He imagined the bowl's contents: bits of coagulated fish soup sticking on the woman's skin—or perhaps the bivalves had infiltrated so deep into her cranium that they now spilled from her mouth, devouring the moldy remains of her final meal.

For a moment, a pang of guilt hit him. Could this be his fault? Could this plague be somehow linked to the relic he had abandoned in this city eons ago? Had it twisted itself into an item of worship for the denizens of Neph and gained influence over their flesh, their lands, their sea? Could it be that pieces of a primordial god develop a sort of insidious sentience to affect the things around them if imprisoned for too long?

Alan followed his gaze. *"Jesus Christ.* Call *this* superstition?"

"You fear the dead, kid?"

The young man gave him a sharp, don't-patronize-me look. "I fear what *made* them dead."

He was right of course. It did not look good. But Jack had to reassure him somehow, and lies mingled with bits of truth always seemed the most effective. "It won't harm us. This is a plague that slowly works its way on those long residing here. But our roots are not in this place. We are—"

A sudden chill crawled up Jack's spine. Something pulled him like a fishing hook, drawing his gaze upward. The stars pointed down like spearheads, glinting through a misted ceiling. A voice projected from the moon, whispering into Jack's mind.

Jack...

Sweat beaded his forehead, cold as ice. The other gods. They were here. They had sensed the relic's presence and knew he would come for it. The rot was their doing.

"You all right?" Alan asked.

Jack looked deep into his eyes and saw himself there. He saw Alan's future, running in dark velvet with starlight around him, living eternity in fear of the things that lurk at the fringes of creation.

Jack put a hand over his own chest, feeling his human heart. Alan's immortality had to be severed by night's end, before he ever came to know the truth of his origin. For him to spare Alan the life he had lived, Jack had to obtain the relic. Tonight.

He clenched his fingers around the cutlass' pommel as figures approached from the mists, then relaxed as he recognized them. Gulltail, his quartermaster whose goatee's shape and color had earned him the name, stood before him, leading the small reconnaissance group Jack had sent out earlier.

"Captain."

"What's the report?"

Gulltail shook his head. "Dogs all over the streets. Dragging pieces of dead, tearing them apart. Dragged them right off a plague pit. The dead, all purple in the face" —he spat—"wrong, twisted." He proffered a grimy sedge hat. "We lost Tai Yoen. Found this by the ruins of the church on our way back." Then he leaned closer, lowering his voice. His breath reeked of tobacco abuse. "Mister Simmons says he saw what happened. Says the earth swallowed him."

Jack regarded the hat. He knew Tai would be the first of many to die here. It weighed on his soul. But there was no way around it.

"Mister Simmons also says crabs are stealing his knives," Jack whispered back. He raised his voice to the crew. "The Tehnon and its riches lie at the core of the city. Ripe for the taking with no one alive to defend it. You want to die old in your bed with a whore's tit in your mouth? Look alive!"

They marched on through the fog. After a while Alan whispered, "Something's off, Jack. You have that look."

"I always have a look. It's how I keep from stepping into a trap."

"No," Alan said, scratching his neck. "Not that look. It's the one you have when you're staring up in the sky like you've seen the devil."

Jack placed a hand on Alan's shoulder, eyeing the teardrop around the young man's neck. "We're almost there, Alan. One last treasure hunt."

They entered the square of the city, the great fountain dry and cracked, houses lying in ruins on all sides. Yellow branches jutted out of the fissures, like tendrils from krakens frozen in time.

Jack recognized the seeping rot from another dimension, a dimension he knew was the realm of a tyrant god. He inhaled using a muscle left unused for centuries, the cosmic cord joining his immortal core to his human body. Primordial blood flowed through his veins, and he tasted iron. He stopped to avoid risk to his human vessel, exhaled into his palm, and pressed down on the pavement to slow the spreading rot.

He glanced sideways at Alan, who looked back and frowned with worry. There was no way Alan would suspect anything. He'd never learned what Jack really was, and it would only seem coincidental in his eyes.

The earth rumbled and hummed, the yellow branches wiggling like serpents. With the sound of rock cracking, Alan sank into the earth. Jack leaped out, grasping his hand. More men went under all around.

"Push," Jack said.

"Can't move my bloody legs," Alan said. His other hand pushed down on the pavement, cracks formed around it, and it sank like ice giving way.

Jack put both arms around his shoulders, feet pressing hard against the side of the pavement that was still solid, and pulled. It was like pulling up an anchor. He had to use his remaining primordial blood. He banged his boot on the ground, making the earth below shake and loosen its grip.

Alan's feet emerged from the trap. He grunted, grasping a gouge that extended from wrist to elbow. His breeches were grimed with yellow-green filth. "Bloody *death* trap," he said. "You dragged us to a goddamn death trap."

Jack's brain muddled, his throat and muscles ached. Using his power after so long took its toll.

As the earth swallowed men from all around, Jack heard a voice, like a whisper in a cave.

Jack of all trades, Jack of many skins. Are you ready to pay the price?

Deeper into the city, the rot had melded the streets and earth into a swamp. Houses slanted like sinking ships, rusted tendrils of iron drooping down from the remaining walls. Jack trudged ahead, waist-deep in mud, tracing the walls to find solid ground beneath the runny earth. The air reeked of spoiled meat and mold, itching the skin.

The whisper of the tyrant god played over in Jack's mind. He glanced back to make sure Alan was close. He wanted to grab his hand, to feel him there, but it would not do in front of the crew.

"Move faster, you scurvy dogs," he said. "Hold onto the vines, stay close to walls and beams. The swamp will not claim you there."

He could sense the unrest among his men, but they did as they were told. He knew they didn't have the guts to stand up to him, for they did not know what he was. But they were all afraid of him. All but Alan.

"You selfish madman," Alan said.

"Alan," Jack said, turning to look into those deep-set eyes. Not ancient like his own, but fierce. "Have faith in me."

"Faith? Men are dead. Those remaining are just afraid to turn back."

"And what about you?"

The young man hesitated. "I stand by you, Jack. Always have. But the men are not dispensable. Nothing could be worth this."

But it was worth it. And he had to make sure Alan would never know why.

Jack squinted. The blurry outline of a giant cube appeared in the middle of the moldy lake, crumbled steeples sinking around it. The Tehnon.

A sludge gurgled around the men. A green mass shot out—an emaciated man grimed with muck, yellow branches jutting out of his flesh like tree roots out of rock. Arms flailing, he attached himself to one of the men and pulled him under.

Jack grabbed Alan's hand, ushering him forward as the swamp bubbled like boiling gruel and humanoid creatures shot out of the earth. One attached itself to Alan, who pushed back against the remains of a wall, wrestling with the creature. Jack brought out his cutlass, then froze as he recognized the scar across the humanoid's eye, the mark Tai Yoen had gotten in the Battle of Tasmi. The land was spitting his own men back at him, minds muddled and zombified by the primeval poison.

Something grasped Jack's legs and pulled him under.

For a moment, the world became dark. His brain pulsed and his ears buzzed. A tsunami of primordial blood flowed through his cosmic cord, moving from his immortal core through the abyss and into his fragile vessel. A sharp pain trickled down from his brain to his heart, spreading to his bones.

Ethereal serpents lashed out of his mouth, slashing the creatures around like whips. He saw Alan through the muddy soup and coiled a tendril around him. With his other appendages he pierced the sinking wall. As he scaled upward, he saw the teardrop necklace, floating like an eel. He grabbed it and emerged to the surface.

Once he reached the wall's crest, his appendages vanished and he balanced himself, holding Alan over his shoulder like a sack of flour. His muscles vibrated. He could hear the pump of his own blood.

"W-what the hell?" Alan said. "Jack?"

Muffled screams came from the swamp. Jack looked down. Gulltail looked up at him, grimacing as grimy hands clutched on and pulled him down. Could he save anyone if he jumped now? If he used his full power?

Pain seared his throat like hot iron where the tendrils had come through. The godly voice of the tyrant god still echoed in his mind. He squeezed his eyes shut, teeth gritting, fist clenched around the teardrop. He had to preserve his energy; he was already at his limit.

"I'm sorry," he whispered.

Jack ran. In front of him appeared the crumbled gates of the Tehnon, faded arabesque patterns around its frame. A great glass dome bulged out of the gallery's roof, parts of it reduced to shards.

He landed before the gates and put Alan down. The cosmic cord convulsed, spasmed, and primordial blood overflowed in his body, bringing him to his knees. He heard his own bones cracking, feeling a bright fire well up in his chest. He slid the teardrop open, revealing the painting of a woman with auburn hair, a man with deep-set eyes like Alan's next to her.

Layla.

He focused on his hard-earned humanity, his love for a woman. The piece of mortality in him. Tears coursed down his cheeks, and the cosmic cord relaxed.

Jack looked at the Tehnon's gate, gaping at him. A rumbling voice called out.

You will return what you stole, Jack. Your rogue journey ends here.

Moonlight made green by the mist slanted through the dome of the great gallery. The smell of old wood and the drier atmosphere were a welcome relief from the pungent swamp. Crumbled exhibits cluttered the hall: the wooden frame of a large boat, the limestone statue of an obese man, a clay goblet held by a great hand.

The hall brought dreaded memories to Jack, of the time he was always on the run. It felt like only yesterday, like the last centuries had never happened.

His body pained him. The primordial blood still coursing in his veins gave him some relief, like cold water on a wound. A little primordial blood could relieve the pain of what an excess of it caused—like drinking rum to fool the mind from hangover nausea. But it did not heal.

"My necklace?" Alan said.

Jack handed him the wooden teardrop.

Alan put it in his pocket. "I should have stopped you. They trusted their lives to you, and you betrayed them."

Jack's heart panged. "Fearful men driven by greed. There was no trust involved."

Alan snorted. "And that justifies it all, doesn't it?"

"I did what was necessary."

"*Necessary?* Our crew is dead! What *are* you really, Jack? How can you—oh, *damn* it hurts." The young man kneeled, grasping his arm.

From the wound Jack saw wooden branches popping out, tiny as the paws of a newborn kitten. He knew this sickness. He had to act fast.

"Be silent, save your energy," he said, moving his hand to hoist Alan up.

"No," Alan said, brushing Jack's hand away. "You will tell me. What the *hell* are you?"

"Have it your way."

He moved away, toward the end of the room, footsteps bouncing off the walls. Alan's voice rang out. "Don't turn your back on me, you bloody coward! Answer me!"

Jack recognized the ruined staircase leading to the chamber where he'd hidden the relic an aeon ago. His boots parted thick cobwebs as he descended the stairs. It was dark, but the relic pulled him.

He touched something flat, like a display case, feeling the dust sticking to his fingers. He punched. Glass shattered. Maybe he'd cut himself, maybe he hadn't, he was too overwhelmed by his other pain to realize. He flexed his hand around the long pole. It tugged at his primordial blood, burning it within his veins.

As he returned to the light of the main chamber, light shone on the relic. The Primordial Scythe. The Tooth of Azathoth. Its great handle shone pristine silver, untouched by time, its edge a dark crescent devouring the light.

Alan lay by the clay pot statue, curled in a fetal position. His eyelids drooped and the tiny branches wiggled in his arm. "What's happening to me?"

"You're going to be fine."

Jack clutched the scythe with both hands and struck the air as a miner strikes ore. The blade stopped mid-strike; cracks formed around it like some invisible glass. Jack sliced, and a black rip appeared. A portal between dimensions. A portal into the realm of primordial chaos.

He pushed his hand into the stygian world and gripped his fingers around a ball of dark matter. He dropped his scythe and spat into the ball, molding it into a salve. He crouched over Alan, grasping his hand.

"No," Alan said, pulling his arm back, grimacing. "You will. Tell me. What you are."

Jack exhaled. How to make him understand? "The foam of the sea conjures bubbles endlessly. Think of your world as one of those bubbles. I come from the tight space in between them." He pointed at the black rip quivering mid-air. "I sprout from chaos, much like you did, only I was a direct consequence of it with no parents behind me.

It's mind-bendingly rare, but it does happen. That's how gods are born."

Alan stared at him, mouth agape. "You're *mad*."

"Doesn't matter if you believe. That's your answer." He glanced at Alan's diseased arm. "Want to live past the hour? Then let me look after you."

Alan hesitated, but as the wound wormed with spindly appendages, he thrust it out to Jack and turned his head. Jack touched it gingerly, spreading the inky black salve over the wound.

"Ah, damn it all, it burns like hell."

"Close enough."

Jack pulled out his coat and formed a pillow, leaning Alan's head on it. Alan mumbled something incoherent about gods and monsters and drifted asleep. Jack took the teardrop from the young man's pocket and clenched his fist around it, feeling the wooden curves embellished on the surface, feeling it warming him inside with the flame of mortal love.

For a moment, his mind went back to that woman's corpse, slowly decomposing over her last meal as tiny mollusks worked on her brain. Was he doing the right thing? Cutting out Alan's immortality, subjecting him to the bounds and limits of one existence. Was it truly the correct thing to do?

Then Jack's gaze fell on the rift he had torn open, a dark scar by the clay statue. A low hum emanated from it, like the slow rumble of a coming earthquake. A tenebrous world that devoured all it touched. He remembered the time he'd sprouted out of chaos, in a place without time, where everything happened at once. Jack remembered The One Who Brings Suffering and the pain from his whip that flashed from a thousand timelines at once. The One Whose Gaze Sees All and how every time Jack had tried to escape, he'd find one of the yellow eyes looking at him across infinity. The One Who Breaks Creation, The One That Devours Light, The One That Shapes Entire Worlds. All the spawns of grotesque chance, spawns of chaos incarnate. Children of Azathoth. All of them pompous gods that craved obeisance, sought dominance, thrived on fear.

He would not have Alan suffer as he did. Those gods would never find him. The scythe would sever Alan's cosmic cord, his link to his heritage. It *was* the right thing to do. Eternity is heavier than death.

Hours passed. Alan was still out cold, but his color seemed to brighten. Jack pocketed the teardrop and removed the black salve. Rotten bits of wood stuck to the sludge as he peeled it off, exuding a smell of rotten onion. His heart sank. The wound had disappeared as he'd expected, but now a fissure cracked the skin in its place. No blood came out; it was more than a wound, a breaking of his very soul. A deep voice rumbled from the cracks.

Naive little Jack. Did you not feel the taint of my blood in the darkness?

The world shook, a thudding like the march of elephants. With every thud, dust fell from the statues and fissures appeared in the walls and air, spreading like the cracks of a frozen lake slowly giving way beneath a massive weight. The air smelled of heated metal. The sound of an object cleaving the air behind him made Jack whip about, his scythe clashing with the mace of The One Who Breaks Creation. The other god stood twice as large and clad in armor. There was no head, but his neck and shoulder formed one mass—a rough pyramid. A misty red snake extended from his back and vanished to the skies. His cosmic cord. His voice rang with power like the bells from a cathedral.

You will return my scythe. And you will answer for your crimes in Tenevra Rond.

"I committed no crime," Jack said.

Are you so taken with this human guise that you would respond to me with words that are not yours?

Jack grinned. Perhaps the very act of defiance against this entitled, overwhelming god brought some odd, twisted mirth up his throat. "I am this guise now. Human to the bone. In my heart."

Jack pushed back. Pain jolted from his brain to his limbs as snakes poured out of his mouth, flattened and joined, weaving themselves into a veil that covered him, obscuring his presence. He ran behind the statue of the obese man.

Insolent rat. You leave our realm behind, abandon the universe you were tasked to protect, godless, fatherless. *And you would dare tell me that you left it all so you can live eternally pretending to be something you are not?*

The mace smashed through the statue. Debris came hailing down on Jack as he rolled over and under the boat's frame.

And that this form suits you? A guise that rots and dies? Why?

"The shackles of eternal responsibility fit a tyrant god like you quite well. But *I* never asked to sprout from chaos, nor to be a god of any universe. All I ever wanted was freedom."

A tyrant? You dare?

Jack crawled slowly over the edge of the boat's frame. "I've been to your world. I've seen how your worshippers tremble to look at the sky for fear of seeing your form. Their lives are worthless."

You, the most remiss of all the gods, dare lecture me? *They do well to fear, as do you, One Who Hides From Gods.*

The god drummed his mace into the air with both hands, and booming sounds came as if he were ringing an invisible gong. The air rippled and the walls cracked, fissures crawling up to the ceiling. The roof came toppling down in slabs and Jack dashed over Alan, cutting clean through the piece hurtling his way. As it split into two smaller slabs falling on either side, the tyrant god charged him. Jack dodged and veiled himself once more.

The entire building collapsed, revealing a burning sky filtered by yellow-green mist. Cracks formed and punctured the skies. Fire poured out of the cracks, flaming tendrils mingling with the mist, searing Jack's flesh. Time itself had fragmented. And between the cracks, he saw a vision of the past.

"Burn the witch," a man's voice said.

"Death to Satan's harlot!"

Their voices were familiar. Jack's heart drummed.

You cannot hide, Jack, your mind is open, exposed as the timeline of this universe you spent so long in.

"I'm sorry, Jack," his departed wife said.

He told himself the words were just sounds and heat. No longer real.

It's Layla, your beloved wife. That's her voice, Jack. I can make her pass through this moment over and over again.

Flames licked up his skin. A sour scent came to his nose, like rotting fruit—like the rotting fruit he'd found back then, the lemons, oranges, and tomatoes slowly decomposing in the summer heat, sprawled on the floor of their home. The last groceries Layla ever purchased.

Her screams raged on and Jack shut his ears, tears streaming down to his beard. If he had stayed by her side back then, she would not have had to die. If he had stayed, he'd never have to return to that abandoned home, redolent with the stench of lemons and oranges and death.

"You have to share your wisdom with the world as you have with me, Jack," she had said to him.

"Lustful creatures driven by greed don't deserve such knowledge, Layla."

"Am I a lustful creature, then? Driven by nothing but greed? Maybe I also deserve to be devoured when the dream of Azatho—"

"Don't speak his name. And it's not like that. You're different."

She had placed a hand on his cheek then. After eons in the human body, her touch was what made him feel human for the first time. Every time she touched his cheek or kissed his lips, it made all the darkness of the world dwindle and give way to sunlight. "They *can* be better," she'd said. "*You* can make them better."

And so he had tried. *By the Old Ones,* had he tried. Humanity bore the potential for light to exist, however dim. It was worth a struggle. But when he had returned from one of his trips, he found charred remains in the village square. Jack had given Layla balms to heal the sick. In return, they called her a witch and burned her at the stake. All the darkness of eternity seemed to return then, condensed into one moment: the sight of her blackened carcass on the pyre.

Jack killed them all.

There was one among them he'd spared, a farmer with wispy balding hair and a tremble to his lip. He was touched in the head somehow, perhaps from age, perhaps disabled from birth, perhaps a bit of both. The grotesque touch of foul luck. "Her spawn is still out there," he had said to Jack. "Her belly bloated one day, born the next. Seed of the devil."

Jack found their baby, hidden safely in their secret basement. It had the eternal cord, the heritage of a god's descendant. Jack coiled the teardrop necklace around the baby's tiny neck and left the village behind, shifting to another form: a braided beard sliding down his chest, wrinkles forming in his face like scars to mark his pain, a long coat dark as night.

"No one will dare lay a finger on you," Jack had whispered to the baby. "Alan."

An evil voice snapped him back to the present.

We sprout from chaos to bring order, the tyrant god said as he approached Alan's shivering form—unconscious still. *A spawn of a god, raised as mortal. You went to such lengths for this frivolous life. Let us see how attached you really are to your human guise.*

He raised his mace high in the air, and Jack threw himself forward, taking the hit on his shoulder to protect Alan. The cracks broke through the human skin, the pain seeping into his core. It felt as if his arm had been sliced by a dozen searing knives.

You would go this far?

"You cannot begin to imagine."

Tendrils poured out of Jack's mouth as the searing pain spread in his body. They wrapped around the three cosmic cords, pulling them together and weaving them into one great rope.

What are you...?

A tendril grasped the teardrop from his pocket, wound it around his scythe. Jack heard his wife's screams. He felt the piece of his mortality pulling at his cord like an opposing magnet. As the tyrant god raised his mace again to strike, Jack slashed the cords clean with a swipe of his scythe.

The cords writhed like headless snakes, and Jack felt as if a chain attached to him had snapped.

The tyrant god rumbled. His cord severed, he had no human brain to cling to. There was no face to be surprised—a god had no need for surprise, no need to impart emotions to another. His upper body toppled over, a boulder smashing to the ground. The earth shuddered, the ghostly voices faded, and the cracks closed.

Jack could not feel the immortal core anymore. He looked at his hands, realizing this body was the entirety of him now. Humidity dense around his now-mortal skin, only a bare remnant of primordial blood soothed his pain as his limbs fissured like dry earth.

He looked down on Alan, whose wound had vanished along with his cord. Alan was free. His immortality had been severed. Jack caressed his son's hair.

Alan's eyes cracked open. "What are you doing?"

"Acting human. It's been a long time since I've done so."

The young man's eyes widened as if he had remembered something. "*You*—you said. You're a god."

Jack looked around, using his scythe like a cane to support himself. He slashed the air with the dark crescent, forming a vertical rift. From the rift, sunlight shone through. Beyond there was verdant hill with a lone oak tree.

Jack's muscles vibrated, the soothing flow of primordial blood fading away, but it was not pain it left behind, only numbness all over. He saw flakes flowing away from his body in the wind like dead skin.

"Jack..." Alan said.

"Go," he said. "You are free, Alan. There is nothing to fear."

"Jack, what's happening to you?"

"Everything has to end eventually. Else there is no point. Even gods may die, when they have reason."

"I can't just leave you here."

Peels of skin and flesh flew off him, ashen like burned-up wood. "It's my time, Alan. Go. The portal won't last long, my power is fading. There is no escaping the swamp by normal means."

Alan shook his head. "No."

Jack grasped his shoulder and tried to push him away, but there was no power left in him. "*Go!*"

A part of him wanted to tell Alan that he was his son from another life, but he bit his tongue. It would not help to know now. He wanted Alan gone.

The young man moved away. He looked at the rift, then glanced over his shoulder at Jack, tears glistening on his cheeks. "You always were a selfish bastard."

Jack looked up, and for a fleeting moment the mists formed a gap through which the moon shone, a perfect silver disc floating in the night sky.

When he looked down again, Alan was slipping through the portal toward a new life. In his mind's eye, Jack saw Alan in a meadow, running free under the sun. He saw him fall in love, have children, achieve things, grow old.

He smiled. His body was weightless, as if he were flying among the stars once more. The human guise dissolved, the entirety of him drifting away, descending in ashes over the primordial swamp.

Respect Your Elders

Adam L. G. Nevill

WE WERE NEVER in any danger from the meteor that soared between Mars and Jupiter and fireworked through the solar system. It was too far away and winding towards extinction within the sun's heat. Even the scattershot of debris, blasted from the nucleus by cosmic winds and flickering for a few million kilometres behind the incandescent head, posed no threat to anything but our satellites, and one or two space stations.

The debris was incinerated by the earth's atmosphere, producing the spectacular flares that endured throughout that messy, heaving July; so vivid to eyes unhindered by light pollution on land and sea, day and night.

But as the massacres began, the strange coinciding of the slaughter with the comet transformed the latter into an augur. An omen our forbears would have been all over with prophecies and interpretations. But none in the modern world imagined the horrors the shooting stars precipitated. None conceived of the epochal rearrangement of our species that was about to commence.

Before the massacres, I tended to shop every three days. I was never a hoarder during the Covid pandemic. Unless food exports were disrupted, I wouldn't break a sweat. So by the time it was unsafe to do anything but conceal oneself—which occurred by noon on the fourth day of the great slaughter—I'd finished my meagre provisions. They amounted to a dusty tin of bamboo shoots, uncovered from the back of a cupboard, eighteen months out-of-date, and a can of lentil and smoky bacon soup that nearly made me cry with pleasure. For dessert, I crammed six chocolate liqueurs into my maw. An ancient Christmas gift. I loathed such things, but a hungry old man like me couldn't afford to be picky.

I had plenty of water, though I didn't use the hot taps in case the whoosh of the boiler was heard outside, or a wisp of steam escaped the vent.

In conventional real estate terms, the demand for homes in the village was always high. During the massacres there was a property boom.

The first violent incidents occurred late on day three. I heard sounds of violence up the hill and saw a plume of smoke, but there were no sirens. Many more invaders arrived on day four and initiated a free-for-all. The killing was incessant. Stragglers were annihilated on day five. What I came to regard as the accompanying exaltation and madness among the wretches was sustained and relentless.

Once the neighbouring properties in this cul-de-sac were occupied, and the ecstatic celebrations eventually waned, I suspected that some of the invaders would return to investigate this overlooked building, and any smaller properties that had appeared unappealing during the initial frenzies. Someone who missed out on one of the flashier places on the hill would eventually return and settle here. Bored and hungry, they'd break in and realise that the house wasn't a dump after all. No longer fooled by the overgrown gardens or the tired facade, they'd make themselves at home. I was sure of it.

As I clung to the floorboards behind the water tank in my loft, whimpering and listening to my neighbours' screams, it dawned on me that I couldn't hide in the building's cavities indefinitely while bloodstained murderers mooched and rutted to that infernal music, or sat glassy-eyed and gibbered. Concealment and coexistence were not sustainable.

But where to go?

I was the only one with a broken front path, who liked his borders grown together for the birds and insects. The misfit who swapped lawns for beds of native species. I liked to believe my gardens self-regulated. To be honest, my rewilded property was an eyesore. Bit of chaos to upset the stifling order and conformity of my peers. And yet, the tangled state of my gardens had saved my life.

I was alive. I existed. That was all that mattered by day five. And somehow, I was still breathing on day six. We all want to live, especially after hearing the shrieks of the mob that encircles and encloses, the piteous wails of its victims before the hollow thuds as heads are staved and split like melons.

I'd crawled into the cavity beneath my own roof on day three, then spent the following three days in the stifling loft, pissing into an empty water bottle, as my neighbours succumbed. A vigil that provided me ample time to consider the ultimate meaninglessness of rules, restraint, private property, individual rights, and the sanctity of human life. When the pack descended into a blood frenzy, much like the society we'd all taken for granted, all I was, had been, and owned became irrelevant.

And yet, living moment by moment through an ongoing extermination, each minute one is spared is both thrilling and pregnant with unbearable hope.

The dishevelled front of my house was investigated on the evening of day six, but once more my overgrown gardens sufficed as an effective deterrent. Richer pickings must still have existed in the village, in the two adjoining hamlets, and in the nearest town from where the local contingent of assailants poured.

I only ventured outside and into a world reshaped by murder once I'd eaten nothing for the best part of two days. Gathering the courage to leave the loft consumed hours. Hunger drove me out the backdoor on all fours, two hours after midnight. I was reduced to a rat that blinked baffled eyes at an alien place, streaked by cosmic rockets and alive with drums and incessant piping blaring from every phone and set of speakers within the perimeter of the village.

I crawled along the patio and through the grass and down the fence line.

The air stank of greasy smoke and cooling fat. They'd burned some of us alive.

On the distant main roads, a hiss of scattered traffic. Bestial whoops occasionally pierced the night from elsewhere. Solid objects randomly exploded in nearby streets. A door. Furniture pushed from an upper storey. A windscreen.

They'd seemed inexhaustible over the previous two days, but there was always less activity after sundown, and the pauses in the carnage were more frequent approaching midnight. Interludes that were not so tense with the expectation of being observed. A hideous notion of someone outside, listening for your movements indoors. Twice I'd seen figures through gaps in the eaves of the roof, passing in the street before they'd paused and stood briefly on my front lawn. Looking at the house, they appeared to extend the uncanny interrogation of their senses into the humid spaces in which I crouched, blinking with terror and incomprehension.

I'd held my breath, squeezed shut my eyes, until their feet had scuffed away.

Up there: white streaks and flashes in the sky. A barrage of intense light. As if some great angle grinder showered sparks above the earth's atmosphere, incandescent debris fell upon us from the freezing dark. Shrapnel from a comet, passing through a cosmos ninety-three billion light years wide.

Mankind's roof was burning.

On the sixth night I tried to stop looking up. Yet still I flinched, anticipating an explosion above the earth or an impact on the ground. Would the meteorites strike us forever? And make permanent the insufferable feeling of exposure and the pittance of agency that I commanded, for no more than a few feet from my loft space?

The entire firmament was a hideous oppressor. I'd graver matters to preoccupy me below, but that flaring canopy had gradually encouraged my belief that it was the work of a thing all seeing and cunning; cruel and insane like the acolytes it had recruited below.

I suspected the sky was a great lens through which we were being observed by a form as sadistic and mindless as the hundreds of millions of its devotees. As the torments intensified around me, and my wits unravelled, I sensed a growing direction. Guidance from above to create chaos below. Had we not always anticipated such in our faiths and myths?

At the top of the garden, one side of a fence panel could be pushed into the rear of Doug and Joan's property. I crossed the border behind my neighbours' summer house and entered a damp, shadowy runnel. I crept among slugs and the hedgehogs who devoured them. Cat urine abraded my sinuses. Small stones pierced my knees.

I crawled a few feet, stopped. Listened. Then slithered a few feet further, praying that the sounds erupting from my empty stomach didn't carry far.

Hatty and Malcolm at the back of me had been hanged when the mob poured through the village on day four. They were still swinging inside their conservatory.

For some unfathomable reason, each had been dressed in one of Hatty's nightgowns, their faces painted ochre with deck stain. As they were tormented, their hair was spiked with adhesive into starry crowns. From a stepladder, they were then kicked into empty space, ankles and wrists tied. So if you are in any doubt as to why I wormed the earth with the snails, sniffing for sustenance, you hadn't seen those two bulgy, tarred faces drifting in space. Electrical extension cord anchored them to the ceiling. Peering between the attic eaves and looking south across the fence and over the treetops, I'd been able to observe their tufted black heads at my leisure.

Doug next door was pulled apart on his putting green of a lawn. They pegged him out and used the electric saw, which always set my teeth on edge during Doug's incessant pruning, to trim his torso. Secateurs finally squelched inside his joints to cut his limbs free of their sockets. He was alive until his second arm hung by a thread. Inexplicably, they first painted him with white emulsion, then carefully fashioned a meticulous series of symbols in red paint across his chest.

Before the cutting commenced, he never stopped offering them money. I was surprised he had so much.

I never saw them take his wife. I suspected, wrongly, that she'd succumbed indoors, silently. That woman would do anything to avoid embarrassment. No begging and soiling for Joan. Perhaps a stoic's pride beneath the executioner's hand axe was preferable, her chin raised in absurd dignity. The DIY store's label still attached to the wooden handle.

I'd heard slamming and glass breaking next door, two days before, in the afternoon. All the doors remained open at the back. Blackly vacant. No lights.

Most of the wretches had stopped drinking so much by the evening of day five. A fatigue, I prayed, was taking hold. As the mad, elated shrieking wound down in twilight, they took to that vacuous star gazing. Some would be unconscious. But during that hot night, and those that followed, I never knew whether I would find them slumped or compelled to stare into space. Nor did I realise then how unreceptive they were when so absent and morose, or stricken by wonder, like the innocents they no longer were, or could be again.

And yet, in the anarchy and misrule of the first week, no great strategy had revealed itself. No considered tactics. Organisation was ad hoc. Like starved animals, they seemed driven to kill, to take what belonged to others, to make room, to conquer resources. Selfish instincts were never articulated beyond direct action. But as this biblical slaughter had erupted across the planet, many victims shared my suspicion that the lines of communication were being directed from elsewhere. Something was giving orders. Or blithely, idiotically, and thoughtlessly presenting a bad example to the young.

Only fanatics would countenance such a fantasy. But not all diseases are bacterial or caused by viruses. Not all viruses are written with genetic code, nor organic and tangible. Pandemics take various forms. Simple ideas cultivate pestilences of aberrant human behaviour.

We, the elderly, were simply bewildered, as if suddenly shelled from afar by an unknown aggressor. Our routine and unremarkable existences were transformed into front lines before we were aware we were at war. Invaded by our own.

Doug was a dark lump on the grass between two flower beds. I made sure not to look to my left as I crawled around him.

Into the uneasy dark of their kitchen, I crept.

And there I came upon Doug's hideous wife, Joan, in the kitchen. We both flinched when we happened upon each other. By then I was even suppressing exhalations. And I'd spoken to no one but myself since day two.

She looked terrible and unfamiliar enough for me to struggle to recognise her. She'd been sick, some time before, down the front of the clothes she'd worn for days. Her feet were bare and grubby. Frantic eyes in a grey face took me in, flitted away, returned to stare.

"Doug…" she said.

"Have you any food left?" I whispered.

"I won't look."

"I can. Keep your voice down."

"I won't look. He's there, isn't he? Might he be alive?"

"Sorry. No." I shook my head. "I'm starving."

"They've been in and out. In and out. Two of them stayed here. The things they were saying…"

"Where are you hiding?"

"They left the fridge door open. Everything has spoiled. I can't eat… I saw his leg…"

I looked inside the three nearest kitchen cupboards. The doors hung open. Stacked tins and packets of pasta. Bags of flour. Curious cooking oils and spices. A loaf of artisan bread that wasn't green. Even biscuits. Saliva spilled from the side of my mouth.

Joan stepped between me and the counter.

I recoiled at her stench. Stepped back.

She was furious, fists balled. Some colour had returned to her face. "You can't have it! You're no better than them!" This brought to mind her berating me about my unruly gardens and the tree branches at the borders extending over the fence, the broken paving slabs at the front.

"It's ours!"

"Whose?"

"Mine. Doug's. How dare you come in our home!"

Her tone irritated but the volume of her voice trumped my annoyance. "Ssh," I said. "They're everywhere."

"Don't you dare tell me to be quiet in my own home."

"Not yours now."

She didn't acknowledge that and looked away instead, as if listening to some faint transmission. I slipped around her. Seized the loaf.

Her small fist struck the side of my face.

I knocked her away. "You stupid, petty little bitch! Your husband is a fucking torso on the lawn."

Her demeanour changed from enraged to inquisitive. "You've seen Doug? Is he all right?"

She was as mad as a snake. Even crazier than I was. I took the biscuits, one tin, and withdrew from the room.

Joan followed me. "Let me get my coat. I'll show you exactly what is required with that buddleia of yours. It's all over our side again. I won't have it!"

A door slammed. Next door.

"Don't," I pleaded, and motioned, with outstretched hands, for her to stay put.

She followed me like a child.

Eager feet kicked gravel on the drive outside.

I fled. Through the living room, dining room, conservatory, and into the garden, the victuals clasped to my bony chest.

Behind my route, Joan's front door swung wide.

"They're all on drugs," Doug had said to me, as the cosmic shrapnel flared white in the firmament above us, on the second day of the killings. "Half of them don't know what they are. Girls. Boys. These websites they're on. Chatting instead of working. What they call it? Facebook? Computer games..." He went on, explaining it all, berating, his eyelids squeezing shut like clenched fists to emphasize each idea that he pushed out of a white beard, trimmed prissily.

He was in uniform that day. Pink polo shirt, predictable logo. Tailored golfing shorts. Expensive loafers. No socks. An immaculate garden framing a self-gratifying arse, whose affluence and privilege was founded on the inflated value of his former properties. Like mine. He often recited what he'd bought for trifling amounts, then sold at exorbitant prices. How he'd always done "the smart thing."

Pitched himself as a wily entrepreneur. Always ahead in a game in which the foolish competition floundered.

Since the news broke yesterday, I'd seen him pacing about his fussy front garden, hoping to catch the eye of a neighbour or passerby so that he could unload. By the time he reached an analysis of social media and gender identity, he'd already been orating for some time. Working out his shock. His outrage. His fear. And he'd been on his podium for twenty minutes to make me understand why *it* happened.

Boredom expanded a heat from my gut until it felt like heartburn. I became aware of aches and minor discomforts. Started to fidget.

"Knifing each other in London. Faces full of metal…"

The moment I returned home from spending the morning having my withered pecker massaged in order to sink balls-deep into a Thai girl for five minutes, whom I frequented in town, Doug loomed. And was on me.

I smelled of sex, wanted a shower, needed to distract myself with pottering. I always pursued trivial routines after paying for sex, to placate a residual idea of my dead wife that I always sensed in the house as an admonishing, sullen presence. She'd been gone six years. Fussing about also assuaged my instinctive shame and disgust. Though that never lasted long.

Like almost everyone else the day before, I'd watched the news until midnight, the endless analysis from experts. They'd been shipped in to process the atrocity for us all at home. I'd swapped between seven news channels, checked online papers on my phone and tablet, googled down rabbit holes on my laptop. Like a repeat of 9/11, the terrorist attacks in Europe, Syria, the Australian wildfires, the first months of the Covid pandemic, the storming of Capitol Hill, Russia's invasion of Ukraine, I'd sat in safety and comfort and watched a generally dissatisfying but unthreatening world lose its shaky balance and topple backwards into history.

I'd fallen asleep on the sofa and woken the following morning, restless and aroused, with a crippling backache. Then headed into town to work the stiffness out and change my oil with the delectable Anong.

But who'd be young today? I felt an impulse to announce this to Douglas as he'd ranted. At me. But I remained silent. Objections would prolong his spiel and provoke personal slights, assured by any disagreement with him. As with most people I encounter, familiar or unfamiliar, my neighbour was incapable of listening. I'm 73 but have a sense that I have mostly been silent since my late forties. Around that age, my decades of listening to others began. As did my years of suppressing yawns, shuffling, humouring the speakers with nods, until finally holding up a hand. "Gotta fly."

Being in the audience and not on stage, for performances I never wished to attend, is exhausting. Tedium is fatigue. Mercifully, my wife had a quiet, melancholy soul and we rarely argued, though of my habits she disapproved.

I'm not sure what it is about me; an expression, perhaps? But within moments, the few who even bothered to acknowledge my existence made a decision that my role was to listen. To them. That I was a vessel into which they'd pour their personalities. You learn nothing by jabbering, but you become aware of so much by remaining silent. I think this gave me a head start in understanding the slaughter.

"Tattoos. All over. What they gonna look like at our age?" He went on. And on.

I've been aware for years that if I ventured so much as a quick interjection in any exchange with another, a fragment of my sentence contained a keyword that incited a speaker to indulge in yet another anecdote, or bout of one-upmanship, or idea, or assumption about me, or criticism, judgement, explanation, monologue.

We live in the age of the agent provocateur, the autodidact, the pedant, the attention seeker. In the attention economy, I am penniless. But I was content with penury.

I stopped listening to Doug and harboured a hot fantasy about obliterating him with a tool from the shed. An implement with bludgeoning capabilities. While his wife, Joan, screamed. And then, like the ageing white chimp that I am, I'd stove her skull in too. And pull her limbs off. Bury them together, under their roses, before taking a piss on the disinterred soil.

Wishful thinking, when only days later I would see his limbless torso, painted the colour of his extension? I now investigate that murderous impulse and ponder its significance. I can only assume that my fantasy possessed a more universal quality than I had hitherto suspected.

Maybe we all had it in us. I was too old to wield much of a blow. My back would have crunched like a rotten branch. But others, many, many others, were not so decrepit. The younger one was, the more potent and concentrated the desire to savage, to open the sluice on suppressed grievances. To redden.

There were too many of us. All milling. Wallowing in our resentments. All over the world.

Doug begged for desecration.

I suspect, to many, we all did here.

That's one of many things about the atrocities, at the beginning, that troubled me: I wasn't surprised enough. My generation had just gone on and on, year after year, kept alive or revived by free or private healthcare. Shut away in the winter with wine, TV, hobbies, heating on full. Out in the spring for garden centres. Pottering. A cruise. Spain. Considering the vast global and domestic imbalances, the grotesque inequalities and injustice in a loaded game, could all of that have continued forever?

And, oh God, we were dull in that neighbourhood. Sour. Regimented by routine. Oppressed by a consensus of our own devising. Standards and shared values erected like a wall to keep out anyone who wasn't exactly like us, or wasn't as fortunate as us, when little of that accrued affluence was of our own making.

"They're all flakes!" Doug's voice rose. "They wouldn't get away with it in Russia or Saudi Arabia."

Neither would you.

"You can see why the Yanks have so many guns…"

But who'd be young, Douglas? I'd wondered, in a familiar train of thought. We have most of the money and property. In every town and city and village, we have the best of everything. And the best of the coasts, the countryside. The best buildings, vehicles, the best of every service. We're first in line. We're preposterously prosperous. Who, or what, we vote for always wins. We're the luckiest generation of our species and have been since apes climbed down from trees seven million years ago.

And thus, as I'd watched what happened on day one, in that exclusive residential village in Dorset, and from a variety of angles, I did suspect that things had finally come to a head. All that was required was for *something* to remove restraint, and to instil a temporary madness, a hysteria, a rabid viral idea. Chaos.

After the first hammer fell upon the first disbelieving face in that retirement village, the footage from Dorset was widely shared online. In minutes. Smartphones uploaded their shaky-cam footage, those blood-spattered set-pieces, before the first news channel managed a single stuttering report.

"Anyway, gotta get on, Douglas. Few things to do." Like washing off the scent of lube, perfume, and sweat before diving back into the fallout from yesterday's news. I hadn't been that fearfully excited since the London riots.

As suspected, me calling time on his broadcast irritated my neighbour. "You still haven't sorted out your front path," he said, nodding at the rubble.

Whatever.

In the early morning hours of day eight, I trembled down the loft ladder for the second time on rickety legs, in search of sustenance. I'd finished the loaf by then, the can (of fucking lychees, which I loathe!), and there were now only six biscuits left in the packet that I'd taken from Joan's kitchen. My house, mercifully, had remained empty of all but me, and no matter how much of a temptation my bed and the shower had become, I'd stayed inside the fetid loft and sweated under the roof beams.

Our visitors, or occupiers, had been active again in the village. No one was left to kill by then, but a form of celebration had lasted most of the eighth day and evening, set to *that* music, blaring from car stereos and phones.

Like hippies, the young invaders now wandered freely about our lawns and streets, hand in hand, with beatific smiles and blood-spattered clothes. There had been a fire in the next street that morning. At least one car went off with a bang. A pool party had raged up at Tim's, on the hill, the biggest house in the village. Though it was an unusual gathering in which they had all screamed themselves silent amidst the weird hammerings and piping of their chosen soundtrack. By then, I was even humming the music that the mob had killed to from day one.

Music that scored the first videos posted online. Clashing, steely, industrial drums. Bass synths bubbling like earth tremors below what might have been folk pipes, even flute music that swarmed like angry bees around the rhythm. Discordant, then wonderfully and simply melodic. A racket, but inexplicably compelling, which made my heart race and my old feet tap the floor. A composition that seemed to make time go faster and suck the air out of wherever it was played. Circular, repetitive, maddening. The cacophony orbited until the piece reached speeds that briefly disintegrated comprehension, before it began again. That piece of music was the anthem of July, the greatest terror in mankind's history.

Some frantic, noisy sex occurred in the house at the back of my garden too, no doubt watched by the corpses of Hatty and Malcolm, who were still tethered by their necks inside their conservatory.

Distant gunshots or fireworks had marked the afternoon, and a big group of eleven-year-olds must have stripped the village shops of confectionary and convenience foods. I'd seen them at midday. They passed the house, each one clutching a jangling, buzzing phone in one hand, their loot tucked in the other paw.

Garden of Eden. Just take what you want.

Like a nocturnal mammal, I traced my previous path up the garden and down Doug and Joan's to the open back door. Doug had been in the sun all day again, so I pulled the neck of my shirt over my nose and mouth as I staggered by.

All I could think of was the rows of foodstuffs, neatly stacked in columns in their kitchen cupboards. They had a deep freeze in the garage too, and I wondered if I might actually risk something hot. I couldn't remember my oven ever making noise. Oven chips, I fancied. A steak. Garden peas. Desire made me dizzy and dulled my senses enough to nearly walk across the legs of the girl sitting on the floor of my neighbours' lounge.

I stopped, said, "Oh," and began to shake, certain that my end was imminent.

Burning flesh. Smashed heads. Amputations with garden tools. Stretched necks. Would they paint me first with creosote?

The scruffy girl sat cross-legged before the coffee table, staring into the space to the right of me, though it took me a few seconds to establish that. Her eyes were open, but she didn't see me. She wore an electric blue bikini top and was quite beautiful. Tanned, a recipient of pedicures and manicures, tight jeans, but all stained with dirt and viscera. There was an open case beside her, filled with clothes taken from shops, jewellery from houses. A bottle of raspberry flavoured vodka.

As if prompted by my presence, she began to speak, though not to me. But, perhaps, at me, as if my presence, as usual, had provoked a monologue from a stranger. Her accent was regional, the tone questioning but fraught. "And it's in them coloured dusts... we's going down... where stone animals is wrestling... is a cave thing but you can't breathe in the dark of it... all underwater... people behind people, behind people, and I can see through them all... going in."

"Marching, like. All walking into grey things, then black things, then swirly things..." the boy said. When he spoke my bowels near gave out. He sat near the door and stared at the opposing wall. "You see faces in them green lights that is going up when you blink, then drifting down. Mouths is moving... they ain't birds or people, who's in the sky. Going round and round the big chair. Thought they was burning bits. Bats..." He wore no shirt and used a rucksack as a backrest.

Their gibberish continued as I stood before them in silence. I didn't dare move. An encrusted handsaw and hammer with hair attached to the ball-peen lay within reach of the boy's dark, soiled hand. The girl had been using a steak knife.

Joan was upside down on the stairs. Through the living room doorway I could see part of one arm and that mop of thick white hair.

Bitch.

I took one slow step backwards. Stopped. Took another step without removing my eyes from either of them.

"Is them mountains here?" the girl asked nobody. "Which country?"

"I seen me mum and me dad and they had no clothes on," the boy said, "and they was running around them dunes with black grass by the foggy water... There's millions and millions of white people with no clothes... It's a mouth, a mouth of music, that they're swimming inside..."

I left the way I'd come in.

Day two, I revisited the footage I'd seen on the first day. It was on constant repeat, and I sat through more analysis. Calmer, with fresher eyes after a good sleep and fabulous tune-up downtown with the Thai girl, I found myself fascinated by the faces, the very expressions of the young assailants. I wasn't alone. One clip had been watched ten million times before take-down. A truncated version, however, remained available at credible news sources.

Those kids were laughing. Real eye-watering belly laughter, with moments of suffocation fear. How old were they? Mid-teens? And the upper age limit for their collaborators was pushing the late twenties, even early thirties. But no older. Gen Alpha, Gen Z, and young millennials heavily represented.

Their age struck me as significant. In chaos you look for patterns. Patterns imply sense, process shock. Equally poignant was the age of their victims. Boomers and my own Generation Jones. Who else were you going to find in a luxury retirement village?

And what surprised me immediately, with only a smidgen of discomfort, was the sobering fact that once I'd seen a few dozen seniors pushed that fast in wheelchairs across a flat roof and over the edge—or dragged across the ground, or set ablaze in their nightwear, or sat lolling and stained inside cars after their escape attempts had been thwarted, or just lying with obscured faces on heads too soft and wet—was that I had to keep looking. Intently.

Not dissimilar to a good session with internet porn, I suspected that a sweeter spot existed somewhere. Out there. Something even better than a video or picture that can make you shiver to the marrow. It exists.

Sickened by horror and fear, maybe. But I was ecstatic with euphoria at the sight of violence when I was not the victim. That was intoxicating. Never anything that good on Netflix.

The first victims reminded me of my neighbours. That factored into my reaction. Ever since a faction complained to the council about my gardens, led by Doug's wife, Joan, I'd wanted nothing but the worst for them all. I once told her that her husband should put her out with the bin bags for collection. She'd thrown a trowel at me. It hit the fence. Curiously, Doug never brought up the incident.

But I digress. One hundred and fifty people were murdered in that luxury compound. Despatched with handheld weapons. Some beaten dead with fists and hands. Though when that one kid used a fire extinguisher, all the others around him started casting about for weapons. Monkey see, monkey do. By that time, they'd hurt their feet, ripped their trainers. On teeth.

Low-tech executions, each one. And conducted in just over thirty minutes flat. Though, apparently, there had been some kind of occupation first, resulting in heated verbal exchanges between the staff and residents, who'd rolled up their sleeves and demanded that the intruders leave the premises. That was the trigger the youths had been waiting for; almost certainly hoping for. And in they went. Fast and furious. Animal bloodlust. Pack mentality. No firearms. A Neolithic killing frenzy.

They killed one woman by swinging her head into a cement wall. A group of four held her by her scrawny ankles as she shouted, "Let go! Let go!"

Thump.

I'd be hearing that sound for days until I heard far worse, on the other side of the garden fence.

But how the first footage made my legs shake! My excitement was terrible, unhinged. I wasn't feeling at all like myself, but the prospect of some huge event, or ruction, made me breathless. After all the excitement with the meteor shower and now this! I'd never seen anything like it, though I'd read of worse in the twentieth century, from the Russian Civil War onwards. But for those of us who'd never endured revolutions, invasions, civil wars, famines, or extreme deprivation, this was quite new. And it all kicking off in the next county too. That made me sit up straight.

From what they knew by the first evening, the mob wasn't an organised group. Not a cell or cult. Beyond shared interests online, which excluded political affiliations or even noticeable political bias, most of the killers were strangers. They were just pissed and, inexplicably, went full *Einsatzgruppen,* as if that luxury complex was a hamlet in Romania in the middle of the last century. They Hotel Rwanda'd the entire exclusive retirement village. No survivors.

And that was hard graft, though the method of mass murder was not exclusively utilitarian. But creative. Abstract. Inspired by rage but designed to entertain the aggressors. Or so I thought at the time. That behaviour was novel. Unique. I have never underestimated our capacity as a species for inhumanity and horror. But all that weird dancing? Lots of it. Prancing. Blood-flecked faces leering into the camera. Swivel-eyed fanaticism. Grotesque vandalism ending in a fire they were still trying to douse when I went to bed, nervous yet strangely euphoric.

Only days later did I wonder, as my own sanity unravelled, if the culture of slaughter was intended as tribute to something else.

Saturated and bloated by the onscreen depravity for two days running, if you included the repeats and new footage I'd watched throughout day two, I ended up in my garden with the birds and a book. Smug, secure, I read for a bit, then dozed, only to awake in the cooler air of sundown to the sound of multiple televisions drifting across the hedges, fences, and decks. Every flat screen had the volume up.

Everyone was inside on a beautiful day, glued to their screens. I detected the odd raised voice of a viewer too, though not what was said. But the tones were aghast. Somewhere, a woman wept.

The noise reminded me of the World Cup, the one when England did well, and Wimbledon each summer. They liked tennis around those parts. Loud voices intermingled with loud TVs. I imagined they were all watching the footage from the retirement village. Hadn't they had enough? Or was there a new development? More footage released?

Curious and weary, I wandered inside to establish what had consumed my neighbours.

The obliteration of the back door woke me.

By day ten, I was sleeping during the hot, dry days and shivering awake in the dark to scrounge for food or to sit alone, fretting, while eating what I'd scavenged the night before.

Below the cross timbers and the small section of floorboards, I heard them walk through the rooms of my home. Drawers and cupboards and wardrobes were investigated. Beds tested. None spoke. Their silence was terrible.

Someone jumped up and down and scraped the loft hatch with their fingertips. At that I bit my forearm to stifle my whimpers.

The entrance to the roof space was controlled by a mechanism unlocked from below by a pole, with a metal hook affixed to the end. I'd taken that up with me. But pushing the door from below could unlock the hatch and the ladder would descend.

Had that youth been taller, or bothered to find a chair to stand upon, my disgusting vigil under the roof would have ended that evening.

Inexplicably, the jumper gave up.

Another group was standing in the garden. They'd raised their coloured faces to the flashing sky. Security lights on my fence flood-lit their star gaze. Teenagers. Four boys and two girls who looked like they'd been pressing grapes with their hands. They were talking, but not to each other. Like the two teens in Joan's living room, they channelled what many later mistook for drugged gibberish. I heard snatches.

"Beautiful... it's not enough... they'll leave us... pipes are playing on the other side..."

I was too insensible with fear to take much notice, and knew I must leave. Not just the house but the village. I needed to go where no one wanted to be.

The descent of the ladder through the loft hatch, I assessed, would have been noisy enough to break at least one of them from a trance, and it would only take one. So I disengaged the ladder from the steel mounting. This meant I would have to drop from the hatch, at ceiling height, to the floor below, and make as soft a landing as I could muster.

I didn't know how many of them were inside the house either, nor where they were located exactly. I'd be too visible by day, when they were most active. Most of the houses in the villages, by then thoroughly cleansed of their former owner-occupiers, were now resettled. I'd seen the lights, heard the parties. I had new neighbours, but not the ones I'd wished for. And there was no longer anything better on offer than my tousled cottage. I had to go then, or die when they roused.

Hanging by my frail arms from the loft hatch, I watched my feet hover a few feet above the landing floor. My impact would be noisy and I feared the snapping of one or both ankles. And despite the agony in my arms, I was unable to let go. So I swung there, tears trickling down my gritty face.

"I'm staying. I won't go outside," a young voice said to itself from my bedroom. "Sky's too big. I can see them going into the mouth."

I finally let go and crumpled to a crouch, panting like a dog on a hot day.

Following the video uploads during the first three days and nights, the idea and methods for murdering the elderly went global. Fast. By day four, the slaughter reached critical mass and, like the heart of a star, appeared self-sustaining and inexhaustible. A permanent state. Would they continue until we were all dead? And if the fuel of hatred eventually burned out, and the head smashing ceased, there would be a black hole. Everything we had ever been as a species would fall into that void and become nothing.

On day three, I awoke to new atrocities in every time zone. Under the duvet, bleary with sleep, though never for long, I would extend an arm to collect my phone from the side-table. Gather the phone into the warm gloom of my nest. And pull down the notifications menu.

London. Bristol. Birmingham. Nottingham. Cardiff. Newcastle. Liverpool. Manchester. Glasgow. Oh, Glasgow, you made my eyes water. And then the smaller cities. And many towns. *Fuck the rest of the world. It's happening here!* And whatever was happening had assumed a terrible global momentum—even the Scandinavians—that I desperately wanted stopped. *You've had your fun, and so have I, but it's getting closer to home and I don't like it.* I couldn't even look at the footage from Russia and China. My God. Anyone over forty was fair game.

In the UK, the villages and coastal resorts, those preserves of the elderly, were dealt with later in the first wave; initially by the young gig-economy staff, then by the expansion of roaming bands. They bussed each other out or rocketed out to the sticks in long columns of stolen private vehicles. Every kid, youth, and young adult had Google Maps on their phones. All owned phones, or quickly acquired one, or upgraded. And there were so many seniors to get through.

By the end of day four, nowhere was safe and the spate of massacres erupted faster than news sources could monitor, let alone verify. But even the little that was reported by credible broadcasters defied comprehension. The sheer scale of it.

Sixty million died in the Second World War between 1939 and 1945. But in the twenty-first century, the younger half of the planet euthanized, we suspect, over four hundred million of the elderly in a little over two weeks. That accounted for just under half the world's population born before the mid-1960s. The surviving half, of which I am an ecstatic member, hid. Or was hidden by sympathetic members of Generation X.

By the dawn of day four, the traffic was busier. Some of my neighbours fled but merely drove into congested roads that became killing bottles. At that juncture, I understood something paralysing (until the need to reach the toilet fast had me fleeing like an old gazelle to my ensuite bathroom): there are simply too few police officers, paramedics, and soldiers in the world to respond to a planet-wide cull. When the younger generations turn against the eldest, pretty much simultaneously, there was little that anyone in authority could, or would, do.

Few tried to stop the rabble. What could they do? Bomb their own? And many in authority collaborated. The younger staff, particularly those underemployed, were insidious allies. Swept up by the fervour, the music, they were even suspected of putting on transport services to those harder-to-reach areas.

The human race, between the ages of approximately thirteen (though multiple reports exist claiming that many of the butchers were younger, and I saw eleven-year-olds playing with dead bodies) and the mid-thirties (the upper age limit also became fluid, as partisans in their forties raised hammers in service of the crusade) destroyed those over sixty. Or, more precisely, anyone that looked old and happened to be within reach was culled.

When young, wild chimps, too often slapped and bitten and resentful of their low status, exchange glances, in that look is a communication and a new possibility: the old alpha isn't as hard as he thinks he is.

What can stop us? All of us?

A defenceless creature of the night, I scuttled from shadow to shadow. Crossed roads and struggled down grass banks. Froze upon verges at the very murmur of a distant engine or disembodied voice shouting at the sky. "We're all going up and coming apart in the spinning!"

I crawled around one paddock near a large farmhouse, in which a group sat in the dark, alone with their visions. None called out or seemed able to tear their horrified gaze from the shooting stars. They muttered to themselves, or their mouths moved but released no words.

Careful not to make a sound, I withdrew. I clambered over fences and tore my trousers, then hobbled over night-bruised fields, where cattle lowed the soundtrack of bestial nightmares. Shivering if I stopped to catch my breath and clutch at my heaving, painful chest,

I kept moving. Eventually my stagger became a fretful inching, along hedgerows and minor roads, until I reached a little church and vandalised hamlet. The lights in the buildings were doused. I counted five bodies in the road and three outside cottages that opened onto a tiny green.

Finally alone, I slumped against the church wall, as if seeking sanctuary in the wrong century, and gasped for a while. The church was derelict, padlocked.

Above my head the clear black sky was raked with those infernal pyrotechnics. As the interstellar dust, ice, and minerals peppered our orbit, then ignited and vanished, I looked up in wonder, as I had done on the first night, though now with madder yet wider eyes.

I entertained thrilling, terrifying notions. I was struck by how we moved through space with countless inert bodies and forms; that we were connected to the incomprehensibly large and ancient cosmos. All of it moving. I was stricken with a brief recognition of the size and depth of space, the myriad fragments within it, the perpetual motion of orbits, the great maelstroms up there, the speeding ice, gas, and rock. Evidence of such insensate, chaotic forces, forged billions of years ago in the cosmos, touched my primal core. Awe engulfed me.

During the first waves of shooting stars, I had merely feared collisions. Impacts that would bring to a sudden end our teeming, industrious, polluting, and fractious activities. Now I truly understood that we mattered to nothing but ourselves. We were akin to the bright but dying tail of the meteor. Visible for a while, then not.

By that church, I found no escape from despair, from the height of morbidity. How fragile had been the ties that bound us, even in the West. How quickly what was taken for granted was eroded. We'd seemed destined to destroy ourselves, limping a few decades from the world wars of the previous century, but never secure from nuclear annihilation, collapse, or climate catastrophe. But who could have imagined that our uncherished and disenfranchised youth would wield the fatal blow?

So reduced, witless and exhausted, I formed a better notion of the monumental presence I'd sensed for days and its satanic whims adrift in our orbit. Beyond the shooting stars and inside the void, the presence took no recognisable form. It was the very droning and screaming of the void, the oppressive temperatures and speeding debris, and the depths of unbreathable darkness. Stars and planets had formed within its chaos, and to it they would return in frozen silence. All above and around us were its components and the ether through which it screamed, on so many wavelengths and spectrums that did not register in our undeveloped senses. Its distant power had intensified briefly here, close to the earth, and rearranged things on a whim.

The outer reaches of my thoughts became unbearable.

For thirteen days the frenzies churned red and wet until the mass hysteria, like the meteor shower, ebbed and the energy of the killers ran low. Or disgust and reason inexplicably returned. Or their own loved ones were discovered to have been put to the sword (approximate statistics eventually claimed that the murder of grandparents by their grandchildren tallied a little over twenty million, though the figure is rising).

The variables that contributed to the slaughter, and its end, are too numerous to identify, though are being fastidiously and delicately identified by those with the stomach for it; mostly Gen Xers in surviving academic environments. The same dilemma applies to the reasons why the carnage ceased, and so abruptly, with few reports of senior citizen culls existing beyond day seventeen.

When the young are asked why they did it, they claim to have taken no part, or to remember nothing of that time, or to have hidden refugees. Amnesia is common, as are notions that they were lucidly dreaming. The belief that it was all faked gains popularity, in spite of evidence to the contrary. Justification for how so many of them came to be rich homeowners, and more independent, varies and takes many forms. There are the attacks on capitalism and arguments for the necessity of fairness, and conspiracies that the houses were empty anyway. Mostly, there is a great silence. There are threats. There is trauma. There is disbelief. Spiritual awakenings, which resemble few religions that existed before, flourish. But the normalisation of the new situation and a desire to fixate on the future, to not get hung up on the past, is the most baffling response of all.

I struggle to recognise my own species.

The cessation of intergenerational hostilities was followed by months of smouldering cremation pyres and mass grave burials, organised by horrified, bewildered, and extremely wary authorities, at local and national levels.

But had not youth corrected an imbalance through chaos and established a new order? One they would dominate? A new generational order that gave youth full primacy over age. And from that infernal, inhuman insurrection, a new world rapidly evolved. Within it, the young suddenly owned everything besides what Generation X nervously clung to, and whatever leftovers seeped to the older Millennials.

After the cull, the young owned the property and land of the deceased, and acquired their possessions, their vehicles, their nest eggs, assets, and electoral primacy. The latter evidenced by the mandates of the rash of new, youthful governments. Since the bloodshed, even those Gen Xers and fence-sitting Millennials who'd sat paralysed and traumatized through it all, or spent that terrible period protecting their parents with any effective weapon at hand, behind barred doors, have been known to surreptitiously extend their own borders or occupy bigger houses up the road.

The very question of *Where were your children in July*? is taboo and will be for some time. The post-extermination amelioration by the middle generations, who took no active part in the slaughter, forms another chilling consequence.

But considering this event dispassionately, and its monumentally complex aftermath, there aren't enough courts or prisons to process and accommodate the accused. And after what happened, who'd even dare to make an arrest? Might the cull be repeated?

There has been no official declaration of a pardon or amnesty, as well as a reluctance to investigate. That would take forever, in each and every country, considering the scale of the slaughter.

My own theories horrify me.

At the beginning of that July, I think civilisation in the twenty-first century was a rubber band that had been stretched as far as it would allow. It must either snap, or retract back a few centuries, to when life wasn't so sacred and anything could happen, and often did. At least for a while. Only a cataclysm could address the imbalance.

Resentment is the most common and powerful and corrosive emotion known to man. It is borne of uncertainty about one's place amongst others, and its desire is to unleash chaos.

Vengeance is narcotic, even when it incorporates self-destruction. We'd made a world that so many wanted destroyed. In socioeconomic terms, the killers achieved their aims. On this I concur. But I have also arrived at other conclusions.

Amid myriad theories addressing the causes of the cull, few venture explanations for the culture of annihilation that accompanied it. The dancing. The painting of corpses; the decorated condemned, the offered. That music, the drums and pipes. The sheer joy of torture. And when it ceased, I believe that the will of what drove them to crucify, hang, bludgeon, and burn had simply moved on. Away it had dwindled, following as random a trajectory as that of its arrival. How else can one address the amnesia of the killers?

During the internecion, there were no factions, committees, secret police, revolutionary councils, paramilitary. No evidence of a governing ideology, nothing centralised. But they acted as one, driven by the same ecstasy in bloodshed, vandalism, transgression, and the destruction of boundaries. They killed for days then slept for days, while others surged to break down doors and ferret out the defenceless, incapacitated, and vulnerable. They hunted as one mighty organism with billions of legs and arms, they broke out in orgiastic frenzies, and they slew, and slew, and danced while they did it. Danced to the barrage of fast drums and mad, near discordant piping. Idiot anthems that blinded them to reason or compassion. Ants around a queen in the sky, exalted by the fiery wisp of her mighty tail, miles above, rocketing through the anarchic, freezing cosmos.

And when they weren't involved in wet work and excess, they became motionless and muttered vague, disjointed observations of the wonders and horrors and nonsense that was screened upon their minds.

Like a hint of smoke in the air of an unpleasant winter day, drifting from a distant fire that rages, perhaps the equivalent of a noxious fume visited our overheating planet to replace order with chaos? In turn, chaos again became a kind of order in which none could look another in the eye.

I wonder if something in our complex organic programming at genetic level was triggered. Perhaps a cosmic phenomenon compelled so many to revel in cruel and brutish depravity, as if in the service of second-guessing the will of old gods. Sophistication and reason were abandoned to mirror the suggestions of a deity's formless and unpredictable transcendence.

There must have been something above and beyond us that July, guiding our own transformation. And if it was not a god, then was it a shred of a force that grazed the earth, cast away from a form that we hadn't encountered in our brief existence of a few million years? Was this an accidental glancing blow? Like the physical nature of the cosmos, was such an intensification of chaos merely random? A foreign object passed the earth and we collapsed? Within one month? I'll never know.

I'd also wondered, as I lived on scraps and skulked by night, and peered through cracks to watch the red business commence on the landscaped gardens of my neighbourhood, was the impulse that led to such a cull part of a deity's immanence? Its latent presence within us all, since our origins? Were we connected to it? Did a sleeping potential beg revival, to momentarily pause the direction of our species' travel? To adjust the organisation and fate of civilisation?

Considering what I lived through, and how I survived like a rat, I could be forgiven for thinking anything at all. Or excused for finding consciousness, thereafter, unbearable.

These days, we senior citizens that survived tend to look down anyway, and shudder at any murmur of a housing crisis, or youth unemployment, or some inequality in status, for we know who will be blamed. There is little resistance to the new regime in England, or the capital gains taxation on senior citizens that has rinsed so much money back into the economy; nor do we pose any obstruction to the confiscation of our assets and our enforced exile into publically funded accommodation, for our own safety. The lucky few live with their children. Some Gen Xers rant about stolen inheritances, but when you're uneasy around your own eleven-year-old, and those missing two weeks, perhaps you become grateful for what you have.

As I've alluded, most survivors have been herded into social housing and retirement villages, where we are often forced to erase the blood stains of the previous occupants, before making uneasy homes amidst their ghosts. Some of us sleep four to a room. Or rather, four of us keep each other awake at night. Those who have lost their minds, and those who have kept most of their wits, tell their tales of how they survived.

And for a while now, the skies have remained clear.

About the Contributors

Nathan Carson was raised on a goat farm in the backwoods of Mid-Valley Oregon but has called Portland home since 1997. He is an accomplished music journalist, booking agent, FM radio DJ, founding member of the long-running doom band Witch Mountain, published weird fiction author, and a MOTH StorySlam Champion. More info at www.nathancarson.rocks or @nanotear.

Matthew Cheney is the author of the collections *Blood: Stories* (Black Lawrence Press) and *The Last Vanishing Man* (Third Man Books) as well as the nonfiction books *Modernist Crisis and the Pedagogy of Form* (Bloomsbury Academic) and *About That Life: Barry Lopez and the Art of Community* (punctum books). His stories have been published by *Nightmare, Conjunctions, The Dark, One Story, Weird Tales,* and elsewhere.

Ruthanna Emrys is the author of *A Half-Built Garden, Winter Tide,* and *Deep Roots,* as well as co-writer of Tor.com's Reading the Weird column with Anne M. Pillsworth. She also writes radically hopeful short stories about religion and aliens and psycholinguistics. She lives in a mysterious manor house on the outskirts of Washington, DC with her wife and their large, strange family. There she creates real versions of imaginary foods, gives unsolicited advice, and occasionally attempts to save the world.

Brian Evenson is the author of a dozen books of fiction, most recently the story collection *The Glassy Burning Floor of Hell* (2021). His collection *Song for the Unraveling of the World* (2019) won the Shirley Jackson Award and the World Fantasy Award and was a finalist for the Los Angeles Times' Ray Bradbury Prize. Previous books have won the ALA-RUSA Prize, the International Horror Guild Award, and have been finalists for the Edgar Award. His new book of stories, *Good Night, Sleep Tight*, will be published by Coffee House Press in 2024. He is the recipient of three O. Henry Prizes (one for "Mudder Tongue", which originally appeared in *McSweeney's*), an NEA fellowship, and a Guggenheim Award. His work has been translated into more than a dozen languages. He lives in Los Angeles and teaches at CalArts.

Richard Gavin explores the relationship between dread and the numinous. His short fiction has been collected in six volumes, including *grotesquerie* (Undertow Publications, 2020), and has appeared in many volumes of *Best New Horror* and *The Best Horror of the Year*. Richard has also authored several works of esotericism for distinguished venues such as Theion Publishing, Three Hands Press, and Starfire Publishing Ltd. His latest book in this vein is *The Infernal Masque* (Theion Publishing, 2022). He resides in Ontario, Canada. Website: www.richardgavin.net.

Maxwell I. Gold is a Jewish American multiple award nominated author who writes prose poetry and short stories in cosmic horror and weird fiction with half a decade of writing experience. Three time Rhysling Award nominee, and two time Pushcart Award nominee, find him at www.thewellsoftheweird.com.

T. Kingfisher (aka Ursula Vernon) is the award-winning author of *Digger, Nettle & Bone*, and *What Moves The Dead*. She lives in North Carolina. When not writing, she is usually somewhere in the garden, attempting to make eye contact with butterflies.

Lauri Taneli Lassila is a Finnish author of poetry, aphorisms, essays, and speculative fiction. In the fields of horror and the weird, his idols are H.P. Lovecraft, Samuli Paulaharju, and Clark Ashton Smith.

Akis Linardos is a genre writer trapped in the body of an AI scientist. Trying to explore as much as he can of this unlikely reality, he has lived in four European countries throughout his academic career. His fiction's been published by Apex Magazine, The Maul, Grendel Press and more. Find him on Twitter @LinardosAkis.

Samuel Marzioli is a Filipino-American writer of mostly dark fiction. His work has appeared in numerous publications and podcasts, including the Best of Apex Magazine, Flame Tree's Asian Ghost Short Stories, Dread Machine, and LeVar Burton Reads. His debut collection, *Hollow Skulls and Other Stories*, was published by JournalStone Publishing. For more information about his work, check out marzioli.blogspot.com or @marzioli on Twitter.

Adam L. G. Nevill was born in Birmingham, England, in 1969 and grew up in England and New Zealand. He is an author of horror fiction. Of his novels, *The Ritual, Last Days, No One Gets Out Alive* and *The Reddening* were all winners of The August Derleth Award for Best Horror Novel. He has also published three collections of short stories, with *Some Will Not Sleep* winning the British Fantasy Award for Best Collection, 2017.

Imaginarium adapted *The Ritual* and *No One Gets Out Alive* into feature films and more of his work is currently in development for the screen.

The author lives in Devon, England. More information about the author and his books is available at: www.adamlgnevill.com

Lena Ng lives in Toronto, Canada. Her short stories have appeared in eighty publications including Amazing Stories and Flame Tree's *Asian Ghost Stories* and *Weird Horror Stories*. Her stories have been performed for podcasts such as *Gallery of Curiosities, Creepy Pod, Utopia Science Fiction, Love Letters to Poe,* and *Horrifying Tales of Wonder*. "Under an Autumn Moon" is her short story collection.

R.B. Payne's earliest story can be carbon-dated to his seventh year on the planet. His story *Eddie G. at the Gates of Hell* (written much, much later!) was well-received in the Stoker-nominated *Midnight Walk* anthology about a decade ago. About 25 stories later, (he is admittedly a slow writer), his work has appeared in a multitude of magazines and anthologies including the Stoker-nominated

Miscreations: Gods, Monstrosities and Other Horrors. Other tales have appeared in *18 Wheels of Horror, Madhouse, Hell Comes to Hollywood II, All-American Horror of the 21st Century, Times of Trouble, Monk Punk,* and the original *Chiral Mad* volume.

A nomad by choice, R. B. Payne lives in Paris, France, with his wife, dog, and cat. He can be found at the local *brasserie* where wine and conversation impede the writing process but provide an endless source of story ideas. Online, he is at www.rbpayne.com.

Jamieson Ridenhour is the writer and producer of the popular audio drama *Palimpsest,* the author of the werewolf murder-mystery *Barking Mad* (Typecast, 2011) and writer and director of the award-winning short horror films *Cornerboys* and *The House of the Yaga.* His ghost play *Grave Lullaby* was a finalist for the Kennedy Center's David Cohen Playwriting award in 2012. His newest play, *Bloodbath: Victoria's Secret,* premiered in October of 2021. Jamie has a Ph.D. in Victorian Gothic fiction. In addition to publishing scholarly articles on Dickens, LeFanu, and contemporary vampire film, he edited the Valancourt edition of Sheridan LeFanu's *Carmilla* (2009) and wrote a book-length study of urban gothic fiction, *In Darkest London* (Scarecrow, 2014). He has taught writing and literature for over twenty years, currently at Warren Wilson College outside of Asheville. He lives in North Carolina with his wife and three dogs.

Erica Ruppert, HWA, SFWA. lives in northern New Jersey with her husband and too many cats. Her first novella, *Sisters in Arms,* was released in 2021. Her short stories have appeared in magazines including *Vastarien, Lamplight,* and *Nightmare,* on podcasts including *PodCastle,* and in multiple anthologies. Her debut collection, *Imago and Other Transformations,* was released by Trepidatio Publishing in March 2023. When she is not writing, she runs, bakes, and gardens with more enthusiasm than skill.

Richard Thomas is the award-winning author of eight books— *Disintegration* and *Breaker* (Penguin Random House Alibi), *Transubstantiate, Staring Into the Abyss, Herniated Roots, Tribulations, Spontaneous Human Combustion* (Turner Publishing), and *The Soul*

Standard (Dzanc Books). His over 175 stories in print include *The Best Horror of the Year* (Volume Eleven), *Cemetery Dance* (twice), *Behold!: Oddities, Curiosities and Undefinable Wonders* (Bram Stoker winner), *Lightspeed, PANK, storySouth, Gargoyle, Weird Fiction Review, Midwestern Gothic, Shallow Creek, The Seven Deadliest, Gutted: Beautiful Horror Stories, Qualia Nous, Chiral Mad* (numbers 2-4), *PRISMS, Pantheon*, and *Shivers VI*. He was also the editor of four anthologies: *The New Black* and *Exigencies* (Dark House Press), *The Lineup: 20 Provocative Women Writers* (Black Lawrence Press) and *Burnt Tongues* (Medallion Press) with Chuck Palahniuk. He has been nominated for the Bram Stoker, Shirley Jackson, Thriller, and Audie awards. In his spare time he is a columnist at Lit Reactor. He was the Editor-in-Chief at Dark House Press and *Gamut Magazine*. For more information visit www.whatdoesnotkillme.com or contact Paula Munier at Talcott Notch.

Donald Tyson lives and writes on Cape Breton Island, at the tip of the province of Nova Scotia, Canada. He is the author of numerous works on magic and the occult, both fiction and nonfiction, among them the Alhazred series of books, which consists of collections of stories and novels that follow the adventures of a youthful Abdul Alhazred, author of the *Necronomicon*. His short horror fiction appears regularly in S. T. Joshi's anthology series *Black Wings* and has been gathered in two collections, *The Skinless Face* (Weird House Press, 2020) and *Cruel Stories* (Weird House Press, 2023).

Multi-award winner **Kaaron Warren** has published five novels and seven short story collections. She's sold over 200 short stories to publications big and small around the world and has appeared in Ellen Datlow's Year's Best anthologies. Her latest book is the novella "Bitters" from Cemetery Dance.